A TOUCH O... R OF
HOP...
BUT THE LON... DAWN
IS FRAUGHT WITH PERIL. . . .

Warakan—Years ago his only hope to escape his family's enemies was to flee into a bleak and icy isolation. Now, as possessor of the sacred stone, he must make a choice: use his newfound power to avenge his past . . . or find a path to peace for the People.

Jhadel—Warakan's sole companion in the wilderness, the ancient shaman may be blinded by age, but he sees the future with an inner light. Lying near death, he extracts a vow from Warakan that will send his pupil on the ultimate vision quest.

Xohkantakeh—Once a great warrior, now an aged outcast, he alone provides for his tiny clan of three females. He knows too well that the time has come to find someone to replace him. But the price of failure could be the doom of his family . . . and all he has lived for.

Ika—Tall, strong, bold-hearted, she loves Xohkantakeh more than her own life. But she is now on the threshold of womanhood, and with it comes change. To follow her destiny could mean losing the love and protection of the only man she has ever known.

Quarana—Voluptuous, passionate, and deceitful, she too depends on Xohkantakeh for survival. But she has one secret desire and she will use all her wiles to achieve it . . . even at the cost of a noble warrior's life.

Katohya—Once called Ta-maya, the woman of Xohkantakeh has known more than one love in her long, tumultuous life. Now she has found true happiness at last. But the shadows of a dying age are encroaching, and she may soon be asked to sacrifice all that she has ever longed to possess.

BANTAM BOOKS BY WILLIAM SARABANDE

The First Americans Series

THE
FIRST
AMERICANS

FACE OF
THE RISING
SUN

WILLIAM SARABANDE

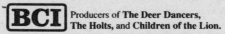

BCI Producers of **The Deer Dancers,
The Holts, and Children of the Lion.**

Book Creations Inc., Canaan, NY • Lyle Kenyon Engel, Founder

BANTAM BOOKS
NEW YORK • TORONTO • LONDON • SYDNEY • AUCKLAND

Face of the Rising Sun
A Bantam Book/October 1996

ISBN 0-553-56030-1
Published simultaneously in the United States and Canada

Bantam Books are published by Bantam Books, a division of
Bantam Doubleday Dell Publishing Group, Inc. Its trademark,
consisting of the words "Bantam Books" and the portrayal of a
rooster, is Registered in U.S. Patent and Trademark Office and in
other countries. Marca Registrada. Bantam Books,
1540 Broadway, New York, New York 10036.

PRINTED IN THE UNITED STATES OF AMERICA
OPM   10   9   8   7   6   5   4   3   2

*To and despite the memory of Edward A. Murphy
and his inimical law . . . over and around which
this author has maneuvered for the past year.*

The Great Lake

The Great River

The Great River

- ▲ The Drowned Camp
- △ Xohkantakeh's Winter Camp
- ○ Place where three rivers meet
- ◇ Place where Warakan is washed downriver
- ← To the Far Gorge and Land of the Ancestors

© BOOK CREATIONS INC. 1996

Mountains that Walk

- ∙∙∙ Tundra
- ∴ Grassland
- ∧∧ Forest

Mother of All Rivers

The High Plateau

Warakan's Cave

Great Forest

LAURENTIDE ICE SHEET

Area shown on main map

North America c. 12,000 years ago

R. TOELKE '96

PART I

IN THE COMPANY OF WOLVES

1

He went from the lodge. Quietly and in stealth he went, although secrecy was against his nature, and he cursed the need for guile that sent him alone into the Ice Age night.

Clad in the furs and skins of beasts, he stood beneath the stars, a giant of a man on the far side of youth, telling himself that from this moment on, no matter what happened, he must be young again, strong again, unafraid again.

The world is changing. Nothing will ever be the same. On the hunt to come, if you are to take the prey you seek and return alive to speak of it, you must be all that you have ever been: Xohkantakeh . . . bold hunter and warrior of the People of the Land of Grass!

He stared into the darkness. He did not feel bold. He felt tired, and old. The Land of Grass was far away; youth was farther still, and less attainable.

And now Great Paws has sensed your weakness as a stink upon the wind. He has crawled from his den beneath the snow and mocks you as he prowls the broad hills and steals once more from your snares and caches.

Xohkantakeh's eyes narrowed within the protective recesses of his wolfskin hood as an image flared within his brain. Furred and fanged and standing to a height that made even a giant of a man feel small, the vision burned behind his eyes and seared his tongue with the name of its kind: *Bear.*

3

He fought the urge to retreat into the warmth of the lodge and won, but not easily. *For the sake of your woman and daughters, you must go forth to hunt this Bear, this Thief, this Great Paws!* His brow furrowed in response to the unspoken command; it was the only part of him that moved.

Dire wolves were howling on the ridgetops and in the benighted hollows of distant hills. In the pulsing glow of a red aurora, it seemed to Xohkantakeh that both earth and sky were awash in blood. He grimaced at the inadvertent comparison and gazed upward, observing stars whose positions in the sky assured him that it was spring even though he could feel the hard chill of the winter snowpack beneath his trisoled moccasins. His gut tightened; there was something unnatural about the endless cold, about the unseasonal progression of springtime stars across the bloodred winter sky, and about the coming of the great bear into his hunting grounds now, at a time when . . .

His thoughts stopped in midflow. An owl was sounding in the tamaracks beyond the palisade of dry reeds and deadfall that he had raised to keep wind and predators from his winter camp, making him shiver. In the lore of his people, Owl flew before Death. Unnerved, Xohkantakeh squinted across the compound to see streams of airborne ground snow misting toward him through breaks in the palisade. The wind had breached his defenses. With a sinking heart he knew it was only a matter of time before Great Paws did the same.

"Not while I live!" The vow was a muted snarl. There was boldness in it, and defiance, but dread quickened the beat of his heart as he visualized the enormous tracks he had come across yesterday while journeying alone to the closest of his upriver cache pits. He had not told his woman or two surviving foster daughters of his find. The day had been too special. With his youngest girl confined for the first time to the hut of blood and his eldest girl and beloved woman busily preparing for the celebration that would honor Lanacheela's completion of her first menses, Xohkantakeh had not had the heart to tell them. Shaken and weary as he had been when he returned to camp, his voice would have betrayed his fear of an animal whose foreclaws alone left marks in the snow that exceeded the length of his hand.

A long, willful intake of freezing air steadied his nerves. He knew this bear, this Great Paws, this high-shouldered, short-faced bear that had once moved in and out of the seasons of his life as elusively and dangerously as a haunting. During long-gone moons beneath which he had broken with his tribe and led his little family southward along the great river, there had been times when, feeling himself watched, Xohkantakeh would turn and look back across the miles to see the bear standing like a tawny mountain in the mists of distance. Scarred along its right flank and face, Great Paws would heft its girth upright onto hind limbs as thick as trees and stare back at Xohkantakeh; like a man the bear had stared, like a warrior challenging another of its own kind to combat.

The memory jolted the giant. There *was* something unnatural about the animal. He had suspected it then, and he had been certain of it yesterday when, after having seen no sign of the beast for over a full hand-count of years, he had looked down at the massive impression of the scarred right forepaw in the snow and known that only one bear in all the world could have made it.

His mouth tightened with shame. How many times had he discovered that monstrous track and, having no desire to confront an adversary of such appalling proportions, hurried his woman and daughters from hunting grounds he would have preferred to make his own? How many summers had passed since the looming presence of the beast had so frightened Xree, the youngest of his foundlings, that the child fled into a marsh and drowned? And, after that never-to-be-forgotten day, how many nights had he sat up until dawn, knowing that the beast followed, waiting in vain for it to fall afoul of his snares or baited meat, feeling it circle his camp while his loved ones slept and he raised a mighty fire and kept his spears at the ready and sang bold songs to inform the bear that he was not afraid, even though his blood ran cold?

Too many, conceded Xohkantakeh. Scowling, he found himself unable to number the hills, valleys, and rivers he had put between his family and Great Paws since realizing that if he traveled far enough during the time when bears lay sleeping beneath the winter earth, Great Paws could not follow across the frozen land, except in dreams.

But this is no dream, for him or for you, thought Xohkantakeh. *Great Paws has awakened once more. He has risen from the earth and crossed frozen water and winter land to find you. And now he is close, so close that even if you were to break this best of all camps and run from him again, he would follow. The time has come for you to stand up to this bear. Too long has he hunted and shamed you. For your woman and daughters, you must finish him!*

Xohkantakeh growled quietly. The wolves and owl were silent now. Another bird raked the red darkness with its cry. He looked up but did not recognize the call or the small, sharp-winged form momentarily silhouetted against the stars; but in the dark, hemorrhagic light of the red aurora, instinct told him that the omens were bad for him this night. *Very* bad. He should not leave the compound to hunt. And yet . . .

Great Paws is out there. If he has not come afoul of the snares you set for him yesterday, he will snout out your camp and devour the last of your winter stores. It is the way of his kind. In his eyes, the woman and daughters of Xohkantakeh will be meat. You must protect them. Soon the sun will rise. By then you must be far from here, lest those who call you Man and Father attempt to prevent you from doing what should have been done long ago. When you return to this camp with the hide, flesh, and fat of Great Paws, your females will rejoice, knowing that Xohkantakeh is a warrior once more!

A sudden restlessness was on him; there was fear in it and a heady, almost intoxicating impatience. His gloved hands were shaking as he took his spears, braining club, and spear hurler from where he had left them upright in the snow against the main lodge, next to his eldest daughter's exquisitely made smaller lances.

A dark sprawl of eyebrow arched toward Xohkantakeh's hairline as his glance held on Ika's weapons. He had taught the girl well; in all his days he had never made lances as fine as Ika's. Now, as he appraised them, he had no doubt that the girl would insist on going with him if she knew his intent; her zeal for hunting was surpassed only by her extraordinary strength and skill, and she was afraid of nothing that he knew of. Nevertheless, he could not allow her to accompany him on this hunt, not under this bloodred sky. Not when Great Paws prowled hungry after his long winter sleep.

Again Xohkantakeh growled to himself. Ika was not going to be happy about being left behind, but the time had come to make the girl remember her gender and her place in the order of life. His massive shoulders curled into a shrug of begrudging acquiescence to circumstances beyond his control. Soon, like her younger sister, Ika would become a woman. In the hunting grounds of their ancestors, the laws of the Ancient Ones forbade females to make or use spears. He had found it a reasonable commandment in a land of many warriors, but not so in this vast, uninhabited country into which he—a renegade and outcast—had led his woman and adopted daughters so many winters ago. The memory was unsettling; since turning his back on the land of his perpetually warring ancestors, Xohkantakeh had found good cause to break many old taboos. Now he found himself wondering if the spirits of the Ancient Ones were punishing him, after all these years, by sending out of endless winter a marauding bear to make a shambles of his world.

The possibility rankled him. He countered it with unspoken, righteously indignant justification: *Only a fool would not have taught his woman and girls the forbidden skills when he had no sons left alive to hunt at his side!* And now, thanks only to his defiance of tradition, the giant knew he could go beyond the palisade secure in the knowledge that as long as bold, brave Ika was within his encampment, his beloved woman and youngest daughter would be safe and

fully capable of fending for themselves until he returned
from the hunt.

And if you do not return? The question took Xohkantakeh off guard; he had not considered it before, nor would
he consider it now. The time had come for him to be a warrior once again. Great Paws was waiting.

Ika awoke with a startled gasp. Hope, bright as a newly
kindled lodge fire, brought a smile to her wide face as she
sat upright on the bed of piled skins that she usually shared
with her younger band sister. Lanacheela did not sleep beside her this night, nor was she likely to share Ika's mattress again. Ika's smile became a frown. It was cold in the
lodge. She shivered within the old bison-hide sleeping
robe she and Lanacheela had shared since childhood, that
long-gone day when Xohkantakeh had stood against the
will of a war chief to become Outcast and Renegade rather
than see the orphaned children of slain fellow warriors
abandoned under a Starving Moon. There had been three
of them then: tiny Xree and frail Lana, sisters by blood,
and Ika, half-breed spawn of a Land of Grass warrior and
his captive from the distant and despised Red World. In
Xohkantakeh's band they had been loved in equal measure, and the giant had called each of them Cheela—
Daughter. Now, shivering, she remembered the new
blanket that had been given to Lanacheela when she left
the main lodge to enter the smaller, conical shelter re-
served for Xohkantakeh's menstruating females. The
frown becoming a jealous scowl, Ika visualized the luxuriant, lightweight robe of matched winter rabbit skins that
her foster mother, Katohya, had fashioned in the way of
her Red World people, snaring the animals herself, lovingly choosing and curing the pelts, working them until
they were soft and as resilient as . . .

No! Ika would not let herself think of the wonderful
robe that she, as Eldest Sister, had long imagined would
someday be her own. There was something much more
wonderful to consider now: The white bird had flown within
her dream and summoned her from sleep with its cry! Ika's

heartbeat quickened. She was smiling again as she hugged her knees and held her breath, listening, waiting for the bird to call once more. Moments passed, and though she could hear the wind prowling the compound and harassing the treetops beyond the palisade as, far away, dire wolves sang harmonies to the night, the bird of her dreams did not call again. Ika released her breath and opened her eyes, disappointment weighting her more heavily than the timeworn bison hide.

"What is it, Ika? Can it be dawn so soon, child?"

Child! Ika winced at her foster mother's familiar endearment. Yesterday she would have warmed to it; now it bruised her pride. "No, Katohya," she replied quietly, straining for patience with the older woman's insensitivity even though she would have preferred to shout in protest. A quick pull of air steadied her nerves and cooled her temper. Xohkantakeh had long ago made it clear to his daughters that he would tolerate nothing less from them than kindness and respect toward Katohya. The woman, although born of another tribe, was the daughter of a chieftain and—under her girlhood name of Ta-maya—had known more than her share of hardship and sadness before becoming the giant's slave and, in time, his woman. And so Ika sighed and said politely, "It is not yet dawn. I did not mean to wake you. Return to your dreams, my mother."

"And you to yours, dear one," responded the woman softly, exhaling a sleepily contented yawn. "Once the sun rises we will have no time to squander. There is still so much to do. Lanacheela will finish bleeding in three days, perhaps four. Our new-woman gifts and feast foods must be ready for her when she comes reborn from the lodge of blood. Ah . . . how I have longed for the day!"

Ika's mouth puckered into a knot of frustration. She was fifteen! No matter how hard she tried, she could not understand why the forces of Creation were preventing her from menstruating while honoring with first flow one who was younger by nearly two full winters. "I am Eldest Sister!" she blurted, unable to stem her feelings of resentment. "The new-woman robe and gifts and feast should be for me.

Lanacheela is not worthy to be a woman. She is not brave! She is not strong! She does not have the endurance to hunt at Xohkantakeh's side as Ika hunts! She is a small, slothful girl who is too lazy to lift sinew from a fresh kill without tearing it, or even to dehair a hide properly. Why have the forces of Creation honored her before me, Katohya? It is not right! It is not fair!"

"Ah, dear one, this woman learned long ago that the forces of Creation shape the world as they will. Who among any of the Three Tribes may say what is right or fair? The People war and scatter like seeds before the storms that beset us all. The Four Winds blow. Life flows like the great river. And who can see beyond the edge of the world to know where the wind and waters may pour forth in the end?"

Shaken by Katohya's predictable but unwelcome logic, Ika nearly cried as she said with a defensive ferocity born of pure longing, "But the white bird has flown within my dreams! This can mean only one thing. Soon I will join my sister in the lodge of blood. Soon I will also be reborn as New Woman. I am worthy!"

"Ah . . . the white bird. Yes, I remember the tale. It is not surprising that you would dream of it now, child." Another yawn. Then, gently and kindly, "You must not be envious of your sister, dear one."

Ika trembled with shame and angry annoyance; Katohya knew her far too well. "It was more than a dream!" she insisted.

"Perhaps. It is difficult to be sure of such things. Go back to sleep, child. Rest. Soon enough, if the tale of the white bird is true, the winged one will come to you in the full light of day when we all can see and hear it and be glad for you."

A lump the size of a small fist formed at the back of Ika's throat, constricting her breathing and bringing tears to her eyes. Katohya did not believe her. Hurt and indignant, she flared, "The tale is true! When the white bird flies in the light of day, then this girl will shed a woman's blood and the bird will speak Ika's new-woman name! It will be a name of great meaning and importance! This the

Four Winds promised my *real* mother on the day of my birth!"

"Yes, child. So you have told us. Many times."

Ika fought back tears and sought a sympathetic ear in the darkness. "Tell her, Xohkantakeh!" she demanded, wondering now, for the first time, why he had not stirred in the darkness or spoken before now. "Tell Katohya that my words about the white bird are true words!"

Silence.

Then Katohya's gentle voice again. "Xohkantakeh has gone from the lodge to hunt, child."

Ika was incredulous. "Without me?"

Katohya's sigh was one of strained forbearance as she adjusted her slender form beneath the bed furs that she usually shared with her man at the far side of the lodge. "You are not Xohkantakeh's shadow, Ika. He whispered to me in the darkness that I was not to wake you. He does not need you at his side as he seeks a new-woman gift for Lanacheela. I think it will be some small, special animal of his choosing, a creature whose blood, meat, and pelt will represent our hopes for the new woman at her honor feast."

Ika half choked on envy and despondence. *Not my hopes!* she thought, knowing that when her sister emerged from the lodge of blood to be feted, purified in sacred smoke, and given an adult name, Lanacheela would be New Woman. Never again would the younger girl be called Daughter by their father. In this tiny band in which Xohkantakeh was the only male, Lanacheela would be his wife, a sexually mature female who would open her body to his and—if the forces of Creation continued to favor her—in due time give Xohkantakeh the gift that Katohya had failed to give him: a son to replace those who had died in battle among warring tribes to the north, a son to make his spirit sing with pride, a son to hunt for him when he grew too old and weak to hunt for himself and his females.

Ika could not imagine the giant ever growing too old or weak to hunt, nor could she understand why he needed a son when he had her to hunt at his side. Her wide, plain

face worked with emotion. She knew the giant had outlived
two wives and all his offspring, and she would never forget
his compassion for "useless" female orphans. Now, many
winters later and far from the hunting grounds of murderous, ever-battling tribes, while Lanacheela sulked and
whined about coming to womanhood in a land without suit-
ors, Ika could not comprehend how her ungrateful sister
could even think of other men. Surely no man could be
taller, stronger, or more caring of their needs than their giant! When Xohkantakeh was within the lodge, Ika found it
warm, bright, and safe, even when the fire lay banked and
cold and lions roared outside in winter darkness. When he
smiled or nodded in approval of some small thing she said
or did, the sun shone in the girl's heart even though storm
clouds blanketed the world. When he singled her out to
hunt at his side, openly favoring her above Lanacheela and
behaving toward her as though she were the son Katohya
had failed to give him, pride swelled Ika's meager breast
until she could barely breathe for the sweetness of it. And
when they walked together beneath the stars, Ika knew that
Xohkantakeh was the Great Father Bear in the firmament
of her sky, and she wanted nothing in life other than to
be, as he so often called her, his Little Bear, bound by love
and loyalty to walk forever in the shadow of his might and
wisdom.

*But if Lanacheela becomes Xohkantakeh's woman and
gives him a son, will he still favor Ika and find her worthy to
walk in his shadow?* The unspoken question made the girl
light-headed with dread. "I must join my father!" she declared. Fearing nothing in all the world save the loss of his
love, she fumbled in the darkness for her gloves, outer garments, winter moccasins, snow walkers, and hunting bag.
"He must know that my place is always at his side no matter
what—"

"You cannot go alone into the night, child!"

"I am *not* a child! I have dreamed of the white bird. It
has called my name. I must tell Xohkantakeh. He will believe even though you do not—and he will be glad." Pulling
up her socks of softest fawn skin, then shoving her feet deep
into her heavily soled, thickly insulated knee-high moc-

casins, Ika rose and wriggled into her hooded, multilayered hunting tunic.

"What are you doing, daughter?"

"I *will* hunt with my father!"

"He has forbidden us to go alone beyond the palisade!"

"Rest a while longer, Katohya, and do not fear for Eldest Daughter. I will be back with Xohkantakeh soon enough, with whatever small, weak thing he has chosen to be a fitting gift for my sister."

"Beware of your tongue, Ika. It is as sharp as a spearpoint. But remember that it is rooted in your mouth and, if used to hurl words unwisely, may well cut you more deeply than it offends the object of your derision!"

"I speak only the truth!" Ika snapped as she turned on her heels and, ignoring Katohya's further protests, went from the lodge, only to stop dead in her tracks.

It was cold, so cold the girl felt as though she had just been slapped. Startled by the painful sting of the wind, she hurriedly drew up her hood and pulled its thick foxtail ruff forward around her face as, for a moment, she suspected that the very air was repudiating her fractious manner toward Katohya, her contemptuous words about her sister, and her blatant disobedience of Xohkantakeh's command not to venture beyond the palisade alone. The moment passed. Ika felt foolish as she wondered how she could not have expected the cold embrace of the wind. It had been winter for so long she had almost forgotten what it was like to go from the lodge into the warmth of a summer night. Now, however, as she shoved her hands into her gloves and looked around, she was surprised to see that although stars were still shivering in the fading darkness of a sky that glowed pink in the light of a dying aurora, the first hint of dawn was blushing upon the world. She smiled, her mood instantly soothed by the promise of a new day and by the familiar starry form of the Great Father Bear sprawling across the sky with the Little Bear at his side.

"So, too, shall it always be with Xohkantakeh and Ika!" she informed the starry twosome. "One cannot hunt without the other!"

She took a step forward, then paused, squinting into the wind, her smile gone. Wolves were singing far beyond the palisade; their voices came from all around.

"The pack is gathering," warned Katohya as she came from the lodge bundled in her bed furs against the cold.

Ika made no reply. Cocking her head and holding her ruff slightly open, she listened to the long, deep, steadily ascending monotones and could not remember a time when her band had not shared the hunting grounds of wolves. The animals were as much a part of the natural order of her world as the coming and going of the wind or the passage of clouds across the sky; as long as they were heeded and guarded against, there was no need to fear them. Indeed, Xohkantakeh had taught her to observe and learn from the ways of wolves, for he believed they were much like men and that, in the country of their kind, hunters would always find meat so long as they remembered the wolves' potential not only to lead to prey but to turn upon a careless hunter and make meat of him, or *her*.

Ika raised a speculative brow. She had killed and eaten the flesh of many an animal, including wolves, but she could not recall ever coming close enough to her own death to imagine herself as meat. Yet now, hearing the wolves' song, she shivered a little, for she knew that Katohya was right: The pack was gathering, summoning the sun and one another to the hunt.

"They are many," Katohya observed.

"But they are far away," countered Ika, listening intently to the subtle differences in pitch that told her she was hearing the vocalizations of at least eight different wolves. One among these stood well apart from the others, alone, it seemed, raising sharp, broken ululations from the summit of a hill that lay just to the west of the encampment.

"Listen," urged Katohya. "I have heard that wolf before. Always it cries alone. And always from the western hill. If I did not know better, I would swear that it is not a wolf at all but a dog trying to win acceptance into the pack."

Ika had only the vaguest memory of dogs. There were none of their kind in this far land to which Xohkantakeh had led her little family.

She cocked her head to the opposite side. There was something distractingly plaintive about the odd cry. It touched a deep inner nerve of sympathy and roused disturbing memories that refused to coalesce into clarity. Ika frowned. After only a few staccato wails, the wolf with the cracked voice was silent, and, inexplicably, she was glad.

"Come back into the warmth of the lodge, child."

Child! Again the hated word. Ika glared down at Katohya. The woman was half her size and carried her life spirit within a frame as slender and delicate as that of an antelope, but with little of the muscle to match. Although Katohya's face was lost to darkness within the tent she had made of her bed furs, the girl could nevertheless imagine her earnest expression and was in no mood to tolerate her falsely placed concern. "I will hunt with Xohkantakeh!" she declared as she moved to tie on her snow walkers.

"I will not let you go!"

Ika snatched up her spears. "I will not let you stop me!" Casting a jaundiced eye toward the conical brushwood shelter within which her sister lay sleeping, she brazenly followed Xohkantakeh's tracks to the palisade and beyond.

"Ika!"

The girl ignored her foster mother's call. She would answer for her lack of respect and disobedience later. Xohkantakeh was hunting without her! He needed her! She knew he did, and so she hurried across the snow-mantled land. It seemed to be welcoming her, affirming the rightness of her purpose as, from across broad hills and within dark primordial forest, the wind sang with the wolves. Ika raised her voice and sang defiantly back to them both:

> *"Yah hay! I am Ika! I come!*
> *Hay yah! To walk with Xohkantakeh, I come!*

Hay yah! See this girl come boldly into the wind!
Hay yah! I am Ika! I come unafraid of wolves!
Yah hay!"

The words and drumbeat cadence of her striding-forth-alone-across-the-land song silenced the wolves and emboldened the girl's heart. Her young spirit exalted in her own courage, in the savage splendor of the Ice Age winter world, and in the joy she found in being alive and a part of it. The rolling surface of the snowpack was hard and granular beneath her feet; it yielded excellent purchase to her willow-framed, sinew-webbed snow walkers. Using the butt end of one of her spears as a balance prod, she deliberately kept her steps long and purposeful lest potential predators mistake her solitary condition for weakness. At last, weary of her song, she sent her voice across the miles like an invisible lance, slicing distance with the sharply articulated cry of her father's name.

"Xohkantakeh!"

Again and again she called. Soon he would hear. Soon he would answer. He would wait for his eldest daughter, who would tell him of her dream and share her gladness in it. They would hunt together, and then, seeing her strength and skill and daring, Xohkantakeh would know that although Lanacheela was the first of his daughters to enter the lodge of blood, Ika was the one most worthy to be his new woman. She trembled to think of it.

The wind had dropped. Ika stopped, silence surrounding her. It was as though the world and sky were holding their breath, waiting for the sun to rise and a new day to be born. The moment was transcendently beautiful. She threw her arms wide, rejoicing in it until a raven came winging toward her out of the east, its long dark wings bearing it northward as they sliced soundlessly across the sky above her head. Somewhere alarmingly nearby, a wolf howled, once.

Ika winced, stiffened as a surge of adrenaline heated her blood and caused every nerve in her body to bristle. Spears at the ready, she turned and looked around. Close to her left rose the broad, windswept dome of the stony hill from which she had earlier heard the solitary wolf raise its odd, broken ululations. She squinted upward at bare, snow-spattered, virtually treeless scree. If the now-silent howler was there, she could see no sign of it. Nevertheless, she swallowed hard, knowing all too well that this did not mean that the beast was not there, watching and taking measure of her vulnerability from behind a boulder or the scabby-barked trunk of a weather-stunted tree.

"Hmmph!" she exclaimed. Even though she knew full well that where there was one wolf there were probably others, she reminded herself that she was armed with well-honed lances that were stronger, sharper, and more dangerous than the teeth of any wolf. As long as she walked wisely and warily and gave no sign of fear or vulnerability, she had no reason to be afraid of their kind.

She went on. Under the rapidly fading star glow of the Great Bear in the sky, the wind gusted now and again out of the north. As she walked into it, calm returned to Ika's spirit. She was smiling again when, with a start, she paused before a looted cache pit and looked down on the enormous tracks of an animal. Great bears walked not only in the sky but also in the world of Man—and of these huge, solitary, potentially man-eating marauders Ika was afraid.

Her mouth went dry; her heart was pounding at the back of her throat. Surely her father was not hunting such a dangerous animal? Surely this great bear could not be the feast gift that Xohkantakeh intended for her sister? *Surely* he would not put himself at risk for Lanacheela unless he loved and honored her more than life itself?

"Aiee!" Ika cried. "She is not worthy! *I* am not worthy! Nothing in all of this world or the world beyond is worth the loss of my father's life!" Yet even as she spoke, she saw that the tracks of the man did indeed overlay the paw prints of the great bear. Despairing, she hurried forward on the trail.

"Xohkantakeh! Wait! You must not hunt such a beast alone, my father! Xohkantakeh!" There was panic in Ika's voice, in her scent, in every movement of her body, but the

fear she was experiencing was not for herself; it was for
Xohkantakeh. She kept on her way, uncaring of the danger
to herself.

But the wolf cared. As the frightened girl followed the
trail of the man, the dark-pelaged bitch caught the scent of
prey on the rising wind and followed.

Xohkantakeh had come far since leaving the lodge. Without Ika to consider, there had been no need to restrict the
length of his stride, and although he allowed himself an occasional pause in which to catch his breath, he had made
good time. The sun had not yet risen above the eastern
hills, but now, with the benign light of morning ripening
upon the world, the encampment and looted cache pit lay
behind him, as did the first of the two snares he had set the
previous day.

The giant frowned as he stomped on. Great Paws was
headed for the river. Somewhere a wolf howled and a
young girl cried his name, but Xohkantakeh heard nothing except the ragged suck of his own breath as, lost in
thought, he reflected sourly on the hours he had wasted
contriving his snares. The first, set in a narrow, south-
facing creek drainage overgrown with young trees and old
deadfall, had been the most promising. Bear sign had
been everywhere: claw and tooth marks in trees debarked
and girdled by the animal in its search for sap; upturned
logs, disemboweled by the bear's patient probings for
grubs and winter-sluggish rodents; bits of tawny fur tufting the underside of branches beneath which the beast had
passed; and here and there the telltale look and stink of
urine-stained snow and long, wrist-thick tubes of frozen
excrement.

Xohkantakeh had been sobered by the certainty that
he walked within the hunting grounds of Great Paws.
Pausing to look over his shoulder many times, he had
worked as quickly as he could to fashion a strong rope
from three lengths of thong he had retrieved from the
looted cache pit. At one end of this line he had made a slip

noose large enough to ensnare the head of the largest bear
he could imagine, and when he had done this, he made it
larger still. After securing the other end of the rope high
around the trunk of a sturdy young black spruce that he
hoped would bend rather than break when stressed, he had
spread the noose across a thicket of low-growing hardwoods. Into the thicket he had tossed half the wedge of
well-aged bison fat that was to have been his afternoon
meal. In order to reach the fat, the bear would have to enter the thicket—and in doing so pass through the slip
noose. There were sturdier and more dependable snares
for large predators, but for a man working alone with
minimal supplies in dangerous surroundings, the slip
snare was the age-old and most reliable way. If Xohkantakeh had been lucky, Great Paws would have ambled
into the snare and strangled himself in his frantic efforts
to be free.

His face tightened. He had not been lucky. Sometime
early last night the bear had been drawn to the snare by the
smell of the rancid fat. Somehow—by cleverness or pure,
blind-sided good fortune—Great Paws had pulled the noose
free of the trees, entered the thicket, consumed the bait, and
gone his way unharmed.

Now the bear tracks in the snow led Xohkantakeh
north, out of the trees, away from his second snare. Grumbling against aching limbs and labored breathing, he seriously regretted not having taken the time to secrete a bone
skewer inside the fat. If he had done this, his worries
would be over, because the bear would now be on its way
to a slow death from perforations in its intestine. He exhaled restlessly, wondering how he could have overlooked
so simple and deadly a hunting trick, then conceded that
Great Paws had never been lured into taking baited meat
before; always some other animal found the "prize" and
died instead.

Truly, he thought with a shiver, this bear *was* more than
a bear!

The tracks led on. His feet felt as though weighted with
stones. Then, slowly, he found himself distracted and

pleased by the look of the land. It was a high, wide island of undulating plain rolling away between the trees. Its openness reminded him of the hunting grounds of his ancestors, and of his youth. He smiled, forced himself to lengthen his stride, thinking as he walked that, in summer, there would be grass in this place, grass so tall that even a giant of a man could move unseen as he hunted the great migratory herds of big game animals that roamed back and forth across the world, opening pathways through the grass so that Man and other large carnivores could follow and make meat of them.

The corners of Xohkantakeh's broad mouth flexed. He reminded himself that grass or no grass, the big herds did not come this far south; forest and bogland kept them to the north and west. Yet, in his mind's eye, teeming rivers of big game ran before him across the golden prairies of the past: mammoth, camel, long-horned bison, high-leaping pronghorn, fat-bellied horse, and giant elk with antlers as broad and many-branched as the crowns of ancient oaks. Xohkantakeh saw them all. And he saw himself, young again, strong again. Unafraid again.

Brandishing his spears, he uttered a bellowing whoop of pure delight in the moment, for with memories of youth came newfound strength and the startling realization that he was glad the bear had not fallen prey to his first snare, glad the animal had led him out of wooded country so that he could run like a youth once more beneath open sky, and glad Great Paws was still alive.

"You have dared to come from the winter earth to challenge me!" he roared. "This time I will not turn away! The spear of Xohkantakeh will taste the flesh of Great Paws before this day is done!"

A low laugh rippled out of the giant. He was following the bear with an eagerness for confrontation that should have troubled him. Not since his first solitary hunt as a boy on the brink of manhood had he felt quite so focused and—yes, there was no other way to describe it—reckless and free.

He was running now, loping like a wolf, heading into the wind on the scent of Great Paws until, suddenly, the land fell away before him. Just in time, he stopped dead in his tracks. His great body barely won the battle for balance and control as he found himself poised at the edge of an abyss. He gasped. His hand tightened around the shafts of his spears as he surveyed the broad vistas of snow-covered hill and plain that stretched beyond the edge of the promontory to which Great Paws had led him.

"Is this how you would make an end of me?" he snarled to the unseen bear. "It will not be so easy for you!"

The wind in Xohkantakeh's face was much stronger now, out of the north, cold and spitting alluvial grit. Through squinting eyes he could see the river, white, stark. Though frozen solid, it remained a living force resting with deceptive passivity within the mile-wide embankments that held it an easy captive during its long winter sleep. And there, on the tableland above the closest embankment, he could see a herd of musk oxen defined in the first rays of sunrise blazing cold yellow above the eastern ranges.

Xohkantakeh salivated at the thought of the rich red hump meat that could be won by a man who dared risk hunting such prey. His eyebrows rose. Irony touched him; he was risking far more than being gored by an ox this day. He took a cautious step forward, leaning outward to scan the tracks of the bear. Telltale imprints led from the promontory down a precipitous but passable ridge, then skirted the peripheries of broken stands of spruce and tamarack.

"Hmm," murmured the giant, struck by the realization that the bear could have vanished into the trees at any time. Instead, Great Paws was keeping to open ground, laying a trail into the river valley that a blind man could follow. His brow came down. An animal screamed on the open land he had left behind—an antelope, perhaps, or small deer, he thought fleetingly. But his attention was focused ahead and far below. He could not have looked away if he tried. There, where land and trees met the river on a broad, stony floodplain, was the bear.

"Great Paws!" The name of the beast left Xohkan-

takeh's lips as an exclamation not so much of recognition
but of incredulity. Even from this great height and distance
he was stunned by the size of the animal as it slowly stood
upright on its hind limbs and looked straight up the wall of
the promontory toward him.

He stared.

The bear stared back.

For a moment, just before the beast dropped to all
fours again and turned away, Xohkantakeh knew that he
was looking into the eyes not of a bear but of a man—no!
of a warrior!—challenging another of his own kind to final
battle.

As the bear disappeared into thick, low-growing scrub
growth, Xohkantakeh knew that Great Paws was inviting him
to follow. He knew this as surely as he now understood that
this hunt was to be his last. His head went high. He felt no
fear, no remorse. With the certainty of death came a sudden
and oddly soothing sense of disconnection from all he had left
behind: woman and daughters; the warm, comfortable, well-
made camp—indeed, *all* the untold numbers of warm, comfortable, well-made camps he had raised over the past many
years, in which he had greeted every dawn with the ghosts of
warning and regret whispering at the back of his mind:

*In all of this world beyond the world of warring tribes,
you are the only man.*

Walk wisely, Outcast.

Walk warily, Renegade.

Forget that you were once a warrior.

*What does it matter that your woman and daughters
must surely name you Woman behind your back? You have
chosen to lead them into this land of no people. When you
go forth to hunt you must do so with your wits and seek only
small or stupid game that presents no challenge to your skill
or daring because if you are killed or injured and can no
longer bring meat to your females, they will surely die.*

Xohkantakeh shuddered in frustration. "No more!" he exclaimed, weary to the marrow of his bones of worrying about
the welfare of others and certain that the last thing he wanted
was to survive this hunt, return to the encampment, and be

obligated to celebrate the maturity of Lanacheela, on whose young body he was expected to make new life and thus increase his worries and responsibilities.

Xohkantakeh's eyes narrowed. Time weighted him down. He thought of the many eager, soft-thighed young women with whom he had lain and enjoyed a warrior's privilege of first blooding, of the wives he had loved and outlived, of the sons he had seen killed in battle, of the daughters and hunt brothers who now walked the wind forever and awaited his coming to the land of spirits.

A sudden thrill went through him.

Has not Owl called to you in the light of last night's aurora?

"Yes!"

Have you not trained your females to hunt, and are your daughters not at last mature enough to survive without you?

"Yes!"

And is not a hunter of the People of the Land of Grass entitled to one last good kill before he dies?

"Yes!"

And if you end your days as meat in the belly of a bear, then will you not have died a warrior, facing a worthy enemy once more before your woman and daughters see the weakness that has been growing in you during the past moons?

"Yes!" Again a tremor went through him. Now, while the renewed strength of youth invigorated his spirit and the long-forgotten drumbeat cadence of a warrior's heart gave courage to his blood, it *was* time for him to die. But not before he made an end of Great Paws. For the bear as well as for the man, this would be the final conflict.

He raised his arms. The sun was rising above the eastern hills. He faced it, welcomed it, and made his death song boldly.

"Let the eye of Father Above behold Xohkantakeh on this his last day! Let the spirits of the Ancient Ones behold this bold hunter and warrior of the People of the Land of Grass! Let the ancestors prepare to take his spirit to the sun and, with him, the spirit of the great bear who

will threaten the woman and daughters of Xohkantakeh
no more!"

Ika was paralyzed with dread and confusion. How could she
have been so clumsy? How could she have allowed herself
to trip and fall and then cry out like a foolish child? Perhaps
Katohya was right about her. Perhaps she was still a child
after all.

No! She would never concede to that! But perhaps she
would never have a chance to concede to anything again.
With her spears scattered just out of reach and her left foot
caught in the lacings of a broken snow walker, Ika found
herself on her knees looking straight into the eyes of the
biggest, blackest, ugliest wolf she had ever seen.

Head down, tail tucked, the animal stared at Ika. As the
girl looked into the menacing eyes of the advancing carnivore, her image stared back at her out of the beast's fixed
and ravenous eyes. For the first time in her young life, Ika
saw herself as meat. For the second time in the last few moments, she screamed.

The sound startled the girl as much as it did the wolf.
The animal jumped, yipped, and then lowered its head and
lifted its lips in a quivering snarl. It held its ground, but
something in its eyes and stance and scent had changed; its
posture was defensive now. Sensing this, Ika was suddenly
emboldened. Scrambling to her feet, she kicked out as hard
as she could, smashing the animal across the face with her
broken snow walker.

Wide-eyed, she could barely believe her eyes or good
fortune. The wolf yelped and ran! The force of her kick had
somehow untangled the laces of the snow walker and freed
her foot, and even when the broken walker fell in two pieces
on the snow, the wolf kept running, back across the way it
had come.

"Aiee!" Ika exhaled with relief, almost laughing
aloud. How bold she was! How daring! "If only Katohya
were here to see this daughter's bravery and resourceful-
ness. No 'child' could make a wolf run in fear!" Self-

satisfaction warmed her heart. The feeling, however, was short-lived.

In the dazzling light of the fully risen sun, Xohkantakeh's voice came to Ika on the wind. He was chanting, the sound like thunder rumbling over distant mountains. The girl turned and saw him, arms upraised, standing between her and the sun. Bewilderment furrowed her brow. He had not heard her first cry, or her second. And yet he was so close!

"Xohkantakeh!" she called for what seemed the thousandth time since she had left the lodge.

There was no reply.

Ika frowned. Why did he not turn to welcome her? There was only one way to find out. With a sigh of resolve she bent, hurriedly untied her other snow walker, slipped it off, and tucked it under one arm. After retrieving its damaged mate along with her spears, she plodded anxiously across the snow to the giant's side. "My father, I have come!" she called. She looked up at him, relaxed in the closeness of one whom she found as indomitable as a mountain.

Xohkantakeh did not move. Head high, arms raised to the sun, he stopped chanting but made no other response.

"My father . . . ?" Ika moved to stand between the giant and the sun, where he must surely see her as she tugged lightly at his tunic.

Still no response.

"The white bird has summoned me from my dreams!" she told him, taken suddenly with rapturous delight, certain that her joyous revelation would win his complete attention.

Nothing.

Ika was hurt and confused by his utter disregard; it was as though he were pretending she was not there. Fighting mixed feelings of inadequacy and indignation, her quick temper suddenly flared as she took hold of his tunic and tugged again, this time as sharply and imperatively as she spoke. "Lanacheela is not the only one of Xohkantakeh's daughters to be honored by the forces of Creation. Soon Ika will also become a woman! The white bird will return to fly in the light of day. You will see. Ika is strong! Ika is brave! Ika will be the one to make sons for Xohkantakeh. Strong, brave sons. And then Lanacheela—may she be Mother of Daughters Only—will hunt with Xohkantakeh to honor Ika . . . if Lanacheela is not afraid!"

The giant's body stiffened.

Ika babbled on, wanting him to know how much she loved him and how worthy she was of his favor. "Katohya told me you did not need me to hunt at your side this day, but I have seen the tracks of the one you follow. Aiee! I would not let you hunt such prey alone. I have driven away a black wolf! I will not be afraid to . . ." The exuberant rush of words died in Ika's mouth as she saw her father turn down his head and slowly—in a way that made her think of a great and fearsome eagle roused from sleep—fix her with purely raptorial eyes.

"Perhaps it is time you learned to be afraid!" he warned, rage twisting his mouth into a grimace.

Ika had never seen Xohkantakeh so angry. Stunned, she told herself his mood must surely pass. She tried to produce a smile that would calm his anger; it was no use. Not even the black wolf had appeared so menacing, and it had been set to devour her!

"Have you forgotten that I have forbidden you to go beyond the palisade alone?" Xohkantakeh demanded.

"I . . . no, but I—"

"And did Katohya not tell you to remain at the lodge?"

"Yes, but I—"

"Her words were *my* words!" he interrupted fiercely. "When you disdained her request, so also did you disdain me! And now you dare to stand between me and the sun . . . to shatter my song of intent to the Ancient Ones . . . to turn me from my purpose."

"No, Xohkantakeh! Never! Without you beside me, there is no sun! Your song is my song! Your purpose is my purpose!"

He stared. Something in her words had touched him. Deeply. But not for her good.

Holding his gaze, Ika felt herself shrivel with dread. A disturbing fire smoldered in his eyes. Blacker and more dangerous than the stare of the wolf, it terrified her. A moment later it blazed up, and she saw madness in it.

"Is your purpose mine, then?" he challenged, taking hold of her shoulder and shoving her with uncharacteristic roughness toward the edge of the promontory. "Come! Hunt with me! We will soon see!"

2

"Bring her to this place!" cried the shaman. "Now, Warakan! Before it is too late!"

The young man turned. What had the old man just said? The words swept through Warakan's mind before he could grasp them, startling him from his early-morning reverie as they came from the depths of the cavern in which the ancient one secreted himself each night like a little brown bat retreating from the light of day. Warakan's handsome face tensed with impatience. He knew he was being unfair. Jhadel loved light as much as any man; it was from cold that he sought escape, from the bitter, soul-numbing cold that gnawed at his ancient bones and fed upon his sanity.

Sadness touched Warakan as he waited for Jhadel to call again. Silence brought a familiar sense of loneliness and frustration. He had emerged from the cave in the troubling light of a red dawn to stand in an encircling windbreak of young oaks, within which it had become his habit to greet the rising sun. He did not want to return into the cavern. He did not want to see to the endless needs of one for whom yesterday, today, and tomorrow were hopelessly entangled in the mists of a mind that had once been as brilliant as sunlight flashing on clear crystal. There was no talking with such a man—not real talk, not talk that eased the spirit and brought laughter to the heart. And so Warakan stood alone within the grove on the broad, stony terrace above the frozen creek, watching the sun rise above the cold heights of the eastern plateau, then facing West Wind, inviting her to comb his hip-length hair with cool, invisible fingers while she sang through the forest and filled his nostrils with the scent of the distant mountains and sunstruck grasslands of his birth.

"Warakan! Where are you, Warakan?" the shaman cried again. This time, although the holy man's words were clearly audible and far less strident, a quivering, almost ephemeral lightness of tone betrayed the disorientation of the very old.

"I am here, Jhadel. Outside. In the grove." Compassion softened facial features that might have been considered too perfect for a would-be warrior except for the small scars at the sides of his mouth and a crooked bump in the bridge of his nose that bespoke a long-healed break. His long, obsidian eyes narrowed as he fixed his gaze on the entrance to the cavern and waited for the old shaman to come tottering from beneath the jutting brow of the streamside cliff in which they had sheltered the past two winters.

Warakan knew he was expecting the impossible. For eight long years he and Jhadel had lived and traveled together as a band unto themselves. Following mammoth and occasional man sign from one hunting camp to another, at Jhadel's insistence they had deliberately put the country of warring tribes behind them and journeyed eastward beyond the edge of the world. Through broken expanses of spruce forest and mixed grassland they trekked, across fly-infested muskeg, over rolling tundral barrens, until they found their way blocked by a cold and monstrous body of water. In hopes of finding a climate that would take the ache from Jhadel's brittle bones and restore some small semblance of strength to his failing body, they turned south along the banks of one of several mighty rivers. Warakan could not have said just when they turned east again, following migratory game into the green deeps of a primeval woodland unlike any they had ever seen. More hardwood than evergreen, the forest was home to

birds, beasts, and all manner of green growing things
whose names and ways they did not know. The trees broke
the back of the cold wind that had until then been so much
a part of their lives—a hard, grit-laden wind that blew constantly from its birthplace in a towering mountain range of
ice that rose beyond the northern barrens with its feet
firmly planted in the great lake Jhadel believed to be the
Mother of All Rivers.

The young man's brow rose thoughtfully. Life Giver,
the great white mammoth totem of the People, had disappeared into those mountains of ice. Warakan would have
hunted the tusker long ago, for the spirits of the Ancient
Ones had promised invincibility in war to the one who
dared to hunt, slay, and consume the flesh and blood of the
great white mammoth. Jhadel, however, had other ambi-
tions for him.

Warakan's brow slumped as he surveyed his surroundings. The southeastern forest had proved warmer than the
broken woodlands to the north, and it was rich in small,
unusual kinds of game, but not even a shaman of Jhadel's
skill had been able to prevent Time from finding their
place of seclusion and working its will upon them both.
Warakan had been a boy of nine when Jhadel forced him
from the country of their ancestors. Now he was a man in
his prime. Jhadel's once hawk-sharp eyes were white with
blindness, and of late he was so unsteady on his feet that
he no longer even tried to negotiate the distance between
his bed and the entrance to the cave without Warakan's
support.

Touched by pity for himself as much as for Jhadel,
Warakan sucked in a ragged breath. Suddenly distracted by
changing light, he gazed upward. High above the trees a
dark form was soaring before the sun, setting shadows shifting back and forth across the world below. Shielding his
eyes with the back of his hand, Warakan recognized the ma-
jestic silhouette, the slow, arrogant stroke of mighty wings,
the intermittent flash of opalescence as sunlight snagged
brown neck feathers and transformed them into a collar of
shimmering gold.

"Brother of Sun and Moon! Mediator between the pow-

ers of Earth and Sky! Golden Eagle!" Warakan spoke the
names of the sacred raptor with reverence, instinctively
touching the eagle feather he wore braided into his forelock.
He had not seen or heard a golden eagle for many a long
moon and, until this moment, had been convinced that the
great raptors of the grasslands and western peaks sought
neither meat nor nesting sites in the closed canopy of the
eastern forest. "Ah," he exhaled with the pure pleasure of
again seeing a creature that, in the hunting grounds of his
ancestors, had been the preeminent guiding animal spirit of
both his father and grandfather. Indeed, he believed with all
his heart that the golden eagle feather he wore in his hair
had come to him as a gift from the sky spirits on the day his
grandfather, Shateh, chieftain and shaman of the People of
the Land of Grass, was betrayed by his own warriors and
slain by enemies in the stronghold of the People of the
Watching Star.

Memories flared. A firelit cave. The beat of war drums.
A mortally wounded man lying close to the dead body of
another. The stink of death and perfidy. Blood—everywhere, blood. And in the shadows, a shaman lurking,
watching, eyes sunken and steady with intent beneath a
crown of raven feathers as a taloned hand extended to a
battered captive clinging to the embrace of a dying grandfather.

"I have not forgotten my vow to avenge you, Shateh!"
proclaimed Warakan. A moment later—as the eagle cried
and banked and disappeared into the face of the rising sun—
he was overcome by a devastating sense of loss and frustration. He was seventeen. In the distant land of his ancestors
he would be a warrior by now. He would have a woman,
perhaps even more than one, and children, most certainly all
sturdy, aggressive young males like himself. He would possess slaves whose subservience and fear of him would be
living proof of his prowess in battle. And yet here he stood
beyond the edge of the world, bound by loyalty to an old
man's needs, while Shateh remained unavenged and those
who had abandoned, betrayed, and slain him no doubt lived
on to mock his name!

Warakan moaned softly. He wondered how many had

survived the grass fire he had set loose upon the wind to devour his enemies while he and Jhadel fled for safety on the other side of the flames. How he lusted to know! How he envied the eagle its freedom! How he yearned to follow its flight, not eastward over the high plateau into unknown land, but into the west! His spirit ached to avenge the dead and to return home as a proven warrior.

"Warakan!"

Jhadel's summons made the young man wince. His mood had changed; the golden eagle no longer set shadows upon the earth, but they remained within Warakan's spirit as he deliberately stood his ground, knowing that if Jhadel had his way, he would never possess the woman of his dreams or hunt the totem, much less return to the land of his ancestors as an avenging warrior. He sighed angrily. He was sick of mothering the old Peacedreamer, of listening to his endless tales, of feeding him, bathing him, dressing him, of carrying him outside when the weather allowed so that he could sit, bundled in his decrepit bison-hide cloak, withered face upturned to the sun while his thoughts ran free among recollections that only the ghosts of his own youth could follow.

A sharp twist of guilt caught Warakan off guard, dangerously close to the brink of wishing the ancient shaman dead. He was appalled at his selfishness. Jhadel had given up everything for him—betrayed the trust of his own tribe, turned his back on comfort, disdained the privileges of rank—and all to save the life of a captive boy in whom he imagined the potential for future shamanic power. Warakan did not share Jhadel's vision of the future, but he could not deny that the holy man had saved his life. How could he not reciprocate by caring for Jhadel until, at last and inevitably, there was no longer need of his care?

"Warakan!"

"I am coming, Wise One!" Warakan called back, even as he hissed annoyance through strong white teeth. In moments he was out of the grove and inside the enormous hollow that opened like a great gaping mouth in the south-facing creekside cliff. Long shafts of sunlight spread across the floor of the cave and illuminated the vaulted interior. Warakan followed the light to where the old man sat upright, wrapped in his bison hide, on a mattress of skins piled atop several layers of old woven matting. A dark, grizzled old she-wolf lay at his side.

The wolf looked up.

The old man did the same. All beaky nose and wide, gaping, seamless mouth, Jhadel resembled a defeathered little bird ready for trussing as he "stared" up at Warakan out of sightless eyes that showed white in his tattoo-blackened face. "We thought you had abandoned us," he said matter-of-factly and reached to lay a hand upon the head of the wolf.

Warakan flinched. "When have I ever given you cause to believe that I would be less than loyal?" he snapped defensively. "And surely Sister Wolf knows that I would not leave one who has walked with me since I carried her as a pup from a burning enemy encampment in the days when you and I first traveled together."

"Hmm. You were then only a pup yourself. Now you are a man . . . a man who, I think, still yearns to be a wolf."

Warakan frowned. Jhadel was blind, but somehow he did not need his eyes to see into the inner workings of his companion's heart. Feeling vulnerable to the old shaman's stare, the young man turned his own gaze to the wolf. She thumped her tail. Warakan felt her affection for him even though he knew that if he were to summon her to his side, she would not come. These past days and nights, Sister Wolf would not leave Jhadel except for brief forays from the cave to relieve herself or hunt up a quick meal of rabbit or mice. This meat she invariably consumed on the spot, then regurgitated in the cavern at the foot of the old man's bed, for it was the way of wolves to share the bounty of a successful hunt with the young or sick among the pack. Jhadel always thanked the animal and explained that, since appetite had left him, she must reconsume his portion of the feast lest it be wasted. Now, as Warakan held the steady, yellow-eyed gaze of the animal, it occurred to him that when the old shaman's spirit left his body to walk the wind forever, there was a strong chance the spirit of Sister Wolf would follow. He did not want to think of it.

"Come," Warakan said to the old man, shivering a little in the damp cold of the interior as he scanned the upper cave walls and ceiling, which had begun to stain and seep. Last year it had been the same—the damp and the dripping, sure signs that the lower layer of the winter snowpack was melting and percolating downward through the earth. Soon it would be spring. Warakan could feel it in his bones and said as much to Jhadel. "Soon the White Giant Winter will leave the forest. Come, I say. You stay too much within the shadows. The sun is up. I will help you outside."

"No!" Jhadel was adamant. "My juices rest content; I have no need to release them. But you must go! You must bring her here, into the forest beyond the edge of the world where warring tribes cannot harm her!"

Warakan raised an inquisitive brow. Were these the words that had roused him from his earlier reverie? It seemed so, but they made even less sense to him now. He shook his head. "You have told me as many times as there are feathers on the back of a teratorn that Mah-ree, woman of the Red World shaman, Cha-kwena, is not to be my woman."

"And so! Her man has followed the great white mammoth totem into mountains of ice where no one will ever find him, or her. But someday their children will come out of the rising sun, and—"

"I will not wait for their return," Warakan interrupted coolly. "But someday I will find Cha-kwena. And I will take his woman!"

"She is *not* the only woman in the world!"

"For me there is no other."

"Bah! For you there is one who will come out of the sun! One who will walk with wolves! One who is in danger now and for whom you must . . ."

"Abandon you?"

The old man trembled, pulled his robe tighter around himself, and closed his eyes. When he opened them again, with a start, his expression was that of one who had gone to sleep in one place and awakened to find himself transported somewhere else entirely. "What? Where . . . ? Are you still with me, Warakan?"

"Yes, Jhadel." Warakan dropped to one knee before the old man and laid a reassuring hand on his bony, fur-covered shoulder. "I am still with you."

"Ah. It is good." Extending his face, Jhadel sniffed the air with broad, camel-like nostrils until, reassured by the familiar scent of the young man, he nodded, smiling. "We thought you had abandoned us." Resting one shriveled hand atop Warakan's, with the other he patted the wolf's head.

Warakan rolled his eyes as he realized that the old man's limited power of reason had just come a full, very small circle. So it was to be the same today as on other days, he thought forlornly. The old Peacedreamer's mind was drifting; at any given moment it was impossible to tell where his thoughts stood in time.

"Where would I go without telling you first?" Warakan asked gently.

"Back into the world of warring tribes! Back into the west to retrieve the magic spearhead of white chalcedony . . . a white spearhead to kill a white mammoth!"

"You made me bury that weapon and leave it behind many a long winter ago."

"Because it would be the death of you! But it is still there, in the high gorge, under the Watching Star . . . and in your mind. You would seek it. You would use it. And when the totem was slain you would return to the camps of the mammoth hunters who bore you. To the lodges of your father Masau, Mystic Warrior of the People of the Watching Star, and to the hunting camps of your grandfather, Shateh, shaman and chieftain of the People of the Land of Grass."

"You speak of the dead, Wise One."

"I speak of those who were enemies in life but whose spirits live on in you, Son of Two Tribes, for in the days and nights before the caul of blindness thickened over my eyes, I would look upon your face and form and see Masau and Shateh as they were in youth. It was as though they were alive again. Never in all my days have I seen a resemblance so strong. And I tell you now that someday you will look with their eyes upon the land of the ancestors, upon the hunting grounds of the People of the Watching Star and the People of the Land of Grass, and you will see that country not as an avenging warrior—but as a peacemaker and bringer of unity to all!"

"Never." The whisper sliced Warakan's spirit and made it bleed with the need of vengeance against those who had scarred his face and slaughtered nearly everyone he had ever loved. "Those who slew my father and grandfather, and those warriors of his tribe who abandoned him to his enemies, will die at my hand. This I have sworn!"

"Hmmph! And is this what Eagle asked of you just now as he flew into the face of the rising sun?"

Warakan gaped. "How . . . ?"

"I am blind but not *deaf* to the cries of my winged brothers and sisters of the sky! But you are both, Warakan, and your thoughts and dreams shame the memories and quell the hopes of the spirit warriors and shamans from whose loins you have sprung!"

"Shateh's spirit cannot rest upon the winds until it is avenged by one of his own blood!"

The old man gave a low exhalation. His head swung from side to side on the slender pillar of his neck as he fixed Warakan with his blind eyes. "When you were still a wild pup who walked with a bear and taunted your captors and dared steal the sacred stone talisman of the Ancient Ones from Mah-ree of the Red World, Medicine Woman of the Third Tribe, I watched you and took measure of you and knew you were the one into whose care the talisman was destined to come. The keeper of the sacred stone is Shaman above all shamans. The guardian of the sacred stone is also the guardian of the spirit of the People. And yet sometimes I wonder if I was wrong about you, for in all the long years that have passed since then and now, although I have tried to teach you everything I know, you have not yet learned to think as a shaman, Warakan!"

Seething with frustration, the young man gripped the

talisman suspended by a length of sinew around his neck. As hard as granite, as rough as old bone, and no larger than his thumb, the sacred stone of the Ancient Ones lay within the rough press of his palm like a stabbing tooth torn from the mouth of a young lion. "When I have hunted and slain Life Giver, the great white mammoth totem of the People . . . when I have won the woman of my heart . . . and when I have taken vengeance in Shateh's name upon my enemies in distant grasslands that lie beneath the eye of the Watching Star, perhaps then I will be Shaman!"

"Terms? You would dictate terms to the forces of Creation? Never! You may wear the sacred stone, Warakan, but I tell you now that the forces that dwell within the talisman speak through this shaman's mouth when he says that as long as the life spirit of Jhadel dwells within his body, you will not be an avenging warrior!"

"Then die, Peacedreamer, and let me live the life I was born to live!" Warakan shouted in a spurt of uncontrollable anger. Instantly contrite, he caught his breath, but it was too late to call back his words.

Jhadel recoiled as though struck. Pained incredulity widened his eyes and twisted his mouth as he gasped, "You wish death for me, and on the stone?"

"No, Jhadel! No!" Warakan quickly released the talisman, for his palm felt burned by it, as did his conscience. "If the spirits within the sacred talisman listened to me, you would be young and strong again, and we would be far from the depths of this cursed forest, feasting on the flesh of the great white mammoth. Mah-ree would be with us, and my enemies would be—"

"Enough!" A violent shiver shook the old man.

Warakan stared in disbelief as the ancient one's eyes bulged and his breath snagged in his throat; a moment later he sagged sideways and collapsed in a furry heap.

Sister Wolf was on her feet, tail tucked, nuzzling the old one, then taking hold of his furs with her foreteeth and pulling. But there was no response. "Jhadel!" cried Warakan. On both knees, he moved to cradle the old man in his arms.

The pallor of death was upon Jhadel's face as he opened

his sightless eyes and reached weakly for the young man's hands. "Ah, Warakan . . . we thought you had abandoned us."

"No, Jhadel. I will not abandon you."

"We must share the same vision and hope for the future, you and I!"

"I . . ." Warakan could not bring himself to continue the argument now. Although conciliation ran against the grain of his character, he had learned long ago that deception could be masked with truth. For Jhadel's sake he nodded and said placatingly, "Yes, Wise One. I share your vision."

Bony fingertips sought the young man's face and rested on his mouth. "You cannot use words to confound me, Warakan. Old I am, and dying now, I think, but I am still a shaman. I do not need eyes to see through you into your heart. You have shared my vision, yes, but you have not said that you would commit your life to the fulfillment of my hope for the peaceful unification of the Three Tribes."

Warakan exhaled; he was trapped and knew it. "Then I will say it now, Jhadel, and vow that it will be so if this will ease your—"

"No! You will not speak lies to appease my spirit." The old man's hands went to his own face, crossed, and lay trembling over his eyes. "Go!" he commanded. "Seek Golden Eagle, Brother of Sun and Moon, spirit guardian of your father and grandfather! In the way of the knowledge seekers of our tribe, call from the sky the sacred bird so that you may take and eat of his life. Through his blood and flesh, the spirits of the dead will speak. Perhaps you will listen to them as you will not listen to me. Perhaps you will then understand that what I ask of you demands more courage than the momentary valor of a warrior facing a single battle. And perhaps then you will know what Shateh and Masau both knew at the moment of their deaths: that Jhadel's hope for the future of the People is the *only* hope." When next he spoke, his voice was a thin wheeze. "Go, Warakan. And when you have done what I ask, return to me with a cloak of Eagle's wings that will carry my weary spirit to the sun!"

Warakan was shaken. Jhadel was dying; there was no

doubt about it. "I will not leave you, Wise One! Not to seek an eagle, or to search for a woman, or to hunt the totem that would grant me the power to take vengeance upon my enemies! I will stay. I will build up the fire to warm your spirit as well as your bones. I will bring you food and water. You will be strong again. You will see! Soon White Giant Winter will leave the land and Warm Moon will rise once more. Your favorite foods will be for the taking: sweet fern shoots and birds' eggs and the tender meat of fawns and young rabbits. Why, if all that you have said about the sacred stone is true, you are going to live forever! And do you know why? Because once, long ago, when I was still that wild boy who walked with a bear in the forest, I called upon the Four Winds and asked them to let you live as long as the mountains! On the power of the sacred stone I wished it! Did you know that, Jhadel?"

"Hmm." Jhadel did not move, but the long gash of his mouth puckered into a droll smile over the rubble of his few remaining teeth. "I knew, but not even mountains live forever, Warakan. Upon rock does Lichen feed while the Cold Sisters, Snow and Ice and the Great Nagger, Howling Wind, work with Rain and Sun until that which was once granite-hard and sky-high is reduced to only a handful of pebbles lying at the bottom of the river of life. This is the great Circle of Wisdom, the great Joy and the great Sadness, the great and unchangeable Teaching that all must learn and abide."

Warakan stared, sobered. "I will not leave you!"

"Sister Wolf will stay at my side. I will not be alone. There is food enough for several days in the parfleches and on the drying frames, and there is water in the bladder flasks. I will eat. I will drink. I will sleep. You need not fear for me. My spirit has assured me that it will not leave my body to walk the wind forever until the Northern Dancers set their campfires in the sky to light my way along the Great Star River to the cloud lodges of the ancestors. So go. Go now. And do not look back until you have accomplished that which I have asked of you."

Warakan winced as he remembered the auroral glow

that had drawn him from the cave before dawn. The Northern Dancers! When had he last seen their fiery dance across the sky? Memory did not serve him, not that he would have told Jhadel about the omen if it had. His brow furrowed. Deep, even breathing told him that the old man had drifted into dreams. Slowly he settled Jhadel amidst his sleeping furs and rose to his feet, aware of Sister Wolf's steady appraisal.

"I must go. And you must stay, as Wise One has commanded," he said. The animal lay down, placed her grizzled head across Jhadel's bedding, and watched Warakan over folded forepaws as he filled his fire horn, then took it up along with his fleshing dagger, medicine and hunting bags, a pair of spears, and the long, narrow, beautifully designed snow walkers Jhadel had crafted for him.

"I will seek communion with Eagle and return as soon as I can. If luck is with me, I will bring fresh meat for us all!" Warakan left the cave and stepped into the cool, sweet, welcoming air of morning, smiling with relief. Death lived with the old man inside the cavern. Life was here, beneath the sun, in the embrace of West Wind as she sighed through the grove from which the happy conversations of migratory songbirds were promising the advent of spring . . . a spring that most likely would be Jhadel's last.

Warakan's heart lurched. *Soon you will be alone with only a wolf to keep you company, and only a vow spoken to grant peace to a dying man will hold you captive to his foolish dreams.* Despite his yearning to be free to go his own way in life, the premise was devastating. "I will not think of it!" he declared aloud as he walked on without looking back, finding solace and strength in the warm bearskin robe. It was worn and tattered around the edges, but he had not the slightest doubt that the power of the great short-faced bear had come to him when he slew the beast on his first hunt, skinned it, ate of its heart, then took pity on its cubs and managed to raise to adulthood the male of the twosome as though it were, like himself, an orphaned human being. The memory both pleased and saddened him; he wondered what had become of his tawny, unruly "child" in the years since it had grown to maturity and sought its own kind in grasslands far to the northwest.

"May it be that you survived the great fire, and may we meet again, Bear Brother!" he said. With one hand curled around the sacred stone, he shouted the remainder of his wish upon the rising wind. "And may your enemies tremble in fear of you in the hunting grounds you have chosen as your own!"

3

The bear came unseen onto the tableland above the great river. Slowly, on silent paws, it advanced across broken snowpack, concealing its form and scent in thick underbrush and a favoring wind until, suddenly, it exploded from the camouflage of bare-branched willows. With one paw and then another it hooked the hind limbs of a hugely pregnant musk ox that had been grazing apart from her herd, much too close to the trees.

"Great Paws!" A startled Xohkantakeh spoke the name of the beast that had been the source of his nightmares for so many years. Glad for any excuse to pause and catch his breath, he observed the bear from his hard-won position on an outcropping just above the base of the promontory. The descent from the summit had not been especially difficult, but on the narrow ridge, steeper than anticipated, he had focused all his thoughts on finding safe footing for himself and the girl as they proceeded downward across ice and loose scree. His anger toward his daughter had soon cooled, and after a while he had even forgotten the object of his pursuit—until its reappearance from the undergrowth elicited an exclamation from Ika.

The giant frowned. The bear had burst so suddenly from the trees that he had not immediately recognized the blur of tawny yellow as it charged from cover. Indeed, until this moment, Xohkantakeh would not have believed it possible for an animal of such awesome size to move with such speed. Now, however, as he watched the bear bring down the musk ox while the rest of the herd broke and scattered, its power and agility were undeniable, and there was no mistaking the specific identity of the scarred, high-humped boar.

"My father knows the name of this bear?" whispered Ika as, descending carefully onto the outcrop, she pressed close to Xohkantakeh's side. "My father sees its great size and strength and still dares hunt it? Ah, my father is even braver than this bear!"

Xohkantakeh was not pleased by his daughter's words. "I know the name of this bear," he conceded and, surprised to find himself feeling neither brave nor daring, regretted the descent from the promontory. He would have been more comfortable observing the carnivore from a much greater height and distance. *For Ika's sake, not your own!* he assured himself. But he had to admit that his zeal for the hunt had left him. Great Paws was even bigger than in his memories. Under the snows of the past many winters, while Xohkantakeh had grown old in the lodges of his females, the solitary boar had grown into its prime and doubled its size.

"Ah, look at him, my father!" Ika spoke as though at prayer. "He is as big as the great star bear in the sky! And do you see how wisely he has chosen his prey? The cow is . . . *was* with calf. Aiee! See how easily he has opened her and pulled the unborn calf from her belly! Look at how he takes and eats of the tenderest meat!"

The girl's observations should not have disgusted the giant. If anything, they should have roused a heartily covetous appetite. Among the big-game seekers of the Land of Grass, the fetal meat of oxen, mammoth, bison, and all other large grazing animals was prized above hump steak, tongue, liver, heart, and even eyes.

Suddenly light-headed, he steadied himself with his spears. His heart was pounding in arrhythmic leaps that forced him to fight for breath while he watched the musk ox cow attempt to rise in defense of her calf even though her back limbs would not serve her. Although disemboweled, she managed to pull herself forward on her knees until her forelimbs buckled and she collapsed on her side, bleating while the great bear sat upright like a man, feeding upon the full-term fetus that lay still alive within the torn casing of its amniotic sack.

A great, uncontrollable trembling overtook Xohkantakeh, as though he had become the prey upon which the bear was feasting. He could smell the breath of the beast, feel its weight pressing him, its claws and teeth tearing him. Despite the cold wind, sweat oozed from his pores as he imagined how it would be to die at the discretion of Great Paws, to be mauled, mutilated, all the while looking helplessly into the face of Death as it devoured him. Was this the end he had been seeking for himself in the bloodred light of this morning's dawn? Somehow such a death no longer seemed an appealing alternative to the rigors of life.

"Xohkantakeh, look! The great bear rises!" exclaimed Ika in an excited but circumspectly hushed tone. "There. He will finish the mother ox now! But look . . . wait! He turns toward us. Aiee! I think we are seen!"

The girl's last declaration sounded too much like a scream. The giant winced, certain that, even with the wind in their favor, the bear would hear Ika's words. He was not mistaken. The beast pulled itself into an upright stance, hunched its neck, then dropped to all fours and charged.

Xohkantakeh heard himself gasp as, a heartbeat later, the bear came to an abrupt halt and, amidst flying ground snow, flung itself once more into an upright and thoroughly belligerent stance. The animal's actions produced in Xohkantakeh an emotion that he had, until now, thought alien to his nature: terror. How invasive it was, and alive—like an invisible being expanding inside him, all light and heat, searing his senses, prodding him to fling wide his arms and break into a panicked run. For the second time this day, he stared into the eyes of Great Paws.

The bear stood rigid.

The man willed himself to do the same.

The girl looked wide-eyed from one to the other and, in several fluid motions, quickly positioned a lance in her spear hurler and stood ready to throw.

As Xohkantakeh fought back the beast of panic, for a moment he was certain it would break him. The moment passed. He continued to stand his ground.

With a huff and a shaking of its mighty head, the bear dropped to all fours and ambled back to its feast.

Xohkantakeh relaxed, but only a little. Had he seen contempt in the eyes of the beast? At that distance he could not be sure, but he knew that when Great Paws had risen to face him, the bear had twice exposed its heart and might now be lying dead had he shown the presence of mind to nock a spear into his hurler and throw. Anger replaced terror: anger at himself, at the bear, and, illogically, at Ika. He turned on her, shoved her down hard, and ignored the pained exhalation of surprise that rasped from her lungs as he accused, "Your careless words nearly drew the hunter from its prey, and to us instead!"

"He would have to come uphill to us, my father," said the girl, rubbing her shoulder, her manner subdued. "Such a great bear may be swift on level ground, but he has much meat, fat, and bone to heft up this slope. I think he would run slowly and give us time to take aim with our spears and hurlers. I am not afraid of this bear you call Great Paws! Not as long as Xohkantakeh is at my side and we can hunt together like the big and little bear in the sky and—"

"Do not speak so much!" Xohkantakeh was infinitely annoyed, not only by the girl's failure to apologize and her irksome habit of informing him of the obvious but by the realization that, while he had been frozen in terror, she truly had not been afraid! Her bravery demeaned him. Indeed, thought the giant, it was long past time for Ika to be reminded of her gender and rightful place within the order of life. "Last night I left the lodge alone, free of the threat your female presence would bring to my special intention for this day," he told her, jerking her to her feet by the back of her hunting tunic. "Until you followed uninvited, Ika, I had no cause to fear that which now feeds upon the mother ox. Were it not for your disobedience, perhaps I might already have made my kill—not only for Lanacheela's honor feast but to prevent Ox Killer from coming close enough to our encampment to raid our cache pits, or worse!"

"But I could not let my father hunt such a great bear alone! You might have been hurt, or even killed!"

"I am an old man. Old men die, Ika. It is the way of the world. And can you truly believe that I would dishonor Great Paws, and myself, by hunting such prey with an immature female at my side?"

Ika was visibly stung. "Soon I will be a woman. And you are not old! You will never be old, my father! You are like Great Father Bear in the sky. In Katohya's stories of her Red World People it is said that Great Father Bear will live forever, hunting across the night with his Little Bear beside him, the two of them holding up the black robe of the sky, fishing together for stars to eat as they—"

"This is not a time for stories!" Xohkantakeh appraised the girl with measuring eyes. How bold she was, how physically strong! What a son she would have made, what a warrior! But she was not male. She was female, and although she was no beauty, her unstinting loyalty and stubborn need to be at his side touched him deeply. He wondered what she would think of her "Great Father Bear" if she knew that the naïveté of her childish proclamations had just given him the excuse he had been looking for to justify his own need to retreat. "You will not live to be a woman and I will surely not live forever if Great Paws has his way!" Without another word he turned and started back to the heights of the promontory and the relative safety of the highland beyond.

Ika followed.

The ascent of the promontory was by its very nature more physically demanding than the descent had been and, where thick layers of loose stones underlay wide, scabrous patches of ice, also more dangerous. The giant soon paused and, breathing hard, told the girl to go ahead. "If you grow weary you may lose your footing," he explained in a surly tone. "I would not have it said that I was not behind you waiting to catch your fall."

"I will not grow weary! I will not fall! I . . ." The words died in Ika's mouth. Xohkantakeh was glaring at her. As she looked up into his slitted eyes, she realized that her confidence had sparked not admiration of her strength and daring but the same dark, frightening anger she had glimpsed before descending from the escarpment. Bewildered and suddenly afraid of him again, Ika swallowed hard and obeyed without hesitation.

On and on went the girl. She carried her snow walkers slung across her back, with two of her lances stuck laterally through the sinew webbing, and used the strongest of her three spears as a staff. She did not look back. She did not speak. Guilt, confusion, and regret walked within her. The emotions were foreign to her and made her so inexplicably sad that she wanted to cry; this need was also strange and puzzling, for try as she might Ika could not remember the last time she had shed tears. With a sigh she tried to find comfort in the fact that, although angry with her, Xohkantakeh was still following. She could hear the deep, deliberate suck of his breath, the heavy strike and occasional slip and recovery of his rough-soled winter moccasins on rock or ice. Now and then, when the way ahead became exceptionally steep, he closed the distance between them until the girl could feel the heat of his breath at her back. She was grateful for this until she heard his low, unarticulated curses. She was certain he was muttering in frustration because his concern for the safety of a disobedient daughter had forced him to turn his back on the hunt on which he had set his heart.

Ika wondered if she had ever felt as unhappy or contrite. She wanted to turn, to tell her beloved foster father that she was sorry for diverting him from the hunt for Great Paws, but she was afraid to speak lest the terrible anger she had seen in his eyes be loosed to strike her down as cruelly as any of his spears could have done. She shivered to think of it and wondered which would be worse—to be killed by him or to suffer the permanent loss of his love. Surely the latter, she thought. When he commanded her to stand aside while he went ahead to cut shallow footholds across a stretch of ice over which they had earlier descended on their buttocks, as Great Paws had done, Ika obeyed without question.

She watched him brace his massive limbs and bend to

his task, using the long, lanceolate stone head of his heaviest spear to chip away at the ice. How tall he was! How powerful! Surely, thought the girl, in all the world there was no man to equal Xohkantakeh. She marveled at the way he kept tirelessly at his work, loved him with her eyes and spirit and hoped he would feel her love penetrate his fur garments and enter his heart, where surely some small semblance of forgiveness for his eldest daughter must lie.

Disappointment formed into a lump at the back of Ika's throat. If Xohkantakeh felt her loving gaze, he gave no sign of it. He kept chipping away at the ice, forming one foothold and then moving on to hack out another, sending fragments of ice flying until, at last, he paused and leaned against the shaft of his spear, head down, breathing hard. Ika cocked her head as she observed him. He had loosened his wolfskin hood, so that his long, graying hair blew free in the wind. In his heavy hunting coat of winter-killed bison hide, he looked like a snow-dusted, shaggy woodland bison snorting and heaving for air. The girl found herself wondering why a man of such power had not hurled his spear at Great Paws when he had the chance.

Xohkantakeh was still straining for breath. It took Ika a moment to realize he was exhausted, and, seeing in this an opportunity to please him, she hurried forward.

"I will help you, my father!" she announced, beaming up at him.

"The work is done!" snapped the giant. "Xohkantakeh has no need of children to help him!" He stood erect, adjusting his hunting coat and glaring down at the girl as though he were, indeed, a great and shaggy forest bison looming over a tenacious little woodland fly that had just shown the bad judgment to bite at his pride.

Ika hung her head.

"Go!" Xohkantakeh commanded. "Back to the top of the promontory! Now! And place your feet carefully lest you slip and fall and my efforts on your behalf be wasted!"

Gored by the invisible horns of her father's disdain, Ika moved obediently ahead of him once more. She had slipped and fallen once this day and would not allow herself such carelessness again. But Xohkantakeh had not seen her fall. Why, then, had he twice cautioned her about losing her footing? Although she accepted full responsibility for being the cause of her father's animosity, Ika could not comprehend why he was behaving as though she were a clumsy, inexperienced child and not the daughter he had raised to hunt boldly at his side. *Aiee!* she lamented in silence. *I have seen the white bird in my dreams and dared to drive off a black wolf this day, but my Great Father Bear no longer finds this Little Bear worthy to hunt as an equal at his side!*

Then they were atop the promontory again. The distraught girl watched Xohkantakeh amble past her without a word. When he lowered himself onto a nearby rock, Ika took this as a signal that she was to do the same. She looked for the nearest snow-free outcropping and, suppressing a sigh of relief, seated herself and dangled her limbs over the edge of the promontory. The muscles of her thighs, calves, and ankles burned from the strain of the long and tedious ascent, but she would not complain, nor would she rejoice at how good it felt to be off her feet lest she give Xohkantakeh further cause to think her a weakling.

Far below in the sunlight, the valley of the great river stretched between snow-whitened hills that seemed to be holding up the entire curving sweep of the horizon. *How beautiful it is!* thought Ika with a despondent sigh. She drew back her hood to expose her face and neck, inviting cold air to comb through her long, unbraided black hair and dry the perspiration that had formed along her scalp. The breeze was as unexpectedly soothing as it was invigorating. Despite her mood, the girl's senses quickened to the stimuli of the magnificent natural world: light, color, the scent of trees and ice-encrusted land and river, the feel of sun-warmed stone beneath her gloved palms and haunches. She tilted her head and opened her mouth, drinking in the wind, tasting the sweet breath of daylight. Feeling rejuvenated, she smiled until, startled, she saw a raven wheeling overhead.

Ika's smile became a frown. Where Raven flew, so also flew Hawk and Teratorn, Condor and Eagle. All were predators and carrion eaters. She turned her gaze back to the valley. The herd of musk oxen had come together in a rest-less brown circle on the far shore of the river, well away from the place where the bear had settled in to feed. Even from this great height and distance she could see Great Paws hulking over his feast like an enormous hummock of autumn-yellowed grass.

Her stomach growled again. Visions of food swam be-fore her eyes: sun-cured strips of trail meat, dried berries, palm-sized meatballs rich with suet and marrow, red and sweet with chokecherry juice, each bound tightly within its own little traveling packet of oiled intestine. And musk ox meat! Steaks! Innards! Eyes! Fetus meat!

The girl's belly growled. With a start she looked to see if Xohkantakeh had heard. He was balanced on his heels a few paces away, his forearms crossed over his thighs, lost in apparently troubling thoughts as, still breathing hard, he stared morosely across the river valley from which they had just come. If he had brought travel-ing meat with him, he had not spoken of it or offered to share. Indeed, Ika realized that he had not said a word since his last cautionary remark about not slipping and falling down.

As though I would do that twice in one day! she thought indignantly. *I am not Lanacheela. I am Ika. I am strong. I am sure of foot. And . . . and I am hungry as a warrior in one of Xohkantakeh's tales of the Land of Grass!*

The comparison brought a wry grimace to her face. The warriors in Xohkantakeh's tales walked many days and nights without growing weary. They traversed hills and plains, mountains and badlands, followed mammoths and mysterious totems and sacred talismans, and all the while fought enemies as indomitable and dangerous as themselves. But never did they lose their footing and fall down! Never did they complain about being hungry, although Xohkantakeh claimed that dur-ing hunt feasts a warrior from the Land of Grass could eat more than half his weight in meat.

Ika sternly reminded herself that if she was hungry it was her own fault for giving no thought to food before setting out on her impetuous, misbegotten trek from the lodge. With another sigh she pulled her legs from the abyss and crossed them. Tucking her moccasined feet beneath her thighs, she eased her snow walkers and spears from her back, then stretched languorously and, acknowledging weariness, closed her eyes. The sun was high. The wind was cool. The moment was sweet. Ika basked in it and, since there was no food to be had, resolved to take nourishment from the sun and wind and the gleanings of her own imagination until Xohkantakeh told her what to eat.

And then he spoke. "It is a good thing I am not a carnivore of another kind, Ikaree, or you would make an easy meal for me!"

The startled girl batted open her eyes at the sound of the familiar but seldom-used endearment. Ikaree. Little Ika. He rarely called her that these days, and never when he was angry. Hoping to win a smile from him, she leaped to her feet, only to discover that her feet had gone numb. She would have toppled into thin air had Xohkantakeh not pulled her back by the scruff of her neck. The girl's face flushed with shame. How could she have failed to hear her father's footfall in time to rise like a respectful daughter and properly greet his approach? The answer was immediately evident. As her eyes took in her surroundings, she saw that the sun had moved. Shadows were longer, and the wind was colder. "Ah!" she exclaimed in surprise, realizing that her feet were not the only part of her that had fallen asleep! Looking up at Xohkantakeh, she started an apology, but the words died in her mouth. Never had she seen him look so tired. His broad, craggy face was so drawn with fatigue that it appeared on the verge of cracking. Her eyes widened. Was it possible that her father *was* growing old? *No! Not Xohkantakeh!*

"Look!" he commanded, pointing to the valley below.

Ika's glance followed his gloved hand. On the far side of the river the herd of musk oxen had tightened their circle, and a good-sized pack of dire wolves had appeared on the opposite shore at the edge of the floodplain close to where Great Paws was still feeding. The bear looked up. Squinting, Ika counted ten wolves trotting forward into the wind, including one darker beast that moved well back from the others. Recognizing the animal, she raised her own hand and pointed. "The black wolf!" she exclaimed.

"Hmm." Xohkantakeh raised an eyebrow. "The wolf that howls in the way of a dog and follows the others in hope of someday being one of the pack."

"You have seen it before?"

"I caught sight of its long dark flank disappearing over the crest of the western hill some moons back."

Ika stared, rapt. The wolves were breaking rank, separating into smaller units of two and three; save for the black wolf, they all resembled one another—pale faces, mottled gray backs. Their heads were down as all but the black made a brazen foray in the direction of the bear. Great Paws stood erect, menacing with its size the canine force that dared invade its feeding space. As though a communication had passed among them, the wolves stopped, arrayed in a loose half-circle around the bear.

With the trees at its back and some fifty man paces between it and the nearest wolf, Great Paws fell into a quick, blustering lunge and then stood upright again, arching its neck, shaking its great body in warning. The wolves backed off but did not turn and run.

Ika's heart raced in anticipation of what must happen now. But long, tense moments passed, and wolves and bear remained as though frozen in time and space. Then, slowly, a single gray wolf began to advance. With its head lowered nearly to the ground and its eyes fixed on the bear, it came forward one cautious step at a time, raising a paw, holding it suspended, then placing it gingerly down and holding it steady on new ground before raising another. Ika counted six such tentative yet audacious steps before the animal paused and sat down in dangerously close proximity to Great Paws. The girl caught her breath, stunned by the incomprehensible behavior of the animal.

A low rumble of approval rippled through Xohkantakeh. "He is brave. A warrior wolf! Do you see how he has informed Great Paws that he is Head Wolf? Do you see how he has said to Great Paws that the valley of the great river belongs to his pack, that he is unafraid of the bear who has come hungry from beneath the snow, and that the bear may eat the meat of the ox he has taken but only at the sufferance of the wolf?"

Ika frowned; she had not seen this at all. "How can you know his thoughts, my father?"

"Because in time beyond beginning, the People and the Animals were one. Wolves and men belonged to the same clan, and our ways are still much the same. We live in tribes and follow the same game. On the vast hunting grounds of yesterday, our ancestors were warriors together. If you had been watching with your heart and spirit as well as with your eyes, Ika, you would have seen Wolf and Bear look at each other and speak through mind and body in the way of their kind. There will be no death for either this day. Each has decided to go his way in the valley of the great river where there is enough meat for all."

An amazed Ika watched her father's prediction come true. The wolf rose, turned, and trotted away. Tail up, it led the pack back across the way it had come while the great bear dropped to all fours and dragged the mutilated carcass of the musk ox into the cover of the trees.

"Great Paws will be long at his feast," Xohkantakeh said. His face was set and grim as he added, "When the meat, blood, fat, and marrow of the ox have become a part of the bear, he will bury what is left and come from the trees, stronger than before, his life force renewed by the death he has made."

Ika was sobered by the thought. "Then we must hunt him before he comes from the trees?"

Xohkantakeh's gaze remained fixed on the valley as he said thoughtfully, "Tonight the wolves will cross the river. Tomorrow they will hunt big meat, meat worthy of warriors. As a pack they will hunt the musk oxen. The cows are heavy with calf; they will be slow, easily tired. The wolves will take much meat! The young and old among them will not go hungry. And if Head Wolf falters or falls injured under flying hooves and gouging horns, others will be there to take his place. It is because he knows this that Head Wolf runs bravely, his heart strong and bold for the good of all, regardless of danger to himself."

Ika cocked her head. "Xohkantakeh is Head Wolf! And Ika is all the hunting pack you will ever need! You have taught me well, my father, and because of this you may hunt as boldly as you will and feel strong in the knowledge that this daughter will hunt beside you, as sure and unafraid as any wolf!"

The girl's exuberant proclamation brought an unexpected response from the giant: sarcasm. "Katohya and Lanacheela must rest easy in our camp knowing that the only man in their world has raised up such a comfort as you, my little Ika, to protect them against the likes of Great Paws if I should fall!"

"You will not fall! But I *would* protect them! I am no longer 'little' Ika. I am taller than both Lanacheela and Katohya, and I tell you, my father, the white bird *has* come to me in my dreams. Soon I, too, will be a woman! Then I will be even stronger and bolder with my spear than I am now, and—"

"Yes!" Xohkantakeh cut her off sharply. "You will be a woman like no other! Too long has this man refused to acknowledge the inevitability of this!"

Ika was hurt. Somehow she sensed an insult in his pronouncements and could not understand why he was staring down at her as though at a stranger.

"In the land of the ancestors, the laws of the Ancient Ones forbid females the use of spears," he told her.

"This is not the land of the ancestors!" she reminded him, taken aback by his mention of the old law. She had forgotten it.

"No, it is not," he conceded. "Nevertheless, Ika, once you become a woman, the spirits may well be offended if I continue to allow you to hunt at my side with the weapons of a man!"

The girl's eyes widened with incredulity. She could not believe her father was seriously thinking of denying her the use of spears when he had spent years instructing her in their mastery. "Who else will hunt with you if I am not allowed at your side? Katohya is not young. Lanacheela is not strong."

"Yes, and so, exactly!" Xohkantakeh replied, squinting upward, distracted by the raucous cawing of ravens harassing a golden eagle in the sky overhead. "Carrion eaters gather," he observed, watching the birds circling before the gradually setting sun. "Tomorrow they will feast on the leavings of wolves. They will not follow us as we return to our encampment. In the meantime, there is little daylight left. We will pass the night here. I will see what I can do to mend your broken snow walker, and then we can sleep a while without worry, for on the heights we will be safe from Great Paws, who will spend many days and nights sating himself on the flesh of the ox before he seeks us out again."

Ika was aware of a dull ache at the pit of her belly. Xohkantakeh's talk of meat and feasting caused her to once again long for food, but when she started to ask if he had brought provisions, she quickly swallowed her query. He had a strange, troubling expression on his face.

With a weary sigh Xohkantakeh dropped to one knee and sent a melancholy gaze across the valley. "Perhaps there is a reason why Great Paws has chosen to follow me once more?"

Ika was puzzled by his question, but she did not reply. He had spoken so quietly, to the wind it seemed, as though she were not beside him at all.

"Perhaps the forces of Creation have sent Great Paws rising from the snow not to be feast meat for Lanacheela but to show me how vulnerable I have made my daughters and woman by breaking the laws of the Ancient Ones and setting myself apart from the protection of my band."

A growing feeling of unease caused Ika to hold her breath as she waited to discover just where his postulations were leading.

"Perhaps the great scar-faced bear brings fear to my spirit and shame to my heart as just punishment for abandoning my chieftain in the land of warring tribes?"

Appalled, Ika tried to speak but found herself tongue-tied. What was he saying? *Fear? Shame?* Surely Xohkantakeh knew neither emotion! And how many times had she heard him say that, after the death of the great war chief, Shateh, he had chosen to turn his back upon his tribesmen because they had chosen an unworthy man to be chief in Shateh's place and because, although he knew no fear of battle, he was weary of their warring ways?

"Perhaps the time has come for me to make peace with Great Paws and return with my woman and daughters to the land of the Ancient Ones, where there will be others to protect them and—"

Ika gasped. This was too much to bear in silence. She broke in with a hot protest. "No! Katohya has told us that if you were to return to the land of the Ancient Ones you would be slain by your own tribe as punishment for your defiance of those who would not heed your wisdom! We need no protection in this good land to which you have led us, my father. It is a land without war, without enemies!"

Xohkantakeh shook his head. "Time is my enemy, Ika. And make no mistake, daughter, Great Paws has declared his intent to war upon my family and my spirit if I choose to remain in this land with no people in it."

"*We* are people!"

"One man, one woman, two young females . . ."

"We are a band! We need no others! Together Xohkantakeh and Ika can war on Great Paws before he wars on us! And when we have finished him, we can carry his meat back to our encampment wrapped in his own yellow hide as an honor gift for Lanacheela—even though such a small and lazy girl as my sister is not worthy of such a feast!"

Xohkantakeh's long eyes narrowed in solemn introspection. "What a brave and loyal daughter I have found in you, Ika. May it be that when we reach the land of the ancestors we will find a young warrior who is worthy of you."

Ika was shocked by the idea, and hurt by the suspicion

that she had just heard mockery in his words. "What need have I of a young warrior?" she demanded, wishing her lower lip would stop wobbling as, for the second time this day, she found herself fighting back tears.

"You know nothing of men, daughter."

"I know you!" Ika declared with a ferocity born of a love so intense it brought her to her knees beside him. "It is enough! It is everything! In all this world and the world beyond, there is no man to equal Xohkantakeh!"

4

Darkness . . . no stars, no moon . . . only long, tattered, wind-driven clouds scudding above the snowy plateau upon which Warakan sat in his bearskin robe, close to the small fire he had just raised inside a natural, circular windbreak of boulders.

The young man looked up through the breaks in the evergreen boughs with which he had roofed his shelter. He frowned. He did not like the look of the night. The clouds, thickening by the moment, had begun to take on the bruised, bilious look of thunder bearers. Snow would come before dawn; he was as certain of this as he was that his fire would not last until morning.

No matter, he thought. He had not left the depths of the forest in search of wood or warmth. He had come onto the cold, windswept, virtually treeless plateau in search of Eagle, and for now the meager flames would suffice, fed with scraps of deadwood collected on his journey from the cave.

His eyes narrowed. He was no stranger to these heights. Toward the end of the previous summer, he had tracked a white-tailed deer uphill for a day and a night through the humid forest, following the animal onto and across the high plateau. Here he had rejoiced in the cool wind and open sky, giving exuberant chase until he brought down the deer with one of his spears. As he stood over it, a curious family of chubby, stumpy-tailed lemmings peered at him from behind a clump of leathery gray tussock grass. As often happened in hunting grounds beyond the world of warring tribes, Warakan had been taken aback by animals staring at him as though they had never before seen a human being. When, seconds later, the lemmings suddenly scattered in obvious fright, he had known that their action had been motivated not by fear of him but by terror of the shadowing wings of an eagle soaring overhead. Then, as now, Warakan understood why he and Jhadel often saw the great raptors riding the thermals over the plateau. Regardless of the season, there was food for their kind on the open heights.

And now, thought Warakan, *there is food for me.*

"Seek Golden Eagle, Brother of Sun and Moon, spirit guardian of your father and grandfather! In the way of the knowledge seekers of our tribe, call from the sky the sacred bird so that you may take and eat of the life of Eagle. Through his blood and flesh, the spirits of the dead will speak."

Warakan had not forgotten Jhadel's words. He wished the old man warmth, wellness, and a full belly this night. His hands closed around the sacred talisman of the Ancient Ones as he looked down. Between him and the fire lay the object of his search.

"Eagle . . . Brother of Sun and Moon . . . Mediator between the powers of Earth and Sky! I, Warakan, son of Masau, Mystic Warrior of the People of the Watching Star, and grandson of Shateh, war chief and shaman of the People of the Land of Grass, thank you for yielding your spirit to me!"

It had all gone so easily: the long trek through the forest; the sighting and stoning of a squirrel—necessary bait meat in the entrapment of Eagle; the gradual climb upward along the bed of the stony creek with his snow walkers dangling over his shoulders. And then the final ascent, around the frozen falls, past the fork, to the headwaters of the creek and beyond, onto the plateau. He had taken no food or water. Jhadel had long ago taught him that a spirit seeker often required up to four days and nights of fasting before his body and mind were cleansed and transformed into worthy receptacles for the visitation of spirits. Many times they had fasted and sweated together in skin-covered lodges of bent willow, enacting sacred rituals, bathing their bodies in the thick, sweet steam of heated urine-and-water-moistened rocks and the pungent smoke of burning sage, fragrant grass, and balsam needles. Many times they had shared their dreams and visions in this way, weighing and evaluating the will of the spirits and trying always to understand and do only that which was pleasing to the ghosts of the Ancient Ones. But with Jhadel alone with Sister Wolf in the distant cave, a disconcerting restlessness had come upon Warakan. When he had seen the tall, tight circle of monolithic boulders, he recognized immediately their potential as an eagle trap and, although his fast was not even a full day old, had known that the spirits were offering a great gift.

Under other circumstances Warakan would have rested and prayed a while before setting himself to the considerable labor of digging a pit as he had seen eagle seekers do in the faraway hunting grounds of his people. The memory of the exact method and ritual had been dimmed by time, but his mind had a way of sometimes being able to see around corners into the past, and he had no trouble imagining himself marking out the desired space, his hands bound so that his palms would not be blistered by the effort, then digging deep with his dagger, piling loose earth and snow on his robe, then dragging it away to reassemble into mounds resembling the convex tunneling of ground-dwelling rodents. A man might labor for a full day to hack out a suitable pit trap, and when this was done, he would still have to cut branches and lay them across the trap to conceal it. Then he would hide underneath after securing the bait atop the branches, a tempting morsel to lure from the sky any hungry eagle in search of an easy meal.

The circle of boulders, however, offered a natural pit. After securing tree limbs across the top of the tall, inwardly leaning monoliths, Warakan had opened the belly of the squirrel so that its death scent would be released, then tied the furry little body to the branches with a twist of thong. That done, he entered the stone circle from the side and concealed himself, one of his spears at the ready to poke away unwelcome carrion eaters that might fancy the bait intended for Eagle.

He had expected to wait until dark and then, perhaps, if luck was not with him, for many more days and nights. Seated with his back to cold stone and his spear positioned upward, he had recalled eagle seekers who were forced to bait their trap several times before being rewarded in their quest, and others who suffered the displeasure of the sky spirits and returned home empty-handed. Thinking of Jhadel lying weak, vulnerable, and alone, Warakan had gripped the sacred stone and made prayers for quick success in his endeavor.

As though by magic, Eagle had swept down from the sky to claim its prize. In a single instant the young man instinctively released stone and spear, reached up through the branches with gloved hands, and boldly snatched a taloned foot. He pulled the startled raptor down, amazed at its strength as, shrieking and flapping its mighty wings, it fought him . . . to no avail. In seconds the bird's neck was snapped. With the great feathered body suddenly limp in his grasp, Warakan watched the life force fade from the golden eyes as the sun slipped below the western rim of the plateau and long, chilling shadows filled the space between the boulders.

Now Eagle—Brother of Moon and Sun, Mediator between the powers of Earth and Sky—lay dead before him.

Now Fire—raised only moments ago from the single live coal he had carried from the cave in his moss-lined fire horn, then nurtured with dried grass and feathers brought in his medicine bag for this purpose, and sustained on deadwood carried up from the forest—warmed him.

Now Wind—breath of the living world and sky, elemental union of the four dynamic powers of Creation—sang beyond the boulders, and Warakan listened to its song and imagined that he heard the sighing of spirits across the plateau and in the forest far below.

He swallowed hard, reminding himself that he had come onto the heights in search of spirits and that, as the son and grandson of war chiefs and shamans, he must not be afraid.

"It will be done in the old way, as Jhadel has requested,"

he said. Taking up the last few pieces of deadwood he had laid at his side, he added them to the fire one by one. "May the spirits of the Ancient Ones be with me in the light and warmth of Fire, which I have raised to their honor!" he intoned. In the hot, bright glow of the flames he took his dagger and cleansed the stone blade in heat and smoke, then laid open the eagle from throat to gullet and eviscerated it in what he hoped was the traditional and acceptable manner of the vision seekers of his tribe.

The scent of warm death rose into his nostrils. He drew it in, knowing it was all that remained of the life force of the great raptor whose heart he now removed. "May the heart of Eagle, Brother of Sun and Moon, now live again and beat strongly in the heart of Warakan!" He raised the organ above the fire; blood dripped, spattered, steamed, then smoked. He placed the entire heart in his mouth. It would not do to defile it by cutting or dismembering it; the man who consumed the heart of an eagle must be man enough to devour it whole. The taste of the organ was sweet, its texture smooth. Warakan bolted it and felt it descend into his innards, warm, sleek, empowering. Next he took the tongue of the bird and swallowed it. Last came the eyes. As with the heart and tongue, he bolted them whole lest he risk destroying or defiling their power by masticating them between his teeth.

"Now has Warakan taken into himself the brave heart, straight tongue, and all-seeing eyes of Eagle! Now does Warakan—son of Masau, Mystic Warrior of the People of the Watching Star, and grandson of Shateh, war chief and shaman of the People of the Land of Grass—ask the spirit of Eagle to fly from this world to the world beyond on the sacred smoke that will now be born of Eagle!" The declaration made, Warakan used both hands to break and fold back the breastbone of the raptor. Then, slowly, he spread wide the great wings and lowered the bird until its hollowed chest and belly cavity lay directly over the fire. He knelt back in self-imposed darkness. He waited.

Soon the scent of charring flesh was strong. When he could see smoke beginning to seep from beneath the outstretched wings, Warakan leaned forward and lifted the bird, allowed smoke to rise from half-smothered flames, and then fanned both fire and smoke with the wings. In moments the little circular refuge he had made of his eagle trap was filled with smoke. The young man breathed it in as he rose, mounted the dead eagle upright on the head of one his spears, and used it to move aside the branches that walled off the sky.

"Rise!" Warakan commanded the smoke and bird, using both hands to steady the weight of Eagle as he raised the spear. "Now Warakan sets the spirit of Eagle free to fly upward on sacred smoke, to spread its wings upon the Four Winds, to call forth the spirits of Shateh and Masau so they may make known to Warakan what is in their hearts so and on their tongues, and what their spirit eyes see in the future for one whose life has sprung from their blood and loins!"

Later he would wonder if the spirits chose to favor or rebuke him in that moment, or if what happened next was only the mindless coupling of rising warm air with a downfalling blast of cold night wind. Suddenly it seemed as though an enormous invisible hand had descended from the sky to push the smoke back within the circle of stones, condensing it, stirring it madly until the young man found himself choking in the lung-searing miasma.

Blinded and unable to breathe, Warakan broke from the shelter of the boulders, still carrying Eagle mounted firmly on the stone head of his spear, and staggered into the cold, clear night air. His bearskin robe protected his body from the cutting edge of the wind, but his eyes burned so painfully that, weeping, he threw aside his spear and began to rub them.

It was in that moment that Warakan first heard the forces of Creation speak and smelled the rank ozone stink of their breath. With a deafening crash and an explosion of light that penetrated through his skin to his brain, lightning struck the stone circle from which he had just fled and sent his spirit hurtling into oblivion.

There were ghosts in the forest.

Warakan heard them singing. He opened his eyes. The

full face of the moon stared down at him out of a now cloudless sky. He stared back, disoriented, wondering just where he was and why he was lying flat on his back with an ache in his head that numbed his senses. He tried to rise, failed, then, groaning, tried again. It took him a moment to steady himself, and as he did, he winced because the soles of his feet felt as though they had been scalded.

"Impossible!" he exclaimed, lifting one foot and then the other, tentatively pressing each only to find to his amazement that the bottoms of his knee-high, thickly insulated moccasins were scorched. But the soles of his feet were not so sore that he could not stand or move about on them. Relieved and perplexed, he took a few steps and looked around.

Moonlight bathed the plateau. Far to the east, thunder rumbled: the source of ghostly voices, he thought as lightning flashed, illuminating clouds that had moved on to settle over unknown hills and distant horizons. This was not, however, what held his attention. As he turned back toward the circle of boulders, he saw with a start that the largest of the monoliths had been rent in half.

"Impossible!" he exclaimed again. His hand went to the sacred talisman at his throat, from which he took comfort and strength of will as he hobbled forward to take a closer look.

Dread filled him, slowly and absolutely.

Death. Warakan dared not speak the word, but it was on his tongue. Spirit Sucker, eater of life, had been here. He knew it, sensed it, smelled its lingering presence—and saw its moonlit afterglow in gray whiffs of oily-looking smoke that rose from the very place where he had not long ago been sitting before his little fire. Yet only when he paused before the lightning-sundered boulder, shards of scorched rock arrayed around his feet like so many splinters cast off by a stoneworker's hand, did he understand the enormity of what had transpired there.

Warakan's hand tightened around the talisman. Few men are given the opportunity to look upon the place where they would surely have met their death were it not for the intervention of circumstances beyond their control or comprehension. He swallowed; his mouth had gone dry. What would Jhadel have said were he at his side now? he wondered. The largest of the monoliths had been halved; one side had fallen, the other had been shattered, and the entire circle inside the stones had been blasted into the earth. He could not recognize any of his belongings. His extra spear, fire horn, dagger, snow walkers, and hunting and medicine bags had all been transformed, vaporized, and then somehow annealed by the heat and power of lightning into a dark, oily, gravelly powder.

Warakan knelt. The pain in his head had vanished, but the bottoms of his feet still hurt, the surface of his skin ached as though with fever, and although he was not cold, he was shivering inside his bearskin robe. Slowly, thoughtfully, he fingered up a portion of the blackened ground and knew that if wind, smoke, and the heavy air of night had not combined to drive him from this place, he would be lying here—transformed in a fiery instant into a part of the mountainous plateau along with his bearskin robe, the eagle feather of Shateh, and the sacred stone talisman of the Ancient Ones. And blind old Jhadel, who might have borne witness to Warakan's death in dreams, would also die alone, deprived of the cloak of Eagle's wings in which the ancient shaman hoped to set his life spirit free to fly to the sun.

"Neither mountains nor men live forever, Son of Two Tribes."

Warakan turned at the unexpected sound of an unfamiliar female voice. He blinked. Surely this time his eyes were tricking him. The shattered monolith had been real enough, but there, standing in the moonlight with his spear held upright in one hand, stood a woman unlike any he had ever seen. He gaped. She was tall and as broad of shoulder, slim of hip, and deep of chest as a man. She was also as naked as at the moment of birth. His jaw went slack. Although the opulent female comeliness of her body was worthy of awe, it was her face and the hair on her head and woman bone that took all of his gaze. These, he saw at once, belonged to no human being. The woman had feathers! A closer look at her hands and feet revealed thickly plaited skin and hooked talons that were the perfect complement to her head, which was that of an . . . "Impossible!" Warakan exclaimed for the third time since waking.

She laughed. "Have you never seen an eagle spirit before, Son of Two Tribes? Your will and words have called me here. Or are you going to tell me that you are not the one who lured me from the sky for the purpose of slaying me?"

"I . . ." He blinked again and shook his head, refusing to believe what he was hearing and seeing.

"Kya!" She exhaled in disgust, fixed him with the yellow eyes of a raptor, clacked her beak at him, and mocked, "Did you imagine me male? Yes! Of course. As though there were no females among my warrior kind!"

"I . . . I . . ." He could find no words.

"Kya! Can you not say a simple thank-you to Eagle, who is 'Brother of Sun and Moon, Mediator between the powers of Earth and Sky'? It is I who whispered to Wind and Smoke this night and told them to conspire together to drive a would-be warrior from the highest point on the great plateau before Lightning stung the circle of tall stones. Kya! I tell you, Son of Two Tribes, you will not live a long life in this world if you do not learn where *not* to take shelter when you are under thunderclouds!"

"You . . . you *spoke* to the wind? You . . . you *told* the smoke to—"

"On the head of your spear you impaled my body! Into the night you raised me up out of the sacred Circle! Out of your mouth your tongue sent words commanding me to fly to the world beyond this world and summon forth the warrior spirits of your ancestors so they might make known to Son of Two Tribes what is in their hearts and on their tongues, and what their eyes have seen of the future of one whose life has sprung from their blood and loins! This I have done!"

Warakan looked around for other spirits; there were none to be seen. He gawked at the eagle woman, disbelieved his eyes again, sought words that would break whatever spell was on him, and again failed to find them. "I . . . you . . ."

"Kya!" She cut him short with a snap of her beak. "Is

this some new and inarticulate language of your own devising? What kind of would-be warrior is this who stands before me? You wear the skin of a great bear, yet your own skin shivers and burns with fear and trepidation! You wear the flight feather of my sire in your hair—a gift from your grandfather, whose warrior spirit rides the Four Winds with the Ancient Ones and who, through me, has summoned you to this place where you might be given the gift of Vision and understanding—but are you worthy of this Insight, Son of Two Tribes?"

"I . . . yes! But . . . but I . . ."

"Kya! You have consumed the tongue of Eagle and yet you cannot speak! You have eaten the eyes of Eagle and yet you will not see! You have devoured the heart of Eagle and . . . and . . . kya! It is contagious, this stammering of the man tongue! Enough talk. Let us discover if the heart of Eagle truly beats in the breast of this would-be warrior! Come!"

"But . . . I . . ."

"Kya!" The exclamation was a clear command for silence as she turned and strode off toward the east.

Warakan gaped after her. He expected to see wings on her back; there were none. She did not fly away. She strode like a warrior setting out for battle, bravely, defiantly, fearlessly. He found himself shaking his head, still not convinced she was real. How could she be?

A woman with a human body and the face, hands, and feet of an eagle? A woman with feathers sheening her head and tufting her female place? A woman striding naked and barefooted across the snow upon long, smooth, supple human legs with high, rounded buttocks rising and falling like two matched moons?

The sight of her set the warm ache of man need loose in Warakan's loins even as his questions convinced him that such an apparition as Eagle Woman could not exist. And yet the young man clearly beheld the grotesquely beautiful form moving off across the plateau, growing smaller and smaller as she lengthened the distance between them. Then, with a start, his eyes fastened on his spear. Thanks to the

lightning bolt, it was his only weapon now and might mean
the difference between life and death on his return through
the forest to the cave. He scowled. Eagle Woman was holding it upside down, using the projectile point as a snow
prod. "Wait!" he called after her.

"I will not wait!" she called back.

"I will have my spear! You will chip or shatter the stone
point using it as carelessly as that. Spearheads are not easily
made or mended!"

"Kya! Yes, of course. So come and take it from me,
would-be warrior . . . if you dare!"

Warakan had never been able to resist a challenge. He took
great pride in this even though Jhadel had warned him often
enough that pride was a flaw in the nature of Man and might
someday prove his undoing. Now, however, as the young
man followed Eagle Woman across the plateau, his blood
was up, and the last thing on his mind was the old shaman.

He had come far. The position of the moon told him that
long hanks of time had passed since he had first committed
himself to the pursuit of the apparition and the retrieval of
his spear. His sore feet slowed his progress, but only a little,
and although he had almost immediately lost sight of Eagle
Woman, her strange tracks were easily seen in moonlit
snow. He followed eagerly, looking now and then to the
stars to determine the direction in which he was traveling.
The brilliant full moon set a silvery sheen across the night
sky, veiling into insignifance all but the brightest points of
starlight: the vast, arching sweep of the Sky River; the
sprawl of the Great Bear; the flexing length of the Great
Snake, whose open jaws pointed to the one star around
which all the others turned—the Watching Star, the North
Star—by which a man could find his way or lose it forever.

*All that is bad comes from the north . . . all that is dark
and cold . . . all that has to do with death and danger.*

Warakan's gut tightened in response to his unbidden
thoughts. The moon was so bright he could not see the
Watcher. *But it sees you,* he assured himself. He hated the
star, remembered that, although he had been born into a

tribe whose chieftains and shamans looked to it as a source of eternal power, all that had ever been hard and cruel and painful in his life had come to pass under the cold, glinting constancy of its authority: the death of loved ones, the shaming of self, the loss of everything that had once centered his life and made it worth living . . . until he discovered the renewal of spirit that came to a man when he committed himself to revenge.

The latter thought brought a smile to his lips. *Someday!* he vowed. Wishing on the sacred stone that the moment of retribution was at hand, he went on more doggedly than before until at last the footprints of Eagle Woman led him from the heights into a dark, downwardly sloping expanse of broken forest below the eastern rim of the plateau.

Here, brought short by the darkness and no small measure of fatigue, he paused to catch his breath. It was a moment before he realized that he had lost her trail. He frowned, tried to pick it up again, and in his search turned and began to double back along the way he had come.

And then, as in a long-forgotten boyhood nightmare, he saw them.

Backlit by the moon, his enemies burst toward him through the trees. In war feathers and body paint, their ankle-length hair streaming over their shoulders and their war dogs barking and in full battle array at their sides, the tall, tattooed warriors of the People of the Watching Star and the equally tall, painted warriors of the People of the Land of Grass came leaping and bounding downhill toward him with their massive spears held high and his name a war cry on their lips.

Stunned into immobility, he stared in disbelief at the sight of twice a double hand-count of men coming to a sudden halt and aligning themselves in a single menacing rank above him. "Warakan! Son of Masau of the Watching Star!" a single voice called out.

Warakan took a backward step, squinting up through trees and moon shadow as he tried to see which of the warriors had spoken. With the moon behind them and their paint and tattooing masking their features, he could not tell. But the voice had been familiar.

"Warakan! Grandson of Shateh of the Land of Grass!"

Warakan scowled as recognition dawned. The speaker was Ranamal, a woman-beating warrior and tracker of great reputation among the People of the Land of Grass. Warakan had never liked or trusted the man. "I do not need you to tell me who I am!"

"Warakan! Defier of shamans!" This voice was deeper than the first.

Warakan's face twisted in astonishment. "Maliwal?" What was his father's only brother among the mammoth-hunting People of the Watching Star doing here? He was earless, his face ruined by hunt scars. If there was ever a man more hideous to behold, Warakan had not seen him. He shook his head, grateful for the masking of moonlight but perplexed, for he had long thought Maliwal slain in the first of the great wars that had cleaved the Three Tribes forever.

"Warakan! Bear Slayer!"

Warakan flinched at the sound of yet another familiar voice. "Teikan?" Incredulous, he spoke the hated name, truly puzzled now, for he had seen Teikan die beside his grandfather at the hands of Shateh's enemies in a place of war and betrayal known as the Valley of the Dead.

"Yah hay, Warakan! Why do you stare?"

"Hay yah, Teikan! Why is it that you still live?" he shot back. He wished he felt as bold as he sounded.

"Behold!" Maliwal called, pointing down with his spear. "The grandson of Shateh stands rooted and quakes like a sapling in the wind!"

"There is no wind," observed Ranamal. "It is fear that shakes him!"

"Then let us cut him down," Teikan suggested. "He has called to us upon the sacred stone, and we have come at his command to answer his need for vengeance. But clearly he is not fit to stand against us, this Warakan, this Son of Two Tribes and betrayer of both!"

"No!" protested Warakan, hurt to the quick by the unfairness of the last three words. "I will not hear that from any man!" Righteous indignation took control of his tongue. "I *am* Warakan! I am son of Masau and grandson of Shateh! I am slayer of the bear whose skin I wear and defier of any shaman who chooses to set me upon paths I have no wish to follow! But I have betrayed no man who did not first betray me or mine!"

"You betrayed us all!"

Warakan cocked his head. The words had come from many mouths speaking as one, and he knew he must refute them. "As a boy I would not stand aside while my sister was sacrificed to the Watching Star. Nor would I be silent as she was flayed and fed as a sacred offering to our people even as my father, Masau, was slain. Who among you was there, eh, beside Maliwal? Who ate of their flesh and would have eaten of mine had I stayed among you? Yes! Proudly I turned my back forever on the People of the Watching Star and placed my loyalty in another camp, with another tribe, with those among my grandfather's People of the Land of Grass, who then betrayed him and me!" He paused, raised both fists, and shook them at those who stared down at him. "*You* are the betrayers, all of you . . . sons of the Two Tribes . . . eaters of human flesh and despoilers of honor!"

"Life must eat life to sustain life!" slurred Maliwal.

"So turns the great Circle!" The affirmation was shouted in unison from every warrior's mouth.

Suddenly they were moving forward again, a wall of men and slavering dogs. Warakan caught his breath. He saw the glint of moonlight on bared canine teeth and spearheads of black obsidian and in human eyes flashing white with the intent to commit slaughter. And now, focusing on his own bare fists, he experienced a sick, sinking feeling in his gut as he remembered that he had neither spears nor dagger with which to protect himself.

"Fool!" The accusation sprang unbidden, but well deserved, from his own mouth.

Someone laughed. A female voice.

Startled, Warakan remembered that there were female shamans among the People of the Watching Star and that they could be crueler and more dangerous than the warriors who swore allegiance to them. He stood his ground. He would not be accused of quaking before a woman!

"Kya! Who do you take me for?"

Warakan blinked as, from out of nowhere, it seemed, a golden eagle plummeted through the trees to swoop between him and those who were now almost upon him.

"So you would take single-handed vengeance on the combined forces of the warriors of the Two Tribes, would you? Kya! Now Warakan will see where his self-centered need must lead him!" The eagle banked downhill and disappeared into the trees, but not before dipping its broad wings to slap the top of Warakan's head so hard he was nearly brought to his knees. "Follow!" the bird commanded. "Or has Jhadel wasted these past many years on one who rightly names himself Fool? Kya! Can it be that the Son of Two Tribes prefers to die rather than commit himself to the peaceful reunification of the tribes and the fulfillment of Jhadel's hope for the future of us all?"

Warakan was stunned. Peaceful reunification of the tribes in the face of advancing warriors who were now unified against him? Commitment to the future when, at this very moment, spears began to fly and he found himself standing in a rain of lances amidst the thundering war cries of enemies? Eagle Woman must surely have lost all reason! Having no wish to die, Warakan whirled on his heels and broke for the cover of the trees.

Too late.

A war dog was on his back. He bent forward and deftly twisted his body, throwing the surprised animal off and to one side, only to feel himself struck from behind by a spear. He cried out as he lurched forward, shocked—and not only by the power of the blow. The spear's projectile point had sliced straight through his back and emerged through his breast to pierce his tunic.

Staggered by the impact and by the sight of a spearhead protruding from his chest, Warakan dropped to his knees and tried desperately to pull it free. It was no use. The lance was lodged tightly in his body, and the stone head was slippery with his blood; its long, narrow, exquisitely sharp edges cut his gloves as effortlessly as they had sliced through his flesh. He held his hands away from the momentarily cleansed spearhead and, with a start, saw that it was

unlike the others his enemies used. It was not black obsidian. It was white chalcedony of the finest quality. Only once
before had he seen another to equal it. "A white spearhead
. . . to slay a white mammoth or . . . a man?" Warakan felt
himself blanch as he remembered Jhadel saying that the
weapon would be the death of him. And now, to his horror,
he saw the pale point disappear in a sudden fountaining of
thick, dark, arterial blood.

A wave of nausea swept through him. "Ah!" he exclaimed, astounded by the realization that nothing he did
now would stanch the flow from such a wound. His enemies had dealt him a mortal blow, and now, despite all
Jhadel's hopes and dreams, there was to be no future for
him at all.

The slope upon which he stood was steep. Too steep.
Warakan stared down through the trees into a lake of impenetrable shadow. He was dizzy, light-headed, sucking air
through his teeth and finding no nourishment in it. The
ground seemed to be rising to meet him. He knew he was
going to faint, but, with the eagle feather he wore braided
into his forelock drifting before his face, he also knew he
would not easily yield to such weakness.

"I am Warakan . . . grandson of Shateh . . . son of
Masau. I will die on my feet . . . facing my enemies . . . in
the way of a warrior!" The words rasped from his throat. He
could taste blood in his nostrils, mouth, and the back of his
palate as, still clutching the spearhead that protruded from
his breast, he fought his way to his feet. The effort cost him.
Until this moment his wound had been anesthetized by
shock; now the beast of pain awoke and set itself to devouring his senses. Warakan gasped, rocked on his heels, and
nearly swooned. Nevertheless, defying pain, he turned to
glare contemptuously up at those who had again paused in a
single line above him. "Warakan knows no fear of you!" he
wheezed. "Come! Fight me. Man to man. Bare-handed, as I
am unarmed."

They laughed at his bravado. "You are dead!" they told
him and, smiling, loosed their dogs on him.

Warakan managed to turn and move away quickly just

as the first of the animals leaped for his throat and, unable
to correct its downward trajectory in time, hurtled headlong
into a tree instead. Anger gave the young man a surge of
strength and courage as he scrambled madly downhill, for
although he knew he was dying, he found it preferable to
fall and break his neck than to be further dishonored by his
enemies and devoured by their dogs. Cursing both beasts
and men as cowards, he wished Sister Wolf were at his
side. Old as she was, her great size, strength, and wisdom
would have made her a living weapon with which he could
have turned and fought his adversaries with some semblance of honor until death overcame them both. *But no!
She deserves a better death than this!* he thought. Sensing
the dogs closing on him, he was genuinely glad that Sister
Wolf was safe with Jhadel in the cave. The old Peacedreamer, at least, would find comfort in her presence at the
moment of his death, and then, after a lifetime of loyalty to
her human pack, Sister Wolf would be free to seek her own
kind at last.

The dogs were at his heels. The spear in his back was
agony, but somehow Warakan managed to kick back, hard;
he felt his heel make contact with flesh and bone and was
gratified to hear a startled yelp and then the voice of a man
calling back the dogs. He was not in the least relieved.
Lances were again raining through the trees, and his kick
had thrown him off balance and taken the last of his energy.
He was already stumbling when a second spear found his
back and, striking deep, impelled him forward. The force of
the blow was explosive; he felt the air go out of him as he
went down, flailing his arms and grasping at branches to
stay his fall. The effort was futile. He had lost all ability to
control his muscles. The branches slipped through his fingers, tore off a glove, and slapped cruelly at his face as he
tumbled helplessly head over heels down the tree-columned
slope.

He screamed when he heard and felt the first of the two
spears that protruded from his back snap off against a tree.
The pain was so violently overwhelming that he did not feel
or hear the shattering of the second lance; indeed, his con-

sciousness expanded into a blaze of pure light, then collapsed into absolute blackness. He felt and heard nothing more until he came to rest in a heap at the bottom of the lake of shadows.

Somewhere lightning flashed.

Somewhere thunder rumbled.

Somewhere a wolf howled.

And somewhere an eagle called, "There is another way! It lies under another star! Follow into the face of the rising sun, Warakan, Son of Two Tribes! Kya! If you dare!"

Warakan did not respond. He lay as in a dream that must be endured but could not be altered. His body involuntarily twitched against pain, but he was otherwise unable to move. Under the shadowing wings of an eagle, he felt his life bleeding out of him while the war dogs of his enemies swarmed from the heights to devour him.

Once again there were ghosts in the forest.

And once again Warakan heard them singing. Only this time when he opened his eyes, he knew he must be one of them.

He sat up with a start. He felt no pain and could no longer taste blood in his mouth or sinuses. Amazed, he stared down at his chest and impatiently parted his robe with both hands. The spearhead was no longer protruding from his breast, nor were the ill-matched skins of his tunic torn or bloodied. He looked over his shoulder, scanned downward over the tawny fur of his bearskin, and saw no lances in his back. A feeling of prickling unease came over him.

"I am a dead man," he whispered. Aware for the first time of the beat of ghostly drums, he reached for the sacred stone; as always he was reassured by touching it even though he could no longer see how the talisman was of any protective value when it had just allowed him to be slain by his enemies.

Slowly, uncertainly, he rose to his feet. A shimmering

pall of ground mist undulated around his ankles and
stretched away in all directions. Above his head, the
canopy of the forest arched like the ceilings of many a
smoky sweat lodge within which he and Jhadel had
sought communication with the spirits from the world beyond the world. But this forest was unlike any Warakan
had ever seen. With a startled gasp, he realized that it *was*
a lodge—a long, wide, columnar dwelling of such immensity that he could not see high enough to fix the actual
apex of its roof or—although four tiny glimmers of light
showed to the east, west, north, and south—have said
which, if any of them, marked the places of entrance and
egress. "I am in the world beyond this world . . . in
the lodge of the Four Winds and the dwelling place of the
ancestors!"

A soft wind was rising, parting the mists before him.

"Come . . . see . . . *know!*" sang a voice from the mists.

Warakan looked around for Eagle Woman. She was not
to be seen. But far to the east the ground fog was thinning; a
tiny glimmer of light was growing larger, brighter, rounder.
Warakan recognized the sun and, with a sharp jolt of intuition, felt himself borne toward it and knew that he was
Eagle now!

On broad wings he rose into the face of the rising sun,
looking down on the winter earth out of the great and infinite lodge of the world beyond the world.

Mountains. Valleys. Mighty rivers. A land of ice and
frozen lakes, ponds, and endless forests stretching away to a
body of water so vast not even an eagle could fly over it. All
this Warakan saw. And more.

The Four Winds took him, turned him, bore him upward
on vast whispering tides of air until he learned to use his
wings and banked hard to the north and west. Onward he
flew, until the distant flickering of a single campfire on a
promontory above a great river caught his eye. Then ground
mist closed in and Warakan found himself borne eastward
once again.

The sun was rising rapidly now. The long, soft shadows
of dawn were seeping across the world below. Warakan

soared high, set his own shadow across icy barrens, stunted woodlands, and wind-scoured tundra. Then, with a start, he hovered on the wind. A mammoth walked below. A white mammoth! Huge, massive, it plodded forward like a living mountain, a beast with tusks as long as great trees and a voice that echoed up to him like thunder rumbling in the sky.

"Life Giver!" Warakan cried in recognition of the totem.

"Follow the sun to the place where Dawn is born, and it shall be so!" thundered the white mammoth.

Warakan's breath was coming fast and sharp. There, striding beside the great mammoth, was the Red World shaman, Cha-kwena, in his sacred owl-skin headdress and rabbit-skin robe. At the shaman's side walked a woman: small, sure of step, striding out as purposefully as the man. Warakan's heart lurched much too painfully for that of a dead man. He had almost forgotten how deceptively fragile and lovely Mah-ree was. And how much he loved her!

"Mah-ree of the Red World People!" Warakan called.

The couple below gave no indication of having heard him; they walked on, holding hands, smiling at each other.

Warakan grew so angry that he was unaware he had positioned his body and wings for a ferocious earthward dive. "Mah-ree is for Warakan!" he shrieked. "Do you hear me, Cha-kwena? On the sacred stone of my ancestors and yours I have vowed that this will be so!"

The wind was cold in his face, stinging his skin and eyes as he plummeted through gathering clouds. But suddenly the clouds congealed around him, and he could no longer see the world below. Tears stung beneath his lids. The foolishness of the words he had just spoken struck him, more sharply and cruelly than the spears of his enemies had done. The sacred talisman of the ancestors *was* his, but for what purpose? He was a spirit now, no more a man, and Mah-ree walked below, warm and alive, the woman of the Yellow Wolf forever!

"No!" Warakan raged. In a fury of jealous frustration he

sharpened the angle of his body and stretched back his
wings to hasten his descent. Headfirst he streaked downward, boldly slicing through the clouds, tearing them with
his beak, cutting them with the narrow edges of his mighty
wings until they began to bleed rain and he heard them hiss
in protest of his passage.

He was not sure exactly when he first caught sight of
the small, predominantly white bird. One moment it was
not there; the next it emerged from the clouds and flew directly into his path. He saw the flash of startled eyes and
the gape of a red beak, saw short, dark legs extend as
though seeking a frantic landing in thin air as long, mist-
pale wings oared the clouds and maneuvered desperately
to turn the sleek body from harm's way. Warakan was
moving too fast to stay his flight; he struck the hapless
creature from the sky and heard its cries of dismay as it
fell to earth.

"Eee ka!" called the white bird, a strange and unfamiliar
cry. "Eee ee eekaaree! Eee kaaa . . . ee kaaa!"

Warakan did not look back.

Faster and faster he flew. If, like the white bird, he were
to fall through the clouds and strike the earth, what matter?
He was a spirit now! He would rise again with the mists!
But first he would touch the flesh of his beloved Mah-ree
once more and soothe himself in the warm brown pools of
her antelope eyes and . . .

The cloud cover broke wide. Momentarily blinded,
Warakan veered sharply upward. His vision returned in
shards of bright, hurtful light that only gradually coalesced
and allowed him to focus downward through clear, cold air.
He could see the earth far below, but the mammoth was
gone, and there was no sign of the shaman or the medicine
woman.

Now he saw the phantoms whose ghostly song had
twice awakened him. In the shadowed hollows of the hills
they gathered, strangely clothed figures moving in the mists,
murmuring, dancing, beating upon invisible drums. When
they turned up their faces and their eyes met his, Warakan
had not the slightest doubt that he was looking upon an assembly of the Ancient Ones.

"Warakan!" They spoke his name in greeting as they looked up, pointing skyward.

"Brother of Sun and Moon!"

"Son of Two Tribes!"

"Guardian of the life spirits of all whose blood now flows in the veins of one who flies with Eagle! Behold the ancestors! As in time beyond beginning, the People are one!"

With the eyes of Eagle Warakan saw them rise and proceed in a single column to where a man clad in the skin of a black-maned lion stood with a large, wolflike dog on a vast plain that somehow shivered like water in the light of the rising sun. A tall, spear-carrying woman dressed entirely in the pelts of wolves was at his side. Beyond them, the land stretched away into the mists of morning, and all across the land the campfires of uncountable bands sparkled like wind-stirred embers cast out of the sun.

Warakan caught his breath. How beautiful it was, the land to the east, how welcoming. But as the man in the lion skin looked up, Warakan was shaken. The stranger's face was Shateh's, as it must have been in youth. And Masau's. And . . . his own!

A mammoth trumpeted somewhere far to the east. Warakan could not see the tusker, but the man in the lion skin raised an intricately carved bone bludgeon and, with the woman and the dog at his side, gestured the People on.

"First Man! First Woman! We follow! Always and forever!" The exclamation went up out of innumerable mouths as the ghosts of the Ancient Ones followed the man into the face of the rising sun.

Warakan trembled as he watched them go. They were leading him to the totem! They were showing him the way to the shaman who had stolen the woman of his heart and then had dared once again to vanish with her and the great white mammoth into the mists. "I will follow!" he declared.

His spirit quickened as he flew after them, borne by the certainty that he had discovered the purpose of his transformation. As Eagle he could follow where no man could go.

As Eagle he could fly beyond the edge of the world! As Eagle he could swoop from the sky and with his talons tear into the tough hide of the great white mammoth and fill his beak with the flesh and blood of the living totem! Would he then be transformed again and, as legend promised, become a warrior incapable of failure when at last he brought vengeance to those who had slain his father and grandfather, and humiliated him in the forest only scant hours ago? The prospect thrilled and excited him. He laughed aloud. "Yes!" he cried into the wind. "Yes! It shall be so!"

"Never! As long as the life spirit of Jhadel dwells within his body, Warakan will not be an avenging warrior!"

The familiar words and voice of the old Peacedreamer slapped the young man so hard they made his conscience bleed. But only for a moment. Warakan scowled down out of the sky, saw an ancient man hobbling along at the end of the column of ghostly ancestors, and told himself that one old man was much the same in appearance as another and that he was only imagining the familiar form.

"I will have my revenge!" he cried to the forces of Creation and hurled himself into headlong flight until . . .

"Kya!" Eagle Woman spat contempt at him as she rose out of the clouds to bar his way with outstretched wings. "It is not for this that I whispered to Wind and Smoke on behalf of a son of the Two Tribes! It is not for this that I deprived Lightning of human meat! It is not for this that I called forth the Ancient Ones from the lodge of the Four Winds! And it is not for this that I yielded my eyes and tongue and heart to a would-be warrior! Have you seen nothing with my eyes, Warakan? Kya! No! You have not seen. You have not learned. Your tongue tells me that your heart is not yet worthy of true Vision!"

And suddenly he was an eagle no more. With a gasp Warakan felt himself falling, plummeting earthward. "Eagle Woman . . . have pity . . . help me!"

"Kya! I have done that, would-be warrior. Now you must help yourself!"

But try as he might, he could not stop his fall.

The earth rose to meet him.
In an instant Warakan knew no more.

The chittering songs of small birds, the soft sighing of the
morning breeze, and the barely audible drips and gurgles of
meltwater oozing from beneath the winter snowpack into
the earth: These were the sounds that woke him.

Warakan's eyes batted open. Dazed, he stared up at a
dawn-washed sky. Eagle Woman was no longer there. If
ghosts still sang in the forest beyond the high plateau, he
could not hear them. After a moment he realized that the
drumbeat pounding quietly in his ears was the steady, rhythmic beat of his own heart.

His head ached. The bottoms of his feet burned. He
groaned and started to prop himself on his elbows, only to
see a lemming sitting on his chest, peering curiously into
his eyes with its nose and whiskers twitching. Startled,
Warakan bolted upright. The fat little rodent scurried
off with a frightened squeak as the young man looked
around and saw that he was exactly where Lightning had
left him.

He rubbed his eyes, pulled his bearskin robe around his
shoulders, and looked around again. He saw the circle of
stones, the shattered monolith, and his spear lying on the
ground with the eviscerated body of the golden eagle impaled on the point. All were lightly powdered with a thin
dusting of new snow that had fallen during the night. He
got to his feet, went to the lance, took it up, and, after flick-
ing away snow with his fingertips, fixed his gaze on the
dead eagle.

"Was it your spirit that came to me in dreams?" With his
free hand he reached up for the sacred stone. His fingers
curled around it as he remembered wishing on the talisman
for the forces of Creation to grant him the gift of Vision.
Sobered, he realized that the gift had been given, but he was
not at all sure he liked or understood its meaning.

"An eagle with the body of a woman leading me
across the night in the light of the Watching Star . . . my

enemies setting their dogs on me and ending my life with their spears . . . the great lodge in the sky . . . the white bird flying before me as though it could turn me from my purpose, even as the Four Winds carried me into the mists from which I glimpsed the Red World shaman and my Mah-ree happily following the totem into the face of the rising sun with First Man and First Woman and the Ancient Ones . . . and . . . Ah, of course! It was Jhadel's vision, not mine!"

Suddenly angry, Warakan glared at the eagle, convinced that the old shaman had tricked him somehow, for surely his dreams had been nightmares terrible enough to turn any man from thoughts of vengeance. "But I am not any man!" he declared fiercely. "I am Warakan, son of Masau and grandson of Shateh! With my own hands I have slain Eagle, Mediator between the forces of Earth and Sky. I have taken its eyes and tongue and heart into myself. And now Jhadel will have his cloak of eagle's wings! Let him fly into the face of the rising sun if that is what he truly desires! As for Warakan, when that old man walks in this world no more, I will be free to go my own way, to dream my own dreams, and to seek my own vision of the future!"

The words filled him with a new sense of purpose. Carrying the charred body of the golden eagle high upon the tip of his spear, he smiled as he turned for home.

The rising sun was warm at his back.

The ghosts of his nightmares were silent.

And last night's snow had been almost completely transformed into morning mist when, far to the west, a wolf began to howl.

Warakan paused. "Sister Wolf . . . ?" His smile vanished as he recognized the tones and subtle nuances of his old companion's ululations. Sister Wolf was singing a song of lamentation!

A wave of intuition staggered Warakan. Jhadel was dead. He knew it, felt it, and cried out against the unwelcome knowledge. "No!" Jhadel was old and infirm and often a tiresome burden, but Warakan was astounded by the depth of love that he felt for him now. In all the world

Jhadel was his only friend. If he were dead, then Warakan was the cause of his demise, for he had wished Jhadel's death upon the sacred stone, and the talisman had answered his prayer.

He felt sick. Now it was shame that burned him. "What kind of man wishes death to a friend?" he asked himself as he hurried on.

Although the eagle staked to the end of his spear did not move or breathe a word, Warakan heard the spirit of the raptor answer: "Kya! A would-be warrior . . . who cares for nothing and no one except himself."

5

It happened so suddenly that Xohkantakeh had no time to confront the demoralizing fear that had been gnawing at him since Great Paws had crawled from beneath the snow to prowl the broad hills and steal once more from his snares and caches.

"My father!"

Ika's imperative scream shattered the giant's self-deprecating reflections as, trudging homeward behind her, he looked up just in time to see Great Paws break from the trees and charge toward them.

The moment seemed to hang suspended in time. With that strange, bright burst of visual clarity that often accompanies shock, Xohkantakeh saw that, with the bear almost upon her, Ika had already hurled a lance. And instead of turning and running for her life, she was levering back to throw another even as the first glanced off the scarred side of the bear's face. She held her ground. What a daughter he had in her! Never was a warrior born with a braver heart! Now her second lance was flying. It struck deep into the shoulder of the charging animal. With a pained whoof of surprise, the bear came to an abrupt halt and turned back its head to snap at the offending spear. In that instant Xohkantakeh saw the throat and upper chest of the beast exposed. Without so much as a breath of hesitation, he sent his three massive, fire-hardened spears flying one after the other with all his strength behind them.

The bear went down.

Ika, holding her third lance poised overhead, stood frozen before the huge, tumbled mass of tawny fur.

Xohkantakeh felt horror take him. Any moment the monster would find its footing! It would rise! It would move on the brave-hearted girl who now stood before it, shaking like an aspen in a gale.

"Run, Ika! Run!" commanded Xohkantakeh.

She did not run.

He raced forward. Somehow, without consciously willing himself to loose his heavy, stone-headed braining club from the slip thong that held it to his leather waistband, Xohkantakeh found the weapon in his left hand as he snatched the lance from his daughter with his right. He shoved her back, put himself between her and the bear, and smashed the braining club against the bear's skull with one hand and thrust the girl's lance deep behind the beast's ear with the other. Even though the animal did not react, Xohkantakeh leaped back, dragging Ika with him until he achieved what he could only hope was a safe distance.

They waited.

The bear lay motionless.

And still they waited.

Then Ika whispered, "Look, my father. See how blood comes from the great one's wounds and mouth, a gushing flow with no heartbeat to set it pulsing. His eyelids and nostrils do not quiver. And no breath lifts his sides."

Xohkantakeh nodded. The girl was right; the bear looked to be near death. "Stay here," he told her, then moved cautiously forward until he stood close enough to the source of his nightmares to touch a forefoot with his moccasined toe. The paw was limp, lifeless.

"Xohkantakeh's spears have set the great one's spirit free upon the wind," observed Ika, pressing close to his side.

The giant felt the girl trembling against him and was only briefly annoyed by her failure to remain where he had commanded her to. The body of the bear had all his attention. Only in his nightmares had Xohkantakeh been closer to Great Paws. Now he found it difficult to comprehend how truly enormous the animal was. "Only three spears and a pair of girl's lances to kill such a bear as this?" It did not seem possible.

"Xohkantakeh's great spears and mighty braining club brought down this bear, not Ika's slender lances."

"Hmm." The giant pondered the girl's statement. He suspected that the bear had been dead before he struck it with his club, but Ika had a valid point: In this far and uninhabited land beyond the edge of the world, it was easy to forget that in accommodation of his own great size he made his spears longer and heavier than those of other men, and he doubted there was a man anywhere who could heft his club. "Even so," he sighed, "I had begun to wonder if this bear was not somehow more than a bear, more than flesh and blood, bone and sinew, fat and fur . . . but a spirit, perhaps, that followed my trail season after season and slipped my traps as easily as mist wafting through a noose, a phantom that would not be killed before it first killed me."

A tremor shook Ika as she looked up at him. Her hood was back, and in the light of the morning sun her wide face was tense and unnaturally pale. "He was a great bear, my father. Surely this is why he followed you. Surely Xohkantakeh is the only warrior in all the world worthy of releasing the spirit of Great Paws to walk the wind forever."

Xohkantakeh was pleased. His brows arched as he appraised the enormity of his kill. "As Great Paws was surely a warrior worthy of releasing mine," he conceded, infinitely grateful that this had not happened and at the same time inexplicably saddened to see the great bear reduced to a lifeless pile of meat and fur and bones. Puzzled by his reaction to the death he had made, he shook his head and said to Great Paws, "You should have been content to stay beyond the edge of the world, in the Land of Grass that lies beyond the great gorge, beyond the many hills and mountains and frozen waters I tried to place between us. And you should have been content to feast upon the meat of ox instead of abandoning that kill to wolves so that you could seek the meat of this man instead. Once too often did you come from the snow to follow me and steal from my snares and caches. No more will you shame me before my woman and daughters by threatening them and forcing me to break down my camps and move on. Now it is you who are shamed. You should not have challenged me, for now, surely, Great Paws will follow Xohkantakeh no more!"

"But you have taken his life, my father! Now, in the way of the warrior hunt tales of the Ancient Ones, if you summon the spirit of the failed challenger, is not the power of Great Paws bound to return from the world beyond this world to live in Xohkantakeh forever?"

The girl's earnest question took him aback. "Yes, and so, exactly!" How could he have forgotten? He nodded vigorously. "If we summon his spirit in the way of the Ancient Ones, the spirit of the great bear will be honored slave to Xohkantakeh! He will roar and hunt again in me at my command!" Exhilarated, with one foot braced on the massive beast, he began the process of honoring the bear's spirit by removing his weapons from its body.

It was no easy task, for his spears had gone deep. The first had penetrated the bear's throat, entering just below the lower jaw, running straight through the neck, and severing the spinal column and the life-sustaining cord that lay within. One pull on the spear told Xohkantakeh that the weapon's stone projectile point—a deadly sharp lanceolate flake as long as his extended hand—was lodged between the two massive upper-neck vertebrae. He gripped the spear shaft with both hands and twisted hard to the right and then to the left several times before he could pull the loosened shaft from the sinew-hafted foreshaft to which the point was attached. He would retrieve both later, during butchery.

"He could not have survived such a wound or risen to fight you after receiving it," observed Ika.

Xohkantakeh grunted agreement and handed the spear to her. She stood dutifully by as he turned his attention to another of his weapons. He saw at once that, although it had entered close to the first, it had done so at an angle that allowed the point clear passage past the breastbone and into the chest cavity. He drew it out with relative ease and, recognizing the pink, bubbly organ tissue that clung to the foreshaft, knew at once that this spear had pierced a lung.

"This wound would also have killed him in time," said Ika, taking the weapon.

He nodded and plucked the girl's two shorter, lighter-weight lances from the bear and handed them to her. She took them, but without comment.

Now, as Xohkantakeh fixed his gaze on his third spear, although he meant no disrespect to the spirit of Great Paws, he allowed himself a smile of satisfaction. He had driven this lance straight through the bear's heart.

"The killing wound!" declared Ika. "Surely, in all this world, only Xohkantakeh could have made so skilled and powerful a throw!"

The giant's smile broadened. The girl had no experience of the world; nevertheless, he could find no cause to disagree with her. He knew he had thrown his spears more effectively than he would have dared dream possible, given the number of his years and the soul-numbing stress of the moment in which he had been forced to hurl them. As he pulled the lance from the heart of the animal that had been the source of his nightmares for all too many years, he was overcome by a sudden feeling of euphoria. Yesterday he had been ready to die. Today he felt reborn, young again, powerful again, truly a warrior once more!

"Yah hay!" he cried, raising the bloodied spear to the sky. "With this spear Xohkantakeh—once of the People of the Land of Grass, now man of Katohya and father of Ika and Lanacheela in this Land Beyond the Edge of the World—has loosed the life spirit of Great Paws to roam the wind! Now Xohkantakeh calls back the great bear he has slain. Now Xohkantakeh opens his own spirit and says: Come, Bear! Walk again in the world of the living! Walk with Xohkantakeh! This man who has slain you has proved that he is a worthy receptacle of your power!"

Holding the weapon in both hands, Xohkantakeh shook back his hood and turned in all directions so that the Four Winds and the forces of Creation would not fail to see who called into the infinite or know what one "old" man from the Land of Grass had done this day.

And then he laughed.

Not at the powers of the infinite.

Not at the bear that lay dead at his feet.

Not at the girl who was staring up at him in wide-eyed astonishment at his unseemly mirth.

Xohkantakeh laughed at himself, because in this moment he realized that all of yesterday's fearful omens—the call of the owl from the tamarack grove beyond the palisade, the bloodred sky at dawn, the sight of ravens and eagles gathering overhead in the blue light of evening—had portended death for the bear, not for the man who dared hunt it! And he understood beyond a shadow of doubt that the spirits of the Ancient Ones had not sent Great Paws to make a shambles of his ordered world; they had sent the bear to test him and thus prove to him that, despite his years, he was still all he had ever been: Xohkantakeh, bold hunter and warrior from the Land of Grass!

His broad face split wide with a grin as, for the first time in longer than he could remember, he thrilled in anticipation of returning to his encampment with the meat and hide of an animal in whose killing he could again take pride. No rabbit, this bear! No antelope or deer! No dim-witted sloth, or shy forest bison, or fat-tailed giant beaver! This bear was Carnivore, big and dangerous! How his beloved Katohya's eyes would shine when she saw the skin of the beast that he would soon bring into camp! How sullen little Lanacheela would gape—and perhaps even smile—at the piles of meat he would place before her to honor her new-woman spirit! How the feast fire would burn! How the fat of the great bear would smoke and spit and grant light and nourishment to those who looked to Xohkantakeh for sustenance. And how strong would be the sons he would make on New Woman when he lay with her on the newly fleshed skin of Great Paws!

A shiver of expectation went through the giant. He lowered the spear and was both distracted and gratified to feel the warm rising of his own shaft. Long had it been since he had felt this much stirring in that old bone. Still again he laughed. The power of the bear was his already, transforming him, strengthening him, returning to his body the needs of youth! It would be good to lie again on a new woman, to initiate a loved one into the pleasures of mating, to make new life, and to see the yearning of his beloved Katohya fulfilled in the laughter of children squalling around their camp once more, even if these little ones were not her own. Now that he had regained confidence in his ability to protect and provide for his band, the thought of children—especially of sons—was no longer unappealing.

"Come," Xokantakeh commanded Ika, impatiently gesturing for his other weapons. When she obediently placed them in his grasp, he was surprised to find that her hands were shaking. "What is this? My bold little Ikaree still shaken and afraid? You whose spirit is not unlike that of the slain bear? This cannot be! Come now, daughter. We must honor Great Paws as we prepare to transport him to the encampment where his meat and hide will be the most worthy of honor gifts for your sister."

Ika wanly attempted a smile, but a wobbling chin defeated her; she lowered her eyes and bowed her head.

The giant reached out and lifted her face with the crook of a gloved thumb. "Death has come close to us both in the light of this morning's sun, daughter. It is only natural that its presence has shaken the female in you. But Ika walks with Xohkantakeh. Surely you have seen that there is no need for you to be afraid!"

Ika *was* afraid, but she could not—would not—tell him why. She dared not admit her fear even to herself. They worked together in silence, opening the bear, removing the quickly perishable innards to lighten the massive body for traveling and prevent spoilage of the meat on the long journey home. These they respectfully interred beneath a mound of snow.

"As Great Paws has come into the world from his den beneath the snow, so will this small part of him now be returned to the womb of Mother Below," said Xohkantakeh. After commanding Ika to lower her eyes lest her female life force weaken the power of his invocation on behalf of a male spirit, he added, "May the forces of Creation accept and honor this offering even as we honor the spirit of the great bear from whom it has been taken."

"May be it be so," Ika responded with a hurt little twist to her voice, for never before had he commanded her to look away when he offered invocations of thanksgiving after a successful kill. Her display of weakness on the promontory had caused him to see her as a female, a lesser being; no longer would things be the same between them. She remained on her knees, eyes obediently lowered, knowing that Xohkantakeh was now raising the heart of the great bear to the sun.

"May the power of this great heart now live again in Xohkantakeh!" he implored, then lowered the heart to his mouth and began to eat.

"May it be so!" affirmed Ika with profound solemnity. With hope for the fulfillment of his prayer pounding in her breast, she knew that her father would not offer to share the meat. Even though she was weak with hunger, she would not allow herself to covet it. The heart of the great bear was for the one who had slain it; it would beat in Xohkantakeh now. And in this knowledge the girl rejoiced, for it banished the fear that had so shaken her.

He ate slowly, purposefully. Ika dared watch him, albeit through lowered lids, her own heart swelling with pride in him.

He startled her by extending to her the last small morsel. "For the one who stands before the challenging bear and does not run away!" he declared.

Ika stared at him in surprise at this unexpected generosity. "But the kill was Xohkantakeh's!" she protested.

His eyes narrowed with disapproval. "And the spirit of the great bear now speaks through me to say that Little Bear will share in his power! Ika will not disobey the spirit of Great Paws! She *will* eat!"

The honor was great. So was the potential for anger she saw in Xohkantakeh's eyes. Half swooning with pleasure, she leaned forward and accepted the morsel into her mouth from his fingers. She ate, not hungrily but, as he had eaten, slowly, with awe and respect and infinite appreciation. There was power in the meat; she could feel it. Trembling with renewed strength, she looked straight into her father's eyes and proclaimed, "Now we share the same heart! Now may it be that we are truly like the Great Bear and Little Bear in the sky! May Xohkantakeh and Ika always hunt together!"

His brows rose, then fell. "May it be so . . . until you become a woman and can hunt with a spear no more . . . or until the power of the bear and the forces of Creation give me sons to hunt at my side."

The words took all the joy from Ika's heart. Again she lowered her eyes and fell silent. When he commanded her to rise and help him make a meat drag, she obeyed without question. With the rope he had made of thongs retrieved from the looted cache pit they fashioned a harness of sorts, then attached it beneath the shoulders and head of the great bear. They set off together, hauling their monstrous burden toward the encampment.

"In the Land of Grass we would have dogs to pull this meat!" Xohkantakeh muttered. "When we return there, we will have them again, and my woman and daughters will not be burdened by—"

"We do not need dogs!" Ika interrupted, dismayed to realize that the killing of the bear had only intensified his desire to return to the land of warring tribes.

"Tell me this when we return to camp, Ikaree, and perhaps I will believe you."

The weight of the great bear was brutal. They rested often, and although Xohkantakeh proclaimed deference to his daughter's needs and not his own, Ika knew the truth. She wrestled with it as they both wrestled with the weight of their burden, and soon fear returned, even though Xohkantakeh celebrated with wheezing song the feast meat he was bringing to honor his youngest daughter and gladden the heart of his beloved Katohya.

"Sing, Ika! Be joyous in this burden we carry!" he commanded, displeased and puzzled by her solemn silence.

To please him, she obeyed, but there was no joy in her

heart. The bear was dead. Great Paws would threaten her band no more. Soon Katohya would smile her gentle smile in renewed appreciation of her man. Soon Lanacheela would have the new-woman feast of her dreams. Soon Xohkantakeh would make sons on her sister and forever take pride in the knowledge that he had slain the beast of his nightmares. But Ika would forever be haunted by the knowledge that she had shrieked her father's name and warned him of the charging bear *four* times before he heard her cries. And she would never forget that by the time he finally responded, his reaction had been so slow that, had her own lance not struck the beast and caused it to stop and turn its head—thus allowing Xohkantakeh's spears to make their killing wounds—they would both be dead and Great Paws would perhaps even now be on his way to their encampment—not to *become* a feast but to *make* a feast of Katohya and Lanacheela.

Now, as she trudged along beside her father, Ika's spirit ached. For the first time in her young life, she acknowledged that the giant was no longer the man he once was. *He is old. He is slow. And he is nearly deaf. Aiee! Even with the heart of the great bear beating inside him to make him strong and sure of himself once more, I do not think he will live forever.*

She felt sick, weak, bruised, as though the bear had somehow managed to batter her body and pummel her senses. Later—long after the sun had gone down, long after she and Xohkantakeh had settled into a cold camp to eat sparingly of fat and meat sliced from the belly of the bear, long after the giant curled himself in his bison-skin robe and gave himself to dreams that made him smile— Ika sat awake. She was so tired. Her back and limbs ached. There were blisters on her palms and across her shoulders and brow where the drag rope had chafed her skin. Hurting, and too deeply disturbed to sleep, she listened to the howling of a lone wolf, watched the stars grow bright, and saw the constellations of the Great and Little Bear with new eyes.

Perhaps the small bear walks in the shadow of the giant

*not because it seeks strength in the great one's shadow, but
to be the eyes and ears of one who is so old he cannot hear
the approach of danger or see his way across the night.*

Ika was so saddened by her thoughts that, despite her
warm clothes, she shivered and felt tears burning inside her
nose and stinging behind her eyes. She snuffled, drew a
hand across her lids, and then tensed suddenly when she
saw a shadow pass across the stars. It was gone in an instant, but not before she caught the bright, white flash of
starlight gleaming on long, pale wings and, even as the
shadow disappeared, heard a bird shrilling in the darkness.
"Eee . . . eeka . . . eekaree . . . eeka . . ."

Ika caught her breath. "The white bird!" She snapped to
her feet and cried out, "You call my name at last!" A sense
of wonder filled her, of gladness so intense that the aches
and pains of the day fell away. But despair brought them
back in a rush. "No! Not now! You cannot come to me now!
My father needs me! I cannot be a woman yet! Who will
hunt beside him and—"

"Hmm . . . what is it you say, Little Bear?" Xohkantakeh
rumbled as his lips made the smacking sound of one only
half roused from sleep.

"I . . . nothing, my father. Nothing." A sob rose in Ika's
throat. Stifling it, she moved forward, well away from the
sleeping man.

Staring breathlessly up into the night, the girl waited for
the white bird to reappear. Moments passed, but the bird did
not return, and Ika's heart tightened with a pain so terrible
she thought she would die of it. "But I cannot die," she
whispered to the stars.

Comprehension dawned, bleak and cold as the heart of
the darkest winter morning. The white bird had come. It had
called her name—her *childhood* name, not her new-woman
name. Tears coursed down Ika's cheeks as she understood
at last why the forces of Creation had seen fit to prevent her
from becoming a woman. Xohkantakeh had sworn that once
she shed a woman's moon blood he would be forced to deny
her the use of a spear.

"But by the light of this morning's sun I have seen that
just as the Great Bear in the sky needs his Little Bear to hunt

at his side, so Xohkantakeh needs Ika to hunt at his side, to be his ears and eyes when danger threatens . . . until the sons my sister will bear him grow to manhood." A sigh of remorse escaped her lips as she went to her knees in the snow. "By then I will be old before I have ever been a woman at all! But Xohkantakeh will have his pride. And for now Ika will be his son. He needs no other."

6

A life was ending. A circle was closing.

Warakan could feel it happening. As he hurried through the sunlit forest, his breath was rasping in his throat and the soles of his feet ached, but he paid no heed to either impediment. A day and a night had passed since he left the high plateau, and now he cursed last night's fatigue-born carelessness that had sent him down the wrong fork in the creek. The error had doubled the time it should have taken him to return to the cave.

"Jhadel!" he cried. "I am coming with the cloak you asked for, and with tales of Vision to share! Wait for me, Jhadel! Please!"

He quickened his pace, certain that if he failed to reach the cave in time he would be shut out of the final pattern of the old Peacedreamer's life forever. There would be no good-byes, no last touch of hands, no words to soothe the spirit of an old friend along the trail to the world beyond this world, and no way to ease the pain of the young man who would be left behind.

"I will not believe he is dead!" Warakan cried to the wind and forest as he kept doggedly on his way. "Not yet! Not without the cloak of eagle's wings to carry his spirit upon the Four Winds and into the face of the rising sun!"

Shadows were growing long around him; he moved

through them, weak-limbed and light-headed but resolute. "Jhadel will not die until I return, and then the meat of the eagle will restore his strength as the heart of the eagle has restored mine!"

Fatigue brought him to his knees. His bearskin robe lay so heavily upon him that for a moment he could have sworn the animal was alive once more and deliberately pressing him to the earth with its monstrous weight. He shrugged off the thought and, after a few deep breaths during which he clutched the sacred stone and asked the spirits within to renew his strength, soon felt strong enough to rise. "I must go on! Peacedreamer *cannot* die! I will not let him! On the sacred stone I vow that I will give him back his will to live!"

The shadows grew longer. Once again weariness became too heavy to bear, and yet this time Warakan bore it. He would not pause. He would not slow his pace.

Jhadel was waiting.

It was nearly dark when Warakan at last came through the trees to see Sister Wolf sitting dejectedly on the terrace above the frozen creek. He paused, waiting for the wolf to bound forward to greet him, but although she pricked up her ears at the sight and scent of him, Sister Wolf did not move.

Premonition settled like a stone in Warakan's belly. A cold sweat broke out on his brow. For hours now he had been hearing the wolf's intermittent howls coming through the forest—four short cries, a long silence, another four cries, and then silence again. Half a lifetime of living with the animal had taught him that this was the sound of her kind when distressed and calling others of her pack to aid her. Struck by the unwelcome possibility that he might now be the only member of her pack, Warakan pulled his bearskin close around his shoulders. "No!" he declared. "I will *not* believe it!"

He hurried to his old friend and was surprised to see her quiver, lay back her ears, yawn, lower her head, and tuck her tail at his approach. "What is it, sister of my pack? Why do you speak apology to Warakan?" He dropped to one knee and scratched behind the grizzled ears as she lay her head and forepaws on his thigh. "Why have you not stayed with Jhadel in the cave as I commanded?"

The wolf whimpered and nuzzled his hand.

Warakan saw blood on her snout and paws, and her claws were worn as though by excessive digging. "What is this? And . . . *this?*" Distracted by the sight and scent of a small pile of regurgitated deer mice lying close to the animal's flank, he exhaled with revulsion. The dead rodents were not fresh. Now he knew why Sister Wolf had left the cave: She had gone to hunt up a meal for Jhadel.

"If Jhadel were dead, Sister Wolf would not have gone hunting for him!" he exclaimed, allowing himself a smile. He doubted there was ever a wolf cub or sickly old wolf anywhere who had a better caretaker than Jhadel had found in this animal. Yet, as he fingered her paws and accepted her gentle licking, he was puzzled by her behavior. She had not run to greet him. She showed no interest in the eviscerated golden eagle mounted on his lance, and he could not understand why she had deposited her food offering for Jhadel outside the cave instead of bringing it inside to him as she always did. Unless, of course, she intended it as a gift—not for the old Peacedreamer but for the returning young vision seeker.

Warakan got to his feet, touched by this display of generosity. "I thank you, Sister Wolf, but I have eaten the heart, tongue, and eyes of this eagle. Now you and I will see our Peacedreamer grow strong once more upon its sacred flesh, and we will hear him speak no more of Death or of . . ."

Sister Wolf took hold of one of his moccasins and tugged him toward the entrance to the cave.

"I know the way!" Warakan told her, pulling his leg free of her tearing teeth. He sensed an unnatural tension in the animal's movements as she trotted off. When she paused and stared back at him, he knew she was asking him to follow. "I am coming," he told her.

Sister Wolf *bruff*ed once in reply, then turned and disappeared into the darkness of the cave.

Warakan stared after her. He could not move. Holding

his lance upright, he swallowed and was surprised to discover that his mouth had gone dry. After his long race across the land, he found it strange that he could not now bring himself to take another step, even though he knew that with only a few more paces he could settle himself on his bed furs, pull off his moccasins, and blissfully rub his feet before stirring up a fire and cooking a meal for himself and . . . "Jhadel!" he called, and waited for an answer.

There was none.

He called again.

There was still no answer.

With his free hand Warakan clutched the sacred stone. Suddenly he saw himself emerging from the cave in the light of a bloodred dawn, and clearly he heard Jhadel say:

"I will sleep now. You need not fear for me. My spirit will walk the wind forever and dance with the Northern Dancers as they light my way along the Great Star River to the cloud lodges of the ancestors in the Land of the Four Winds!"

Warakan gasped. He released the sacred stone as though it had burned him. It was instinct, as much as magic, that told him what awaited him within the cave. Yet he would not listen. *Could* not listen. His thoughts were in tumult as, with his head held high, he followed Sister Wolf into the cave.

Darkness.

The sound of the wolf moving up ahead, whining and digging and growling to herself as, somewhere in the gloom, water dripped into an unseen pool.

The scent of moist earth and mud and cold stone and unsettled dust and . . .

"Ah!" Warakan cried aloud. Ten long strides into the dark but heretofore familiar interior, he had stubbed his toe on a rock that should not have been there. The pain was overwhelming. Grabbing his toe and cursing the offending rock, he hopped up and down until his eyes grew accustomed to the gloom. He froze in place.

There was not one rock on the floor of the cave; there were many: large rocks, small rocks, rocks as big as mammoths, embedded in oozing, stone-impregnated mud.

Warakan stared, lowered his foot, and saw that, although Sister Wolf was just to his right, he could go no farther into the interior. Ahead of him, beyond the debris on the floor, was a wall of stone and mud. The roof of the cavern had collapsed, burying all that lay beneath.

"Jhadel!" As panic overtook Warakan, he slapped his lance against the wall, clawed at the rocks, and began to fling them aside.

He dug until his gloves were in shreds, until his hands were raw and bleeding and he knew that by the light of day he would see bone through the tips of his lacerated fingers.

He dug until his breath came in shallow, wheezing drafts. Sagging in exhaustion, he gasped and shook and sobbed the name of the old man again and again.

"Jhadel . . . Peacedreamer . . . Wise One . . . shaman of the People of the Watching Star! Can you hear me? It is I, Warakan! I have returned with the skin of a golden eagle with which you may fashion the cloak that will carry your spirit to the sun! Jhadel! You said you could not die without it! Jhadel, please . . . I take back my death wish as many times as there are stars in the Sky River! On the sacred stone of the Ancient Ones I take it back! Jhadel! You promised you would not die until I returned! I do not want you to die. Answer me!"

There was no answer save the low, worried whining of the wolf.

He turned back to the wall, attacking it now, digging until he reached a monolith no human hands could move. In a desperate rage, he pulled the eagle from his lance, threw it aside, and, using the spear as a lever, tried to heft and move the boulder. It was no use. The stone head of his weapon cracked, the boulder settled in the mud, and the spear shaft snapped, throwing Warakan backward. He landed hard and wept like a child as he staggered to his feet, shouting, "By the forces of Creation, I am Warakan, son of Masau and grandson of Shateh! The sacred stone of the Ancient Ones is mine! Where, then, is their power? How can I save Jhadel's life without it?"

Sister Wolf whimpered in the darkness and licked his hands. Somewhere deep within the wall, there was a rumbling followed by a terrible sound of falling rock and settling debris. Warakan tensed. The cave trembled. The wolf yelped. And the young man ran for his life as the cavern began to collapse around and behind him.

All night long Warakan sat within the oak grove. Bundled in his bearskin robe, he leaned against the largest of the young trees and, looking up through bare branches, watched the slow progression of stars moving inexorably toward dawn. He knew by his ruined gloves and the pain in his shredded fingertips that what had just transpired in the cave had been no dream or vision. He had wished upon the sacred stone for the death of Jhadel to free him to go his own way in the world, and his wish had been granted. The old Peace-dreamer was surely dead. And now Warakan was alone beyond the edge of the world with only a wolf to keep him company and no one to tell him how to order his life or in which direction to set his feet when at last he chose to travel on.

He shivered. At his side Sister Wolf looked up at him and, sensing his misery, offered up to the night a sorrowful ululation that touched Warakan's spirit with a desolation that made him want to howl with her. His grief was too deep; it constricted his throat. He could not move, could not weep, could not form a single word or thought to console himself or the faithful animal beside him.

Listening to her lamentation, he closed his eyes and was not aware of drifting off to sleep. He did not dream.

And then, shivering and hurting inside his bearskin, Warakan felt the Four Winds stirring all around and heard Jhadel whisper in his ear:

"Not even the mountains live forever, Warakan."

With a start he opened his eyes. The first rays of sunlight were playing in the bare, wind-riled branches above his head, and a golden eagle was cutting an ever widening circle against the sky. Although his mood was black and his body ached, Warakan leaped to his feet. "Jhadel!"

"Kya! Son of Two Tribes, see now the great Circle of Wisdom, the great Joy and the great Sadness, the great and unchangeable Teaching that all must learn and abide."

Warakan's heart was pounding. He raised his hand to shield his eyes from the glare of the morning sky. The eagle was gone. He waited in vain for its return, then scanned across the terrace to the cave entrance. Shocked, he saw that it was no longer there. The great, gaping mouth in the side of the cliff had closed completely, swallowing all that lay within. And yet, somehow, Warakan knew that Jhadel had found the body of the eagle and made of it a golden cloak upon which his spirit was even now flying into the face of the rising sun.

Tears of joy and sorrow stung his eyes. He let them fall. Now when Sister Wolf howled, Warakan howled with her until his spirit was sated with grief. Exhausted, he hunkered on his heels and watched the sun rise high over the northeastern plateau. With all that he owned buried with Peacedreamer, he realized that a new life was beginning for him and trembled as he thought of all that lay ahead.

He made a fire. It was no easy task. He found kindling beneath an encrustation of snow that covered the high dome of a muskrat's long-abandoned lodge, and there was plenty of standing deadwood to be had, but dragging the muskrat's booty of dried fodder and breaking off usable pieces of deadwood proved an agony to his aching body and tattered hands. Nevertheless, he placed one end of a small dry branch into a nest of dry grass and spun the branch back and forth between his palms until the resulting friction raised sparks. After blowing these into flame and patiently feeding larger and larger sticks of deadwood into his little pyre, he maintained a constant smoke upon which he sent his prayers upward to the lodge of the Four Winds, prayers of thanksgiving to the old Peacedreamer who had saved his life, raised him to manhood, and taught him all he knew.

He was not sure when he felt the Four Winds shifting, but the sun stood high, and he knew that the time had come to journey on.

"Yes," he conceded. Noting the absence of Sister Wolf, he whistled for her.

She came obediently.

Warakan raised an eyebrow, surprised to see that this time she had a dead rabbit in her jaws. When she dropped it at his feet, he thanked her, then added, "Perhaps if you had brought such fare to our Peacedreamer, he might have been more willing to eat! But then, in truth, we both know that he no longer had the strength or will to chew such meat. Many were the rabbits I brought him, and quail and winter songbirds and fat-breasted gobblers, too! And yet he would not, could not, partake of them."

The wolf cocked her head.

Warakan's talk of food made him remember that he had not eaten in days. He took up the hardwood stick he had been using as a fire prod and poked the embers in the fire circle. When the coals glowed, he added the last of the wood and placed the rabbit over the flames to singe. Since he had no blade with which to skin and gut it, he let it burn, turning it often with the fire prod until the morning air was rank with the stink of burning hair and hide. Commanding Sister Wolf to stay where she was and refrain from eating the meat until it was suitably cooked, he sought evergreen branches from nearby saplings, then returned to the fire, skewered the blackened rabbit on the fire prod, layered it between two thickly needled fir branches, and returned it to the flames. Now smoke rose from green wood, flavoring the meat as it cooked.

Sister Wolf salivated.

So did Warakan.

Soon the flesh of the rabbit was dripping pink juice. The young man kicked it from the fire and rolled it in the snow to cool it. When he could handle it, he tore it into pieces and shared it with the wolf, giving her prime portions because she was his sister and the maker of their feast.

Warakan watched her as they ate together. "It is good," he said. "It will give us strength for the way ahead."

Soon, feeling strong again, he noted that the Four Winds had settled and now blew from the west. There was meaning in this. He nodded, rose, looked toward the high plateau, and, recalling the visions he had seen of his own death in that place, knew that he would not return there. "We will walk into the West Wind," he told the wolf. "We both know the way back to the high gorge where long ago, at Jhadel's command, I buried as fine a spear as any man could wish for, a spear with a killing point of white chalcedony—a magic spear made to slay the great white mammoth totem, whose flesh and blood will make me invincible when at last I am ready to take vengeance upon our enemies."

"Kya!"

Startled, Warakan looked up, but above the trees the sky was clear, free of clouds, free of raptors and of spirits circling before the sun on golden wings. He frowned, certain that guilt had turned his imagination against him. Pressing a hand against the sacred stone, he cried, "Forgive me, Peace-dreamer, but your life is over, and mine is just beginning. And now, lest the spirits of my ancestors wander the wind forever dishonored by their enemies, I must do what I have sworn to do!"

He stood very still, waiting—for exactly what, he could not have said—but at that moment the smell of the cooking fire was strong in his nostrils, and as his hand drifted down, a profound sense of loss and loneliness overcame him. He longed for the companionship of his old tawny friend, Bear Brother, and yearned for home—for wide northern skies and the sweet yellow grassland of summer; for the laughter and camaraderie of young men his own age, gathered around cooking fires over which the hump meat of bison and the steaks of mammoth sizzled and spat sweet fat while camp dogs, dirty-faced children, and crop-haired slaves hunkered close, waiting for the leavings. Closing his eyes, he trembled as he hungered for that which he had never known—a woman opening her robe to him, a small, soft, antelope-eyed woman to whom he had given his heart long before Cha-kwena, shaman of the People of the Red World, stole her away to follow the great white mammoth beyond mountains of ice that rose from the lake Jhadel had believed to be the Mother of All Rivers.

"Jhadel," Warakan sighed and opened his eyes. The sun

was bright, hurtful. He turned into the West Wind, aware of Shateh's now-tattered eagle feather blowing back over his shoulder.

"Come," he said to Sister Wolf. "It is time for us to return into the land of the living. We are of one kind, you and I, meant to run in pack, not alone!"

PART II

NEW WOMAN— BLACK WOLF— SPIRIT OF YELLOW BEAR

1

Lanacheela was not happy.

Kneeling inside the conical brushwood woman's hut, she scowled as she watched her foster mother reverently place into the fire pit the mosses that had absorbed the last of her menstrual blood. Katohya was singing and smiling, and now she looked up and urged Lanacheela to do the same.

"I have been fasting since my flow began," the young woman snapped irritably. "I do not feel like smiling. And I do not want to sing!"

Katohya leaned back from the fire pit. Fanning the flames with the flight feather of a swan, she appraised her pretty foster daughter out of narrowed eyes, then clucked her tongue good-naturedly. "Lanacheela, your face and form are as lovely to look upon as a spring moon, but your disposition is as nasty as that of a snapping turtle caught in a net or a cornered ferret growling down out of a tree. You must sing! You must smile! Surely your heart must rejoice in the way of all new women of the People when they prepare to come forth from the lodge of blood for the first time!"

"The People? What People? Where are they? I see only you, Katohya."

"Did you not hear Xohkantakeh's soon-I-will-return and all-is-well songs coming to us through the darkness last night? He is close. He will return to us today at last. And I feel in my heart that he and Ika are bringing something wonderful in honor of your first-woman feast!"

"I do not want a first-woman feast."

"Every girl wants to become a woman, Lanacheela."

"Not I . . . not here . . . not in this land of no people!"

"Better here than in the country of our ancestors, where the Three Tribes make endless war and Spirit Sucker walks among the bands bringing death more often than the forces of Creation allow new life!"

"I would not know about that!" snipped Lanacheela, tilting her straight little nose upward. She sighed with dramatic exaggeration and wished that she could drift off with the smoke through the open vent in the roof, across the miles, over the trees, back to the far land of her birth. The longing was painful because she was certain it could never be. "I know only what you and my father tell me in your stories of your own youth." She turned her gaze to the older woman. Katohya was still beautiful despite her rain-gray hair and advanced years. Somehow, the pale scars that lifted the corners of her mouth ever so slightly made her features more appealing—like a perpetual smile, thought Lanacheela as sudden resentment soured her own mouth and curled it downward. "Tell me, Katohya, when you were a young girl in the distant Red World of your tribe, did your mother come to you as you now come to me in the woman's hut?"

Katohya beamed with obvious pleasure. "Oh, yes! It was long ago, Lanacheela, but the grandmothers of my village were right when they told me that a day would come when strands the color of sun on rain would streak my hair and yesterday would be as bright as today within my mind. I remember my mother sitting before me as I sit before you now. I remember the way we shared woman secrets for the first time, and the way she offered up my first blood in smoke to the forces of Creation as I have offered yours, with prayers of thanksgiving and hope of many children."

"And did you then yearn for your first-woman feast?"

"Yes!"

"And did you yearn to be mated?"

"Yes! Oh, yes!"

"To your own *father?*" Lanacheela shrieked the words. Her voice broke, and tears were running down her cheeks. She did not care. The stricken look on Katohya's face brought only small satisfaction to the angry girl, but it was satisfaction nonetheless.

The older woman's head went high, her features softened with understanding. She rested the swan's feather upon her thigh and, absently rubbing the ache in an old arm wound that had never fully healed, closed her eyes and said, "Some things cannot be changed, my daughter."

"I am *not* your daughter!" Lanacheela's face convulsed as she released her frustrations in a hot tide of tumultuous accusation and longing. "Maybe if I were your own true child you would see how unhappy I am! Ah, Katohya! You have told me of your own happy childhood in the faraway red land of flat-topped blue mountains. You have told me of the warm Lake of Many Singing Birds and of how you and your sisters and friends swam naked together and teased the young men who spied on you from the reeds along the shore and called to you by your childhood name—Ta-maya, Most Favored Daughter.

"Ah, Katohya, for Lanacheela there have been no friends! For Lanacheela there have been no young men to tease! For Lanacheela there have only been Katohya's stories of all the things I could *not* have!

"Ah, why have you told me of the many young warriors who wanted you when you knew there would never be a young man for me? Why have you told me of how Xohkantakeh risked everything to make you his own, and then gave you a 'love' name—Katohya, Sweet-Scented Woman—because of the fragrant balsam needles you twisted into your hair when you first journeyed together through the forests that lie beneath the Watching Star? Ah, where is the warrior who will risk everything for me? And why have you told me of the new-woman feast that was yours, and of the way the young men put on feathers and painted their bodies until they looked like wonderful birds as they danced before you and chanted of how they would make your body sing if only you would say yes to their beauty and give yourself to the new life they would make on and for you?

"Ah, Katohya! Why have you told me of the joys of first love when you knew I would never know it? Why have you told me of the sweet ache of wanting a man, and of the sweet sadness that was yours when you left your band with the warrior of your heart to journey to a new life among a new tribe? Why have you told me that you have had not one but *three* loves in your life, bold warriors all, and of how it was for you each time when your body awoke to the fire that comes to a woman when she opens her thighs and takes a man deep into herself and dances the dance of life-making beneath him? Ah, Katohya! Can you not know how I burn when I lie awake in the night thinking of your talk of joys I will never know?"

Katohya's eyes were wide open. So was her mouth. "I . . . I have never meant to cause you dissatisfaction, child!"

"Child? Save that name for Ika. She is eldest, but she *is* still a child! She should be here, shedding a woman's blood, looking forward to taking a new name and being mated to Xohkantakeh! She is his favorite, not Lanacheela, even though I will never again be a child!"

The unfairness of her situation was more than Lanacheela could bear. Feeling utterly sorry for herself, she rose, shook back the fine new rabbit-skin robe that had been her only garment since entering the woman's lodge, and stood resolutely before the fire, a small, naked, nubile young woman trembling in abject misery. "Look at me, Katohya! I *am* a new woman. I have shed first blood. I have breasts. There is hair on my woman bone. And for many a long moon now, when you and Xohkantakeh and Ika lie asleep at night, I have lain awake remembering the smooth faces and hard-muscled bodies of the young warriors of my own tribe. I close my eyes. I call my memories and draw them close around me. I touch my woman bone and rouse the sleeping fire. I dance the dance of life-making beneath a young, smooth-faced, hard-bodied young warrior who is not really there except in my longing for him. And when the dance is done I fall asleep, but the fire in my body still burns, for the young warrior lives in my dreams, and I see his face, so smooth and handsome with youth. I feel his body, so lean and hard and . . . Ah! He is not *old*! He is not my *father*!"

Katohya stiffened. "Xohkantakeh is *not* the father of your blood and body!" she reminded sternly. "And even if he were, since the last days of the great war between the tribes when I was taken captive and badly used by many men, my body has been unable to sustain new life. Xohkantakeh is the only man in this band. It is not a good thing that he should come to his final years with no sons left alive to hunt at his side. And so, in the way of the People since time beyond beginning, the new woman among us *must* be mated. To waste your potential as a life bearer would be an affront to the forces of Creation, Lanacheela. Besides, it is the belief of Xohkantakeh's tribe that only through his sons may a man's spirit live on in this world forever. And so the male children you will bear will perhaps make him strong and proud and, yes, perhaps even young again. We will see."

"I do not want to see! He does not want me. He does not even look at me these days. When I entered the woman's hut he turned his back and growled as though I had done something wrong!"

A smile played on Katohya's mouth. "You have grown up among us, Lanacheela, but you understand so little of those who love you. On the day I became a woman, my father turned away lest I see his tears of sadness at the 'death' of a child, and of gladness at the 'birth' of the new woman I would become."

"Xohkantakeh does not shed tears! Not for me! Not for anyone!"

Katohya's smile disappeared. "It burdens my aging heart to know how easily you forget that it is only because of Xohkantakeh's compassion that you—once a useless child abandoned by your tribe in a time of hardship—have lived long enough to become a woman."

Lanacheela frowned. The reminder cut deep, and the expression of disapproval on Katohya's face was startling—not because it was unexpected, or undeserved, but because it re-arranged the woman's features in such a way as to emphasize the fact that she was old and no longer strong. Lanacheela stared, saw the blue circles of fatigue—or perhaps even ill-ness—beneath the long, still-lovely dark eyes. Never one to miss an opportunity that might advance her own cause, she reacted instantly.

She rose, hurried around the fire, and dropped to her knees before Katohya. "I have not forgotten, mother of my heart!" she said sweetly. "But I *am* a woman now, and you are no longer young or strong, and the old injuries that you received to your arm and leg during captivity pain you even though I have never heard you complain. Xohkantakeh should think more of both of us. Why, if we were to return to the land of our ancestors, there would be many warriors who would not find a new woman, potential life bearer, and pleasure giver useless. And surely there would be many war widows who would be proud to spread themselves for such a man as Xohkantakeh, to give him the sons you say he needs, and to lessen the many burdens of his woman Kato-hya and—"

"Enough!" Anger flashed in Katohya's eyes. "You are right. I am no longer young or strong. My once-broken arm gives little service, but it *does* serve, and what does it matter that the frost spirits fed upon my toes many win-ters ago? I can still walk. I have lived many years, Lanacheela. I have known many men. And I tell you now that I would gladly breathe my last before I would subject my beloved Xohkantakeh to the rigors or risks of such a journey."

Lanacheela glowered. "But—"

"Do not speak of it again!"

Lanacheela moved back, reached for her robe, swirled it around her shoulders, and seated herself on her bare but-tocks, angrily crossing her legs. "Then I will never burn with the true fire that comes to a woman when she opens herself and dances the dance of life-making beneath the man of her choice. I will never know the joys that you have known. I will never experience the—"

"The pain or the sadness that I have known." Katohya laid

the swan's feather across the girl's mouth and smiled lovingly. "Ah, Lanacheela, you may have shed a woman's blood and your body may burn with the fire of a woman's need, but you are still a child. Believe me when I tell you that life is good for us in this land beyond the country of warring tribes from which Xohkantakeh has led us. The 'true' fire of which you speak is sated soon enough, but the love of a truly good and caring man is to be cherished above all else and . . ." She paused.

The triumphant hunt song of the returning giant reverberated through the little encampment and fairly shook the walls of the tiny lodge.

"He returns," slurred Lanacheela, lacing her arms across her breasts and scowling.

"He returns!" echoed Katohya with obvious delight. Dropping the swan's feather beside the hearth stones, she leaped to her feet and limped to the weather baffle, pulled it back, and peered eagerly from the hut. A moment later she stiffened and clapped both hands over her mouth in amazement.

"What is it? What do you see?"

Katohya turned a radiant smile in her foster daughter's direction. "Come, unhappy one! Come and see what our truly good and most caring of all men has killed in your honor even though you say he does not care about you! Come, I say! Behold our Xohkantakeh! He is not young, but no *old* man could have slain so powerful a beast!"

Lanacheela rolled her eyes as she thought disdainfully of the largest, most dangerous meat her father had ever brought into camp—an old stag moose whose meat had been as tough and tasteless as its antlers would have been had they been considered edible. Making a face, she condescended to rise, but her breath soon caught in her throat when she stood beside Katohya and saw the giant and her younger sister hauling the tawny carcass of a monstrous bear through the break in the palisade.

"I must go to them. They will need help with all that must now be done," said Katohya. Turning to Lanacheela, she commanded, "You will stay hidden in the woman's lodge until I return, Lanacheela. Continue your fast. Cleanse your body with ashes from the fire in which your first woman blood has been burned. Today the child, Lanacheela, will die forever, and tonight the new-woman feast will be prepared. When all is in readiness, I will come to prepare you for the dawn. And then, with the rising of tomorrow's sun, you will come from this place reborn!" Smiling, she strode forward into the cold light of the sunstruck winter day.

Lanacheela's heart was racing. She turned, allowed the weather baffle of woven grass to fall closed behind her, and, suddenly breathless, went back to the fire circle. She stood a moment, then knelt, not so much out of obedience but because she was stunned.

"A bear . . . he has killed a bear . . . for *me!*"

Incredulous, she stared into the coals, saw the embers glinting up at her, and found herself thinking of frog eyes blinking red and gold in the light of the band's fire, on a long-gone summer night when Xohkantakeh had encamped with his family at the edge of a misted marsh. There had been fish and birds and deer in abundance. And a bear. Had there not been a bear?

"Yes." Lanacheela shivered within the softness of her luxuriant robe and wondered why she should think of it now, and of that faraway place where Xree, her littlest sister, had drowned so long ago.

She crossed her hands over her throat and gently pressed inward to quiet the beat of her pulse as her eyes turned up to stare at the beams of sunlight that shone down through the vent hole. The old fear was back, the childhood terror, the guilt. "May it be that there is not such a lonely death ordained for me!" Lanacheela implored the spirits of the smoke.

She closed her eyes, bit her lower lip, thought of frogs and darkness and of how it must be to die as tiny Xree had died, wandering off alone into the marsh, blundering into silent, unexpected deeps, gasping and sputtering for help, then going down, down into green, algae-thick water before anyone could reach her and pull her to safety.

Lanacheela opened her eyes in hope of banishing the

memory. It was no use. The moist smell of the marsh would forever be in her nostrils. She would always see herself, four summers old, sitting on a grassy shoreside hummock, singing happily as she braided green reeds into a doll, slapping at blackflies and her bothersome littlest sister until she finally succeeded in driving both away. And she would forever remember how bright everything had seemed when, startled by Katohya's sudden cry— "Bear!"—she had looked up from daydreams to see a tawny ursine form vanish into the willows just as a terrified Xree disappeared below the surface of the marsh and Xohkantakeh, roaring in anguish, hurled his great body across the water. Like some huge, despairing waterbird he dove again and again until Katohya and Ika drew him to the shallows, where they sat together with their arms around each other and he wept for the child he had been unable to save. It was the first and last time Lanacheela had ever seen him cry.

Later, under cold uncaring stars, she had crept from the lodge. She could still feel the wet, rough-edged grasses slip beneath her bare feet and hear the booming of a bittern as she hurried toward the marshy shore and called to her littlest sister.

"Xree! I know you are out there! Come back from the dark water! It is not a good place to hide. Xohkantakeh will keep you safe from bears. And I will make you a doll of your own! Or, if you really want to, you can play with mine. I promise! Xree! Please come back! I did not mean to send you away! Xree!"

Now Lanacheela bent her head, tears sliding over her cheeks as she remembered calling her sister's name again and again. The bittern had fallen silent. Only the frogs answered her cries as she looked across the marsh to see their round little eyes malevolently aglow in the reflected light of the campfire beside which Xohkantakeh sat disconsolately with Ika and Katohya.

"Grwill nah! Geeper bahk! Grwill nah! Geeper bahk!" croaked the frogs in a monotonous litany that set a slow horror rising in Lanacheela as she understood their lan-

guage and realized they were daring her to challenge their
authority to keep her sister a prisoner of the marsh
forever.

"Grwill nah! Geeper bahk!" sang the frogs. "Grwill not!
Geever bahk! Grwill not give her back . . . will not give her
back! Will not!"

And then the bear had returned.

Lanacheela saw it in her mind's eye—a shadow moving in the darkness, a huge and monstrous form huffing
restlessly in the trees behind the lodge, then standing upright on its hind limbs, observing the encampment as
though it were not a bear at all but some scar-faced chief
come from the forest to take command. Xohkantakeh had
hurled a lance and Katohya and Ika were shouting, shaking
their fists, and throwing burning sticks. Lanacheela remembered the whoof of surprise, almost of disappointment, that the great bear made as it dropped to all fours
and disappeared.

The next day Xohkantakeh had commanded them to
break camp and move on out of the hunting grounds
of "Great Paws." Lanacheela did not want to go, not without Xree. Xohkantakeh had taken her forcefully into his
arms and hefted her onto his shoulders, and all the long,
long way southward through the woodlands along the great
river, Lanacheela had wept and looked back for the sister
who had been left behind, alone and abandoned to the frogs
in a dark, deep, misted marsh in a land where there were no
people to remember that she had ever lived at all.

"May it not be so with me!" Lanacheela raised her eyes
and spoke her deepest longing to the smoke spirits, for in
this moment she feared the future more than the past. Tomorrow, despite all her girlhood hopes and yearnings, she
would be mated to an old man. To her own father! She
shuddered. Never would she know the love of the smooth-
faced, hard-bodied young man of her dreams. And soon
Xohkantakeh would die and leave her alone with Katohya
and Ika in a land where there were no warriors to protect
them from the terrors of the misted marshes and dark,
lonely, impenetrable forests that stretched endlessly beyond
the edge of the world.

Lanacheela's teeth were chattering with dread as she drew her new-woman robe around her slender shoulders. Beyond the brushwood walls of the little lodge, Katohya's exclamation of delight was followed by Xohkantakeh's laughter, rumbling like thunder on a summer day. Surprised, Lanacheela cocked her head, trying and failing to remember the last time she had heard her father laugh like that. Something in the sound recalled the vast snow-mantled mountains and wide rolling plains of her distant homeland. Drawn forward, she rose, went back to the weather baffle, and held it aside.

Her eyes widened. Xohkantakeh and Katohya were not only embracing; the giant had lifted his beloved by the waist and was whirling her around while Ika stood nearby, staring up at the body of the great bear that had been raised, spread-eagled, and bound to the palisade. Lanacheela's mouth fell open as her eyes fixed on the hide and head of a bear the color of the sunstruck plains of her childhood . . . a bear scarred along its face and shoulder . . . a bear that had prowled her nightmares for almost as long as she could remember.

"He has killed Great Paws!" she exclaimed, and suddenly her heart was racing once again as hope filled her entire being. "An old man who can slay such a bear—who can risk so much for this new woman—perhaps he may be made to risk even more before he dies?" A slow smile dimpled her soft features. "Perhaps, if not for Lanacheela then for the children I will bear him, he may yet be made to take me back to the land of the ancestors! To hunting grounds that lie beneath the bright sun and open skies! To the country of many people where no one dies alone and where there are no dark forests and sister-eating marshes guarded by frogs! And where, perhaps, I may yet find the young warrior of whom I dream!"

The power of the bear was his.

Xohkantakeh knew it, felt it, and had no doubt that, through the death of Great Paws, he had been reborn.

"No more will we run from this bear!" he proclaimed

to his woman as he placed her on her feet. "His spirit is
our spirit now. As the great white mammoth has been
totem to the People since time beyond beginning, so now
is Great Paws also totem to the woman and daughters of
Xohkantakeh!"

How Katohya's eyes shone as she stood radiantly before
him! How precious was the smile she bestowed upon the returning hunter!

His heart swelled with pride as, in keeping with the
traditions of the Ancient Ones, he allowed silence to settle
between them. In a solemn, ordered ritual, Katohya and
Ika stood aside with downcast eyes as the man who had
slain the bear worked alone to cut from its skin the meat,
bones, sinew, and fat that would sustain his family for
many a long moon to come. And when at last the work
was done, his body ached and the palms of his hands
burned, but the flesh and bones of the great bear were
piled high while the hide and head remained intact upon
the wall of the palisade, mounted high so that Great Paws
might look his last upon the world within which he was
chief no more.

"From this day the great bear will see through your eyes,
my father," said Ika. "He will hunt with your hands. He will
tread the forest and hills in your moccasins . . . for surely his
spirit *is* yours!"

"It is so!" affirmed Xohkantakeh, frowning at what he
took to be an unnecessary statement of the obvious. He
eyed the girl askance. She was slumping on her feet and appeared tired, which was understandable given their long
trek home; less understandable, however, was the inexplicable sadness he saw in her eyes as she offered up a wan
smile. Was this the same bold creature he had seen stand
unflinching before Great Paws? Perhaps her intractability
had not been bravery after all, but only inability to act in
the face of danger? Regretting his earlier admission of
weakness to the girl, and wondering if he had done the
right thing by sharing even the smallest portion of the
bear's heart with a fearful young female, he turned impatiently away and, to his surprise, saw that the sun was setting behind the palisade. The day was done, and Katohya,

her arms raised in deference, had placed herself before the skin and head of the great bear.

"Bear! Hear this woman!" she implored with reverence and a dignity that would have marked her as a chieftain's daughter even to those who did not know her lineage. "You, Bear, I say! You are symbol to the People of life coming forth from the winter earth! It is fitting that you have chosen to come to us now with the gift of your life! May the meat of your flesh and the marrow of your bones give renewed strength to this band in these last days of winter! May the presence of your spirit grant fertility to our new woman! And may your power live in the man to whom you have yielded your spirit so that—even as Mother Below gives birth to Bear each spring—the new woman of this band may be given cause to birth many strong sons to hunt for this family that you have so honored with the sacrifice of your life!"

Xohkantakeh was deeply moved—by pride in his woman and in his own accomplishment. Despite the rigors of the past days, Katohya's words had taken him beyond weariness. "May it be so!" He fairly shouted the affirmation and, forgetting Ika's presence entirely, placed his big hands on his beloved's slim shoulders and drew her close. In a lowered voice he revealed, "But it is for you, my Sweet-Scented Woman, that the spirit of the bear now 'sings' in this man."

Katohya kissed one of his hands, then the other. Her eyes were all for her man now as she raised her own hands and rested them over his. "Tomorrow the new woman will come forth to you with the dawn," she said with a gentle smile that bespoke a mother's love and joy and an aging, barren woman's resignation. "Tomorrow the life spirit of the bear must sing to the one whose body promises renewal to this band. And so now, perhaps, the returning hunter should rest, eat of his kill, and then sleep a while so that the bear spirit will be strong in him and eager to rise and make his song of life rise with the sun?"

Xohkantakeh raised both eyebrows at Katohya's use of metaphor. He would have laughed with delight at her circuitous way of speech had he not feared that a display of amusement might offend the spirit of the slain bear that was "singing" and rising in his loins even now. "I need not wait for the rising sun to fill you with the heat of my need, woman! Come. We will—"

"It cannot be!" Katohya's face flushed as she stepped away from him. "I must attend Lanacheela so that all will be in accord with the forces of Creation when the new woman comes forth to you in the light of the newly risen sun. Until then, Ika and I have much work to do."

"Ika is strong. She will do the work until we—"

"She is a child! She may be strong and tall as a young warrior, but to my eyes she is as obviously tired as are you!" Katohya gestured toward the main lodge. "Go now. Rest. Take food from the boiling bag next to the hearth. It will weight your belly and bring sleep that will still the 'song' of the bear until it pleases the spirits to see it rise in the hunter again!"

"In the Land of Grass, when a man felt the need to come between his woman's thighs, it was said that his very need pleased the spirits."

"This is not the Land of Grass!"

"No. But you are my woman, and I am a man in need."

"In the Land of Grass there were many female hands to do the women's work, but here, tonight, in this far land beyond the edge of the world, there are only Ika and Katohya to do what must be done if tomorrow's new-woman feast is to please the forces of Creation. I am only one woman, Xohkantakeh! Tomorrow you will have another. You *must* save your need for her."

Ika watched him go. He was obviously annoyed, and he glowered at her as he went by. Had he kicked her aside she would not have felt more hurt or left out. Xohkantakeh had made no mention to Katohya of his eldest daughter's bravery on the hunt or her part in the killing of the bear. The closeness she had sensed between them on the promontory had fractured, and she was not sure why. Yet, as her gaze followed him across the compound, she saw that he moved with an ease and resiliency of step that had been absent before their confrontation with Great Paws. Indeed, as he disappeared into the lodge, Xohkan-takeh appeared younger and more powerful than he ever had before.

"There *is* much to be done," Katohya emphasized, her voice strained and cool. "Since your father has seen fit to say nothing of the disobedience that set your feet against my will and upon his hunting trail, I also will say nothing more about it. You have been long away. The feast fire, however, must be laid out now so that it will be ready to be ignited at first light tomorrow. Had you remained in camp to offer assistance, Ika, all this would already have been done—the spreading of the feast mats, the placement of sacred boughs, the arraying of the many new-woman gifts in the place of honor. Now there are also steaks to slice and skewer for the feast, and much meat and fat to prepare and set aside for drying, smoking, and pounding." She paused and looked thoughtfully at the girl. "Of course, if you are too tired from your unnecessary journey, help me to uncover the wood that was set by long ago for tomorrow's special dawn, then rest a while. We can do the bulk of the work later, after I have tended to Lanacheela's needs."

Ika had been avoiding Katohya's censorious gaze. Now she turned toward her. The movement reminded her just how tired she was, but with renewed fatigue came a flaring of righteous indignation. "Unnecessary journey?" She nearly choked on the words. She clenched her teeth lest she blurt out that, had she not followed her father on this hunt, he would most likely be dead, there would be no feast meat in the camp, and Great Paws would still be alive and on the prowl. She shook her head. "Lanacheela has been lying around inside the lodge of blood for more than four days! Tomorrow she will be a new woman! Why can she not help us prepare the feast? After all, it is for her, is it not?"

"Tomorrow the new woman will be honored! She will do no work!"

"Hah! Then it will be like most any other day for her!"

"No, Ika. It will be like no other day in a young woman's life. She will be purified in sacred smoke. She will come forth from the lodge to be mated in the old way of the People! And when the blood of her first piercing has been shed, she will be brought to the fire circle. She will tell of the dreams she has dreamed during her confinement and receive a new name from the headman of this band. Then we will eat of the meat of the great bear that your father has so valiantly slain, and we will celebrate and honor the new woman with the many gifts that—"

"Should have been for me!"

"I have told you before, child, that the forces of Creation shape the world as they will. In time you will be a woman . . . when they deem you worthy to bear your father's sons, not before."

"Worthy?" The word was so bitter on Ika's tongue that it made her want to cry. Again she clenched her teeth. She ached to shout the truth, to hurl it in her foster mother's face. She had faced down and driven away the black wolf! She had stood to a charging bear in order to assure her father a kill that would restore his pride! She had hefted more than twice her share of the weight of that great beast and dragged it home uncomplainingly despite shoulder welts, suppurating blisters, and a heart and lungs strained near to bursting! And all so that Xohkantakeh's newfound self-confidence would not be quashed by the hard reality of physical limitations that might well bring his little family to ruin and death if he ever yielded to them again! Ika's head went high. Having accomplished these things, she knew she could speak of them to no one. For love of Xohkantakeh, it took even more courage than Ika knew she possessed to turn from Katohya in silence now.

They worked together without so much as a shared word until, at last, nearly all was in readiness and stars were shining brightly overhead.

"Rest now, child," Katohya urged, her mood softer now as she sent a conciliatory hand reaching for Ika's in the darkness. "Go to the lodge. I will wake you before dawn. In the meantime, sleep. Dream. Perhaps the white bird you so yearn to see *will* come to you and you *will* soon become a woman . . . a most worthy woman!" Having given the compliment in place of an apology for her earlier sharpness, she hugged the girl and hurried off to attend to whatever secrets would now pass between her and Lanacheela.

Ika remained kneeling on the woven mat that would be hers during the festivities that would begin at dawn. She would not have admitted it to Katohya, but she was too tired to get to her feet, much less stride across the compound to the lodge. She stayed where she was, still holding the last of the little sprigs of sacred sage that had been collected during the band's wanderings and set aside for the moment when they would be fed to tomorrow's new-woman fire. The scent of the dried, silver-leafed herb was both pungent and sweet; she breathed it in as she heard low, excited talk begin in the woman's hut and was aware for the first time of deep snoring coming from the lodge.

Feeling lonely and unwelcome in either shelter, Ika closed her eyes and, soothed by the healing aroma of the sacred sage, was soon fast asleep. Dreams came: of wide, dark, unfamiliar hills across which she wandered unafraid toward the east, where uncountable numbers of tiny campfires glowed like stars on the horizon of her thoughts. A scar-faced bear walked beside her, huge, silent, a companion, not an enemy. A wolf came out of the darkness to walk with the bear, and suddenly Ika saw a pregnant musk ox and heard it scream with her sister's voice as it fell beneath a pack of leaping wolves and was torn to pieces.

"Aiee!" Ika gasped. With the last warmth engendered by hours of hard work finally wearing off, she shivered so hard she awoke with a start.

It was a moment before she saw the lone wolf standing inside the palisade.

Black against white snow, a sizable chunk of bear meat dangling from its jaws, the animal was staring at her.

"You?" Ika stared back, cocked her head, and wondered if she was still dreaming.

Moments passed; neither girl nor animal moved.

"Are you real?" Ika asked the wolf.

The animal kept staring.

Slowly, through the scent of sage, another scent came to Ika. Animal. Canine. *Wolf!* And something more: the smell of injured flesh and . . .

The animal growled.

Slowly, with adrenaline heating her blood, Ika rose defensively to her feet.

And slowly the wolf backed into the break in the brush-lined timbers through which it had come. In less than a breath of time it dissolved into the night.

Wide-eyed, Ika threw the sprig of sage aside as she scrambled to gather deadwood and shove it into the breach. Breathless, as much from fright as from exertion, she leaned back against the palisade and closed her eyes. *The black wolf! It must have followed us unseen from the kill site. The smell of blood and meat has drawn it to our camp, and where there is one wolf there are bound to be others!* She trembled as she realized what might have happened if the entire pack had entered while she had so carelessly allowed herself to sleep in an unguarded camp.

"Never again!" Ika opened her eyes and looked up past the hide and head of Great Paws to the Great Bear in the sky. "Tomorrow this Little Bear will warn Xohkantakeh of wolves," she said resolutely. "We will set traps and . . ." A terrible realization broke through her thoughts. *Xohkantakeh should have known! He should have warned me to keep alert if he was going to sleep!*

A soft and gentle song was coming from the woman's lodge. Ika was glad to be distracted. There were no words, only melody, as Katohya's lovely voice sang for the new woman soon to be born.

Again Ika closed her eyes and stood very still. There was a lump in her throat the size of an oak gall as she stared glumly across the compound at the lodge of blood.

Tomorrow her sister would emerge from it reborn.

Tomorrow, in the moment when the sun showed its full face above the eastern hills, the new woman would be mated for the first time.

Tomorrow the feast fire would be raised for the new woman. Tomorrow all the fine new-woman gifts—the back-rest of woven willow, the fine new awls and scrapers, bone needles and perforators, new moccasins and garments and . . .

Ika shook her head, overwhelmed by the realization that the gifts were nothing to her.

Tomorrow her sister would lie in Xohkantakeh's arms as his new woman and join Katohya as "Beloved" in his eyes. To the girl who had sent all hope of a woman's love away on the wings of the white bird of her dreams, this knowledge was everything, and it nearly broke her heart.

The night wind gusted from the west. Ika was so miserable she actually welcomed its chill. Distracted by the skin of the great bear rubbing and straining against the thongs that held it fast to the palisade, she looked up at the beast she had helped to kill.

The huge, scarred head sagged to one side. The eyes had glazed; there was no color in them now, no threat. Ika could just make out the largest of the bear's upper teeth pointing down between dark lips that appeared strangely benign in death. With no saliva to moisten them, they had gone as stiff as a leather parfleche and almost seemed to be smiling; the teeth that had flashed so menacingly in the light of the sun were dull now, and no more frightening than a collection of broken bone awls, for Ika saw that one of the canines had been fractured and reduced to a long splinter. It occurred to her that the bear must have suffered constant pain from such a tooth.

She frowned, remembering a childhood incident in which she had fallen and cracked one of her two front baby teeth on a stone. She could almost hear herself bawling as though she would die from the hurt, and she could feel Xohkantakeh's strong arms around her as he had taken her on his lap, looped a strip of sinew around the damaged tooth, and promptly yanked it. She had yowled at the resultant pain, but Katohya had given her cool brown river weed to suck and kissed the top of her head as Xohkantakeh told her that brave little "warriors" did not cry. *I was a little girl, a future woman, not a future war-*

rior! Ika wondered if it was possible that, even then, her father had known what she would never be to him. Sadness touched her, and an unexpected empathy for the slain bear.

"Was there one among your kind who cared for your hurts when you were a cub, Great Paws? A mother or father bear to take the pain from a broken tooth, or from the wounds that marred your face and side? Or have you walked the world alone with your pain, with no band or bear brothers or sisters to give meaning to your solitude?"

Ika pressed herself into the hide of the animal and reached to lay her work-worn hands upon one of its huge paws. The fur was cold and as rough to her touch as the inwardly curling claws and the massive, scarred, callused pads. Nevertheless, the girl held her face against the paw and sighed with bittersweet remorse. "I am sorry I tricked you into exposing your heart to my father, but Xohkantakeh needed to kill you more than you needed to live, I think. He will honor your spirit, Great Paws. Truly he will. Your power has made him bold again. He has named you totem along with the great white mammoth. No bear could ask for greater respect than this! But my father is old, as you were old, Great Paws, and he makes mistakes, as you did. And so, as long as he lives, this girl—who has been honored to share with him the power meat of your heart—will remain at his side to protect him and my band from—"

Beyond the palisade, a lone wolf offered a high-pitched howl to the night. The sound was over almost before it began, but Ika recognized the voice of the black wolf and knew that she would never forget or forgive the way it had looked at her as meat when she had been alone and vulnerable on the open land.

"That one will not come into the encampment of my band again!" she vowed and turned her face up to the blind eyes of the slain bear. "I may never become a woman or know the love of a man, but thanks to you, Great Paws, I *have* become a warrior who has faced death and lived to walk away! Now, in the light of the Great Bear in the sky, I will go forth alone to bait the black wolf lest he come again to shame my father. I will go and return before I am missed, for your heart beats in my heart now, Great Paws, and I will not allow myself to be afraid!"

2

There were wolves in the forest.

Warakan, awakened by their familiar harmony, was glad it was made by living beasts and not by ghosts; he had had enough of woodland phantoms for a while. With Sister Wolf beside him, he sat up in the nest he had made of evergreen boughs laid crosswise over the snow within a tight stand of low-growing trees. Grateful for the windbreak and the warmth of his bearskin robe, he listened to the wolves. After a moment, he observed with a profound feeling of satisfaction that came naturally to one who was unarmed, "They are nowhere near."

Sister Wolf trembled.

Warakan slung an arm around her shoulder. "What is it, my old friend? Do you fear them, or do you long to go *to* them?"

She lay down close against his thigh, shivering a little and panting nervously.

Warakan shook his head at what he recognized as indecisiveness, then smiled. When he spoke, his words were a teasing outpouring of affection. "What would you do among that wild pack now, old and tame as you are, my sister? You could have gone to your own kind at any time after I found you so many years ago in that burning camp on the far side of the great gorge. You might have found a mate. You might have borne many a litter and made a pack to put fear into lions if you desired, but you chose to stay with me and old Peacedreamer, and I am glad for that. It would be lonely without you beside me now, for not since my days with Bear Brother have I had such a friend as you among the four-footed kind."

He rubbed her behind the ears. "Perhaps we will meet my brother in the days ahead? It would be good to wrestle again with that fat sack of yellow fur as big as a mountain! And to tell him that, while he has left me to seek his own kind in the Land of Grass, you have been a true friend and stayed with the one who has been both Mother and Father to you!"

The song of the wolves fell away.

Warakan waited for it to begin again. When it did not, its absence left a hollow space within the night that made him feel suddenly alone and so desolate that he felt the need to fill the space with words. "In the land of the ancestors there are many wolves," he informed Sister Wolf. "Some walk upright on two legs and think they are men, but they are wrong. They *are* wolves . . . the worst of their kind! But we will find and put an end to them, you and I!"

Sister Wolf sensed the change in his mood and rooted at his hand, offering the consolation of her presence and, at the same time, showing him that she wanted more rubbing.

Warakan obliged, but without much enthusiasm. An unsettling restlessness had come upon him. "There is so much to do between now and then," he said. "And we have so far to travel—to the high gorge for the magic spearhead, then to the barrens to seek the power of the totem. And then back to the Land of Grass! But perhaps distance can be an ally. It will strengthen us and give us time to plan and make new weapons: lances, a fighting dagger, and a good, well-balanced braining club. These things we must have, for I tell you now, old friend, that as a boy among my grandfather's people I have seen what you have not—men killing for the sake of killing, turning upon one another until the land was red with the blood of the slain and the wind carried the voices of the dying and the killers howled liked wolves and feasted until they could feast no more. When we confront such as they, even though the power of the sacred stone and of the great white mammoth totem will by then be ours, we must be prepared for a difficult and dangerous battle from which there will be no turning back!"

It suddenly occurred to Warakan just how long it was going to take him to complete the journey he was contemplating. How many seasons to reach the gorge from here? At least until summer's end, perhaps much longer. How many more seasons to cross the barrens and eventually—after the totem was found and slain—to return to the Land of Grass and the hunting grounds of his enemies?

He lay down, propped his head on his bent right elbow, and fingered the sacred stone with his left hand as he looked up into the night. "The talisman of the Ancient Ones will show us the way," he assured the wolf, shrugging off the fear that she might not be with him at the journey's end. Above the bare-branched canopy of the forest, the Sky River shimmered across the night. Warakan's eyes drifted, defined the pointer stars of several familiar constellations, then settled on the Great Bear as he remembered aloud, "Among my grandfather's warriors there was a giant. As big as my Bear Brother was that man! His name was Xohkantakeh. He was not young, but he was strong and wise, an honored keeper of sacred Fire within the chieftain's sweat lodge and a great fighter even though he made no secret of his weariness of war. He had little patience with me. In truth, Sister Wolf, more often than not he called me Trouble. But one day Xohkantakeh drew me to a craggy bluff and made me look down upon your kind as they ran wild with killing madness amidst a herd of winter-starved elk, nearly half its members mired at a river crossing."

Warakan paused. The memory disturbed him, yet he allowed it, encouraged it, for he knew that it was leading along a trail of thought that he must follow. "It was not the usual wolf kill, my sister, for that is an ordered thing, a thing *needed* for the survival of all. This was one wolf leading others to the attack again and again even long after enough meat had been taken. This was one wolf setting fire to the pack, enflaming all so that they killed and killed again, savaging their prey—and even one another—leaving many dying elk to wander off, dazed and torn, even as the killers rolled with pleasure in the guts and blood of their many kills. And then a strange thing happened: The killing madness over for all but the wolf that had provoked it, several wolves closed on that animal, and when it challenged the true leader of the pack, it was driven off. The others looked around, tails tucked, confused and perhaps even embarrassed by all the useless death they had made.

"It was then, old friend, that a hunting band of youths of my grandfather's tribe went to drive off the wolves and take what they could of the slain and dying elk. They called me to join them and help make an end of the kill-maddened wolves, whose ways, they said, would forever be a danger to our people. But the giant kept me where I was and told me that what I had just witnessed was so rare among the wolf kind that it was almost never seen by men. And then he asked me if, among the warriors of my own tribe, killing madness had not become so common that it was celebrated in the great autumn hunts when more game was stampeded over the bison jumps than the people could butcher and eat in twice a double hand-count of winters. When I said yes, he asked if, among the People of the Land of Grass and the People of the Watching Star, killing madness had not become a way of life and given a name of honor: *war.* When I said yes yet again, he growled as though he himself had become a wolf and reminded me with great sadness that, unlike wolves, men who provoked killing madness were not reviled or driven from the tribe as traitors to their chieftain. They were made chieftains over all!"

Warakan's head swung slowly from side to side. "This is a truth that Jhadel, shaman and wise man though he was, refused to accept."

The wolf's head rose at the sound of the old Peacedreamer's name.

Warakan looked at the animal's questioning expression and, reaching to rub behind her ears, continued quietly, "Only when we have driven from the tribes those who inspire killing madness against the true chiefs will the peaceful unification that Jhadel so longed for be possible. Those who betrayed my grandfather, my sister, my mother and father, and . . ."

An owl *oo-ooh*ed somewhere in the darkness. Another answered. Then all was still again.

Sister Wolf cocked her head.

Warakan did the same. Jhadel had taught him that a man could never be sure if he was hearing more than mere sounding from an owl. Owl could also be Messenger, one of many animal spirit guides from whose example Jhadel had taught him to learn the attributes of a successful hunter. Owl was Wisdom, clever enough to see by night as well as by day. Owl was Patience, waiting and watching until the time was right to seek its prey. Owl was Treachery, moving through darkness on silent wings to take prey unaware. And always Owl was Death, a presence that assured that there would always be widows and orphans mourning in the camps of Mouse and Rabbit and Snake.

An unexpected thrill went through Warakan as he settled himself more comfortably between the trees. "I will be Owl to my enemies! When the time is right, there will be widows and orphans mourning in the camps of those men who have come as wolves to set killing madness loose among my people . . . and in the lodge of the giant who betrayed them in the last days of the great war!"

3

It was very late. Ika went beyond the palisade. Into starlit darkness she slipped unseen, silently asking the forces of Creation to overlook her willful disobedience of Xohkantakeh's command to never venture from the encampment alone.

The night was still and deep and beautiful. The weary girl breathed it in. The guard hairs of her fox-skin ruff filtered frost and allowed the freezing air to nourish her senses as she paused, pulled off a glove, opened the leather sack that she had brought with her, and took from it one of several palm-sized chunks of bear meat.

Ika stared at the raw, tendinous muscle tissue. In the darkness it had the color of old liver. It lay stiff in the hollow of her hand, not only because of the cold night air but because of the slender, thumb-length bone skewer she had inserted deep within it and each of the other cuts of meat. Once inside the belly of any animal unlucky enough to swallow them, the little lances would be freed by digestive juices to work through the meat and perforate the intestine. Death would come to the animal within a matter of days.

Ika scanned the open land before her. A lone wolf was howling again. She cocked her head and listened. The animal was calling from somewhere atop the smooth dome of the broad, windswept slope that lay to the west of the encampment. She recognized the odd, barklike crescendo. "I know you," she whispered, then cocked her head to the opposite side, for there was something different about the cries of the black wolf tonight. She imagined she heard pain—and something else, something deeply disturbing that she could not quite define.

A shiver went up the girl's back.

Loneliness? Despair? Was it possible that she was hearing human emotions expressed in the song of an animal? Ika knew that if Xohkantakeh were here he would remind her that in the time beyond beginning, in the days when the Animals and People were of one tribe, wolves and men spoke the same language, hunted the same prey, and ate the same meat.

A frown creased her brow. Xohkantakeh was not here. She was glad of that, for if he were, he would be castigating his daughter for once again ignoring his commandment never to venture from the palisade alone. Nevertheless, when she thought of the black wolf's slavering jaws and menacing yellow eyes, she did not regret her disobedience.

"You are *not* of my tribe!" she whispered vehemently to the night. "You are my enemy. You have hunted me. You have looked at me as meat. You have shamed me and my father by stealing from our band while we slept! And now, as I listen to your song, do you imagine that I do not know that you must be calling your brothers and sisters to tell them that there is food for the taking in the camp of Xohkantakeh?"

Resolve filled Ika's heart. Until this moment she had intended simply to stride well away from the palisade, toss the baited chunks of bear meat onto the snow, then quickly return to the safety of the compound before she was missed. Now, however, it occurred to her that the black wolf might not return to the encampment tonight. It might wait on the heights of its favorite haunt, content to consume what it had stolen, deliberately delaying its next foray until her guard was down. If she scattered her bait now, smaller scavengers would surely be drawn by the scent. Ika did not want their deaths; it was the black wolf's death she wanted, badly.

She dropped the chunk of bear meat back into the bag. The wolf had fallen silent, but within her tired mind thoughts were running wild with the hated animal. She suspected that it was watching her, savoring the stolen meat, perhaps deliberately biding its time until all the flesh of Great Paws was portioned, prepared, and set out upon the drying racks for easy snatching by quick and clever jaws.

Anger flared within her meager breast. "You will find Death first!" She visualized the animal coming down from the heights, approaching the palisade on cautious paws, sniffing, salivating, then gulping down her "gift." Again she frowned, realizing now that, even if the wolf took her bait, it would not feel the deadly sting of the skewers until long after it had eaten. It would have time to make another raid on Xohkantakeh's camp, and having been successful once, it would not be so easily driven away a second time.

The black wolf would come in silence.

It would come in the way of its kind. Warily it would wait until it was certain the human band lay asleep, and then—alone or in the company of its pack—the black wolf *would* come.

Ika swallowed hard. If she failed again to prevent the animal from entering the encampment, Xohkantakeh's failing senses might keep him from seeing or hearing or even scenting the presence of the beast until it had again made off with meat or until someone was hurt attempting to prevent its thievery. Then, surely, Katohya and Lanacheela would suspect the truth—that a man who failed to anticipate and safeguard against a plundering wolf was unlikely to have successfully stalked and slain Great Paws single-handed.

"I will not let them know the truth!" The girl jammed on her glove, stepped boldly away from the palisade, and strode into the night. The broad, windswept slope was not so far from the encampment that she could not hope to reach it and be back within her bed furs long before dawn. "I will follow the black wolf there and place my offering

of Death close to the high ground on which he makes his
own camps. I will call him to the gift I bring. He is Wolf.
He is Curiosity. His ears and nose will lead him. But his
appetite and greed will kill him. And then, as he lies
dying, everything will go perfectly for the new-woman
feast tomorrow. The pride and strength of the hunter
depend on it!"

The snowpack, rough and hard beneath Ika's feet, held
her weight, but neither she nor the black wolf left many
tracks upon it.

"A few are all I need!" the girl assured herself, but all
too soon she lost even these upon the broken snow and
stones of the talus slope. Having come much farther than
she realized, she came to an abrupt stop.

Confounded by deepening darkness and increasing fatigue, Ika strained to catch her breath and was not exactly
sure just when she caught the scent of canine urine upon a
heavy downdraft of cold air—or first sensed that she was
being watched.

The hackles rose on her back, neck, and arms.

She stiffened and held her ground as she heard a low
growl emanate from a tangle of high boulders just ahead.
The sound was deep, steady, a tense and resonant warning
that seemed to set the very night to trembling.

Straining to see more clearly, Ika was almost sorry when
she succeeded. There, poised to leap on her from atop the
tallest boulder, the black wolf stood in silhouette against
the stars.

The girl's breath snagged in her throat. Her eyes met
and held the unblinking gaze of the beast. She felt its hatred.
It was going to leap at her. It was going to rip her to pieces
and devour her.

"No," Ika growled back at the wolf. "I will not be meat
for you!"

Slowly, as she took one cautious backward step and then
another and another, her arm moved to position her lance.

The growl of the wolf intensified.

With a jolt of horror Ika realized that she had come
into the night unarmed. In an instant, fatigue and terror
drove all sense of caution from her mind. She dropped the

bag of baited meat, turned on her heels, and ran for her life.

Katohya came from the woman's lodge with a bladder skin of warmed water. Hefting the bone-handled carrier, she paused and looked around. It was nearly dawn. In an hour, perhaps less, it would begin to grow light. It was very cold and still; the air was cutting sharp, yet sweet to her senses after a night spent with Lanacheela within the close, smoky confines of the woman's hut. The girl had at last fallen asleep, and, with all in readiness for the morrow, the woman had left her to the final dreams of childhood.

The palisade and the trees beyond stood black against a sky that had taken on that rarest and darkest of all blues, a color that existed only at the very edge of deepest night and only for a scant run of heartbeats before fading into the somnolent, melanistic gray that eventually absorbed the stars and washed away into morning. Standing alone beneath the stars, her bare hands warmed by the curving contours of the water carrier, Katohya raised her face to the dying night. It was beautiful. Her eyes swimming in the exquisite blue, she felt renewed by its transient loveliness and wondered if the moment was an omen of some sort. If it was, only time would prove whether for good or bad.

A sudden sound disturbed the stillness.

Katohya tensed, listening, and heard a low, quick rustling at the far curve of the palisade. She turned, sent her gaze across the starlit compound, sieving through darkness to see a fur-clad form slip surreptitiously through a breach in the wall, then bend to shove brushwood into it before hunkering down below the skin of the great bear.

Ika! Katohya nearly spoke the girl's name aloud. How could the girl so flagrantly disobey her father's command to remain within the compound unless in the company of another? Why had she gone? For what possible purpose? Katohya shook her head. Whatever Ika had been doing alone in the dark beyond the palisade was a question that would best be dealt with later. Katohya had not come from the woman's lodge without purpose, and that purpose would be more easily accomplished without the presence of the child.

Her brow furrowed. Ika did not appear to have noticed her. She could see that the girl was settling in her furs and preparing to sleep sitting upright against the wall. Her eldest daughter's behavior troubled her these days, but she was glad that Ika was not in the main lodge; what must transpire there would best be done beyond the eyes and ears of an immature girl whose senses would soon be seared by the new-woman ceremony that would take place in the light of the rising sun.

Moments passed. Katohya held her ground until the girl's head went down onto her knees. Moving quietly and slowly across the compound, she barely breathed as she went to the main lodge and entered.

It was very dark inside. She stood motionless as her eyes grew accustomed to the gloom. She could not see Xohkantakeh, but she knew where and how he lay—close to the northernmost curve of the lodge, on his side, his face toward the entrance, his spears within easy reach in the event of an attack. The habits of a man raised in a land of ever warring tribes were never broken. Feelings of tenderness stirred Katohya's heart. She moved forward into warm darkness.

The rhythm of Xohkantakeh's breathing told her that he was still deep in sleep beneath his furs. She knew that the last few days had cost him. She also knew that she would not speak of this, now or ever. His killing of the great bear had restored a part of his spirit that she had feared lost forever— more than his courage, his very will to go on living. To her dying day Katohya would thank Great Paws for this greatest of all gifts.

She knelt, set the bladder flask down carefully, then slowly slipped off her robe and her knee-length winter dress. Naked save for her moccasins and leggings, she raised the closest corner of the heavy bison hide that covered her man, and lay down facing him.

"Soon it will be dawn," she whispered to the sleeping

man. He exhaled and shifted his weight slightly, then made the low rumblings of one attempting to settle back into pleasant dreams.

"Awake," Katohya bade him, her mouth close to his, her breath a warm sigh against his face as her fingers moved upon his lips. "Soon it will be the beginning of a new day . . . for the new woman, for the man within whom the power of the slain bear has been reborn, and also for this woman, who will not lie alone with Xohkantakeh beneath these furs again."

"Hmm . . . ?"

"Hold me. Let me lie close against you in the dark, just you and I, one last time. Let us talk of all the good things we have shared since setting our backs to the land of warring tribes and following the great river into these good hunting grounds. And let us share our hopes of how it will be when the children of our new woman fill our camps with laughter and song and happy games."

"Hmm . . ."

"It is said by the wise old women among my people that the very sight and scent of a new woman ready for mating makes all men young and bold with need to be the first to make life on her. She will be a good woman for you . . . one who will savor mating, for she has told me that her body burns with need of it. I have taught her all the ways in which to enhance her coupling pleasure and yours. Soon, when the sun rises over the eastern hills, she will come to you in the way of the new women of my tribe since time beyond beginning, naked and oiled and eager to color your man bone with the blood of her first piercing. And for this end, my most dear beloved, I have brought warm water to bathe your body." She moved closer, sent her hands moving downward and across his bare skin in slow, circular, loving caresses. "You must be cleansed of the kill before you go to the one into whom you will set the fire of new life . . . with this . . ."

He gasped at her unexpected handling of that portion of his anatomy that had already begun to react to her words. His breathing quickened. His eyes batted open. "Ah, Sweet-Scented Woman, you are my life," he told her, and drew her into a kiss that sent his tongue to speak of that which he would have pass between them now.

Katohya accepted the kiss, but no more. Her body was aflame, and her thoughts were in turmoil. She had come to the lodge not because of her own desires but because she knew that by dawn her man must be aroused to a state of readiness if the new woman was to be successfully mated in the light of the newly risen sun. Weary as she was—and after years of believing that man need was long dead in Xohkantakeh—she had forgotten his behavior toward her upon his return from the hunt. Now, startled by his unexpectedly quick and intensely heated response to her seduction, she placed her palms against his chest and pushed away from him. "The power of the great bear *does* live again in you . . . in all ways!"

"It is so! Come! Open your body to mine. It has been too long since we last—"

"But the power must not be wasted! It must be for the new woman! It cannot be squandered on one who is growing so old that she rarely sheds moon blood and has failed to nurture the milk of life that you have so many times placed into her body."

"Until sunrise I have but one woman."

"And *at* sunrise you must take the new woman when she comes from the lodge of blood reborn."

"It will be so."

"But it is nearly dawn! I came to fire your need for the new woman, not for me."

"Have I brought you to believe that I am no longer man enough to take and fill more than one woman?" He took her wrist and gently pulled her to him. "The power of the bear *is* in me, Katohya." He guided her hand to the hard, hot truth of his statement and, with his free hand moving in provocative exploration of her breasts, whispered huskily, "In the light of the rising sun, the new woman will be mated. But now, Sweet-Scented Woman, Great Paws will not be denied."

Sunrise.

Under clear skies, with West Wind rising and good

omens all around, Xohkantakeh came from the main lodge. Barefoot and naked save for the heavy bed fur that he had slung around his shoulders, he was smiling, for not since youth had he felt so strong, so self-satisfied, so certain of his own worth and potential as a man.

Before him, all was in readiness. A pathway of woven reeds extended before him across the snow to the lodge of blood; another, smaller path branched off at the center and led to the middle of the compound, where wood and kindling for the feast fire had been placed and seating mats and backrests arranged around it. Upon the new woman's newly made mat, gifts had been assembled in a great heap, each intricately wrapped in pounded bark, woven grass, or strips of fur, bound with ribbons of hide and silvery, dried fish skins, and artfully festooned with feathers, bone beads, and shells collected over the years. Xohkantakeh's eyes narrowed with pleasure. Katohya had outdone herself. He told himself that he should not be surprised; she had been looking forward to this morning for more sunrises than he cared to count, and now it seemed only yesterday that he had first heard her worriedly say, "We must begin to prepare! Someday our little girls will come to womanhood!"

"Someday." Xohkantakeh heard his own begrudging reply reaching out of time. Now, as then, it was difficult for him believe that his little girls could ever be more than vulnerable, trusting little foundlings to be looked after, protected, and loved as fiercely as any of his own long-dead children had ever been.

The memory jarred him. He closed his eyes, saw faces from the past, beloved women and sons and a daughter, all slain, all lost to him forever in that far land of warring tribes from which he had fled with Katohya and the foundlings so long ago.

"We are Father and Mother to them now, Xohkantakeh!"

Again Katohya's voice came to him out of time as, behind his closed lids, he could see her, young and earnest and as beautiful as a summer dawn, standing beside him.

"We must ready gifts for the day when they emerge

reborn from the lodge of blood to be honored in the old way of the People."

"Of your tribe or mine?"

"We are of one tribe now. And, in truth, sometimes I think that the forces of Creation have chosen you to lead us out of the hunting grounds of our enemies into unknown and uninhabited lands so that we would become like First Man and First Woman—wandering a new and undiscovered world, Mother and Father of a new generation of the People who will walk and hunt together in peace under a more benevolent sky!"

Xohkantakeh's brow came down. He opened his eyes and stared across the compound, barely seeing it now, for he was disconcerted by his recently acquired ability to recall clearly events that had transpired half a lifetime ago. It was an old man's gift, and he wanted no part of it. Yet sometimes, as now, yesterday seemed more real than the moment at hand. He was certain that when he had first led his little family southward along the great river, Katohya could not have known that she—who had successfully conceived and borne a child to another man, only to see both die—would never again be able to sustain life within her womb. She could not have known that the only little ones she was destined to raise to maturity would be the foundling offspring of strangers. In time she must have begun to suspect and then gradually accept the truth: that although she continued to shed moon blood and never turned her back to her man when he had need of release within her body, her breasts and belly would never again swell or quicken with life. She had been made barren during enslavement to a war band whose members had brutalized and repeatedly raped her.

His mouth tightened. Memories were heavy on his spirit. He tried to shrug them off, but they were like spiders settling in his brain, stinging his conscience with the poison of regret. He had been a member of that war band. He had used her as fighting men invariably used captive women after battle, until one day her grace and dignity captured his heart. Soon it was he who was enslaved. To save her life and return her to freedom among her own people, he had challenged the war chief and fought his fellow warriors until he was forced to abandon his tribe and take her to safety beyond the edge of the world. In time they had learned of the death of her people. Under his patient care she had healed, had grown strong again and able to forgive and, yes, even to love again. She had willingly become his woman and pledged her heart to his "always and forever." In time her hair had begun to gray. In time her confinements in the lodge of blood became infrequent and her features began to line and rearrange themselves with age. But to Xohkantakeh she had grown only more beautiful, and her loyalty and affection for him and their girls never wavered.

Now his eyes focused on the assemblage of new-woman gifts. A smile moved the corners of his broad mouth as he remembered watching Katohya collect shells, feathers, and rare stones and set aside the finest pelts and shining skins of silver fish while the little ones napped or wandered unaware of what she was up to. He remembered the way she secreted her collection in a special pack roll and parfleche, willingly carrying the extra burden from camp to camp until it grew so large that he insisted on adding the bulk of it to his own pack frame. He remembered watching her as she sat cross-legged in the lodge, sewing and weaving and happily humming in the depth of night, working by the light of a sputtering oil lamp toward the day when their sleeping daughters would come reborn as women from the lodge of blood.

"They must know the full, transcendent joy of that day as I knew it . . . as every new woman must know it!"

And he remembered challenging what he then deemed only a stubborn and meaningless fixation with the old tradition. *"In new lands, if men and women are to survive outside the protection of the tribe, they must learn new ways."*

"Yes, and so it must be, but when a girl comes forth from the lodge of blood reborn as a woman, her eyes must shine with pride and her heart and body must sing with infi-

nite delight so that, in days and nights to come, when life grows difficult and children come from her body in blood and pain, the happiness of that day will sustain her."

Xohkantakeh's head went high. How wise was his woman! How loving and compassionate despite—or perhaps because of—the tragedies that had befallen her in youth! And how fortunate were his foundling daughters to have such a shining maternal guide to light their way along the pathway of maturation! Memories fell away. He could feel the warmth of the new day rising at his back as he surveyed the scene before him. No daughter of the Land of Grass had ever been honored with a finer-looking fire circle and assemblage of gifts, or more impressive feast meat. His eyes fixed on twice a double hand-count of bone skewers, arranged and ready for roasting along the perimeters of the fire circle. Each was laden with chunks of prime flesh cut from the body of the slain bear. The beast itself remained staked to the palisade directly across from him, its lifeless head fixed toward the east, its pelt tawny and grizzled around the shoulders in the light of the rising sun.

Pride filled the hunter. Drawing in a deep breath of the morning, Xohkantakeh strode across the compound and, feeling as invigorated as though he had just quaffed blood drawn hot from a still-living "kill," stopped before the bear. The morning wind was cold against his skin as his sleeping fur fell away and he worked to loosen the thong bindings that held the massive hide to the inner wall. In moments the task was accomplished. He slung the bearskin around and over his shoulders and back, positioned the head to face forward atop his own, and brought the forelimbs with their huge clawed paws to dangle over his chest and down below his knees.

The warmth and weight of the uncured, roughly fleshed hide brought an undefinable sensation of satisfaction prickling beneath his skin. The inner surface of the huge pelt was still moist; it reeked of blood and softening flesh. Somehow the stench of death was the essence of his own power. Xohkantakeh adjusted the hide, felt it slip against his own skin, and knew that he and Great Paws were now one. He closed his eyes, luxuriating in the moment, until he was aware of being watched. He opened his eyes to see a solemn-faced Ika standing before him.

She had gathered up his sleeping fur and was looking up at him, sad-eyed and soiled in her hunting clothes, her hair unkempt and blowing raggedly in the morning wind.

"Why does Ika look so unhappy?" he demanded.

"I . . ."

"Why have you not bothered to comb your hair?"

"I . . ."

"And why are you still in your hunting clothes? Have you no respect for the importance of this day?" Suddenly irked beyond words at the girl's inappropriate dress and manner, he thought, *This one will* never *be a woman!* and turned from his eldest daughter to be made breathless by the sight of one who was.

Katohya came alone from the lodge of blood.

Xohkantakeh gaped like an awestruck boy. It was apparent that she, like he, had been refreshed by their earlier coupling; both of them had slept briefly afterward. When he had awakened, she was cleansing his body with warm, sage-scented water. Her touch had been exquisite. He had closed his eyes, savoring it until, her ministrations done, he opened his eyes to find her gone. Now she stood, in a new white dress and moccasins fashioned of the skins of winter-killed female foxes, her hair loose to her knees, her face radiant beneath a wreath of evergreens entwined with last autumn's berries and tufts of dried sacred sage that she had gathered and brought with her from the northwestern grasslands. His heartbeat quickened as he realized that she had dressed and adorned herself like Winter Woman, heroine of the New Woman Coming song that he remembered from the Land of Grass. She was honoring him, showing him by her garment that, although the ceremony to follow was being held at dawn in the way of her tribe, it would now proceed in the way of his. Barely realizing that he spoke aloud, he loosed the well-remembered litany of the Winter Woman into the morn-

ing as he crossed the compound and took his place before
the main lodge:

> *"She comes!*
> *Behold, Winter Woman!*
> *In white she comes!*
> *In silence she comes!*
> *Covering the skin of Mother Below, she comes!*
> *Behold, Winter Woman!*
> *She is Season Ending opening the way for New*
>   *Beginning!"*

Katohya was smiling. A small hand drum dangled by a
thong loop from her right wrist. In her left hand and braced
against her waist was a shell-adorned basket. Long stream-
ers of iridescent fish skin and hide dyed red with the blood
of many kills had been hung on either side of the entry into
the lodge of blood—the first in representation of the wa-
tery womb of life, the second of the blood and caul
through which all newborns must come into the world.
"New Woman, Sun is rising!" she called into the lodge.
"Come forth now through darkness, water, and blood into
the world of light, air, and life! As bear comes from the
earth reborn, come forth, I say, and be received by your
people!"

A head appeared at the entryway—not a face, merely
the top of a young girl's head. The rest of her remained
crouched on hands and knees within the "womb" of the
little lodge.

Katohya uttered a series of groans.

Xohkantakeh found them impressive replications of the
sound a woman makes when expelling a child from the birth
passage.

"Come forth, New Woman!" commanded Katohya
again. "Seasons Ending summons New Beginning!" This
said, she dashed the contents of the basket—blood and water—at the head of the girl so that it splattered the new
woman and the entryway, through which Lanacheela now
thrust herself onto a thick layering of mats spread over the
cold, snow-veneered ground.

"Ay yah!" cried a jubilant Katohya. After tossing the basket onto the unlighted pyre, she began to beat the little drum.

Xohkantakeh responded instantly to the unique and long-unheard rhythm: a single long, sustained beat followed by two strikes in quick succession. His pulse began to race as the pattern was repeated again and again while, slowly, New Woman crawled toward him, head bent forward and tucked to her knees.

His brow came down. Lanacheela, although completely naked, was unrecognizable. Her hair and body had been thickly greased with fat taken from the great bear. Every inch of her skin had been painted red with finely ground ochre. She seemed barely human as she advanced in fetal position, her hair slicked to her head, her body glistening as though encased in a birth caul. She made no sound. She did not even seem to be breathing when at last she paused at Xohkantakeh's feet.

"Behold New Woman, who comes from the womb of Mother Below cleansed of first blood and eager to open her body to the life of the tribe!" announced Katohya with a final flourish of double beats upon the drum. "Now let the headman of this band accept this new woman! Now, in the way of the People of the Red World and of the Land of Grass, let the man be as the stallion and bull and stag of the great herds! Let the forces of Creation flow from this male into this female! Let this band live forever through the new life that he will give to her now!"

Silence.

Xohkantakeh felt it press him. He knew that his beloved Katohya had deliberately enflamed him with her choice of words. He was hard and hot and pulsing with renewed man need. There would be no turning back from what must happen now. New Woman was getting to her feet before him, holding wide her slender arms, displaying her body even as she kept her face turned to the ground. He was grateful for the latter; this was not a moment in which a father chose to look into a daughter's eyes.

She turned slowly before him, allowing him full view of that which had been purposefully withheld from his gaze for many a long moon. He stared with amazement, wondering when and how this awesome transformation had taken place. The small, lithe, virtually featureless body of his foundling had matured into that of a ripe and ready woman. His eyes took in the smooth, taut, tapering lines of her hips and belly and thighs, the fine, full breasts with nipples peaking hard in the cold wind, each encircled by a beguiling pattern of black dots that held his eyes until she turned to show a sleekness of oiled back and full rounded buttocks that took his breath away. She knelt then and, still facing away from him, lowered her hands to the matting, raised her hips, and spread her limbs, exposing the soft moistness of her new-woman place in invitation to be mated.

"Let it be done . . . in the way of a warrior of the People of the Land of Grass!" cried Winter Woman.

Xohkantakeh did not need to be urged on. With the sun in full ascent above the eastern hills and his body clothed in the hide and head of Great Paws, the man caught fire. He *was* a warrior of the People of the Land of Grass! He had killed the great bear! He had eaten its heart! And now, once again, he could feel its power reborn in him as surely as the girl had come forth from the lodge of blood reborn as a woman. His heart was pounding more intensely than any drum. He had not the slightest doubt that the forces of Creation had heard and heeded Katohya's imploration, for in this moment he had become not stallion or bull or stag—but boar! He was all at once Bear and Man, and his male part was erect and alive against his belly, throbbing, seeking, hunting . . . woman.

With a growl of unsated sexual hunger, Xohkantakeh dropped to his knees behind New Woman. She was shivering in the cold air of morning. He growled again. Only scant hours ago he had made love to Katohya as he had not made love to her in years, but what he was experiencing now had nothing to do with affection. Great Paws was alive in him, and the pure, driving, mindless animal need to make new life was on him.

Running his hands over New Woman's oiled flanks until his palms and fingers were slick with the fat of the beast he had slain, he reached to finger her woman place while he bent his head to browse between her thighs, scenting and mouthing the sweetness of her gender until, startled by the sudden invasion of his tongue, she stiffened and tried to scoot away on her knees. He made a grab for her ankles, nearly lost her when his greased hands slipped on her equally slick skin, but somehow managed to maintain his hold. Growling yet again—this time in response to painfully heightened need—with one hand he impatiently positioned himself for penetration while jerking her back with the other.

She cried out as he thrust his hips forward and rammed deep.

"Ay yah!" Katohya shouted and began to beat a new rhythm on her little drum.

With the warm moistness of New Woman flexing tightly around his man bone, Xohkantakeh roared with renewed masculine power, ejaculating and quivering with the ecstasy of immediate and explosive release. He gripped her thighs and, scenting the blood of her piercing, held her fast, thrilling to sensations of an intensity he had not known since youth, working her until he swelled again and, amazed at his prowess, ejaculated again, this time with such force that she collapsed forward, making low, breathless mewings as she panted like a wild camp dog too long deprived of water. A tremor went through him as he continued to grip her thighs; she was still flexing on him, moving her hips, the muscles of her woman place gripping him as she shivered, no longer with cold but with the pleasure he was giving her. At last, drained and more sexually satisfied than he had ever thought possible, he drew out of her.

"It is done!" he declared and rose to his feet, pulling the new woman upright with him, steadying her as he noticed that her mouth was compressed and her eyes shut so tightly that the long lids showed white through the ochre paint that now glistened with perspiration. "New Woman, you will look at your new man!"

She did not look.

Katohya came close, frowning a little until she saw that

his man bone was limp and dark with the girl's blood. She smiled then and, after removing and placing her wreath upon the girl's head, raised both arms to the rising sun. "Now New Woman is born into this world in blood, in the way of the People since time beyond beginning! Now may the evergreens that encircle New Woman's brow remind her of her place in the eternal Circle of Life! Now may she be as ripe and full of seed as the berries that encircle her brow. And when her time comes to walk the wind forever, may there be many sons and daughters at her side to burn the sacred sage she wears, for on its fragrant smoke her spirit will rise into the Blue Land of Sky, where she will live forever among the stars in the encampments of the ancestors!" Katohya's voice broke. There were tears in her eyes as she looked into Xohkantakeh's face with absolute love and radiance. "Now may the feast fire that will celebrate the coming of New Woman to the People be ignited by the man who has placed the fire of his own life inside her, for now, through Xohkantakeh, hope in the future of this band is restored!"

Now was the time for rejoicing.

Now was the time for song.

Now was the time for feasting and dream telling and for the headman to choose a new name for the new woman.

Ika saw no cause to rejoice. Still aching with fatigue and shame over her cowardly retreat from the black wolf, she could not bring herself to sing. She could not lift a moccasin, let alone make herself move to her feast mat; she was shaking so badly that she had to clench her teeth to keep them from clacking and lock her knees lest she fall down.

So this was what it meant to be mated!

Stunned, she wondered how she could ever have imagined it would be otherwise. Had she not seen the restless power of the great stags in autumn rut? Had she not marveled at the sight of stallions in fevered extension, observed lions roaring, biting, and shivering as they joined, and grown puzzled when she saw wolves locked one to the other in copulations that went on for hours? Had there not been violence in those matings? And bloodshed and pain? Sometimes it had seemed so; she simply had not thought about it. She was, after all, of the People; the beasts and birds, the insects and scaled creatures of the earth and water were Animals. She had observed them as an outsider, as one not of their tribe and therefore not connected to their ways. And yet, season after season, she observed the booming, boisterous blusterings and explosive, feather-flying mountings of the marsh birds. She had watched curiously as toads clasped one another and hopped about, "talking" as they made new life. She had peered into shallow pools at the river's edge and saw fish circling frantically together until one expelled the milk of life over eggs laid by the other. She had lain back on moist, dark green, sweet-smelling grass that bordered many a pond and, shielding her eyes with folded arms, listened to the drone of insects and looked up to see blue and red dragonflies hovering overhead, their netted wings shimmering, their slender bodies joined and moving as one in a dance of beauty that touched her spirit and made her smile as she wondered what it would be like to pair with another being and fly away together into the sunlit blue vastness of a warm summer sky. And sometimes, albeit rarely and not for many long moons, Ika would awaken in the close, comforting darkness of the lodge to the breathless gasps and muted groanings of Katohya and Xohkantakeh moving together beneath their bed furs. She would close her eyes. She would listen. And while Lanacheela responded by moving to a rhythm of her own, Ika would grow perplexed and troubled, for although what passed between her parents in the night seemed natural and without threat, it was only then that she remembered that, in time beyond beginning, the People and Animals were of one tribe.

Now, in the light of this morning's sun, she had seen that this was still surely so.

Xohkantakeh was lifting Lanacheela in his arms, enfolding her in the skin of the great bear, and carrying her to the place of honor before the unlit feast fire. How gently he settled the new woman onto her beautifully woven new mat! How tenderly he drew the luxurious new winter cloak of exquisitely matched furs around her slender shoulders! Ika could not believe her eyes. A moment ago he had been roaring and showing his teeth like a lion—terrible and terrifying to behold as he moved over her sister, impaling and devouring her at the same time. Half hidden inside the skin of the bear, it was as though he had become Great Paws, and for one horrifying moment Ika had been certain that Lanacheela would fall and die beneath his mauling as surely as the musk ox she had seen disemboweled by the great bear.

The moment had passed. Lanacheela was still alive. Xohkantakeh seemed to be himself again. A smiling Katohya was now beating merrily upon her little drum.

Ika stood dazed, the unexpected horror of the scene she had just witnessed seared into her brain. The rising sun was too bright; it hurt her eyes. She closed them, wished that she was still beyond the palisade, still stalking the black wolf—or being stalked by it—for surely either would be preferable to being here, a mute and inactive participant in the terrors of the new-woman ceremony. A ragged sigh escaped her lips. How she wished she had never seen it!

She opened her eyes. Xohkantakeh seemed to be back inside his own skin and behaving like a man again, yet tears smarted beneath Ika's lids as she watched him stride to his own mat. She knew he had changed and would never again be the same in her eyes.

He wore the skin of Great Paws as though it had become part of his own body. Leaning forward slightly to accommodate the weight of the massive head and hide, he appeared half man, half beast. Indeed, thought Ika, he might well have been taken for a bear had the wind not blown the forelimbs of the bearskin back, exposing his hairless torso and the lightly furred part from which his man bone protruded, shriveled by the chill of the morning air, bloodied and limp from use.

The girl lowered her eyes, inexplicably flushed and bewildered by her feelings toward him: disgust, disappointment, fear, and a new, strangely disconcerting emotion that translated itself into a throbbing warmth at the pit of her belly. She had seen Xohkantakeh naked before, many times. But never before had she seen him as he had just been with her sister—or as he was now. The raging fury of his mating passion was apparently spent, but there was a new and frighteningly overstated energy to his stance and step. Indeed, he seemed taller, broader, and more intimidating and potentially menacing than the bear Ika had helped him to slay.

"Ika! Come! Take your place!"

She shrank from his invitation. Even his voice was different. It was lower, louder, more assured and commanding than she had ever heard it. Ika felt sick. He was no longer her beloved father, no longer her adored hunting companion. He was no longer her benign protector, Great Bear in the Sky. He had consumed the heart of his prey. He had asked the forces of Creation to allow the power of the bear to live again in him, and she had echoed his invocation. Now, as she watched him kneel before the fire circle and ignite the kindling she and Katohya had prepared earlier, she saw only the furred hide of an enormous bear and knew that the forces of Creation had answered their prayer.

"Aiee!" she exclaimed and, rocking on her feet, was shattered by the realization that Xohkantakeh had become Great Paws.

"Come, child!"

Ika flinched, startled but grateful to find Katohya at her side.

"As life comes forth in blood and violence, so it must sometimes also be for the first time upon a new woman," explained Katohya, enfolding the girl in a maternal embrace and kissing her on the cheek as she whispered with love and understanding. "But I assure you, dear one, that in the blood of mating there is also a pleasure like no other in this life. When it is your time to become a new woman, you will understand. Look. Your sister is smiling. So come now, you must take your place in the Circle of Life as we join together to celebrate the joy of this moment!"

Ika could not find the strength to argue. She allowed herself to be led.

Sun. Fire. Smoke.

Of these things Lanacheela was aware.

Of Ika sitting slumped in her hunting clothes on her feast mat looking as though she had just been hit over the head with a braining club.

Of Katohya beaming, radiant, beautiful in her Winter Woman cloak despite her years.

And of Xohkantakeh urging New Woman to speak now of the dreams that had come to her in the woman's lodge during her last night as a child.

Lanacheela's mouth tightened; her smile disappeared. She did not want to look at him. She lowered her eyes and stared fixedly at the bounty of gifts that were soon to be hers. She would not tell her father that she had passed most of last night anxiously learning new-woman secrets from Katohya. She could not tell him that, afterward, hunger had conspired with dread-filled anticipation to allow only fitful sleep, from which she had awakened again and again, sweated, worrying over all she must do and tolerate if the new-woman ceremony was to go her way. And she dared not ever tell him that she had dreamed no dreams at all.

Her brows arched. Through her lashes she could see Xohkantakeh and Katohya sitting forward expectantly, waiting for her to speak. She did not oblige them. A lethargy born of four days and nights of fasting was so heavy upon her that she could not raise her eyelids, much less form the words that would be necessary if she was to manipulate as well as please her parents. She knew what she must tell them. She had thought it all out last night, and now, in the light of the well-risen sun, the corners of her lips rose in a smile.

The mating she had so dreaded had gone well—much better, in fact, than she had dared hope. Thanks to Katohya's wise counsel on the ways a new woman could not fail to arouse a life maker to his full potential, and because of the older woman's warnings of just what to expect from him if she succeeded, there had been few surprises. The melted bear fat Katohya insisted she slather around and deep inside the opening of her woman place had facilitated penetration and lessened the sudden, hot burst of pain that had accompanied the violence of his first thrust. By keeping her eyes tightly shut and willing herself to imagine that she was coupling not with her aging bear-of-a-father but with the lean, beautiful, hard-bodied young warrior of her dreams, Lanacheela discovered that the feel of a man inside her was extraordinary. There had been pain, yes, but also a maddening pleasure that seemed to singe and awaken every nerve in her body. She loved it. She was emboldened by it. She gave herself wildly to the dance of life making and, had she known the way, would have prolonged it indefinitely. Even now, despite hunger and fatigue and a dull, hurtful throbbing within her newly "opened" woman place, just thinking about it brought the quickening of renewed need—not for Xohkantakeh, not for her father, not for the old man who sat across from her in the skin of a dead bear, but for the Other, for the young man of whom she dreamed, for whom she yearned, beneath whose lean, hard body she ached to dance the dance of life making while he . . .

She looked up, flushed and suddenly distracted by the steady, expectant, and sexually invasive gaze of her father. Never before their joining had Xohkantakeh looked at her like that. *Never!* Lanacheela instinctively drew into her new cloak as though it were an enveloping shell and she a soft-fleshed, vulnerable little mollusk seeking refuge within it.

And still her father stared.

Lanacheela stared back.

A frown creased his brow.

Her heartbeat quickened. It was disconcerting to realize what had just passed between them. It was even more disconcerting to find herself wondering if his frown revealed that he was aware of what she had been thinking. Her eyes widened. If he knew her thoughts then, perhaps he also knew where she hoped eventually to lead him. If he knew, she was lost! If he knew, she would dwell in this land forever and eventually die in it and be left alone forever!

A strange sound broke her thoughts.

Then, "Your dreams, New Woman, you must tell us of your dreams!" pressed Katohya gently, smiling with open amusement as Xohkantakeh's belly continued to grumble. "Only from your dreams will our headman know your new name from the way the spirits have chosen to guide you. Only then may you break your fast on the meat of the great bear that your hungry father has slain in your honor. And only then may we begin our feast and celebration!"

Relief rushed through Lanacheela. She was smiling broadly now. The words she had contrived in the darkness of the previous night came easily to her lips as she lied forthrightly. "I dreamed of the great river!"

"Ah!" The exclamation came from Katohya and Xohkantakeh as from one mouth.

"I dreamed of it flowing *backward!*" Lanacheela went on.

"Backward?" Xohkantakeh's brow was down again.

"Yes!" Lanacheela affirmed with great enthusiasm. "The great river flowed *backward,* but in my dream it was not a river of water. No! The great river was a river of grass!"

"A river of grass?" Katohya's interest was clearly piqued. "How can such a thing be?"

"In dreams all things are possible," Xohkantakeh reminded her.

"It is so!" Lanacheela fervently embellished her lie. "I tell you, in my dream the great river of grass *did* flow backward. At first it ran as green and cool as the balsam needles my mother used to gather in the forests that lie under the Watching Star."

Katohya caught her breath, openly dismayed by the new woman's mention of the one constant star under which so many hardships and tragedies had befallen her.

Aware of this, and of a new tension in Xohkantakeh, Lanacheela rushed on, "Then the great river turned yellow and warm and as fragrant as sweet grass blowing softly under a summer sun. It joined other rivers. All flowed backward across the land and over the mountains until at last they came together in a single great river of grass. There were bison grazing within it! Many bison! High-humped brown cows! Long-horned bulls! And yellow calves whose skins Xohkantakeh once told us made the softest robes of all, especially for babies and little ones! And then the great river of grass turned white and hard and cracking cold, but still the bison grazed upon it, only there were horses grazing with them and camels and elk and a great mammoth and—"

"*Mammoth?*" Xohkantakeh's frown became a scowl.

Lanacheela felt a stab of worry. Did he suspect that she was leading him? No matter, she thought. She had come too far in her deception to worry now. "A white mammoth!" She let the declaration fly and saw with great satisfaction that even Ika sat bolt upright at this bit of news. As stunned expressions of incredulity transformed her parents' faces, Lanacheela added with feigned guilelessness, "Could the great white mammoth have been the totem of the People? Could Life Giver have come to walk within this new woman's dream?"

"There is only one white mammoth," rumbled Xohkantakeh.

An awed Katohya reverently recalled, "Since time beyond beginning he has walked among the People . . . growing old and dying in his time even as it is said that the mountains grow old and die in theirs. But always the great white mammoth is reborn, for he is Life Giver, totem to the Three Tribes until the ending of all days, and it is promised by the Ancient Ones that when he dies forever so too shall the People walk this world no more!"

Lanacheela sucked in a steadying breath. She wished Katohya had not seen fit to recount the old legend. It made her nervous to think of it, and she needed courage now if she was to successfully speak the greatest and most daring lie of all. *May the Four Winds and the forces of Creation not be listening!* she prayed. Feeling well justified in her cause and having never set eyes on the great white mammoth—or borne witness to any tangible evidence that proved to her mind the influence of mystic forces upon her life—she exhaled with confidence and brazened on.

"In my dream the great white mammoth called to me!" she exclaimed and hurried on before she lost courage. "In my dream I clearly heard the totem say 'New Woman will walk the river that flows backward to all good things!' I obeyed and waded, not into water, but into a river of sweet yellow grass within which were many kinds of strange fish that neighed like horses and huffed like bison and trumpeted like mammoth and parted the grass with antlers as broad as those of the stag moose my father once brought to be meat for us. And then, when I paused and looked around, you were with me—Katohya and Xohkantakeh and Ika—and there were others, too, many smiling men and women and children who welcomed the return of the new woman to the land of the Ancestors. The warriors among them lay their spears at the feet of Bear Slayer. They embraced him. They named him Brother and Chief, Warrior and Father of Many Sons!" She paused, lowered her head, looked through half-lowered lashes to see how her lies were settling.

Katohya looked worried. Ika was cocking her head to one side, as she usually did whenever she was unsure or disbelieving. Xohkantakeh stood transfixed, his face rapt, his breathing quick and shallow.

Lanacheela sensed that this was the time to ask, "How shall the headman of this band find his new woman's name within her dream?" And now she posed the question she had been carefully building toward, one she knew could have only one answer. "Rivers of grass that flow backward and upon which feed all kinds of game . . . What can the dream of the new woman mean to this band?"

There was dead silence. It seemed to Lanacheela that even the morning wind was holding its breath.

Then Ika shook her head and declared, "Rivers cannot flow backward!"

Anger sparked like fire off flint within Lanacheela's breast. "Did you not hear Xohkantakeh say that in dreams all things are possible!" She turned an anxious gaze to the giant. "Tell us the meaning of this new woman's dream, my fa—Bear Slayer!"

Xohkantakeh's features expanded with obvious approval of the name his new woman had just called him. Head held high, he adjusted the skin of Great Paws around himself with exaggerated authority. He rose, stood a moment, chewing his thoughts, then twice stalked a restless circle before pausing in somber introspection. Katohya, Ika, and Lanacheela watched him with wide-eyed expectation. At length he said, "The spirits of the new woman's dream have made it clear that from this moment the child who was named Lanacheela, Seed Daughter, is to be called Quarana, River Woman. Since she came to dwell with this band, she has spent much of her girlhood beside the great river, growing strong in the many good hunting grounds to which it has led this band. Now, in her new-woman dream, she has been called to follow the river yet again and so—"

"Backward!" the new woman interrupted anxiously. "In my dream the river flowed *backward* to its source in the—"

"Rivers *cannot* flow backward!" Ika repeated emphatically.

"No, they cannot," agreed Xohkantakeh. "But a man can take his family and return upriver into the land of his ancestors." Again there was silence.

The new woman trembled with a relief so intense that for a moment she was certain she was going to faint. She kept her eyes fixed on the man. Her father was a giant. He had been a warrior in his day, and a hunter of big game on the ancestral plains of his youth. He had fought many battles and brought much meat into the camps of his people. The trust and respect he had won among his tribesmen had made him Guardian of Sacred Fire in the hunting camps of the great war chief, Shateh. And now, despite graying hair and many long years of life, to honor a daughter on this most special of days he had single-handedly stalked and slain the mighty bear. Yet, for all his size, strength, and daring, Lanacheela marveled at his weakness. As she had easily led him in the dance of mating, so she had led him along her meticulously laid trail of lies until he gulped down her self-serving deceit with no more suspicion than an old wolf swallowing baited meat.

But Ika was openly upset by her sister's words. "What kind of dreams are these for a new woman of this band? We cannot return to the Land of Grass! Our father has enemies there!"

Katohya was on her feet. "Ika is right. The hunting grounds in the Land of Grass have always been rich in big game, but the warring tribes who dwell there will not welcome Xohkantakeh! Surely there must be more than one meaning to our new woman's dream!"

Lanacheela opened her mouth to speak lest her mother and sister undo the snare she had so successfully fashioned for her father, but Xohkantakeh took the words from her mouth.

"Bear Slayer's interpretation of the new woman's dream will not be challenged!" he declared, obviously affronted as he glowered down at Katohya from beneath the head of the great bear. "A river that flows backward into many rivers . . . all of them rivers of grass . . . all of them flowing into hunting grounds where Life Giver and the animals that have been meat for our ancestors graze in abundance while the warriors of the People lay down their spears and offer welcome to Xohkantakeh! What else can such a dream be saying to the dreamer if it is not advising a return to old ways and hunting grounds in which enemies will be enemies no more?"

Katohya was shaking her head in disbelief. "But to return northward into the shadow of the Watching Star, to—"

Xohkantakeh waved her to silence. "Bear Slayer will hear no more challenges from his females! The power of Great Paws lives in Xohkantakeh now. And the dream of the new woman is an affirmation of a decision to which this man has already come. Too long have we dwelled alone at the edge of the world! While the great river and its many children remain frozen, we will take the meat and fat of the great bear whose life was given to this man as a gift by the forces of Creation, assemble our sledges, strip down our lodges, and begin our journey back to the hunting grounds of the Ancient Ones!" He paused, brought short by the lurching growl of his belly. He smiled, nodded, and gave the broad, tight span of his midsection a resounding slap. "Hunger speaks from this man's belly. Too long have we allowed the meat and fat of Great Paws to go unroasted. Enough of words! Now is the time to feast! Now is the time to celebrate the birth of Quarana, the new woman of Xohkantakeh!"

Only until we reach the land of many warriors, vowed the new woman as she smiled wistfully up at her father. *By then I will have given you a son. Katohya has said that son makers are valued in the Land of Grass. And so I will surely find a new man there . . . a lean, strong, hard-bodied young warrior with whom I will dance the dance of life making as I will never be able to dance it with you, old man . . . with my eyes wide open!*

4

Warakan moved on toward the distant gorge.

Once out of the protective gully of the creek, the brutal reality of lingering winter struck him. The freezing wind pressed him. He walked on, leaning into invisible tides of lung-searing air as he cursed the cold and tented his bearskin robe around himself, then paused to turn his tattered winter gloves into mittens by tying off and inverting the ruined finger extensions.

Snow lay hard and cutting-sharp beneath his feet. He packed evergreens into his moccasins and continued on his way, still cursing the cold as he praised the spirits of the animals whose pelts comprised his remaining garments, most especially the great, tawny mother bear who had long ago given her life so that he might keep himself warm and alive within her skin.

On and on he walked, longing for spring and for all he had lost to the cave and to the lightning bolt upon the high plateau: extra gloves and winter boots, snow walkers, spears, snare lines, and his tool and fire-making bags. Frustration was bitter in his mouth. He spat it out. The wind blew it back into his face, riming his eyebrows and freezing instantly upon his lashes and the tip of his nose.

Warakan turned out of the wind and, slipping on the slick veneer of the snow, followed the lay of the land downward into a broad, stony, sparsely forested hollow, where he was brought up short by the mad upward fluttering of chickadees disturbed by his sudden appearance in their domain. He watched the birds wing through bare branches like so many feathered gray pebbles hurled against the sky by an invisible hand. When they disappeared into a dark stand of evergreens, he remembered awakening on the high plateau to the chittering of migratory songbirds and the low sigh of meltwater running deep beneath the snowpack. He had been so sure in that moment that spring was on the way! But now, above the trees, the sun shone white in a frozen sky, and the surface of the snow remained granite-hard beneath his feet. Sister Wolf burst proudly through a bare stand of scrub to drop a dead rabbit before him.

"I am not a frail old man who cannot bring down game for himself!" Warakan told her, even though he had not eaten since the last time the wolf had brought him a rabbit, at noon of the previous day.

The wolf looked up and, meeting his gaze, replied out of patient eyes, *Then why do you not do so?*

A defensive Warakan responded, "Soon I will find all I need to make new weapons and snare lines. Then I will hunt big meat for both of us. But for now perhaps you *are* better suited to the hunt than I. And I thank you for this generous offering."

He knelt and accepted Sister Wolf's gift. The buck, as large and heavy as a snow hare, had ample meat on its thighs and shoulders, but the flesh was as taut as old leather, and the animal reeked of the strong, sappy essence of bark and evergreen boughs upon which it had been feeding.

"Starvation food." Warakan knew the meat of this rabbit would be tough, not only because of its winter diet but because it was old. Stiff-eared, brittle-clawed, and scarred from many a mating battle, the animal possessed a cleft in its lip so wide the young man could fit nearly the length of his little finger in it.

Warakan nodded with respect. "Long have the teeth of this Old Father been growing and wearing away and growing again and again! Long has this Wise Man Rabbit avoided the hungry eyes of such as Wolf and Eagle as he boldly made his mark upon the land in the red urine of his kind! Long has he fought with lesser bucks and won the right to mate with the best of does! And long have his children eaten of the green growing things of the summer earth and danced together in the way of their kind under the full face of the winter moon!"

Sister Wolf cocked her head.

Warakan raised the dead rabbit high. "May the life force that has guided and strengthened Wise Father Rabbit through all the many seasons of his life now live in this man and this wolf! May our senses quicken! And may we both live to grow old and long of tooth together!"

Sister Wolf's eyes were fixed on the rabbit as, slobbering, she licked her jaws.

Warakan lowered the rabbit to the snow. "Yes, I know," he said to the wolf. "You are impatient with Man words, but what would old Peacedreamer say if we failed to offer thanks for our kills in the way of the Ancient Ones?"

The wolf was staring down at the rabbit and dancing restlessly back and forth upon her forepaws as she grumbled impatiently to herself.

Warakan raised a brow at her behavior. She made him think of a racer held in check at the starting point of the summer running contest that had been a part of his boyhood training as a hunter in the far land of his ancestors. A wistful sigh escaped his lips. The warmth of his breath was instantly transformed by the freezing air into a cloud that hovered before his face. Again he sighed; again he cursed the cold. Never had summer or the hunting grounds of his childhood seemed farther away than they did now.

The wolf growled, but there was no threat in the sound, only a reminder to the man to pay attention to the needs of the moment.

"I am hungry, too." Warakan was salivating as he removed his mittens, stuffed them inside his robe, and set himself to skinning the buck with one of several fire-hardened bones he had saved from the last rabbit Sister Wolf had so thoughtfully brought his way.

The job could have been more easily and quickly done had he not wished to keep the skin of the rabbit more or less intact so that he could later use it as a carrying bag. Instead of making the usual circular incisions around the buck's neck and limbs just above the paws, then holding the carcass upside down by the hind legs with one hand and working the entire skin down with the other, he cut carefully around the mouth and under the ears. With his pointer fingers meticulously loosening connective tissue beneath the pliable skin, he was soon able to peel back the entire pelt with the ears, nose, paws, and tail still attached.

Sister Wolf came close to nudge with her nose the curious-looking, inside-out, "empty" rabbit.

"This part of your kill is mine, but now much of the rest of it will be meat for you!" After quickly cracking and tearing the rabbit's inner limbs free of the skin, Warakan laid the carcass on his lap while he reversed the pelt and placed it fur-side down on the snowy ground. "Back!" he commanded Sister Wolf, waving her off. Then he placed the carcass breast-side up between his knees, opened the belly, and, after setting the intestines aside for himself since he knew the wolf would not eat them, tossed the rest of the innards over his shoulder to his companion.

Sister Wolf caught the offerings in midair. After gulping most whole, she tossed the liver in the air, then rolled on it before settling in to nip cautiously at the organ as though expecting it to nip back.

Warakan raised an eyebrow at her curious preferences and eating habits as he opened the intestines and ate the contents, then wedged out the buck's eyes and popped them into his mouth. Sucking jellylike juices from the otherwise tasteless little orbs, he cracked open the skull and fingered out the brain, then portioned the carcass and sectioned out the larger bones. These along with the brain would be for later use.

Licking his fingers, he moved to raise Fire from the embers he had carried with him inside a gnarled birch burl that he had kicked loose from one of the white-barked trees that grew near the cave. It was an old fire-carrying technique that Jhadel had taught him: When a man had no decent fire horn or, in winter, could find no large, moist green leaves in which to carry the embers of Fire from one camp to another, he could nestle living coals in a bed of short evergreen needles inside a hollow within the virtually fire-resistant birch burl. Warakan had been lucky; not only had he needed no ax or blade to free his burl, but it had come off the tree looking like an inverted black kneecap, a portable container for the living embers of the prayer fire he had raised for Jhadel. With the burl tucked safely inside his tunic, he had gone through the forest, pausing now and then to pick up kindling and lightweight bits of deadwood and periodically opening his upper garments to lift the piece of bark he had placed as a lid over the sleeping tinders. He would blow lightly on them or give them a stir with a rabbit bone. Now he knew they were ready to be reawakened.

Soon Fire was burning hot on a broad, flat, lichen-scabbed stone, and the flesh of Wise Father Rabbit was cooked and consumed in equal portions by the young man and the wolf. When he had eaten, Warakan carefully cracked the joint bones and extracted what marrow he could with a scoop contrived of a smaller bone fragment. After picking and tonguing this implement clean of every morsel of oily, highly nourishing marrow, he set it aside for later transport. Then, as Sister Wolf rolled on her back after her meager meal, Warakan turned to cleansing and hardening in fire the bones he had chosen for future use.

The work was pleasant. It kept him close to the healing warmth of the little fire. The greasy residue of the meal clung to his bare fingers and salved his tattered flesh, easing the pain as he fashioned a few prods and stabbers from the long bones of the rabbit. The shoulder blades and pelvis made flimsy but usable scrapers, whose curving surfaces he sharpened by carefully rubbing them against the fire stone.

Sister Wolf was on her feet again, whining and sniffing for scraps. As he watched her, he anticipated her discovery of the rabbit brain he had so carelessly left out of his reach. "No! Wait!" he cried, snapping to his feet, too late. She was already bolting it down.

Warakan hunkered on his heels. He knew he had lost the prime softening agent for the carrying bag he intended to fashion from the rabbit pelt. He shook his head, faulting himself, not the wolf. She was still hungry, and Wise Father Rabbit had been her kill, after all. His stomach growled. The meager meal his sister had so generously shared with him had whetted more than satisfied his appetite. Now, as he took up the rabbit pelt and held it over the smoldering fire so that heat and smoke would soften what snow and winter air had already begun to freeze, he wondered how far a man and a wolf could hope to travel, much less survive, on such minimal fare.

He scanned the wind-protected hollow. The cold air of night would settle in such a place when the sun went to its rest beyond the western hills, but the absence of wind would keep the temperature tolerable. Warakan knew it would be a good place to camp. He also knew that without a sustainable source of food there was no reason to stay in it. Indeed, now that Jhadel was dead, there was no reason for him to stay anywhere. Loneliness touched Warakan. He tried to shrug it off by turning his attention to the skin of Wise Father Rabbit. The pelt would have to be properly fleshed and at least cursorily cured if it was to be made serviceable as a carrying bag. He turned it inside out again and set himself to removing raw flesh with his newly made scraper. Not wanting to tear the skin, he worked slowly and carefully, holding the pelt like a glove on his right hand as he manipulated the scraper with his left, keeping the blade at a tight angle, working fragments of meat from the skin in short, precise slices, then fingering up and consuming the shreds of flesh to keep the edge of the scraper clean and sharp.

"Mah-ree of the Red World taught me the trick of this,"

he told Sister Wolf. "In the far land of her ancestors, the skins of rabbits were used for robes and sleeping mats and all manner of garments. You should have seen the fine warm cloak of twisted skins she made for the shaman, Cha-kwena, in the days when . . ."

Warakan scowled. In the brief days when Mah-ree, Medicine Woman of the Red World, had shared a lodge with him and Jhadel, she had cleansed and mended their garments and looked after them as though she were of their blood and band, but she had never made a cloak for Warakan.

"Someday she will!" he vowed. He doubted it was possible to miss that small, dimpled, antelope-eyed woman more than he missed her now. "When I find Mah-ree and the treacherous Yellow Wolf who stole her from me, she *will* make this Guardian of the Sacred Stone a cloak, one cut from the hide of the great white mammoth . . . and from the hide of Cha-kwena if he dares stand against me!"

The intensity of the declaration shook him. The scraper slipped and sliced through the pelt into the meaty pad of his thumb. Warakan hissed in pain, sucked the wound a moment, then worked diligently on until Sister Wolf came close to sniff at the bloody remains of what had once been a rabbit. The young man held up the pelt, admired the results of his almost-perfect workmanship, and saw that his sister's eyes were bright with intent to snatch a meal if the opportunity arose. He chuckled, then rubbed the long bridge of her nose.

"No, my sister, the skin of Wise Father Rabbit must now be 'healed' so that it will make a bag to carry my new bone tools and weapons. They are not much to boast of, but, unlike you, I need more than my teeth and 'paws' to snatch a meal!"

The wolf sat and watched Warakan as he held the skin low over the smoking fire. Quivering with restraint, she hung her head and uttered high little whistles of disappointment.

"I share your hunger." Warakan turned the pelt so that all portions were evenly exposed to the heat and smoke as he explained, more to himself than to the wolf, "If my sister had not gulped down the brains of Wise Father Rabbit, I would now be able to pound them into a mash, mix in ashes from the fire, and rub it into the skin of this pelt. The mash would soften the skin and, after several days of smoking, keep it pliable and weatherproof. But I have no desire to linger in this place, and since I will carry this pelt fur-side out, perhaps it is best if the skin is sealed and allowed to stiffen. There will be less chance of it being pierced by its contents and of my losing my new tools along the way."

The last three words distracted him.

"Along the way to where?"

"To the high gorge!" Warakan replied to a voice that sounded vaguely familiar to his ears. "To the barrens and the hunt for the great white mammoth and my stolen woman! And then on to the Land of Grass, where, invincible in the power of the sacred stone and of the totem, I will seek my enemies and win back my pride and the honor of Shateh and—"

Warakan cut off his words as, with a start, he realized that he was replying to a voice that had come from nowhere. He rose, looked around, then stared uneasily skyward, searching through the broken canopy of the forest for the wide, dark wings of a circling eagle. He saw only broad, cloudless vistas of open sky and the cold, featureless face of a white winter sun. The latter stared back at him, held his gaze, played false with his senses until he was forced to close his eyes against the expanding pain of invasive light.

"And how long shall your journey be?"

"As long as it takes!" Warakan shouted. He opened his eyes and, momentarily blinded, knew that he was again replying to a query that had come out of thin air. "Who speaks?" he demanded.

There was no reply.

Warakan's heart was pounding. Adrenaline was surging in his veins. Blinking hard in an effort to clear his vision, he fully expected to find himself surrounded by the murderous phantoms of the plateau as he placed the pelt inside his robe, took a fighting stance, and with one hand free and the other gripping the bone scraper, saw . . .

That he was still alone within the hollow.

Sister Wolf was on her feet, ears back, tail tucked, eyes fixed on Warakan.

"What have you heard?" he demanded imperatively. "Whom have you seen?"

The wolf's head went down, her shoulders humped high, and her hips drooped a little.

"*Show* me!" Warakan commanded.

The wolf rose, came even closer to the man, and dutifully seated herself practically on top of his feet.

As he met her worried gaze Warakan understood that the speaker he had heard had been himself. He rolled his eyes. Jhadel had not been dead for more than a few days, but thanks to loneliness and hunger he was already talking to himself and having conversations with imaginary voices! He shook his head as he surveyed the cold and desolate land.

"The way ahead is long and difficult," he told the wolf. "We had best be on our way in search of a *real* feast! Again I will ask the spirits of the sacred stone to bring us meat enough to clear our heads and make our bellies heavy and our bodies strong for the journey that will surely test us both!"

And so, after gathering up the embers of Fire and placing them in a fresh bed of evergreens within his birch burl, Warakan placed his new bone tools into his smoked rabbit-skin bag and went on his way.

The day was still in its prime. The sun shone high and white. But the freezing wind was waiting for Warakan beyond the hollow, and the winter snowpack remained hard and granular beneath his feet. This time, however, the young man did not curse the wind or cold, for the land opened wide before him, and he and Sister Wolf soon came to the first of several mighty rivers that lay between them and the country of the Ancient Ones.

Warakan paused and stared ahead. The watercourse was almost too wide to see across, but ravens were circling over the far embankment and well out over the water. He knew by their reflections that the river was frozen solid from shore to shore.

He caught his breath. A gathering of ravens often betrayed the presence of an animal lying dead or dying, but it was not hope of a meal that cleft Warakan's mouth with a smile; it was the sight of the frozen river. In its current state it would be no obstacle to man or beast, and Warakan was certain that he and Sister Wolf could cross it with ease. The profound implications of this observation struck him giddy with delight. He threw up his arms and thanked the White Giant Winter for lingering so long upon the land.

"Stay!" Warakan implored. "Until the last of the rivers are behind us, stay! Until we set our feet northward along the far bank of the great river that pours out of the Land of Grass, stay! And the White Giant Winter will know the gratitude of Warakan and Sister Wolf forever!"

And so, without another word, Warakan moved onto the ice. The wolf followed, although now and again she whistled nervously and paused to look back across the way they had come.

Warakan understood and told her gently, "Old Peacedreamer cannot follow us, my sister. We will not see Jhadel in this world again. So come. Turn your back on the land that lies in the face of the rising sun. There is nothing there for us now. Across the river ravens speak of meat. And ahead lies the country of our ancestors . . . and the fulfillment of my dreams!"

They crossed the river without incident.

The sun, low over the western hills, was in their eyes when they ascended the top of the far embankent. As ravens cawed in the woods up ahead, Sister Wolf pricked up her ears, put down her nose, and began to sniff the snowy ground in obvious excitement. A few moments later Warakan saw fresh moose sign and followed the wolf cautiously into the trees.

There was meat. *Big* meat, more than either wolf or man would have dared hope for. Warakan reached for the sacred stone, pressed it to his throat, and stared in jubilant disbelief at his mired prey.

Huge, exhausted, and vulnerable to predators, the stag moose stared back at him.

"Ah . . . forces of Creation, I thank you for this!" exclaimed the young man.

Immobilized in chest-deep drifts midway down a willow-choked defile, the moose flattened its ears, but its efforts to free itself had already sapped it of energy, and it had evidently made peace with its final resting place in the great Circle of Life. Now—with its frozen limbs hopelessly buried and its bearded head dripping icicles and drooping with fatigue—were it not for the occasional expansion and collapse of its nostrils and quivering heave of its great sides, the animal might have been taken for dead.

Warakan trembled. He had wished for meat upon the sacred stone. "The spirits of the talisman have heard my words!" He felt all at once humbled and proud as he realized that, for his sake, the forces of Creation had created within this great animal a hunger for willow that enticed it across drifts that would not hold its weight.

Joy swelled his heart. "This gift will not be wasted!" Visions of plenty filled his mind. From this moose he would take meat and fat and guts and marrow! From the ribs he would fashion frames for a new pair of snow walkers, and contrive runners for a sled upon which he would carry his treasure in moose meat across the miles with no need to hunt or worry about food for a moon, perhaps longer.

"The spirits of the Ancient Ones are with us!" he proclaimed to Sister Wolf, then said reverently to the moose, "Great Hook-Nosed Bearded Father of All Deer, Warakan and Sister Wolf will honor your life and your sacrifice! Your swift death at my hands will be a gift to you from Wise Father Rabbit, whose meat has nourished me and whose bones I have made into stabbers that will release your spirit! Do not be afraid. Your strength, courage, and endurance will live within Warakan and Sister Wolf until the end of our days!"

Suddenly shaking and salivating with hunger, Warakan

took the birch burl from inside his robe, then knelt and set it carefully in the snow beneath a tangle of scrub growth lest he or the wolf upset it and extinguish the heart ember of Fire that lay within. Rising again, he peeled off his mittens, hung them around his neck by their connecting thong, and pulled his new stabbers from their rabbit-skin pouch. He selected the two sturdiest of several fire-hardened bone prods, then raised a dubious brow. They did not look strong enough now to pierce the tough hide of the moose, unless he could drive them into the animal with all his power behind each thrust. He scanned the defile, knowing that this was going to be all but impossible in deep snow in which, without snow walkers, he was as likely to founder as the moose.

"If I only had my spears, I could make the kill from where I stand!" he said, exasperated, as he bent to set the pouch on the snow beside his fire carrier. Straightening, he was suddenly aware of the chortling of birds above his head. A large gathering of ravens had settled onto the long, outreaching branches of an ancient, winter-bare tamarack.

In that moment, inspiration struck.

"I thank you for summoning me and my sister to this feast!" Warakan said to the ravens. Shrugging off his heavy bearskin robe and taking his stabbers between his teeth, he began to ascend the tree.

The ravens made raucous noises of confusion as they looked at the young man and, not knowing what to make of him, took flight and circled overhead, screaming and diving at him.

Warakan ducked his head. "I am no squirrel to be knocked from a tree by your bullying!" he muttered through the rabbit bones in his mouth. Under a shadowing cloud of ravens' wings and a rain of black feathers, he gradually made his way onto a broad, overhanging branch twice as thick as his torso. Soon, balancing on all fours and holding a bone prod in each hand, he paused almost directly over the moose and cried to the ravens, "Come back! You shall have your share of this feast! But not until Warakan and Sister Wolf have taken their fill of meat so that they will grow strong for the journey that lies ahead!"

Then he jumped—flew, it seemed—and with arms spread wide came plummeting from the heights of the tree to straddle the back of the moose. Reaching around the animal's great neck, he drove his bone stabbers deep.

Sister Wolf leaped forward to take part in the kill, but it was Warakan who threw back his head and howled.

5

Far to the west, the light of the rising sun bathed snow-clad hills, and Ika heard the black wolf cry.

She saw the beast loping out of the east, bounding toward her across the frozen river, its eyes fixed, blood streaming from its open jaws. And yet the girl stood mute and as rooted to the snow-covered earth as a tree, unable to raise either spear or warning. A scream formed in her throat. Too late: The teeth of the black wolf were already piercing her neck, ripping tender flesh until . . .

Ika tore herself from her dream. She looked around, both hands crossed protectively over her throat, and half swooned with relief when she saw that, although it was indeed morning, no carnivore was threatening.

But what would you have done if the dream had been real?

The question was sobering. She had not intended to fall asleep! Bundled in the matted old bed fur in which she had carefully tiptoed from the lodge when the others had finally succumbed to dreams, she had just passed a second miserable night sitting upright against the palisade, this time with a lance across her knees and two others within easy reach lest the black wolf attempt to invade the encampment again before the band began its journey back to the hunting grounds of the Ancient Ones.

The girl's brow furrowed. The thought of breaking

down the lodges and moving on in the dead of winter made every bone in her weary body ache, but if the black wolf returned, she was determined to be ready and waiting. This time she would not run away. This time she would kill the beast before it could make a sound, sling its body over her shoulder, carry it into the forest, and bury it beneath stones and snow so that neither her sister nor her mother would ever know that Xohkantakeh had failed to anticipate its coming.

Now, squinting into the tender light of morning, Ika rubbed the residue of nightmares from her sleep-heavy lids. She told herself that if the black wolf had not come by now, it had most likely taken her bait. It was probably curled up under a rock somewhere on the high hill it had made its own and was even now dying in slow, well-deserved agony.

Ika's mouth tightened over her teeth. Any animal that dared steal from her camp, shame her father, and look at her as meat deserved no better. She allowed herself a smile as she savored a moment of self-righteous hope for the death of the black wolf. The moment passed.

Katohya was emerging from the main lodge. A sudden chill touched Ika's heart as she watched her foster mother quietly close the entrance hide, turn, and pad softly along the woven reed matting toward the central fire circle. Katohya's back was bent, and her limp was more pronounced than Ika had ever seen it. She had replaced her exquisite Winter Woman garments with everyday furs and buckskins and removed the wreath of fragrant greenery and sacred sage from her head. Her hip-length gray hair was unplaited, uncombed, and unadorned. Her head was bowed, her brow creased, her face wrinkled with intense concentration. With her kindling basket balanced slightly askew on one hip, Katohya looked old and as thin and fragile as the light of morning.

Suddenly aware of being watched, the woman paused and straightened. The radiance that had shone from her very being at the beginning of yesterday's new-woman ceremony was gone, but as her shoulders curled back and her head went high, her long, dark eyes fixed her daughter with such strength of will that the girl was stunned. There was love in Katohya's eyes—and disapproval so intense it bordered on condemnation. "I see that the song of the wolf has awakened one who no longer sees fit to pass the time of darkness with her family. Come," she commanded coldly. "Join me. There is much to be done this day."

"You heard a wolf?" Ika grabbed her lances and, in an instant, was crossing the compound. "I was sure I only dreamed it!"

Katohya knelt, set down her kindling basket, and began to busy herself raising a cooking fire from the embers of yesterday's new-woman fire. "It was real enough. A sad and lonely sound. With pain in it, I think." She nodded to herself as she jabbed the well-banked coals with her fire prod, meticulously added kindling grass, then leaned forward to blow the breath of life into the embers through a tube of dried bird bone. When this was done, she drew a few dry sticks from her basket, stacked them in a little cross-braced pyramid, and, when flames began to lick hungrily at the wood, looked up sideways at the watching girl. The repudiation that had earlier been evident in her gaze was gone as she said matter-of-factly, "The wolf we heard this morning cries in a way that reminds me of the dogs in the encampments of your father's people. Ah, daughter! How we could use those dogs now to carry and drag our belongings and the meat of Great Paws when we move on from this good camp!" She sighed as she looked again at the fire and began to add larger sticks. "But it is no use longing for what cannot be!"

Ika knelt beside her. Pretending to watch the sticks go into the fire, she glanced discreetly at the old woman's haggard profile and wondered how she must feel about leaving the comforts of this camp. Her brow puckered with worry. All night long, listening to the sounds of darkness and watching the slow, inexorable migration of the stars toward dawn, Ika had tried to understand why the forces of Creation had given her sister a new-woman dream that would inspire their father to uproot the band, at a time when they had just come into enough meat to make life easy and secure until well past the rising of the Warm Moon. She had come to the conclusion that, had she herself dreamed such a dream, she would have risked the combined wrath of the forces of Creation, the Four Winds, and all of the spirits of the Ancient Ones rather than reveal it. "You are too frail for such a journey, my mother!"

Katohya's eyes half closed. Her thoughts were her own; she did not share them. After a moment, apparently satisfied with the fire, she moved back from the little pyre to rest her slender haunches on her heels and laid her palms on her knees. "The song of the wolf also roused Bear Slayer and New Woman from sleep. Truly the power of Great Paws lives on in your father. He slept hard last night. This was good, for him and for the new woman. It gave her a chance to rest, to heal a little. I gave her salves. They will ease the hurt of that which pleasures her more than I believed possible in one so young. But then, sometimes I forget that when I was with my first man, the fire of first piercing, although gently raised in me, burned so hot and sweet that I thought I would die . . . not from the burning, but when the fire was withheld."

Ika watched as Katohya drew in a deep breath, closed her eyes, and shook off memories in a way that made the girl think of a mare shaking its mane to cool itself as it ran before a hot wind.

A serene and wistful smile moved across Katohya's still-lovely face as she opened her eyes, looked at Ika, and inclined her head toward the main lodge. "The killing of the great bear has made your father young again. Strong again. Listen now, and you will hear him raising a fire of his own within your sister. We must prepare meat for them. They will be hungry when they come from the lodge."

Ika's face tightened as she became aware of the low rumblings of a man and the quick, shallow gasps of a woman coming from the lodge. A vision of her sister and father naked, joined, and moving frantically together like a pair of copulating animals brought revulsion, and jealousy. The latter startled and befuddled her. She had no wish to be in the new woman's place. *Better to stand to a charging bear or leaping wolf!* she thought. And yet, when her eyes strayed across the compound to the main lodge, a strangely unsettling sadness came over her, and all she could think was that, although everything in the encampment appeared exactly the same as it had yesterday, nothing would ever be the same.

From this day on, Lanacheela—Seed Daughter, the wan, skinny, big-eyed little girl with whom she had faced the terrors of abandonment and the joys of adoption into a new band—would be only a memory. Never again would she answer to the name given her by the tribe into which she had been born. Never again would she share the same sleeping mattress with her sister, or put her head together with Ika's in the dark warmth of the lodge to whisper childhood confidences or giggle and sigh over the hopes and yearnings of adolescence.

On this day, Quarana, River Woman, awoke for the first time beneath the bed furs of the man to whom she had been mated. On this day New Woman began her life as a mature female who would in time give Xohkantakeh the sons who would surely eclipse Ika in his eyes forever.

The hurt and disappointment of the moment was almost too much to bear, but Ika bore it. Somehow the pain was less intense when she turned her gaze from the trembling lodge and observed with curt disapproval, "It shakes as though a storm were blowing up inside it."

"The storm of your father's life making," affirmed Katohya.

Ika stared glumly into the fire. *My sister is not worthy of him!* she thought. Then, remembering the violence of the new-woman ceremony, she conceded, "My sister is braver than I thought."

Katohya's features expanded into an amused and understanding smile. "Although you do not believe it now, life making *is* pleasurable, Ika. And, truly, it is always best in the morning."

The girl shivered.

Katohya laughed softly and moved to give her daughter a hug. "In time you will know, child. In the meantime, go now and gather skewers from where we cast them about during yesterday's feast and bring meat for roasting. But first promise me that you will not creep again from the lodge and stay away throughout the depth of night . . . or go alone and without permission beyond the palisade as you did on the night before the new-woman feast. Xohkantakeh would not be pleased to learn that you have again broken the rule that he made for the good of all!"

Ika's jaw tightened, and her mouth turned down. "Xohkantakeh lies with his new woman. Someone must guard the camp."

"Against what? Great Paws is dead. He will not come to threaten this camp again."

"A . . . a wolf might come. He might bring his brothers and sisters."

"If Xohkantakeh had fear of wolves he would have had us set snares for their kind beyond the palisade. So do not worry about such things, Ika. If we are to move on from this camp, we must all be rested and strong, for there is still much meat, fat, and sinew to be prepared for transport. Soon your father will come from the lodge. He will eat before he sets himself to cut the skull of the great bear free of its skin and then position it in a place of honor. The spirit of Great Paws will watch over us as we prepare to break down our lodges, and while we labor together to make sure his hide is properly stretched and respectfully cured so that, in days and nights to come, your father may walk in the skin of Great Paws with ease and comfort. So go now. Bring skewers and meat. And do not worry about wolves. It is not the way of their kind to invade the camps of men."

The new woman cried out in welcome. "Yes! Come to me! Yes! Now!"

He hurried toward her, as lean as a wolf and, in his nakedness and obvious sexual hunger, as beautiful and dangerous.

Quarana was not afraid. She knew there was no need for Xohkantakeh to know of this. Her eyes shut tight, she

trembled with desire for the hard, hot, seeking power of
youthful maleness. And so, while the old "bear" slept and
snored beside her, the young "wolf" came to her out of the
darkness of her dreams.

Silently he came, slipping through a break in the palisade, advancing across the compound, entering the lodge,
and then—while a real wolf howled somewhere far away—
the warrior of Quarana's dreams drew back the bed furs and
stared down.

Quarana reached up to him, sent her hands seeking
over his thighs, upward across the tight span of his belly,
and then downward until her fingers found, stroked, and
enfolded that which he had come to share with her. Remembering Katohya's lessons in woman wisdom and instinctively knowing the unspoken need of the man, she
moved to satisfy it in ways in which she had not been tu-
tored, savoring the moist, salty sleekness of him, pleasing
him and herself until he was transformed and her own
body was afire.

"Enough!" he growled huskily. "No life comes from
that!" He took her by the wrists and lowered her upon the
bed furs. "Let it be like this," he said. He bent, put his
mouth on hers, and sent his tongue to speak of his intent,
then broke the kiss and moved to mouth her throat and
breasts and belly and . . .

Quarana gasped at the loveliness of the feelings he was
giving her, arched to him, welcomed him.

"From this moment may you never again know pain in
this . . ." he said, moving upward over her, positioning himself. "Only pleasure . . ."

And it was so.

Quarana forced herself to stifle a laugh at the expense
of the old bear who slept on, oblivious to her fevered motions and mewings as she yielded to the invasion of the
young wolf. She smiled. Slowly, again and again, the
dream warrior pressed her, penetrated, then withdrew,
venturing slightly deeper with each controlled thrust until,
thrilling to the sensations he roused in her, she cried out
for him to give her more . . . all.

There was pain. It was exquisite! There was pleasure. It was beyond enduring! Quarana, eyes still shut tight, flung her arms around her dream warrior's neck, wrapped her legs about his waist, and danced the dance of life making with him until, sated and sweated and exhausted, she could dance no more.

And still he held her, thrusting, probing, expanding, and filling the very depths of her woman place until he threw back his head and thundered, "The power of the bear *is* in me! Feel it! Take it! The sons I make on you will be the sons of Bear as much as of Man! And they will be sons to make you roar with pride as I roar now!"

Quarana's eyes opened in amazement. The hot, driving power of his maleness exploded inside her. The sound of his roaring shook the lodge. With a heaving sigh, he collapsed onto his side, drew her with him, and, holding her so tight she could barely breathe, shivered with prolonged ecstasy as he gradually relaxed and murmured into her ear.

"It has not been like this for me since the days of my youth when I was sent by the elders of the Land of Grass to learn the ways of life making on the widow women who teach and give young men pleasure. In the blood and flesh of Great Paws—and in the body of this new woman—Xohkantakeh has been reborn!"

"Xohkantakeh?" Quarana stiffened and wriggled free of the man's embrace. On her knees, she stared into the morning gloom and saw without doubt that it was the old bear, not the young wolf, with whom she had been so willingly and ferociously dancing the dance of life making.

Still on his side, he crooked an elbow and propped his head on his hand as he smiled at her, not in the bold manner of a confident lover but shyly, sheepishly, almost like a little boy who has amazed himself by accomplishing something so wonderful that he is hesitant to boast of success lest somehow the very words diminish it. Fixing her with dreamy eyes, with a callused finger he tenderly traced her features and drew a strand of long black hair away from her sweated brow. "Who would have thought that such a lazy child would grow into such a 'hardworking' new woman?"

"Katohya has taught me the woman wisdom of her people!" she snapped petulantly.

"My beloved Katohya is wise and kind, gentle in all ways, beautiful to my eyes and yielding to the need of the life maker whenever it has been pressed upon her. But the things you do with this man, and the eagerness and pleasure with which you do them . . . these things cannot be taught." His finger followed the curve of her shoulder downward, strayed to her breasts and played along the rise of her nipples until they peaked to his touch. When she quivered and leaned reflexively into his handling, he raised a speculative brow and vowed quietly, "I will put the milk of life into these, and someday I will lie beside you, and my sons and I will both do this . . ."

She gasped but did not pull away; what he was doing was yet another new-woman wonder to be savored. She did not want him to stop, and yet, perversely, she could not tolerate the thought or sight of him doing it. She closed her eyes, willed herself to pretend that the Other was with her now—the young man, the lean, hard-muscled, black-haired wolf-of-a-warrior who would someday claim her as his own and take her as far from the lodge of Xohkantakeh as . . .

"You were born for this," declared the giant. Raising his great grizzled head from her breasts, he took her face in his hands and made her look at him. "It will be good with us. At first, when Katohya spoke of what must be between us, I was unsure. Until that moment you were Daughter and Child in my eyes. Until that moment many a long winter had passed since it was last in the heart of Xohkantakeh to make new life. And this winter . . . there was a time, even before the coming of Great Paws, when I knew that I would not see another spring. But my beloved Katohya was right. New Woman has taken winter from the heart of this old warrior. The sight of New Woman takes the chill clouds of doubt from my eyes. The scent of you fires the heat of need in my loins. And the nearness of you causes me to yearn for spring."

There was an earnestness in his face that troubled her,

but only when he stretched and yawned and enfolded her in his great arms did she know why.

"Let us rest a while longer . . . sleep a while more," he said and lay on his back with the young woman stretched belly down upon him. "Perhaps we do not need to be in such a hurry to move on from this good warm camp," he mused, sweeping his hands slowly back and forth across the small of her back. "My beloved Katohya is not young, or strong. Such a journey will be long and difficult for her. And I think now that, although you are so small I could break you in my arms, you are more woman than I ever imagined I would possess again. Maybe it is best to stay here beyond the edge of the world, to keep you from the eyes of other men and for the pleasure of this one old warrior, for the making of my sons . . . foreverrrr . . ."

Quarana's heart went cold. What was he saying? Aghast at his words, she pressed her palms into his chest, levered up, and stared down at him. He had fallen asleep, and in the half light of morning she saw all she feared to see—his timeworn face, his scars, his graying hair, the looseness of his skin upon his giant frame. He was old. He would die. And if he died before the band followed the great river back to the hunting grounds of the ancestors, she would never know the love of the young, hard-bodied warrior of whom she dreamed, nor would she long survive with only a sickly old woman and a half-grown girl to protect her from the lonely death and subsequent abandonment that she feared even more than death itself. "Xohkantakeh!"

"Hmm . . . ?"

"Our sons will be like their father . . . tall as trees, powerful and bold as bears!"

"Yes . . . I see them so."

A beatific smile creased his face. Fighting panic, she reached down and took that face between her hands and raised it from the bed furs. When he opened his eyes and looked at her in surprise, she demanded, "Are these fine sons never to hunt big game in the hunting grounds of their ancestors? Or to learn the ways of life making as you learned them from the women who teach and give pleasure

in the Land of Grass? On whom will they make life if they
grow to manhood in this empty land? Surely my Bear
Slayer would not deprive his sons of the joys that he knew
in his own youth? Nor would he hide such sons away beyond the edge of the world where the spirits of the Ancient
Ones will never see them!"

He shook his head free of her grasp, lay back, and
yawned again. "The spirits of the Ancient Ones are everywhere, Quarana. They see all . . . know all—"

"Yes!" There was panic in the interruption, and a small
sob of desperation. "It is the spirits of the Ancient Ones who
send dreams to this new woman about rivers that flow backward into the hunting grounds of the ancestors!" Scooting
away from him, she reached for a sleek, shining new bed
fur, pulled it around herself, and glared at Xohkantakeh
across the gloom she had set between them. "You *must* follow the way of this new woman's dream, Bear Slayer!"

Silence settled.

Quarana heard something small scuttle in the shadows—a mouse or insect foraging in the dried grasses she
had helped Ika and Katohya stuff between the exterior lodge
cover and the interior liner before the onset of winter. The
insulation exuded a vaguely acrid, moldering scent whenever it was disturbed; she caught a slight whiff of it now,
and of mouse urine.

Her face tightened. She remembered how sweet the
grasses had once been, redolent of moist roots and seeds
and sunlight and, somehow, of the laughter and merriment
with which they had been picked. With a shiver of annoyance, she thought, *Ika's laughter, Katohya's merriment,
but for Lanacheela only misery!* She could still see herself
protesting the rigors of the task while Ika and Katohya labored happily together, finding inexplicable pleasure in
working the sunny little meadow by the spring as they used
their narrow, semicircular stone palm blades to slice the
grass stalks off just above the roots. Soon great hanks of
long, moist strands had lain easily across their forearms—
rather like hair cut from the tails of green horses, Katohya
had said. Quarana scowled as she recalled Ika laughing

with delight at that, then romping about neighing and snorting as though she had forgotten that she was a human girl. When Katohya had joined her, Lanacheela had not been amused at all.

Quarana's hands moved absently over her forearms. She could still feel the way freshly cut grass made her bare arms itch and turn red and bumpy. And she would never forget standing aside, pouting and scratching, while Ika and Katohya teased her as they bound the stalks into tight bundles with long strings of tamarack root. She had helped them carry the sheaves to the encampment, although she had feigned a bruised foot; Xohkantakeh, taking pity, allowed her to rest while Ika and Katohya made several more trips to and from the meadow. When the time had come to insert the bundles between the heavy lodge coverings, Katohya had insisted she do her fair share of the labor. She had obeyed, albeit halfheartedly, for the work was monotonous and raised a sweat, and soon her arms were itching again. At last Xohkantakeh had come to complete the final task—for only the giant could work the grasses into the heights of the sheltering dome—and the three females of his band had enjoyed the luxury of sitting together against the west-facing curve of the lodge, basking in the autumn warmth of the setting sun.

Again a shiver went through Quarana as she remembered that moment. Munching grass seeds and sucking sweet juices from stalks that had slipped free of the sheaves, she and Ika had listened to Katohya's stories of other lands and other people. Then, while Xohkantakeh worked on, they dozed to the cooing of pigeons roosting in the hardwoods while the sweet-voiced woman composed songs about the goodness of this forest encampment, the sweetest camp she had ever known.

Quarana scowled. It seemed as if a lifetime had passed since the pigeons had flown south, and longer still since the last of the geese and migratory songbirds had followed and the hardwoods had gone bare. Under the golden rain of tamarack needles, Xohkantakeh had brought all manner of small furred and feathered beasts to be skinned and butchered and set aside for winter food and warmth.

She had been a child when the first snows blew across the land and she had seen her father standing by the great river looking back along the way he had led his band. She had heard him speak restlessly of "big" meat—bison and mammoth—and of missing the hunting of such game in the Land of Grass, where there were always many hands to lessen the workload of such women as his beloved Katohya.

She had been a child when North Wind came to rake the last brittle, frost-blackened leaves from the birches. Katohya had kept her girls to smoking meat, rendering fat, drying berries, and preparing skins until Lanacheela's spirit ached from the burden of endless labor that made her sister and mother sing with contentment. And while they slept, she would lie awake in the ever lengthening nights, listening to the White Giant Winter shaking the trees as she imagined the young warrior to whom she would someday be mated. As she rubbed the calluses on her palms she yearned for the time when she would dwell with him in a band where there were many more hands to do a woman's work than there were in this one.

And now, at last, she was a woman. The sweet grasses of long-gone summer stank of mold and decay. The young warrior for whom she yearned lay with her only in her dreams. The White Giant Winter still lingered on the land. And the bulk of the meat and fat of the bear, Great Paws, still awaited smoking and rendering.

If I stay in this camp—if I must endure another such winter—I will die of unhappiness and overwork! With a start she looked across the gloom to see that Xohkantakeh was now fully awake and, propped on his elbows, frowning in perplexity at her change of mood.

"What troubles you so, New Woman?"

Quarana stared at him. Long and hard she stared. And when at last she spoke, she did so without hesitation, with the stench of mice and moldering sweet grass in her nostrils. "For Katohya's sake, we must return to the Land of Grass. You are right when you say that she is no longer young, or strong, and I fear that if something were to happen to Ika or this new woman, my beloved mother will

surely perish in this land with no other women to help her
with her work! You *must* follow the way of this
new woman's dream, Bear Slayer! Or I fear that the spirits of the Ancient Ones will be angered. They will not
give you sons . . . and this new woman will pleasure you
no more!"

Something was wrong.

Katohya was not sure just what it could be, but the
feeling was so strong that, under the bright, cold light of
the morning sun, she knelt back from supervising Ika in
the preparation of the bear meat and frowned toward the
lodge.

Ika frowned, too. "Are they never coming out?"

"Soon." But Katohya was not sure. A malaise was on
her; she was restless and worried to distraction. Deep inside
her breast, a slow, subtle beat kept trying to find a voice of
its own upon her tongue.

*We should not leave this camp—cannot not leave this
camp—must not leave this camp! There is meat here, and
fat for the lamps. Our shelter lies close to a spring-fed
stream and ponds that will yield sweet water and suc-
culent fish when the Warm Moon rises once again. The
forest is rich in game, and at night Moon and her
Star Children smile down upon this band. Life in this
camp is good. To return into the land of warring tribes is
madness!*

Katohya gritted her teeth. The decision was not hers to
make. The spirits of the Ancient Ones had spoken to New
Woman through a dream on the last night of her childhood, and Xohkantakeh had interpreted that dream. Yet,
try as she might, Katohya could not understand how the
forces of Creation could possibly be urging her man to
break down his lodges and travel back into the country of
the ancestors now, in the dead of the longest winter either
of them could remember. There must be some mistake!
Perhaps Quarana had inadvertently left out some small
and—to her young and immature mind—insignificant de-

tail that would completely transform Xohkantakeh's interpretation of her dream. Katohya sighed. She knew her man
well enough to be certain that he would have taken this
into consideration. But he was Headman, not Shaman, and
his killing of the great bear had put a new and unsettling
fire into him. Nevertheless, Katohya could not accuse him
of ever having led his band irresponsibly before. Why
should he do so now?

"They have stopped making noises together," observed
Ika sourly.

"They rest now," explained Katohya, grateful to focus
her thoughts on the moment at hand. She forced a smile.
"The pleasure they have found in one another has wearied
them. It is the way of life making."

Ika made a face. "It is another way for Lanacheela to
avoid her share of work!"

Anger sparked in Katohya, much too hot for one who
rarely felt the rise of temper; it flustered her, and she did
her best to bring it to heel. "Lanacheela is no more!" she
reminded Ika. "Quarana, River Woman, has taken your
band sister's place. It is good that the new woman rests. It
is good that she sleeps in the embrace of her man. Maybe
she will reconsider her dream and Xohkantakeh will
change his mind about the way in which it would lead us.
But I tell you now, child, that when nine moons have risen
full and then turned away, if the forces of Creation are
smiling upon this band, the new woman will pay in the
pain of childbirth for the pleasure she now enjoys! And
then, with a baby to care for, she will not shirk her share of
work, and we will all rejoice. So come, Ika, for now let us
work together without complaint and ask the forces of
Creation to make us all strong for the journey that lies
ahead!"

The girl's face tightened. "I do not think this journey is a
good thing for you. You must tell Xohkantakeh again that
you do not smile upon breaking down this good camp and
returning to the country of our enemies. Surely he will listen
to you, my mother, for you will always be First Woman in
his eyes!"

"I am First Woman to your father, Ika, but Quarana is New Woman. Her youth has given him back his pride, and her dream has inspired him with new purpose."

"The killing of Great Paws has done these things!"

"Yes, but know now, child, that the meat of that bear will one day be consumed, and the fine, thick robe that we will make of its hide will in time wear thin. But the sons that our New Woman will give to my beloved will carry his spirit, and through them he will live forever. Already the hope of this has strengthened him. If he says we must follow New Woman's dream back into the country of the ancestors, then we will follow, for I will not speak against him . . . nor will I allow you to do so again!"

"But—"

For the second time since sunrise the doglike cries of a wolf broke the stillness of morning.

Ika's protest died in her mouth.

Katohya tensed, certain she heard pain in the ascending ululations, and such terrible loneliness that it hurt her to listen. "Poor beast," she sighed.

Ika leaped to her feet. "It *is* dying!" she exclaimed in obvious triumph.

A chill went through Katohya as she looked up at her foster daughter. Ika had fixed her gaze westward and was listening to the diminishing cries of the wolf, not as a young girl of any of the Three Tribes should listen—raptly, respectfully, and perhaps even a little fearfully—but as though, somehow, she had become a wolf herself, Xohkantakeh's well-trained "fellow" hunter, a lean, tense, and experienced young carnivore who now stood with head extended, nostrils working, all her senses straining to perceive in the soundings of potential prey any weakness that would lead her to a successful kill.

"What has the death of this wolf to do with you?" Katohya asked, troubled by the perplexing change that had come over Ika. Since returning to the encampment with Xohkantakeh and the slain bear, the girl had been sullen, withdrawn, and more intractable than ever. "I have never known you to find gladness in the suffering of any animal," she added. "This wolf cries for reasons that only those of its own kind can hear and understand. If it is dying, then this is the will of the forces of Creation, but there is no cause for you to wish it pain, or death! It will not be meat for us, nor will its bones yield marrow, nor will its hide make garments for the band."

Ika's face convulsed with emotion as she blurted hotly, "It is the *black* wolf that followed me on the night I left the encampment to join my father on the hunt for Great Paws!"

"Ah . . ." Katohya shook her head and, when the wolf's lamentation ended as suddenly as it had begun, said with gentle repudiation, "The White Giant Winter has been long upon the land, Ika. Wolves must feed in the same way as men, on the flesh of any creature that is careless enough to place itself in the path of the hunter. Did I not warn you of wolves on the night you defied me to run after your father, when he set off alone seeking the feast meat with which to honor your sister?"

Face flushed, the girl replied with a defensive catch in her voice, "Xohkantakeh has taught Ika to hunt at his side, and always have we taken up our spears to seek meat for this band *together*! Why should it have been different on that night, or on any other night?"

"Because your father willed it so. You must learn to obey, Ika, for soon you will be a child no more, and a night will come when Xohkantakeh will take up his spears and leave the lodge to hunt for you."

"No! I will never be a woman!"

"Of course you will! This is as sure as . . ." Katohya paused, distracted by Xohkantakeh's emergence from the main lodge.

"Did you hear the howling?" he asked, still tugging his leggings and smoothing the fall of his winter cloak as he came toward them. "If I did not know better, I would swear I just heard the cry of a wolf that had taken baited meat!"

Katohya heard Ika gasp.

Then the girl blurted passionately, "It . . . it could not be, my father!"

Katohya frowned. Ika's quick and unnaturally high-pitched declaration had begun as an indecisive stammer but had finished in a burbled rush that failed to conceal an underlying edge of panic. Xohkantakeh was looking down at the girl out of measuring eyes. As Katohya gazed at him, it occurred to her that, for a man who had just spent a day, night, and most of a morning pleasuring himself and resting with his new woman, he appeared inexplicably ill at ease.

Looking away from Ika, Xohkantakeh glowered as he scanned the compound. "So much meat on the drying frames! So much more meat still to be made! So much work for so few hands!"

"It is a woman's joy to make meat for her band in a good and sheltering camp," Katohya assured him.

Xohkantakeh's scowl remained fixed. "New Woman *is* right. It *is* time to return into the land of the ancestors, where the hands of many will ease the work of the few."

"The spirits of the ancestors would not have entered my new-woman dream to speak so if this were not true, my fa— my man and Bear Slayer!"

Katohya turned at the sound of Quarana's voice. The new woman, clad in her fine new moccasins and winter robe, was coming toward her from the lodge.

"In the land of the ancestors, my mother would now be sitting in the sun, out of the wind, in the company of other gray-haired women," said New Woman with an air of self-importance and patronizing benevolence. "In the hunting grounds of the Land of Grass, my mother and the other gray-haired women would now be resting their old bones and telling the tales of the Ancient Ones to the many children of the tribe while other women—many *younger* women—tend to the long and tedious task of meat making. Is this not so, Xohkantakeh?"

Katohya gave her man no chance to reply. Twice in the light of this morning's sun she had heard Ika voice concern for her frailty. Now Quarana spoke to her as though she were a feeble old woman who needed to be reminded of the limitations of a failing body. Shame burned Katohya's cheeks and her sense of dignity. Was this how her daughters thought of her? And if so, what then of Xohkantakeh? Had his last impassioned life making on her been an act of love, or only an expression of pity for one who was old and about to be forever replaced in his heart by another?

"Yah!" Katohya cried as she snapped to her feet. Wiping her hands on her stained old buckskin apron, she glared at Quarana and once again felt the unsettling flare of temper toward a daughter. This time she let it burst into flame. "What does one who only yesterday was born into this world as a woman know of the ways of women in the land of the ancestors or the hunting grounds of the People of the Land of Grass? You were no bigger than an antelope fawn when last you saw them! Yah! Only the oldest and feeblest of grandmothers were accorded the privilege of which you speak! Sit in the sun by the lodge and rest my 'old' bones in comfort while others labor! Aiee! What words are these you dare speak to one who has carried you on her back, made your meat, stitched your clothes, healed your childhood ills and wounds, and kept you warm and safe against her breast when the frost spirits prowled the world and the women of your own tribe abandoned you?"

Quarana's eyes had gone round.

Xohkantakeh and Ika were staring at Katohya in amazement.

She was glad. "Yah!" she exclaimed again in disgust of all that her youngest daughter had implied. Standing straight as a well-made spear shaft—and in her righteous indignation feeling just as strong and potentially dangerous—she pointed an accusing finger at Quarana. "You have become a new woman of this band and, if the forces of Creation find you worthy, may well birth sons to Xohkantakeh, but I tell you now that as long as this woman can chew meat, she will make meat for herself, her man, and her daughters. In this camp or any other, this task brings joy to my heart and proves the worth of this woman! As to your own worth, New Woman, you have been a lazy child, and until you bear sons to my man and bend to your work uncomplaining, your value is something you have yet to prove to me!"

The new woman's little nose went skyward. She harrumphed daintily and went to her knees on the matting of woven reed upon which her mother and sister had been working. "Tell my mother, Bear Slayer, that I am indeed a worthy and hardworking new woman."

A droll smile bent Xohkantakeh's mouth. "I will tell

your mother that she has taught you well in all things, and that you have proved to me that there is one task for which you are, indeed, worthy and to which you respond with more enthusiasm than you do to others."

Ika scowled.

Katohya was not amused.

Quarana's nose went higher. "Life making has given me much appetite! I would eat now of the meat that my mother and sister have made for me."

"And for our man!" Katohya corrected as she fought back the urge to kick the young woman. "There is roasted meat skewered and ready by the fire for both New Woman *and* Life Maker. If you are, indeed, a worthy and hardworking new woman, Quarana, now is the time to prove it to your mother's eyes. Rise and remember that your responsibilities to Bear Slayer involve more than opening your thighs to his woman pleaser! Bring food to your man while Ika and I continue to prepare the last of the meat of Great Paws for the long and arduous journey to which your dream has called us!"

A smile played upon Quarana's mouth as, with her eyes lowered, she rose and said, "The journey will be long. The journey will be arduous. I will help my mother along the way."

"Yah! We will see who needs help!" Katohya declared hotly and, as the girl sauntered off to obey, told herself that she had won the moment. Why then, she wondered with a start, did she feel no satisfaction in it? And why did she feel that, although she stood in one place, she had somehow just been led to another?

The sun rose slowly toward noon, bathing the surface of the frozen land in a cold, thin, translucent light that set pale blue shadows across the interior of the compound. Xohkantakeh hunkered close to the cooking fire, observed his world, and knew from the look of the sky and the feel of the air that the interminable cold would last a while longer. Nevertheless, he was certain that the long lean days of winter must soon come to an end. He ate slowly and thoughtfully of the meat

Quarana brought him; he would need strength in the days and nights ahead. The meat was rich with fat, and he was pleased to see that Katohya and Ika had roasted it in the way he liked best: quickly at first, seared until the juices rose red through charring flesh, spitting and spattering as they dripped into the fire to be transformed into smoke; then slowly, turned again and again over wood gone gray with ash as the meat swelled and drew flavor from the smoke and fat oozed and ran hot, until at last the crusted flesh shriveled upon the skewer and, still red with blood deep inside, was ready to be devoured.

He smiled at the analogy he found in this. Balancing his new woman on one knee, he advised drolly, "Learn the way of cooking this man's meat, Quarana, for it is the same way he prefers to be with a woman . . . searing hot at first, then slow, again and again, as it was with us this morning, eh?"

She lowered her eyes.

Sated on meat and woman, Xohkantakeh now offered the last and largest chunk of bear meat to Quarana. It was half as big as his fist, a feast portion that expressed his satisfaction with his new woman. If she was aware of this, she gave no sign of it; hunger led her. As he held the thick bone skewer, he took pleasure watching her and feeling her movements upon his thigh as she tore and gnawed at the meat with her fine, strong, even little teeth and then, trembling with satisfaction, backhanded juices from her chin while she chewed.

How young she is, Xohkantakeh thought. *How good to look upon! And how voracious!* "You are a hungry little ermine in your winter coat of white and black!" he teased. As she pulled the last shreds of flesh from the skewer, he told of how Katohya had spent many a winter day setting secret snares for the animals whose pelts now comprised her new-woman cloak; of the way she had secretly cured the skins and set them aside; of how she had stitched the pelts together in the feeble, ruddy glow of her stone lamp, smiling and humming all the while, her heart filled with a mother's happy longing for the day when her beloved child would be a child no more. "And still she labors . . . for you, for Ika, for me! So go to her now! There is still much work to be done. Help Katohya and Ika to lay the last of the flesh of Great Paws over the drying frames for smoking and curing in the cold air and wind. It is time for you to show your mother and sister just what you can do now that you have been reborn as New Woman!"

"I would rather show you," Quarana said, licking the skewer clean, then releasing it as she smiled prettily and opened her robe to reveal that she was naked beneath it. Raising her hands to oil her breasts with the juices of the meat she had just consumed, she yawned and said petulantly, "The flesh of Great Paws lies warm and heavy in my belly. I would return to the lodge and 'rest' again with my new man. Let Katohya and Ika finish preparing the meat of the great bear that Xohkantakeh has slain. They are better at that work than I. Besides . . ." She made a sleepy little sigh of the word as she cupped her breasts in the hollows of her palms and lifted them in offering. "I think now that perhaps Bear Slayer would like to lick these clean and place his woman pleaser between my thighs again?"

The boldness of the invitation startled him. The new woman's tone and smile seemed somehow as oily as her fingers; instinct warned that if he did not watch his step with her he would slip on the manipulative grease of her provocations. Xohkantakeh's brow came down. What sort of thoughts were these to hold toward a child raised at his fire circle, toward a daughter of his heart, toward his new woman? Surely he was being unfair! He could not blame Quarana for wishing to spread herself for him again when, after the violence of first piercing, he had done his best to bring her to savor the gentler aspects of coupling. If she burned for him now, was the flame of her need not of his making? His head went high as he took pride in his success and rejoiced in her sexual receptiveness, even though he knew that he had come into her so many times since their first mating that his own need was temporarily numbed.

"We will 'rest' together again later," he assured her. "Now go and do as your man commands." He rose, forcing her to stand on her own two feet. "Go, I say. I, too, have much work to attend to if we are to begin our journey back into the land of the ancestors."

Quarana's eyes widened as though, in her laziness, she had forgotten something important and was now startled by a recollection that set fire to her heels. Without another word she turned and hurried to join her mother and sister.

Xohkantakeh watched her scamper off, then stood a while longer, taking pleasure in the sight of his females working together. It seemed only yesterday that he had risked all to save them—the lamed captive woman, the unwanted little girls abandoned to die in the depth of a merciless winter under the uncaring silver eye of the Starving Moon. Pride and love filled his heart. He had brought all but Xree to a good life! And now, led by the ancestral spirits that had spoken through the dream of his new woman, he was certain that he would lead them to a better one!

The People of the Land of Grass will welcome the return of Xohkantakeh, for this man is now all and more than he has ever been: warrior . . . bold hunter . . . and Bear Slayer!

Drawing in a deep breath of the morning, with the scent of slowly smoking bear meat filling his nostrils, he was certain that he had never felt stronger or more confident in the future than he did now.

A smile of infinite satisfaction stretched wide the broad mouth of Xohkantakeh. It was the flesh of his old enemy that his females now smoked and dried in the cold wind of morning, the very essence of the body of Great Paws that he drew into himself with every breath! Never again would he come across the massive impression of the scarred forepaw in snow or mud and know that the beast of his nightmares was following. Never again would he see the towering, tawny form standing like a huge, furred warrior in the mists of distance and flee from hunting grounds he would prefer to make his own. Never again, as the great bear circled his camp, would he sit until dawn raising a mighty fire, spears at the ready, singing bold songs to inform the bear that he was not afraid even though his blood ran cold.

Great Paws is dead!

Xohkantakeh has killed him!

This man has eaten of the flesh of that bear. The blood of that enemy runs in my blood. The meat of that marauder gives strength to my body. The power of that boar lives and rises in my man bone to give life and pleasure to my women. When the People of the Land of Grass again set eyes on this man, they will see and know that the heart of Great Paws beats within the heart of Xohkantakeh! As in the dream of my new woman, they will welcome this warrior. They will give shelter to his females. They will hunt with Bear Slayer, and they will lament that he has been so long away!

Invigorated by his thoughts, he sucked in another lung-expanding breath of the morning. If his females were to be safeguarded on the long journey ahead, there was still a single task left to be done if he expected the spirit of the slain bear to live at peace within the skin of the man who must protect them. According to the traditions of the Ancient Ones, Great Paws deserved and demanded one last honoring. And this task Bear Slayer must begin by himself.

"It will be done now!" he announced. Ignoring the curious stares of his females, he went to the lodge to retrieve his best spear, his skinning tools, and the raw, uncured hide of the great bear. He carried these things outside, then set down the tool bag and spread the bearskin upon the snow, fur side down, with the head of the beast staring skyward and the huge paws stretched wide. Slowly, thoughtfully, he laid his spear upon the hide and began to walk a solemn circle around it.

"Look away . . . look away!" Katohya commanded and, turning, saw to it that both her daughters placed their backs to the sun and to their father.

Xohkantakeh nodded, pleased that he did not have to remind his beloved of her obligations to the traditions of his ancestors. The work to which he must now set himself was between hunter and prey, a male thing, and Katohya had lived among the big-game hunters of the north and west long enough to know that if the eyes of a female fell upon the actions of a male at such a time, his prayers and intent would be sullied, perhaps even nullified.

With his three females turned away, the giant completed his circle and spoke his prayer. "To North Wind . . . South Wind . . . East Wind . . . West Wind . . . Xohkantakeh calls to the Four Directions of the forces of Creation, and to Mother Below and Father Above . . . so that they may see and know that this man fully honors the spirit of the great slain bear that has come to live within his skin! May that spirit continue to give this man strength, wisdom, and courage, and live forever in the sons that the power of our combined maleness will bring forth from Xohkantakeh's women!"

It was no easy task to cut the massive skull free of the furred skin that covered it. Xohkantakeh took his time, anxious to keep the face, ears, and neck intact and still attached to the rest of the hide. At last the skull, lower jaw still connected, was free. He sat with it between his knees, turning it as he worked until the bones and teeth were scraped of all vestiges of tissue and blood. Next he rubbed the skull clean with the ends of his own hair, then rose and held it up to a sun that had long since slipped past the noon meridian.

"Father Above!" he called to the setting sun. "Stay a moment in your descent into the west! Behold your son, Bear . . . your son, Man! We are one! We are the same!"

Only vaguely aware of Katohya's voice urging Quarana and Ika to fetch some thong, Xohkantakeh took up his spear and reverently carried the skull of Great Paws across the compound. In moments the women were at his side. After planting his spear upright in the snow, he used the lengths of thong they brought him to hang the skull above the entrance to the palisade—not as a trophy but in proclamation to the Four Winds, the forces of Creation, and all living creatures of earth and sky that the spirit of Bear lived and was honored in the encampment of Xohkantakeh.

"As the great white mammoth is totem to the Three Tribes, let Great Paws be totem to this band! Let his spirit guard us as we prepare to break down our lodges and return to the land of the ancestors! In this camp, in all camps, from this day to the ending of all days, may the strength, ferocity, and wisdom of Bear protect the women, daughters . . . and future sons of Xohkantakeh!"

A thrill went through him. The prayer was good. And he had not the slightest doubt that the spirit of the bear spoke within his consciousness to communicate full affirmation.

He raised his arms. "Now, let each of us offer a gift that will speak welcome and gratitude to our totem!"

At this command, Katohya, Quarana, and Ika hurried off to select small personal offerings. Soon they were gathered again at the entrance, and Xohkantakeh, who had just placed into the mouth of the skull a cut of meat taken from the nearest drying frame, told them, "This meat we offer in the way of the People of the Land of Grass, so that the spirit of Great Paws will know that he shall not hunger as long as he dwells within this band."

"And this I do in the way of the People of the Red World!" Katohya raised her voice in a brief, sweet, wordless chant of thanksgiving, then said, "May this woman's song be accepted by Great Paws as a gift of praise for his flesh, fat, fur, and bones. Because of these things, this band will not hunger, nor will it lack for tools or light or warmth as the women and daughter of Xohkantakeh journey from this good camp in which this woman had hoped to spend many another spring and summer and—"

"It is not the way of the People of the Land of Grass to stay forever in one camp!" Xohkantakeh reminded her.

She drew in a quick, shallow breath, held it a moment as though to steady her nerves, then released it along with a reminder of her own. "It *was* the way of the Red World People when the camp was good and meat was plentiful and there was no need to move on and put at risk the little ones."

"There are no little ones in this camp!" he said sternly. "And this is not the country of the Red World People! Bah! 'Risk' was unknown to the hunters of your tribe because they were content to bring lizards and vermin to the roasting spits rather than break down their miserable villages and lead their women and children to the grazing grounds of bison and mammoth, where 'real' men would surely have made them fight for their share of 'real' meat!"

Katohya's head went high. "The meat of mammoth is forbidden to my tribe. The great tuskers are sacred! Because we honored them, life was good for us. There was no hunger. There was no war. The sacred stone talisman of the Ancient Ones was entrusted to the shamans of the Red World. The great white mammoth totem, Life Giver, walked in the country of my people. Its herd took shade in our pinyon groves by day, then drank and tusked salt from our sacred springs by night. The crying of babies and wailing of widows in the many villages of the Red World chiefs was not heard until 'real' men came into *our* hunting grounds to hunt not meat but slaves, and the stone talisman of the ancestors, and the totem! The sacred herd was slaughtered and the great white mammoth, Life Giver, was driven from the land to—"

"Those warriors came from the encampments of the People of the Watching Star," he said defensively. Then, regretting his unintended insult to her tribe, he added contritely, "They came to you from beyond the hunting grounds of the People of the Land of Grass. They were the enemies of my people and were not of my blood or tribe any more than were you in those days, my beloved!"

"Yet your people also made slaves of mine," Katohya said with a catch in her voice. "Our own little Ika's mother was a Red World captive, and I have known the 'honor' of being taken by warriors of both of the two northern tribes! Aiee! Can it truly be that, in time beyond beginning, the People were one, Xohkantakeh?"

"Yes!" Quarana put in quickly. "And they lived far from this cold land of endless winter, close to the hunting grounds of which this new woman dreams . . . the land in which there is much 'real' meat, and in which I will birth sons to Xohkantakeh far from this lonely country beyond the edge of the world where there are no people to help with the babies and the old women."

"This 'old' woman has been *happy* in this far country!" Katohya countered in bitter earnest as she raised her eyes pleadingly to her man.

Xohkantakeh was moved. He knew that she was begging him to stay, but he also knew that he could not oblige her. Reaching down to touch her cherished face with a gentle and reassuring hand, he explained as kindly as he could, "You will never be 'old' in my eyes, beloved one, but neither will you bear sons to hunt for this band when I am old. We *must* return to the land of which our new woman dreams. Our Ika will find a man there. Life will be easier for you. And the sons that Xohkantakeh will make on our new woman will grow to be—"

"As in my dreams . . . tall as trees and as bold and powerful as my Bear Slayer!" interrupted a jubilant Quarana.

Katohya hung her head.

Ika eyed her sister as though fighting the impulse to strike her.

Quarana beamed up at Xohkantakeh. "Here, Bear Slayer, take this offering! Attach it to the head of Great Paws so that he may keep it always and know that this new woman, Quarana, makes a gift of the music maker that Katohya made for me of little river shells. Now, whenever any or all of the Four Winds blow, and wherever this band may be, Great Paws will hear and be soothed by the song of the great river along which we will soon travel back to the hunting grounds of the ancestors, where there will be many hands to assist my mother at our woman's work!"

"It is only *you* who complains of work!" snapped Ika with unconcealed venom.

"I am the new woman of Bear Slayer!" an imperious Quarana snapped back with equal fervor. "I have fasted. I have endured first piercing! And unlike my band sister, I have shed the blood of my childhood and am not afraid to follow where Bear Slayer would lead me."

"I am *not* afraid for my . . ." Ika cut her protest in midsentence.

Xohkantakeh took no notice. As he looked up at the skull of Great Paws, the dissent that had flared between his daughter and new woman was a vaguely irritating distraction, rather like the sound of insects droning outside the lodge on warm summer evenings; it seemed of little importance, and of less threat, especially since Katohya "tssked" them both to silence. Xohkantakeh's mind was elsewhere. He had one last gift to offer to the spirit of the slain bear.

Holding his spear in both hands, he loosened the foreshaft from the main shaft with a hard twist. There was a dull, grinding crack of sundered glue and splintering bone; he did not hear this as, casting the main shaft aside, he fastened the stone projectile point—still attached to the foreshaft—to the skull by cross-lacing it through the eye sockets. "To Great Paws, Xohkantakeh gives the spearhead

that cleft the heart of this bear! It was this blade of stone—
first cut from the rocky skin of Mother Below, then shaped,
then hafted, then sent by Xohkantakeh's hand—that freed
the spirit of this great bear to live within this man! Now may
this spearhead protect Great Paws against those spirits who
would come from the world beyond this world to hunt him!
Keep it, my brother, until that day when we are at last called
to hunt together forever as brothers and warrior spirits in the
Blue Land of Sky!"

"May that day be far from this one!" exclaimed Katohya, so shaken by this unexpected reference to death that
she reached to steady herself by laying a palm upon Ika's
broad shoulder.

Again Xohkantakeh had reason to regret his careless use
of words. In the last few moments he had twice wounded his
beloved. Indeed, he thought, the bold and reckless spirit of
the bear was inside him, prowling the recesses of his mouth,
loosening his tongue, and setting his thoughts free upon the
air as though they were projectile points to be hurled at will.
His brow furrowed. He knew as well as any man that Death
must come to all living things, but he also knew that Katohya had seen too much of it in her lifetime. In the Red
World, in the Land of Grass, in the mammoth-bone villages
of the People of the Watching Star, and even in those first
days and nights when they had journeyed south along the
great river, Spirit Sucker was always there, watching, awaiting its chance to feed upon her loved ones, carrying them
away into the world beyond this world. Remembering poor
drowned Xree, Xohkantakeh knew that his beloved would
be hard-pressed to bear another death, another loss, another
heartbreak. He slung an arm around her trembling shoulders
and drew her close. "It will go well with us, woman! You
must not be afraid. Great Paws lives in your man now!"

She smiled wanly. "The journey to the land of the Ancient Ones will be long and difficult. I fear for us all, my
dear one."

"And so, but the new woman's dream must be honored.
The forces of Creation have spoken through her. Do you
imagine that they would now lead us falsely when they have

guided us so kindly these past many seasons?" The question sparked an image at the back of his brain, sudden, unbidden, fire bright.

A warm night.

A firelit camp.

A bittern booming somewhere in the darkness.

Heavy, humid air—black it seemed—saturated with moisture, thick in the lungs, a miasma expanding, alive somehow, sucking the breath from a sobbing man so that he choked like a drowning child.

Xohkantakeh gasped; the intake of air brought no nourishment. In his mind he saw himself surrounded and bound fast by marsh grasses, rough-edged, cutting sharp to his palms, wet with dew in which the light of uncountable stars glinted like the firelit eyes of frogs chortling in the great marsh.

He closed his eyes against the memory, shook his head, and tried to will it away. It was no use. He saw the little girl stumbling alone to the edge of black, reed-choked deeps and heard her call out to a sister who would never answer again.

"Xree! I know you are out there! Come back from the dark water, Xree! It is not a good place to hide! Please, Xree! Come back! I did not mean to send you away! Xree! Do not be afraid . . . Xohkantakeh will keep you safe from bears!"

Again the giant gasped, but this time, with his eyes batting open, he found nourishment in the cold bright air of afternoon and forced himself to will the cruel memory of Xree's drowning into the depths of the past where it belonged. Terror of Great Paws had killed that child. Now Great Paws was dead. Xohkantakeh had killed it. He had eaten its heart. The strength and power of the bear were his. Never again need his women or children fear for their lives when they walked in the protective shadow of Bear Slayer. "Enough of sadness! Enough of worry! Come! We must make the final preparations to move on from this camp. But first, what gift has Ika brought to honor the spirit of the great slain bear?"

The girl was watching him thoughtfully, sadly, it seemed, until she raised her head high and said in a tone that bordered on defiance, "The spirit of Great Paws lives in Xohkantakeh now. And so Ika gives *herself* . . . to hunt at her father's side on the long journey back into the country of the ancestors, where she will never take a man! Ika will be Xohkantakeh's Little Bear . . . forever!"

He scowled. "What kind of gift is this? It cannot be! Find something else! Something the spirit of a bear—and of this man—can appreciate and find worthy!"

6

Warakan thought a great deal about women.

Tall women. Short women. Fat women. Skinny women.

Young and old women, all dragging sledges, all with strong, thick backs bent double beneath the weight of pack frames loaded with the belongings of their band. Ugly and pretty women, slave and free, all singing songs of gratitude to their masters, husbands, fathers, and sons for allowing them the privilege of labor as they trudged contentedly behind their men, alongside the dogs of the band, as females were born to do.

Warakan seated himself on the inviting "bench" of a fallen tree and with a whoof of fatigue jammed the butt end of his new moose-bone lance into the snow. The ice-rimed tree creaked beneath the weight of the young man and the meat-loaded back frame he had contrived from the bones and hide of the giant stag.

Sister Wolf paused before him. Drooping in the moose-hide harness that attached her to the heavily laden sled Warakan had also built of moose bones, she thumped her tail and looked at him, loll-tongued and weary-eyed.

"At least I have you as companion and helpmate, my sister," he said wryly, with a smile of affection.

The wolf lowered her head and uttered the low, squeaky whine that was her way of asking for a head rub.

Warakan obliged. His mittened fingers were healing

rapidly, thanks to the soothing properties of oil extracted from glands he had cut from the moose. As he rubbed the animal vigorously behind the ears, he promised emphatically, "When I retrieve the magic spearhead and slay the great white mammoth, I will possess the power of the totem as well as of the sacred stone of the Ancient Ones. I will take the woman, Mah-ree, from the Red World shaman who stole her from me. She is small but strong, and as a female she will be grateful to carry the bulk of our burdens as we make our way back to the land of my enemies. Once there I will take for myself the women of the men I slay in battle. Many women! Many battles! Strong in the power of the blood of the totem, I will win them all! And even if Xohkantakeh the giant looms against me with his great spears, I will not be afraid. He will die at my hand for betraying and turning his back on my grandfather. His women will be my women. They will open their robes to me by night, and by day they will tend our camps and carry our burdens, my sister."

The boast boomed pretentiously, even to Warakan's ears. Puzzled by the sudden intensity of his words, the wolf cocked her head. Warakan did the same, then looked quickly over his shoulder, disconcerted by the feeling that Jhadel was standing behind him, arms crossed, shaking his tattooed head and glowering with disapproval. His brow furrowed. There was no one behind him. He was alone with the old wolf in the cold light of another dying day, and the realization filled him with such sadness and loneliness that he nearly cried.

Missing the old Peacedreamer more than he would once have thought possible, Warakan turned to meet the questioning gaze of his canine sister. "You will see," he told her. "We will not be alone forever. I *will* have women. And I will have dogs, too—many dogs. And although you are female, my sister, as Wolf you will be Chief among the dog kind as surely as Warakan will one day be Chief among men!"

It was a heady and invigorating vision; the pure arrogance of it made him smile. "It *will* be so!" he insisted and, leaning forward, freed the wolf from her harness. As he

watched her shake herself, then roll like a pup with happy
abandon in the snow, he was as proud of her stamina as he
was of the sled he had made. It was a small, crooked con-
veyance, but as long as he kept the curving rib-bone runners
slick with ice, they slid easily enough across the hard surface of the snowpack while the bulk of his bounty in moose
meat rode high beneath a hide tarpaulin on a flat bed of
shoulder and hip bones.

Now, after carefully shrugging off the meat-laden pack
frame that also contained his birch burl and the makings for
this evening's fire, Warakan bent to remove his new snow
walkers. His mittened hands fumbled at thong bindings and
webbing that were stiff and cracking in the cold. Kicking his
feet free, he planted the snow walkers upright in the snow
and eyed them with disappointment. The bone frames were
not holding together properly, and the cursorily cured
thongs were brittle and torn. He shook his head, forced to
acknowledge that his snow walkers would need additional
refinement if they were to serve instead of hinder his journey. Jhadel would have guffawed with open disparagement
had he seen the results of the hurried and sloppy work his
acolyte had made of what the old man considered an art.

Warakan sighed in resignation. He was going to have to
stop in one place long enough to make the necessary adjustments to his snow walkers if he was ever going to reach the
gorge in which he had buried the magic spearhead, much
less hunt the great white mammoth in distant northern barrens before returning to the Land of Grass to slay his enemies and eventually become chief. The distances he had set
himself to cross were enormous. Frowning, he looked
around, trying to ascertain his whereabouts by the position
of the setting sun in relation to the number and alignment of
the many creeks and hills he had placed between himself
and the cave.

"Ah, Jhadel!" Warakan sighed. Unaware that he spoke
at all, he revealed his thoughts to the spirit of the old man
who would never again call to him from the depths of the
cavern, or travel at his side, or sit beside him on a fallen
tree. "Since crossing the river, I have veered to the west at
the forks of six creeks. By the color, texture, and scent of

the exposed stone of the earth, and by the rise and fall of the land beneath my feet, I am almost sure that I am following our old trail, but two winters have come and gone since we passed through this forest in the depth of a summer so ripe with green growing things that we could barely see the trunks of the trees or the earth beneath our moccasins. In truth, it was as though there was no earth . . . no sky . . . no sun by day . . . no stars at night. Now it all looks so different. So cold. So bare. So . . . empty."

Another sigh escaped his lips, along with a small shiver; his last word had chilled him to the heart. How he yearned for human companionship; for the company of Jhadel; for the gruff and sometimes begrudging affection of his grandfather, Shateh; for the camaraderie of youthful companions long lost to him beyond the edge of the world; and most of all for the nearness of his beloved Mah-ree—antelope-eyed, dimpled, strong little Mah-ree who would be warm against him now, smiling as she linked an arm through his and leaned close, teasing him into contentment as was her way whenever he grew morose.

"The woman of my heart *will* be mine!" Warakan burrowed into his furs to seek the sacred stone. With the talisman curled tightly inside his mittened fist, his heart hardened, and resolve pressed the chill from his mood as he wished for fulfillment of the vow.

"Where is she now?" he wondered aloud.

The wolf rose to her feet and shook herself free of snow. She trotted to the young man and whined in a low, vaguely troubled voice that seemed to say, "I am here, my brother. Why do you talk to thin air and bare bushes and trees? They will not answer. They will not understand. But I am your sister. I am here for you. Speak to me, if you will."

Warakan ignored her. The sun was setting beyond the western hills. His eyes narrowed as he watched it through a haze of distance and bare trees and scrub growth; the small, pale circle of pure light shivered and seemed to hang suspended above the horizon as though ensnared within a web of branches. His brows came together over the scarred bridge of his narrow nose. He knew all too well that when the Warm Moon rose again, the web of branches would swell with sap, buds would burst, and soon the forest would become so green and thick with leaves that the sun would not be visible beneath the trees except as a subtle, diffuse glow tracing an elusive arc above the canopy of vegetation. The thought was stifling. When the Warm Moon rose, the rains would come, the snowpack would begin to melt, and ice would break wide upon rivers, ponds, and lakes. There would be no crossing them after that, only long, tedious circumventions. If he did not reach the far shores of the two mighty rivers that still stood between him and the great Mother of All Rivers, whose embankments he must follow north and then west into the country of his ancestors, he would see summer come and go before the White Giant Winter returned to freeze the waters and allow him to complete his journey and walk once more in the world of men.

Loneliness touched him, heavy and bitter. Warakan drew in a deep breath of cold air and, determined to endure his situation, pulled his bearskin robe defiantly around his head and shoulders. He knew now that he dared not give more time than was necessary to the refinement of his snow walkers. As cold as the air around him was, the Warm Moon *would* rise; it always did. And always the White Giant Winter wearied of his freezing predations and, with alternate sighs and bombast, went his way northward to recoup his power in that frozen land of white mountains in the company of his three sisters, Snow and Ice and the Great Nagger, Howling Wind. In their absence the Moon of Mud would rise; it always did. A man slogging across soggy ground and the thick undergrowth that often overlaid treacherous quagmires could not hope to travel an acceptable distance in any one day, or to pull a sled; he would have to dismantle and transpose it into a two-poled travois for Sister Wolf to drag. Upon this and upon his own back they would transport their meat and belongings to the west; the going would be slow and miserable until they came to the great river that would lead them home. And even then, the way to the high gorge and hunting grounds of the Three Tribes was so far away that Warakan ached to think of it.

Scowling, he watched the sun gradually sink beyond the

hills. It set slowly, as though loath to yield the sky or the earth below to the onset of night. When at last it disappeared, Warakan continued to stare through the webbing of bare-branched trees, certain it was he and not the sun who was ensnared by the winter forest and the vast distances that stood between him and all he yearned to accomplish.

Sister Wolf, sensing his despondency, leaped onto the fallen tree and seated herself beside him, shivering a little when the howling of distant dire wolves broke the stillness of the moment.

Warakan opened his robe, slung an arm around the animal, and drew her close. "We have come a long way together, you and I." He looked up as he spoke, knowing that soon the first pricks of starlight would pierce the blue vault of sky, already washing into gray. "Soon it will be dark. We will eat, then sleep a while before I do what I can to mend my snow walkers. Then we will go on. While the White Giant Winter still lingers upon the land and makes travel easy, we *must* go on! Ah, listen. Your sisters and brothers raise their voices in welcome to the coming night. But where is the mate of *my* heart and kind? Where is my woman now? And how long will it be before I find her and hold her near as I hold you now?"

PART III

BACKS TO THE SUN

1

Ika stopped to watch the sun rise above the palisade.

Xohkantakeh, Katohya, and Quarana did not wait for her. The journey to the land of the ancestors had begun, and they walked northward now. The girl stood alone. She cocked her head and looked for the last time upon the winter encampment, thinking how lonely the circle of timber and brushwood appeared now that she knew she and her band would not return to shelter within it again.

"Ika! Come!" Katohya called.

The girl did not move; leaving was proving to be much more difficult than she had imagined. In this camp she had experienced joy, sorrow, and disappointment so profound her spirit had been bruised and withered by it. Yet, if asked, she could not have articulated her feelings. She knew only that in this place it was as though she—as much as her younger sister—had come through a rite of passage into a new and sobering maturity.

Here, in this place, the last days and nights of her childhood had slipped inexorably away, and she—who would never shed a woman's blood—had not even realized they were gone until it was too late to call them back. Here, in this place, she had seen her petulant, manipulative little sister transformed into a petulant, manipulative new woman. And here, in this place, she had known and lost the love of Xohkantakeh.

Ika trembled. "He will love me again," she said to the rising sun. "He will find his Little Bear worthy to hunt at his side once more. He will! On the journey back into the land of the ancestors I will make it so!"

She trembled again. Now she knew why she lingered in this place: Despite all Katohya's assurances to the contrary, she could not think of the trek to the north without feeling that something about the intended journey was wrong.

To abandon a warm camp in the dead of winter . . . to strip down the lodges before sap swells the buds on the trees . . . to pack up our meat and belongings and trudge northward across the snow to a new life in a distant land among people my father and mother have always spoken of with fear and disdain . . . and all because of my sister's dream! Aiee! It makes no sense. No sense at all.

With her eyes slitted against the invasive brilliance of the newly risen sun, Ika fixed her gaze on the palisade and remembered the many times Xohkantakeh had told his daughters that the spirits of the wind had revealed the will of the forces of Creation when they guided him away from his enemies, southward along the shores of the great river.

Why, then, she wondered, *would these same spirits now speak through New Woman's dream to tell our father to turn around and lead the band northward again?*

Ika frowned. She had no right to question the forces of Creation. They knew everything—all that had happened in the time beyond beginning, all that had happened yesterday, and all that would happen today, tomorrow, and for all the tomorrows to come. They knew. *Somehow* they knew. Katohya said so. And Xohkantakeh insisted they must be obeyed.

Her chin tilted upward. She would not disobey the forces of Creation, nor question her father again; he was annoyed with her enough as it was. Besides, although he was no longer infallible in her eyes, ever since the spirit of Great Paws had come to walk within his skin and New Woman opened herself to the thrustings of his man bone, her father had become a force of Creation unto himself. He was strong again, sure of himself again, wise and powerful and determined to lead his band to a new life.

All this would have been profoundly soothing to Ika's heart were it not for the fact that Xohkantakeh now frightened her more than a little, and no matter how hard she tried, she could not understand what was wrong with their old life.

"Ika!" Katohya called again. "Come, I say!"

And Quarana echoed, "Ika! Why do you lag behind? There is nothing in that camp for us now!"

Ika knew her sister was right. Everything the girl owned, except the lance she had left as a parting gift of respect for the great bear, was packed into her sturdy, antler-framed carrying pack or piled high on the sledges. The skeletal head of the bear would remain behind, mounted on the palisade to guard against any evil-bringing spirits that might otherwise choose to follow the family of Xohkantakeh into the hunting grounds of the ancestors. For all other intents and purposes, the winter camp was no more. The lodges had been stripped and emptied; only the wooden frameworks remained intact. They would stand until wind, weather, and the foraging of animals and insects wore them down, and by then the palisade would be a broken jumble of decomposing wood and grass. Only the skull of Great Paws would remain to give evidence that a small band of the People had once lived, hunted, and honored the life spirit of the great bear in this place. In time even the skull would be gnawed away into nothingness, and all that would be left to speak of this band's brief presence upon the land would be Quarana's little shells and the stone heads of Xohkantakeh's and Ika's lances glinting in the sunlight . . . until they, too, were lost beneath the fall of autumn leaves and needles and the golden rain of the tamaracks.

"You! Daughter!"

Ika's eyes went wide at the sound of Xohkantakeh's voice. He had stalked past her this morning as though she was not there; he had turned his back to the sun and, dragging his sledge, gone his way with his two women walking on either side of him. Not once had he looked back to see if his daughter was following. Indeed, for a long and painful moment the girl had stared after him and nearly cried with the certainty not only that he no longer cared about her but that he had forgotten she even existed. Now he was calling to her. He *did* care! He had *not* forgotten!

"Ika!" he bellowed.

Beaming with delight, the girl whirled around. With Katohya and Quarana standing to his right and left, Xohkantakeh, wearing the skin of the great bear, had paused and was scowling at her. Ika gulped a steadying breath. She would not give him cause for further annoyance with her. Quickly taking up the drag lines of her sledge and fitting the brow band snugly across her forehead, she leaned into her burden and hurried toward him across the snow. There was a smile on her face as, for the first time, she realized that her reluctance to leave the encampment was rooted not only in concern for Katohya and uncertainty about the journey to which Quarana had committed the band, but also in a deep inner need to hear her father call her name, to command her to follow, to show her by his growlings that New Woman had not totally eclipsed Eldest Daughter in his eyes.

"I come!" she cried happily, unaware of the downward curl of his mouth and shoulders until she stopped before him.

"You have been outside the palisade without my consent!" he accused in a barely contained roar.

"I . . . yes, my father . . . to follow you on the night you left to hunt for—"

"*Since* then!" He pointed furiously to the snow-covered ground. "Alone . . . and on the track of a wolf!"

The girl looked down and saw the shallow imprints of her winter moccasins overlaying the paw prints of the wolf. She felt sick. The surface of the snowpack had been rough and hard on the night she had ventured from the encampment to set out baited meat for the black wolf, so rough and hard that she had lamented the scarcity of its tracks. But, as meager as they had been, Ika had found and followed them eagerly, all the while setting down footprints of her own.

"Well?" Xohkantakeh pressed her sharply.

Ika's lower lip trembled. She kept her head down, but somehow she still felt Katohya's worried gaze, Quarana's puzzled stare, and Xohkantakeh's angry scowl. "I . . . I . . ." she stammered. For a moment she thought of telling him that she had gone only a short way in a vain attempt to drive off the black wolf, but her own footprints would soon enough name her Liar. And yet the truth would shame Xohkantakeh in the eyes of Katohya and New Woman. He had not anticipated the threat of wolves, and he had failed to warn his eldest daughter to stay awake and keep guard against them. She shivered. An idea sparked, and she vented it quickly, without testing it first in her mind. "The black wolf came into camp on the night before the new-woman feast. I had fallen asleep outside the lodge. I should have known to stay awake. My father and mother should not have had to command me to do so. The fault was mine. I did not see the wolf until it snatched meat from a drying frame. By then it was too late to stop its thievery, or to keep it from running away to join its own kind, so—"

"Why did you not wake me?"

Again Ika shivered; Xohkantakeh was still growling. "My father was tired after our long trek back to camp with the body of Great Paws. My father was sleeping, resting for the new-woman feast."

"*You* were not tired?"

"I . . . no . . . I am strong! I am brave! I wanted to take the life of the wolf that dared to look at me as meat. And so I went to kill it before it returned with its pack to steal the rest of the feast meat of my sister!"

"And where is the pelt of this black wolf?" Quarana asked, thinking aloud as she said, "I would like such a skin! It would make fine leggings! It should be for me if it came into the compound on the eve of my new-woman feast!"

Anger flared within Ika. "It is not for you! If I had killed it, its pelt would be for me! It is my wolf and—"

"Yah!" With a furious outward swing of his right arm Xohkantakeh struck the girl hard across the chest, sending her backward into the snow. "No man or woman owns the spirits of the game! And what are these words you say to me, Ika? The black wolf is solitary! The pack we saw from the promontory did not welcome it to hunt among its ranks. And why would that pack come here? It is probably still feasting on musk oxen on the far side of the great river!"

Ika was stunned. Katohya was on her knees beside her;

she barely noticed. She was lying spread-eagled on her sledge, blinking up at her father, mother, and sister.

"You shame me, Ika!" Xohkantakeh's face was livid beneath the bearskin hood. "As though a mere female—and an immature child, at that—would have the strength and daring to hunt a wolf when the man who has slain Great Paws did not! Yah! Twice now you have defied me!" He was snarling as he reached into his furs, pulled out a small, tawny fur pouch, and hurled it at the girl. "Here. It is obvious that I have no need of this! Let it be for Ika . . . for one who stood to Bear and Wolf and did not run away!"

The astonished girl flushed—whether from pleasure or consternation, she did not know. Her head was starting to ache, and her chest hurt where he had struck her.

"Take it!" Xohkantakeh commanded. "Keep it! It is made of skin cut from the chin of the great bear. A scraping from the jaws of Great Paws is within it, for it is said by the elders among my tribe that in the jaws as well as in the heart of the great bear reside the spirits of his courage and wisdom. You will wear it, daughter, and heed the voice of these spirits when they remind you of the death to which your disobedience and foolishly placed courage nearly brought you when you stood before Great Paws . . . and perhaps, for all I know, when you ran off and failed to kill the black wolf!"

Ika took the pouch, smooth beneath the mittens that covered her questing fingers. "I—"

"Do not speak!" Xohkantakeh glared at her, squinting into the sun and shaking his head. "Were it not for this man your life spirit would long ago have walked the wind. Were it not for this man you would have perished days ago in the jaws of Great Paws. Now the spirit of the slain bear lives in this man, and the forces of Creation have commanded him to lead his women into the hunting grounds of the ancestors. The way will be long and difficult. So do not put yourself between Xohkantakeh and the sun again, Ika! And never forget that your life is mine to keep or throw away!"

They went on.

No one spoke. The silence was oppressive. Xohkan-

takeh would not allow himself to break it. He knew that Katohya was angry with him; the occasional sidelong flash of
her eyes in his direction spoke more eloquently than words.
And Quarana's sudden eagerness to help her mother with
the single sledge they were pulling together suggested that
she, at least, had been sobered into a new course of action
by his threat. As for Ika, she plodded on with head bowed
and shoulders bent. He did not regret striking or threatening
her; she deserved no less from him. Had he wanted to hurt
her, he could have broken her with his blow. Since his commands had failed to dissuade her from continued disobedience, he had found it necessary to intimidate her through
physical and verbal threat.

Your life is mine to keep or throw away!

It was an old law. In the hunting grounds of his ancestors, an immature daughter lived only at the discretion of
her father until another male came forward to take her from
her parents' lodge.

He shook his head. *As though I would ever harm her!
But even if I bring her safely to the hunting grounds of the
ancestors, what warrior with any pride will want such a
plain and fractious female? Unless he seeks her as he would
seek a good dog—for the virtues of her strength and ability
to breed . . . and for the pleasure of breaking her spirit to
serve his will?*

The question troubled him.

My Ika deserves better than that from any man! He
knew that if she needed breaking, the fault was his. In this
far land beyond the edge of the world, he had raised her to
hunt at his side as though she were the son he would never
have. He could not permit himself to despair for her now because she possessed the bold nature of a warrior; he could
only work to change her on the long journey that lay ahead.

Xohkantakeh's eyes narrowed. A morning wind had
risen with the sun. He bent his head, shrugging a little to
readjust the weight of his pack frame and ease the stress of
the sledge lines across his shoulders. He felt the welcome
warmth of the bear hide over his winter garments, the face
extended outward over his own, the neck, back, and shoulders cutting the chill of the morning, the skin of the fore-

limbs draped over his chest and belly to midway down his thighs, cushioning the press of the sledge lines. What a robe of honor it was! Before stripping and emptying the lodges, his women and daughter had stretched, fleshed, and smoke-cured the raw skin until it was soft and dry as warm sand, then oiled and combed the fur until it rippled and shone like sunstruck autumn grass. The giant smiled. He would walk back into the Land of Grass wearing the skin of Great Paws, and the skin would speak his new name before any man dared ask it.

Bear Slayer! By the will of the forces of Creation I come! In the skin of Great Paws I come! No warrior will turn from Bear Slayer! And no chief will fail to give welcome and honor to Bear Slayer's band!

Heady words. Xohkantakeh's smile tightened; his sense of resolve tightened with it. Beneath his snow walkers, a thin glaze of ice cracked and shifted a little, but the deep, striated underlayers of the snowpack held his weight and allowed the iced runners of his sledge to slip easily behind him.

For how long?

The query, from the deepest recesses of his subconscious, took him aback and turned his smile upside down. The body of Great Paws had yielded much meat, bone, precious sinew, and no small portion of skin-soothing grease, fat for eating, and tallow for the little stone lodge lamps; all of this was now packed and piled onto pack frames and sledges. Once the time of the great melting came, the sledges would become useless and the little band's food and belongings would not be so easily transported. His brow furrowed as he tried to number the hills, valleys, lakes, rivers, and marshes that stood between this moment and the day when at last he would lead his little band home. Failing, he knew that he and his women would be long upon the trail and yearned for the companionship of dogs to ease the journey—high-tailed, deep-chested, thickly muscled, agile dogs to pull the winter sledges and drag the dry-season travois. Suddenly, as he realized this luxury was not to be, the weight of the bearskin, the drag of the sledge, and the press of the pack frame were almost more than he could endure.

"What troubles you, Life Maker?"

The name brought Xohkantakeh's head swinging around. To his surprise he saw that Katohya, not New Woman, was striding close at his side. Her expression was one of concern and love, but although the day was newly born, already she looked tired, and there was an unnatural radiance to her features; her skin and the whites of her eyes glowed pink, as if with fever. Not wanting to acknowledge this, he grumbled, assuring himself that he was only seeing sunlight reflected off the snow onto her face. He turned his gaze forward and chose to make no reply to her query. They knew each other far too well, understood the meaning of every expression, gesture, and tone; this was not a time in which he wanted her to see into his mind, not when there was indecision in it.

"The morning is beautiful in this land that has been so good and generous to us and our daughters," she said quietly.

He did not appreciate her statement of the obvious; he knew all to well where it would lead if he allowed it to go unchallenged. "This is not the land of which New Woman dreams," he told her emphatically.

"But I have been so happy in it!"

He growled; this was the second time she had reminded him of this. What was the matter with the woman? Could she not recognize the dilemma in which she was placing him? "The spirits have spoken, Katohya! How many times must I tell you that you will be happier in a camp where there will be many hands to help you with your woman's work?"

"It was never so for me in the past. Why should it be so in the future?"

"Because you are no longer young. And because New Woman has seen it so. Now let there be no more talk about this between us. The hunting grounds of the ancestors are far from this place. Talk takes strength; save yours for the journey. We *will* go on. By the forces of Creation, it must be so."

Katohya lowered her head. A few moments later she fell
back and, without another word, resumed her place beside
Quarana.

Xohkantakeh kept on, listening to the wind, to his own
footfall, and to that of the women and girl.

Katohya will be strong, he insisted to himself. *If she is
not, Bear Slayer will carry her. We cannot stay in this
land. On my sledge, on my back, or in my arms, Katohya
will return to the hunting grounds of the ancestors! The
women of the Land of Grass will welcome her. The sons of
Xohkantakeh and Quarana will call her Second Mother,
and she will rejoice in the meat they bring to her lodge,
and in the wisdom that has brought her to a better life.
How else can it be for her—or for any of us—when
the spirits have spoken through New Woman to command
this man?*

The land ahead was open between the trees, awash in
the cold, soft colors of the morning. He knew every lichen-
scabbed boulder, the rise and fall of every snow-covered
hill, and something about the familiarity of the landscape
touched him, seemed to affirm the rightness of his presence
in it and to implore him to stay.

Irritated, he lengthened his stride. Growling again, he
told himself that he had dwelled too long in this particular
hunting ground beyond the edge of the world; he could
not remember a time in his entire life when parting from a
good and familiar place had not made a painful little
wound in his heart. Why should it be different now? A
man could not be expected to forget a snug lodge, or successful hunts for small game, or the songs of his females
in the winter dark. Nor could he long refrain from calling
to mind the sight of his beloved woman leading their girls
to gather nuts and roots on mornings when frost patterns
lay like great white spiderwebs across the forest floor, or
the joy he found in sighting the first sleek, shining red
buds of spring swelling along the still-frozen creek, or the
pleasure he took in the endless, ever-shifting variations of
green that formed the canopy of the deepest part of the
summer forest.

Xohkantakeh smiled as he walked on, remembering

long, lazy swims he had taken across cold, fast-running streams and broad deep ponds, diving with waterfowl and river otters, and once even surprising and managing to skewer a giant beaver. How his woman and daughters had watched in amazement as he slogged breathless from the water and choked out a command for them to help him beach his prize. How they oohed and aahed at the tale he told of his underwater hunt. And, when he was unable to haul the bear-sized beaver from the embankment to which he had managed to float it, how they praised his skill and strength as they skinned and butchered the animal on the spot. Later, back within the safety of the palisade, they found cause to exclaim again as they set the rich, fatty tail of the beaver to singe and roast, for few meats were more desired or delectable than this.

He shook his head. The meat of that beaver had lasted well past the last brazen flaming of autumn, and portions of its rendered fat were still being used to keep his females' faces and hands from chafing in the winter wind.

Xohkantakeh paused. His memories were overwhelmingly mellow and gratifying to his spirit, so much so that he scowled resentfully against them as he suddenly realized that—with Great Paws no longer a threat to the band and the power of the bear reborn in him—were it not for New Woman's dream, he would have no desire to leave such a benevolent land as this. And yet, was it not the way of his people to be always on the move from one encampment to another, always on the hunt for the great herds and sacred sage and . . .

A single thin, unnaturally high, pathetically crooked howl pierced the otherwise silent morning, then was gone.

Xohkantakeh's body stiffened, and as he instinctively turned toward the sound, his thoughts of the past fled from his mind. The wind was from the west now, blowing down from the rounded heights of the hill from which he had once caught a fleeting glimpse of a black wolf. His eyes narrowed, and his nostrils widened. The wind was cold this morning, very cold, but not enough to mask the unmistakable scent of putrefying flesh.

Katohya and Quarana paused beside him.

The new woman wrinkled her nose and made a face. "West Wind carries the stink of rotting meat!" she declared.

"Death has come to some large creature on the heights of the western hill," observed Katohya. "And yet it is strange that we see no circling raptors or ravens."

Xohkantakeh's gaze moved to Ika. She was transfixed. Within her ruff, her face was set in a malevolent glare, and her mouth was compressed so tightly against her teeth that her lips had gone white. And yet somehow he knew she was smiling and did not need to ask her why. "It seems you have killed 'your' wolf."

"Yes!" Ika trembled, and now her mouth parted into a smile of undisguised elation and pride.

Xohkantakeh was hard-pressed not to strike her again. "And you have left it for carrion, wasting its meat and pelt, dishonoring its life spirit forever, and thereby dishonoring your own and inviting the wrath of the forces of Creation to fall upon your band!"

The girl caught her breath. "I . . . no! The black wolf was not dead when I left it! It was—"

"Dead wolves do not howl," interrupted Quarana.

"No," Xohkantakeh agreed. Hearing once again the pathetic little howl that had only moments ago broken the silence of the morning, he told her in a fury, "But abandoned puppies do!"

"Aiee!" exclaimed Katohya.

Ika seemed to shrink inside her furs, for she knew as well as any member of her band that there was no greater offense against the forces of Creation than to slay a mother animal and condemn its helpless young to slow starvation or the ravages of predators. "I did not know that he was a she!" the girl cried.

"How could you not have known!" Xohkantakeh demanded, then informed his daughter with a glower of disgust, "By a single look at the flank of the black wolf I could have told you that only a female wolf with nursing young has so thick a coat this late in winter, or one with a tinge of red when seen in the light of the sun! Have you learned nothing at all from the hunting knowledge I have shared with you?"

"I . . . I had forgotten about—"

"Yah!" He wanted no more excuses from her. "Take up your lances! Loose the lines that bind you to your sledge. Go alone onto the western hill. You, not I, will make a quick and merciful end of the children of the black wolf! You will raise sacred fire in that place. You will make songs and offerings to the life spirits of the beasts you have slain and dishonored. Ask them to forgive your careless arrogance, for I cannot. Go, I say! Lest the forces of Creation set their wrath upon us all, do not return to walk with this band until you have made a finish of that which you have so thoughtlessly begun!"

The girl shivered violently, then stood stock-still a moment as though too shattered to take a step. But take a step she did. In moments she was trudging toward the west without having spoken another word.

"Xohkantakeh . . . ?" Katohya stepped close to lay a hand on his arm. "You cannot—"

"Her life is mine to keep or to throw away!" he reminded her. Staring after the girl, he said grimly, "She *must* learn to obey! For her sake as much as for ours." He wondered if his heart had ever felt heavier. Yet slowly, surely, his earlier indecisiveness about the journey was falling, replaced by a new understanding and commitment to the very real necessity for it. He went on to explain, as much to himself as to his women, "The black wolf *was* a solitary . . . an animal that lived apart from the pack, hunting and denning alone for reasons only the wolf kind may know. Sometimes, of late, when I heard its lonely cries in the night, my spirit was moved to sadness, for I knew that it called to others of its kind, to members of a pack to which it did not belong, asking for trust, for companionship, for brothers and sisters to ease the burdens of its days and to lie warm beside it in the cold winter nights. But the pack did not answer in welcome. And so the black wolf lived and died alone, as its pups must now perish in a land where there are none to care whether they live or die."

He paused. It was all clear to him now, the need, the purpose, and the absolute rightness of the journey. Refreshed and renewed, he continued, "And so it will be with us if we remain alone in this far land beyond the edge of the world with no one of our kind to ease the burdens of our days, to offer warmth in the winter of our old age, or to care whether we—or our 'pups'—live or die. New Woman is right. It is a good thing that we turn our backs to the rising sun and return to the land of the ancestors. Unlike the black wolf, we journey into a country where the spirits have promised us welcome. Come. The journey will be long. The sooner we begin it, the sooner it will end."

"But we cannot go on without Ika!" Katohya's voice shook with dread for her child.

"What if she does not come back? Her sledge is so heavy! This new woman cannot pull it!" Quarana stated peevishly. "This new woman is wearied by life making and meat making and by helping her old mother to pack and carry and—"

"I will pull your sister's sledge!" Xohkantakeh was in no mood for New Woman's petulant wheedling, and he was irked by her references to his beloved Katohya's age. "This journey is of your dreams, New Woman! It is only just begun, and you will continue to make life with me and to help your mother pack and carry and make meat until we are *all* old! As for Ika, she has faced down a great bear and twice stood to the black wolf! Now she will learn to face down and stand to her own arrogance and disobedience! This she will do without complaint! And I tell you now that, by the watching star eyes of the Great Bear in the Sky, my Little Bear will be sitting warm and safe among us by this night's fire!"

Morning ripened toward noon.

The little band of three walked on.

The day passed. Dusk settled upon the world.

The travelers paused in gathering darkness to seek a place of shelter for the night.

But Ika did not return.

Katohya was beside herself. In the natural windbreak of a high cutbank of a frozen watercourse, she raised the short wooden poles and skins that would serve her family as a temporary lean-to. While Quarana rested and rubbed her feet, Katohya made fire, for this was the honor duty of the first woman of a man's lodge, and she would not leave it to her daughter. As Xohkantakeh unrolled and spread the sleeping hides, a ravenous Quarana hurriedly saw to the day-end meal. Soon the threesome was seated before the warmth of the little fire, but Katohya could not bring herself to eat so much as a bite of the meat and fat that were being hungrily consumed by her man and his new woman.

"What will our Ika be eating now?" Her question to Xohkantakeh held an edge sharp enough to cut him; it was what she wanted to do.

"My sister has put us all at risk," Quarana reminded her, speaking out of turn as she had begun to do with ease since discovering the authority her new rank afforded her, at least in the eyes of Xohkantakeh. "My sister deserves to go hungry!"

"It is so," affirmed the giant, sitting cross-legged before the fire, chewing slowly and responding quietly but quickly, for the flame of anger Quarana had sparked in Katohya's eyes was brighter and hotter than the flames in the fire circle before him. It must be quelled if the night was to pass in any semblance of peace. "Ika must ask forgiveness of the forces of Creation and the life spirits of the wolves she has slain. I have told her to make songs and offerings. If she has chosen to stay upon the western hill and fast this night, it is a good choice, one I would make were I in her place."

"My Bear Slayer would never be in my sister's place! It is impossible for the man of this new woman to ever be as foolish as Ika!"

Katohya sent a caustic look in her daughter's direction, but the question that left her lips was directed to her man. "How can it be a good thing for a young girl to be sent alone from her band in this land of lions and wolves and bears and—"

"We have neither heard nor seen any sign of lions!" Quarana interrupted. "Our man has said that the wolf pack is on the far side of the river! And why should the women of Bear Slayer fear their own kind?"

Xohkantakeh's face showed his appreciation of his new woman's open adulation.

Katohya shook her head. The last lingering wash of daylight was gone from the night sky; the stars were showing bright against undiminished blackness. "She should have returned to us by now!" she said.

Xohkantakeh nodded; there was a subtle, tightly held tension in his voice as he said emphatically, "She will come!"

But soon the last of the evening's food was eaten, and the fire began to die. The wind grew colder. Xohkantakeh glowered toward the west a while, then gestured impatiently to Quarana. In moments he and his new woman were lying together beneath the skin of the great bear. Katohya remained where she was, with her back to them, banking the coals, knowing by the sounds they made that Quarana was opening her thighs to the imperative press of their man, taking his life maker into herself, enabling his sexual release and thus alleviating the tension Katohya had earlier heard in his voice. A few deep, rhythmic male grunts, a brief cry from the new woman, and the coupling was over. The older woman's brow came down. It had been only that, she thought—a coupling, a quick, hot purging of the senses, perhaps a necessary distraction on a night that would not allow a father's mind to rest as long as his eldest daughter was not safely ensconced with the band.

He does *care. He* is *worried.* Katohya found a mother's relief in her thoughts and a woman's satisfaction in the certainty that Xohkantakeh's mating with Quarana had not been a lovemaking. It had been a joining of bodies, but it had not been a joining of spirits, not a true mating during which a man poured the essence of his mind and heart and very life into a favored woman as he had done when he had taken Katohya before the new-woman ceremonies. A small, hopeful tremor went through her as her hands drifted from the warmth of the little fire pit to the warmth that the sounds of mating had stirred in her loins. Indeed, it seemed that her woman place had remained perpetually warm and quivering with lingering sensations ever since that last tumultuous mating with her man. Katohya's heart gave a little leap. Only once before had her body responded in such a way to a mating; nine moons later, she had birthed a child. Hope flared, but Katohya deliberately quashed it. She would not allow herself to think of such possibilities now.

All was still beneath the hide of the great bear. Quarana and Xohkantakeh had fallen asleep. And Ika had still not returned to the band.

Katohya sighed and wished she could release worry as easily as she exhaled breath. It was no use. She would be unable to sleep until Ika was safe once more within the protective circle of the band. She sighed again, determined to remain outside the lean-to, waiting all night if need be for the return of a daughter who could be no dearer to her heart had the girl been born of her own body.

"Ah, Ika, what keeps you away so long?" Katohya shook her head in despair, rose, sought her sleeping robe, then tiptoed back to the remnant warmth of the sleeping fire, beside which she settled in to keep vigil. Wrapped in her furs, with her arms locked around her knees, she sat facing west, staring toward the distant horizon over which the stars had begun to follow the sun in their sure, steady descent into the mysterious, eternally hidden birthplace of the West Wind. Her eyes narrowed thoughtfully as, shivering a little, she remembered being told by her father that the stars were the campfires of the dead and that, for this reason, she must never grieve over the loss of loved ones, for they would always be with her, above her in the night sky, sitting close to their fires, warming their spirit bodies, waiting to soothe her with their love if she would only look up and remember them.

Let my Ika not be among the stars this night! she implored. Closing her eyes, she was unaware of falling asleep as she drifted in dreams in which her beloved father, mother, and sisters looked down at her out of the sky, smiling, assuring her that all would be well.

"Ika is there."

Katohya awoke with a start to the nearby rumble of Xohkantakeh's voice. He was hunkering on his heels beside her, pointing off to the west where the glow of a small fire could be seen sparking in the wind.

"Hmm," he grunted, openly annoyed with the situation. "She has taken much time before raising fire as an offering to the forces of Creation and to the life spirits of the slain wolves."

Katohya allowed relief to soothe her senses before worry sparked again. "Or as a signal to her family . . . a fire to tell us of her loneliness, or worse, of her—"

"Or of her defiance. It should not have taken her all day to climb the hill, kill a few wolf pups, and offer up prayers and sacred smoke. She should have returned to walk with us long before now. She stays away to make us worry, to make this man regret that he has rightfully shamed her."

"Or she stays away because she cannot return . . . because she has been injured in a fall, or by some beast, and is so badly injured she cannot come to us!"

Katohya's words hung in the air.

For a long while Xohkantakeh remained immobile, staring westward until at last, releasing a ragged exhalation, he said, "If she has not returned to us by the time tomorrow's sun stands high in the sky, I will go and bring her back to the band."

Katohya was not mollified. "And if she is badly hurt, what then? By the time you reach her, it may be too late to bring her back!"

He went before dawn.

Even before the fire on the distant hill flickered and was seen no more, Xohkantakeh set his footsteps to the west. In darkness he walked, and in light. On and on, with never a pause or backward glance until the sun was nearly midway up the sky. At last, with his breath rasping in his throat and the muscles of his thighs and back aching with every stride, he kicked off his snow walkers, slung them over his shoulders, and began to clamber up the broad, familiar slope of talus with the name of his eldest daughter on his lips.

"Ika!"

A bird wheeled overhead. Pale-bodied and sharp-winged against the clouded sky, it seemed to echo his cry, but if the girl was near, she did not answer.

Xohkantakeh's gut constricted against the cold sting of sudden dread. Could Katohya have been right? Could he, in his righteous anger toward a disobedient daughter, have unintentionally sent the girl to her death? *No! Surely it could not be! There is nothing in this place to threaten the child except the ghost of a dead wolf! Had I seen sign of other large predators, I would not have sent her off alone!* "Ika!" he called again, more imperatively than before.

But not even the bird answered him now.

Xohkantakeh swallowed hard, and went on.

The scent of putrefying flesh had stained yesterday's wind; that rank, sweet stink was gone now, replaced by the acrid odor of a recently burned-out fire. It was this scent that gave him hope, along with occasional displacements in the gravelly scree, and drew him ever upward toward the high, rounded, boulder-strewn summit of the hill.

She was here . . . her footfall displaced loose stones . . . she raised a fire . . . she was alive last night . . . and is alive now!

He went on, hope battling despair within his breast as he called his eldest daughter's name. Pausing just short of the summit, he shouted, "Ikaree! You *will* answer your father! Ikaree!"

At the sound of the rarely used endearment, the girl came from behind the tallest of the boulders that stood at the crest of the slope.

She moved as gracefully as a young doe, and when she paused to look down at him out of the furry circle of her hood, her tall, broad-shouldered young body etched against the sky, a turbulent rush of emotions shook Xohkantakeh. Relief. Love. Joy. Pride in having raised such a fine, strong daughter. And an anger so sudden and intense that it obliterated all other feelings. "You are alive! And unhurt!"

"It is so!"

"Then why are you still here?"

"I knew you would come for me."

"I have left your mother and sister undefended!"

"I—"

"No! There are no words to excuse your selfishness and disobedience!" A tremor went through Xohkantakeh as the enormity of his transgression struck his heart. He *had* left Katohya and New Woman undefended! His concern for this arrogant, disobedient female child had put his two women—and future sons—at risk! He felt sick, so shaken that he could barely stand, but stand he did to proclaim to the stunned girl, "Stay here or follow me back to the band. The choice is yours to make, but know now that I will not look back or again risk the lives of my women for such an unworthy child! Your life *is* mine to keep or throw away, Ika, and I have warned you what must happen if you choose to disobey me again!"

"But—"

He waved her to silence and, without another word, turned on his heels and began to stalk away.

"Wait, my father! Please! Wait!"

The girl's plea was a sob. It pierced his spirit as cruelly as any projectile point of sharpened stone could have done; for the sake of his women, for the good of the band, and in hope of future sons, Xohkantakeh would not listen.

"My father! You do not understand! I *have* been obedient! I did not want you to leave my mother and sister to come searching for me, but you commanded me not to return until I had done all that you demanded. And so I have stayed upon the high hill because, although I have buried and honored the black wolf with offerings of songs and sacred fire, I could not kill its pups."

Xohkantakeh turned and, with anger and resolve burning inside him, started back up the hill. "Then I must do it."

"No! You—"

He was at her side. "Do not defy me again, or, by the forces of Creation, you will stay alone in this place forever!

Show me to the den of the black wolf. I will do what must be done!"

With a jagged intake of breath, she whirled and obeyed.

The den was not far. Xohkantakeh would have found the site even if the girl had not led him to it, for the black wolf had chosen well, in the way of its kind. There, just below the summit of the hill, with views of the surrounding land in all directions, the animal had borne her litter in a deep, clean hollow beneath the largest of the boulders. His brow furrowed as he saw Ika go to her knees, burrow quickly beneath the stone, then emerge to face him. Her expression puzzled him as, still on her knees, she opened wide her arms and allowed to spill onto the snowy, stony ground at his feet . . .

"The children of the black wolf!" she announced, beaming.

Xohkantakeh's jaw gaped wide. There, blinking in the sunlight and none too steady on their paws, were four hightailed, deep-chested, thickly muscled, floppy-eared balls of fur that he could have crushed beneath his heels in a moment. But he did not crush them. Instead he knelt, shaking his head incredulously as he stared at that for which he had so long yearned—and despaired of ever possessing in this far land at the edge of the world.

"Let these pups be my gift to the spirit of the great slain bear that lives on in you, my father," implored Ika. "They are a better and more worthy gift than my lance, for these wolves are more than wolves. The blood of the dog kind is in them."

He was stunned. As the pups nosed curiously between his fingers and rooted beneath the bends of his limbs, there was no denying the truth: The markings on their fur and the shape of their fat little faces spoke the truth of their lineage even as Ika spoke the deepest belief of her heart.

"The forces of Creation have sent the black wolf to us, my father. It is they who sent her following me across the snow, and into the encampment! She did not come to make meat of me! She came to summon and lead me to this place where the circle of her life must end so that her pups could come into the care of our band! Ah, my father, now I will not worry about my mother in the long days and nights that lie ahead, for soon the children of the black wolf will be pulling the sledges of Xohkantakeh's women as our band follows New Woman's dream into the hunting grounds of the ancestors and to a new and better life!"

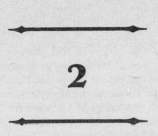

2

Warakan traveled on.

With Sister Wolf at his side he walked into the West Wind, sometimes dragging the moose-bone sledge himself so the old animal would not be unduly fatigued. He had fashioned moose-hide boots for her to protect the pads of her feet from the rough surface of the snowpack, and the meat of the moose kept them both strong. His snow walkers now served him well, requiring only occasional minor repairs and adjustments for the ever-changing terrain. On and on they journeyed. Each step that brought Warakan closer to the land of his ancestors also brought joy to his heart, but sadness, too, because he knew that Jhadel would neither approve of the ambition that drove him nor be at his side to witness his inevitable triumph over their enemies in the Land of Grass.

"May it be that your spirit will someday know that I am right in what I do!" he implored, hoping that West Wind would carry his words to the world beyond this world where Jhadel's spirit walked the Four Winds forever.

In the cold, heavy light of overcast, lengthening days, the young man and the old wolf continued on through ever-changing forest and across ever-changing land until dusk brought them to rest in its shadows. When darkness fell, Warakan raised his fire and, in his loneliness, offered songs to the spirit of Jhadel in the hope of bringing the old man

near to him once more. Sometimes his hope seemed realized, for he had managed to keep embers from the old
shaman's death fire alive within his birch burl, and each
time he summoned flame from those coals, it was as though
the spirit of Peacedreamer was also rekindled. Warakan
would stare into the little fire and imagine that he saw the
old man dancing wild and happy shaman dances in the
flames. It was a comforting image, and he did not feel quite
so alone when he spoke his before-sleep prayers of thanksgiving: thanks to the forces of Creation for his memories of
the old Peacedreamer; thanks for the strength he and Sister
Wolf had gained from the meat, blood, and marrow of Wise
Father Rabbit and Great Hook-Nosed Grandfather of All
Deer; and special thanks, always—in small sacrifices of increasingly odorous moose meat, fed to the fire as a special
show of gratitude—to the White Giant Winter for lingering
upon the land and allowing a swift journey across country
that would be a quagmire come spring.

One cold night, when Moon Mother of Stars looked
down upon their camp, Warakan smiled as the fire burned
low and thought with satisfaction of how far he and the wolf
had come. After carefully banking the coals, he clutched
the sacred stone in one palm, curled up next to the animal,
and drew his bearskin over the two of them. "Perhaps Jhadel
was right about me," he mused aloud. "I have not yet
hunted and slain the great white mammoth totem. I have
not avenged myself upon my enemies. But the blood of
shamans, as well as of warriors and chieftains of two tribes,
flows in my veins. The sacred stone is mine. The animals of
this world and the White Giant Winter heed my commands.
I swear to you, my sister, that soon I will be a warrior and
someday I will be a chief, but perhaps Jhadel *was* right
when he said that I was born to be a shaman. We will see,
eh? You and I, Warakan and Sister Wolf, soon we will see!"

They slept long and deeply. Sometime before dawn, the
wolf pricked up her ears at the sound of distant trumpeting,
and Warakan dreamed of hunting the great white mammoth
totem and of fighting and killing the perfidious, woman-
stealing Red World shaman, Cha-kwena, while a golden
eagle plunged at him with talons extended and screamed:

"It is not for this that I whispered to Wind and Smoke on behalf of a son of the Two Tribes! It is not for this that I deprived Lightning of human meat! It is not for this that I called the Ancient Ones from the lodge of the Four Winds! And it is not for this that I yielded my eyes and tongue and heart to a would-be warrior! Have you seen nothing with my eyes, Warakan? Kya! No! You have not seen. You are no shaman! You are a blind man and must be led!"

He awoke, disturbed, remembering another dream, the same eagle. *A vision? Perhaps.* He was too tired to ponder the possibility. He slept again, and dreamed again, this time of Brother Bear, his big, yellow, scar-pawed boyhood friend, cub of the mother bear whose skin now kept him and Sister Wolf warm at night. It was a good dream. When the first colors of dawn permeated a thin spot in the old hide, Warakan awoke again, refreshed and ready to begin a new day.

Across seemingly endless snow-covered, boulder-strewn, oddly broken hills they continued on their way, crossing many frozen ponds, rivers, and streams before Warakan looked to the stars and knew that the time had come to turn his steps northward toward the lake Jhadel had called Mother of All Rivers.

"When we reach that shore, we will continue northward to the place of many south-flowing rivers," he told the wolf. "May the White Giant Winter stay with us that long, for we must cross these rivers before we can turn westward once again to seek the greatest of all rivers . . . the water that flows wide in the shadow of the Watching Star that will guide us to the high gorge where the white spearheads are waiting—white spearheads to slay a white mammoth. Ah, Sister Wolf, what a day that will be! I will be invincible then, and so will you, for I will share the flesh and blood of the totem with you. We will live forever! You will see. When at last we go against our enemies, there will be no stopping us!"

He was not sure, but it seemed to Warakan that the wind dropped in that moment and that the air warmed a little as they went on. Later, with cold, sluggish tides of dank air bringing a thick fog down from the north, Warakan paused to watch it close in around him and cursed the gathering gray. It stank of rotting ice and decomposing rock, and Warakan suspected from its stench that he was nearing the barrens. Beyond that vast, stony land of grotesquely shaped and stunted trees, he had seen fog sired by the sun and spawned at the feet of the towering mountain range of ice that stood firmly planted in the waters of the monstrous Mother of All Rivers. He cursed again, for he knew that fog born of the barrens was almost inevitably a harbinger of spring. And spring was Enemy, for he had not the slightest doubt that its advent would slow his journey across a collapsing snowpack that would be several moons in melting.

"Go!" he commanded the fog.

The fog did not go; it thickened.

Warakan grimaced in frustration as he sent his right hand burrowing into his furs, sought the sacred stone, and gripped it hard. "White Giant Winter, stay! Fog, go where you will, but go from this land and quickly! Warakan, son of shamans and warrior chiefs, has far to go before his journey and his intent to take vengeance upon his people is done!"

Sister Wolf pressed against his leg and whined softly.

"I know, I know, old friend," said Warakan. "Even wolves are blind in a fog like this!" Unable to see much beyond the extension of his bearskin hood, he found himself wondering if this was how Jhadel had viewed the world through the white membrane that had slowly grown over his eyes and blinded him.

And then, suddenly, he heard a sound: a single short, deep, resonating growl such as he had never heard before. Hackles rose on his back as somewhere ahead—or was it behind, or to his right or left?—a large animal moved unseen within the fog, huffed once, and then was still.

A low growl began to resonate at the back of Sister Wolf's throat, and every hair along the crest of her spine bristled.

A chill that had nothing to do with damp, frigid air

prickled beneath Warakan's skin and caused him to shiver violently as, instinctively releasing the sledge lines, he positioned his lance. Turning slowly, he stared intently around him, trying to see through the mist. He froze. For an instant, surely no more than that, the fog thinned ahead of him, and he caught a fleeting glimpse of something solid in the mist . . . something as pale as bone, as thick as his forearm . . . something long and sleek and extending sharply upward. An instant later the fog closed in, and it was gone.

Warakan's heart was pounding. Save for the sustained growl of the wolf, the silence was palpable. And yet, deep within that silence, there *was* sound. He held his breath, strained to hear, and after a few moments exhaled. Then he heard the low, tense, erratic breathing of a big animal. It was near. Very near. But was it predator or potential prey? He had no way of knowing. His hand tightened around the shaft of his spear. His mouth had gone dry, and now he caught the pungent smell of spruce trees—and of something else, of something warm and alive and reeking of . . .

Another huff.

The wolf's head was down, her snout extended, her ears forward, her tail partially erect, her lips raised and quivering. At the first word or gesture from her human brother, she would leap to the attack.

"Hold, my sister," warned Warakan. "You cannot attack that which you do not see!" Adrenaline was surging in his veins. All his senses were screaming *Danger!*, to no avail. The fog had effectively blinded him. Now, as it continued to congeal around him, it seemed to Warakan that the fog itself was alive, breathing, a single indefinably huge, amorphous gray being intent on confounding and humiliating him as it fingered his face and set him trembling with anger and impotence at his inability to prevent the chill invasiveness of its touch. Again he cursed it and all its undefined threats and mysteries.

And then slowly, so slowly that Warakan was not quite certain it was happening, a slight wind began to stir, and with its coming, the color and texture of the fog changed. It grew lighter and thinner until, gradually, that which had settled so quickly and heavily upon the land began to disperse and form into long, tattered shreds, leaving as lingering evidence of its passage a thin glazing of ice upon the trees, the rocks, and the surface of the snowpack.

Warakan could not believe his eyes. The fog had gone almost as quickly as it had come. He saw the spruce trees now, old trees, many of them dead, mere skeletons towering above the pines and winter-bare hardwoods. And there, lying as though at sleep on folded limbs in the snow, a double hand-count of paces ahead, was the animal whose unseen presence in the fog had caused his heartbeat to quicken and his mouth to dry. Seeing it now brought the same reaction.

It was huge. It was white. It was . . .

"Life Giver!" Warakan exclaimed the name of the totem of his people as the great white mammoth lifted its tusked head and began to rise.

Warakan did not hesitate. In uncountable dreams he had seen this spirit animal coming toward him out of the white mists and white mountains that lay beyond the barrens, and in every one of those dreams he had done exactly what he did now.

"Behold!" he cried with such vehemence that, even in the face of a rising mammoth, the wolf looked up at him and cringed. "I am Warakan!" he roared in direct and unflinching challenge. "Behold the son of Masau, Mystic Warrior of the People of the Watching Star! Behold the grandson of Shateh, chieftain and shaman of the People of the Land of Grass! I come! Call forth your guardian, Cha-kwena, shaman of the Red World People! Call forth Mah-ree, Medicine Woman who walks with mammoth because that shaman has stolen her from me! Warakan will now fight that shaman for his woman! But if Cha-kwena is afraid to come forth, now the totem will die at Warakan's hand, and this man will live forever, invincible and victorious against his enemies, Life Giver to those who will soon name me Chief and Totem!"

The mammoth was on its feet. Out of white eyes it stared at its assailants. Its ears twitching on either side of its long, sloping brow, it extended its head and raised its trunk above short, upturned tusks.

Sloping brow? Short tusks?

"Die!" commanded Warakan. But even as he levered back and hurled his spear with all his strength, he knew that something was wrong. Not with his throw; the spear left his hand in a high, singing, killing arc that would have won the approval of even the sternest of his hunting masters in the Land of Grass. And even when the weapon failed to slice through flesh to make a mortal wound, although Warakan hissed his disappointment, he knew that his spear was, after all, only a moose-bone lance. Without benefit of a stone projectile point, the lance was deflected by the mammoth's hairy hide as easily as though the animal were wearing some sort of invisible war shield of multilayered leather. It was the look of the animal that disturbed him, for standing its ground before him, the great white mammoth was not so "great" as Warakan had imagined; indeed, he had seen long-horned bison that stood nearly as tall. And now, as he reached back to draw another lance from the three he carried, his hand froze in midair.

The mammoth staggered and wheezed. Its legs buckled, and with its head and trunk still extended, it dropped onto the snow as though struck by some unseen but mighty braining club.

Warakan stood stunned.

Sister Wolf was cringing again.

A great whoof escaped the mammoth's lungs, and at the moment it hit the ground, the entire animal appeared to explode.

Icy fragments were flying in all directions. Warakan took a backward step, fighting the urge to turn and run in panic. It was not easy. The old wolf had retreated to a safe distance, but the young man held his ground. The totem had collapsed and vanished into thin air before his very eyes! How could this be?

Squinting through the falling debris, he saw to his amazement that the great white mammoth lay where it had fallen, but it was no longer white; it was a dull, reddish-gray hill lying amidst small clumps of ice and snow that had evidently encrusted its hairy coat, only to be dislodged by the sudden violence of its fall.

Warakan's hand fell to his side. The animal's eyes remained open, but if it was still breathing, he could neither hear, scent, nor see any sign of its exhalations. There was, however, another scent in the air. His nostrils constricted to close off the stench of death as, with the wolf again at his side, he advanced and paused beside the body of the beast.

"Behold . . ." The word was a mocking echo of his earlier enthusiasm as he shook his head and spoke to the elephantine form that lay sprawled before him. "You are not the great white mammoth totem. You are old, and your eyes are white with blindness, and your flesh is wasted away to hair and bones. From the look and stink of you, you must have been lying in this place awaiting the coming of Spirit Sucker for many a long day and night! In truth, I see now that you are not a mammoth at all!"

Disappointment was bitter in Warakan's mouth. The animal that lay dead at his feet was of a kind he and Jhadel had never seen before entering the southeastern forests. Its long, sharply sloping brow and short tusks named its kind: *mastodon*. He chided himself for not recognizing it before; even rimed with snow and ice, the cadaverous old bull was less than half the size of a mammoth and did not have the long-limbed body or high, twin-domed skull that marked its towering cousin.

Warakan cocked his head as he observed the mastodon. He had learned long ago that it was the way of old bull tuskers, be they mammoth or mastodon, to walk alone save when the need to mate was on them. And it was the way of this animal's kind to browse the spruce swamps and wetland forests of the uninhabited eastern woodlands; he had never seen mastodons on the open prairies of the Land of Grass, where his father and grandfathers had hunted the great mammoths with such abandon that the tuskers had all but vanished long before he was old enough to raise a spear against them.

Warakan's eyes narrowed as they held on the fallen beast. Even though his lance had failed to pierce the mastodon's skin, he knew he had killed it; his bold shouts and threats had been enough to so frighten the ancient, sickly animal that, when he had commanded it to die, it had obeyed. He shook his head, regretting his words and knowing that from this moment on he would have to watch his tongue closely, for he must indeed be a shaman.

"I am sorry, old one," he said to the mastodon. "I seek the life of the great white mammoth. I did not want your death. Had I recognized you in time, I would have called upon the powers of the sacred stone and summoned your kind from the forest so that you would have had your cows and calves around you when the time came to set your spirit free to walk the wind forever."

An inner coldness chilled the young man. Loneliness lay so heavy upon his spirit that he could barely breathe as it struck him just how desolate the old bull looked lying in the snow, alone, bereft of herd or even a single member of its own kind to mourn its passing.

So will it someday be for me if I remain alone beyond the edge of the world! he thought.

Sister Wolf, sensing his mood, nuzzled his hand.

He did not feel her nose rooting beneath his mittened palm. West Wind was rising sharply. The thin, clear casing of ice that had been left upon the trees by the passing fog was cracking, falling, raising a sound like that of innumerable music makers of shell and bone tinkling upon the wind. Warakan stood transfixed, watching and listening to the crystal rain, then scanning the grove of dead and dying spruce trees. Unsettled by the overwhelming feeling that Death lived in this place, he found himself wondering if mastodons, too, were doomed to vanish from the earth if men ever came into these forests at the edge of the world to hunt them.

"I will not bring them here, for I will not return to this place!"

The cry of an eagle startled him and drew his eyes upward, but it was the circling and cawing of ravens that held his glance.

"Death does live in this place!" he declared to the old wolf. "Come! We dare not linger lest it find us, too, and suck the spirits from our blood and bones as surely as it did from this old tusker!"

Taking up the sledge line, Warakan went his way with Sister Wolf at his side.

"We have spearheads to retrieve and a totem to kill before we can become warriors and chieftains among our own kind!" he informed his companion.

In the days that followed he looked to the sacred stone for strength and guidance, and by night he dreamed of a lost love and clearing skies within which shone the Watching Star that would help him find his way.

3

Xohkantakeh followed the great river.

Northward he walked, as in Quarana's dream, resolutely leading his women and daughter "backward" toward the hunting grounds of the Ancient Ones. In the skin of Great Paws he was warm, and on the flesh of Great Paws he and his females remained strong. He saw that even Katohya walked steadfastly, her eyes fixed resolutely ahead, her tender spirit emboldened by the meat of the great slain bear.

"It will be good for us, this move back into the country of the ancestors," he told her.

"Since you have said that we must return to the hunting grounds of the northern tribes, may all that our new woman has seen in her dream be true," she replied obliquely. "May the old chiefs sit peacefully with their women and children before their lodge fires. May the warriors who once fought beside Xohkantakeh in the Land of Grass have raised sons to stalk meat and not each other in hunting grounds where the People no longer follow the ways of war!"

Quarana, striding nearby, heard the older woman's words and enthused, "You must not fear, my mother! Truly the warriors of the Land of Grass will welcome so tall and powerful a chief as our Bear Slayer when he returns with his women to the hunting grounds of the ancestors!"

"May it be so, New Woman!" he said and might well have added more to assure Katohya that all would, indeed, be well, but in that moment his first woman spoke up emphatically.

"My Xohkantakeh does not need the affirmation of lesser men!"

"*Our* Xohkantakeh," Quarana corrected.

Ika, carrying the wolf-dog pups stuffed tightly into a sling on her back as though they were human babies, added earnestly, "Great Paws himself has shown Xohkantakeh that he is Bear Slayer, Brave Hunter, and Provider for this band. I do not care what other warriors will say of him, for he is the best and bravest warrior of them all."

The giant eyed the girl thoughtfully. His heart had softened toward her. Since the incident with the black wolf, no father could have asked for a more obedient or respectful daughter. Why, then, whenever she spoke to laud his power, did it always seem to him that she was trying to convince him—and herself—of something of which she was not entirely sure?

During ever-lengthening days of intermittent overcast and cold, stark sunlight, the little band traveled on. Although Katohya made no complaint, Xohkantakeh admitted to Ika that he had never seen a longer winter. The girl rejoiced in his renewed confidence and once again found cause to exalt in the beauty of the winter world and in the joy she found in being alive and a part of it. Each day she hefted her share of the band's load with eagerness, and when the dark came down, she curled up happily with the pups, silently offering invocations of thanksgiving to the black wolf whose death had allowed her to run once more within the circle of her father's life and favor.

Her dreams were untroubled. She saw herself as Little Bear again, and Xohkantakeh was Great Father Bear, the centering light in the firmament of her existence. As they prowled the night hunting for stars to eat, Ika was ever at his side, ready to be his eyes and ears and the strong, steady shaft of his spear if ever the Moon turned against him.

And so it was that she awoke refreshed each morning, happy to tussle with the pups and grateful for the meat of Great Paws that sustained them all. Even Quarana seemed changed by the power of the meat; if she objected to the cold and the rigors of the journey to which her dream had subjected the band, she did not speak of it. Indeed, New Woman did not seem to mind the cold. In the dark her man found ways to keep her warm, and often, during daylight, when pausing to rest in their journey, he would bid her come to him. While Katohya smiled in approval and Ika turned away, Quarana would close her eyes as the giant enveloped her within the skin of the great bear and filled her with the heat of his need. And always, even on the coldest mornings or when still moist from her man's most recent penetration, New Woman was the first to rise from her bed furs, for she who had been the laziest of daughters was now the most eager to assemble a meal, break down the lean-to, and continue on toward the hunting grounds of the ancestors.

Ika was amazed by the change in her sister. *Truly,* she thought, *shedding first blood and being mated* has *made a new woman of her!*

As the days passed, the girl found herself marveling at the sight of Quarana working willingly at Katohya's side. As she trudged ahead of her own sledge, carrying the pups on her back, Ika silently thanked the forces of Creation for her sister's transformation and was anxious for the day when they would be grown and strong enough to carry packs and pull sledges of their own—not for her sake or Quarana's, but for Katohya's. Although the older woman made no complaint about the cold and often broke into carefree song and easy laughter as she walked side by side with Quarana, the two women pulling their sledge together, it was becoming increasingly obvious to Ika that her beloved mother's health was failing. Rare was the morning when Katohya did not pale at the sight of bear meat and wave away her share of food, and often she turned a sickly green and slapped a hand to her mouth in an apparent effort to stifle retching when Xohkantakeh insisted that she eat.

"My woman is not well," worried the giant.

"It is only a passing weakness of the belly," Katohya assured him.

Ika was not assured. Kneeling inside the band's latest lean-to and chewing her morning's portion of smoked meat, she frowned as she looked at her mother. Katohya was sitting with her hands folded in her lap and her eyes turned down in obvious avoidance of the stares of her concerned family. Her face was as gray as the morning cloud cover, and there had been something slightly evasive about her tone. *Aiee,* thought Ika. *She is dying and does not want us to fear for her!*

Quarana gulped down the last of her meat. "I will eat my mother's portion if she has no appetite for it," she offered kindly.

Xohkantakeh, staring fixedly at Katohya from beneath a deeply furrowed brow, grimaced with displeasure at Quarana's greedy generosity. "New Woman will make a belly-easing drink for First Woman." The statement was a command. "Go, Quarana! Bring snow for the melting sack. Ika will raise fire. I will fetch dried goldenrod and the inner bark of willow from the medicine bag and—"

"No!" Katohya looked up with a start. "I would not drink such medicine now!"

His brows expanded. "Then *what?*"

"Nothing. I am well," she insisted. "My appetite will soon return."

"Hmm." His brow furrowed again; he was not convinced. "Ika, wrap your mother's portion of morning meat in a strip of oiled bear gut. She will carry it with her so that she may eat when she is hungry later."

Ika obeyed.

The lean-to was down, the hides and poles rolled and packed onto the sledges, and the band was ready to move on when the girl presented the neatly made packet of meat to Katohya.

"For you to eat later, my mother," said Ika with a smile

of relief. Her mother's eyes were shining, and the color was back in her face until Ika announced proudly that she had added a few good slices of fat to the packet and chosen the best chunk of meat—the one with the most green mold on it—and found herself staring haplessly as Katohya was suddenly and violently sick at her feet.

They journeyed north and west, then north again, following as close to the river as the changing contours of the land allowed. Moon, Mother of Stars, turned her full face to the world below and then looked away. A downcast Quarana informed Xohkantakeh that a hut of blood must be raised, and for the following three days and four nights of her menses she was confined in it. At dawn of the fifth day, the hut was burned and the new woman was cleansed in its ashes, and afterward Xohkantakeh raised her face to his and assured her that, if the forces of Creation so willed it, he would see to it that nine long moons would pass before she had need to ask again for the hut of blood to be raised.

The band moved on.

During long cold days of sunlight they walked, and when the dark came down they rested under stars that continued to promise the advent of spring. A night did not pass in which Xohkantakeh did not join with his new woman in hope of making life on her. And all during Katohya's waking hours, she smiled with happiness, or hummed to herself, or sang the old songs of her people, or invented new songs to suit the happenings of each passing day, for within her heart was a great and wondrous secret joy.

Now, as Katohya seated herself outside yet another newly raised lean-to, she could barely keep from blurting her secret aloud. Instead, knowing that the time was not yet right, she leaned against her backrest and, with a sigh of absolute contentment, bundled more deeply into her traveling robe. The day-end meal was done. And what a fine meal it had been! The wolf-dog pups had flushed a pair of hares. Xohkantakeh had struck both animals dead with well-hurled stones. Ika had rescued the carcasses before the ever-ravenous little pups had a chance to rip them to pieces. Katohya had skinned and prepared the hares for cooking. Quarana had roasted them in the way their man preferred his meat. And then they had all gathered to share the feast—including the pups, to whom went forelimbs and paws, noses, ears, and tails. There had not been much flesh on the hares, but what little there was had been fresh and running with nourishing juices, a welcome addition to the moldering, increasingly rank-smelling bear meat that turned Katohya's stomach even when the nausea that had been plaguing her each morning was not upon her.

She smiled. First Woman of Xohkantakeh would not complain of morning sickness. Indeed, she rejoiced in it as she offered a prayer of thanksgiving—not only as she did at each day's end, in delight of her secret joy and in gratitude to the great bear whose flesh sustained her and her loved ones on their journey—but to the hares, for the goodness of their meat and marrow and, most especially, because the patches of brown in their winter-white pelts told her that the stars were right: Spring was surely on the way!

Spring!

The time of the rising of the Warm Moon! The time when Owl and Ermine and Hare change from winter white to summer brown!

Spring! The time of birth and rebirth!

Shivering with anticipation, Katohya wrapped her arms around her folded knees and began to sing a happy little song, a cadence taught to her by her mother many years before.

> *"Nah ya! Hay hay ya!*
> *Nah ya hay ya hah!*
> *Hah ya! Ya hay nah!*
> *Nah ya hay hay ya!"*

The syllables left her lips in soft yet imperatively uttered phrases of precise and repetitive rhyming. The "words" had no actual meaning for her, nor, she knew, had they possessed definitive meaning for her mother. They were the song words of Red World Ancients, mystery sounds born of a long-forgotten language uttered by the mothers and grandmothers of her distant homeland since time beyond beginning.

"When a woman's joy is great and there are no words strong enough to speak her hope in the future, you must sing as the Grandmothers have taught us to sing, my daughter," her mother had counseled in the never-to-be-forgotten days of her girlhood. *"Sing in the way of the women of the Red World People since time beyond beginning! Sing and the ancestors will hear your song, rejoice in your gladness, and be at your side to keep all crooked, bad-luck-bringing spirits away from the living joy that you carry beneath your heart!"*

And so Katohya sang.

There was so much to sing about. *So much!*

Soon the sun would set. Another day of journeying was at an end. Her man and daughters remained safe and strong. She watched Quarana busily shaking and snapping the bed furs she shared with Xohkantakeh to air and freshen them before she spread them—and herself—for their man inside the lean-to. A giggle drew Katohya's gaze to Ika, who was attempting, as she did at each day's end, to teach the wolf-dog pups to carry the small side packs she had made for them under Xohkantakeh's instruction. Three of the four pups were coming along well with their lessons and were carrying their minimal burdens with what appeared to be a mixture of befuddlement and pride, but the largest, darkest, and most wolflike of the pups had managed to take hold of one end of a loose harness line and, growling ferociously, was tugging at it and circling furiously around and around.

"No!" cried Ika. "Release that line! Aiee, North Wind, what a stubborn pup you are! Stop, I say! What sort of example do you set for your brother and sisters?"

Katohya nodded with satisfaction. Ika's discovery of the pups had changed everything. Indeed, she doubted that any other omen could have portended better for their journey.

Soon the furry little foursome—each named for one of the Four Winds—would be carrying and hauling the major portion of the band's burdens in happy exchange for meat and friendship. As the pups frolicked with Ika in the light of the setting sun, Katohya squinted into the west. The way ahead, which at first she had so feared, no longer seemed strewn with shadows.

She sighed. Weariness was rising in her now. At her side was the willow-wood hoop upon which she had stretched the pelts of the hares. She lifted it, observed and admired her work. She had cut the wood from a nearby stand of young willows. The wood, smooth and pliable and blushing tawny-red with new sap, was not much thicker than a finger. She had trimmed it of budding stalks, then fastened it into a hoop with peelings of inner bark. As she had worked, the strong smell of sap promised the advent of spring as surely as the mottled pelage of the hares had. Katohya's heart had filled with gladness as she bound the pelts fast and rubbed the raw skins with a mixture of melted snow, pulverized hare brains, and ashes. How soft the skins would be when her skilled hands were finished with them! Now, stroking the furry side with her fingertips, she almost wept with pleasure when she thought of the purpose to which they would be put.

"May it be so!" said the First Woman of Xohkantakeh, drawing the hoop to her breast, closing her eyes and nearly drifting into dreams of yearning until the sound of a hammerstone striking rock caused her to open her eyes again.

Xohkantakeh had seated himself on a broad, flat boulder. By the last, lingering light of the setting sun he was chipping flakes from one of several chunks of fine, dark stone he had cut from a hillside they had passed. From these flakes he would make new spearheads for himself, and new perforators, fleshers, and all manner of tools for his women and daughter. Katohya's heart was full indeed as she watched him, so much so that she set aside her hoop and, wanting to encourage his work, began to sing an old, half-remembered song, weaving it of new words and old rhythms and a special strike-and-slide hand clapping that bespoke the knapper's art.

"Clap-slip!
I break!
I am stone!
I sing as I yield to the hand of Man!
Clap-slip!
I break!
I am stone!
I yield like Woman to the press of Man!
Clap-slip!
I break!
I am stone!
I am transformed into new life by the needs of Man!
Clap-slip!"

Xohkantakeh looked up, smiled, nodded in appreciation of her song, then turned back to his work. "It is good. The rhythm puts fire to my hands. Perhaps the stone will hear and feel this and, understanding my need, yield more quickly to its transformation!"

Katohya's face flushed. Perhaps the stone would hear and understand, but she could not comprehend how it was possible for the man not to have seen through to the truth behind the double meaning of her song. Sometimes she wondered if he heard as much as half the words she spoke to him; his concern for the band took all his concentration. Yet, even so, it amused her now to look at him and puzzle over how he—a man who had fathered sons and daughters in the Land of Grass—could have failed to recognize the signs that signaled the meaning of her secret joy or even suspect that he had struck life into the womb of one whom they had both thought barren as a stone until that night before the new-woman ceremony, when there had been lightning in his man bone and, despite her protests, Great Paws had not been denied!

"What is it, my mother?" asked Ika, coming close with the black pup, North Wind, balanced on one shoulder and the other three little wolf-dogs nipping at her moccasins. "Your face glows as though fever spirits are inside you. Are you feeling sick again?"

The girl looked so worried that Katohya felt guilty

about keeping her secret joy from the child. In time Ika would know. Until then, Katohya knew that she must wait until Xohkantakeh made sense of her morning sickness or another moon turned its full face to the earth and then looked away again. By then, if she still had no need to ask for a hut of blood to be raised, there would be no denying the cause of the hard, elongated swelling above her woman bone or the marked expansion and tenderness of her breasts. Not that Xohkantakeh would notice; it was not un-usual for Katohya to miss her monthly shedding of moon blood, and he sated his man need exclusively on Quarana—so often, in fact, that Katohya was surprised the new woman was not yet with child. Once that happened, the pleasures of the new woman's body would be forbid-den to Xohkantakeh, and—with his sexual appetite re-awakened by the spirit of the great bear that now prowled within him—he might once again come to pleasure him-self on his Sweet-Scented Woman. How foolish he would feel when he discovered that she was also forbidden to him. And how proud!

"My mother, are you so weak and sick that you can no longer speak to me?"

Katohya was surprised to see that Ika had peeled off a mitten and was kneeling before her, checking her brow for fever. She took the girl's hand and held it in her own. "You worry too much about me, Ika. Yes, I am tired, but has the day not been long for us all? I am not feeling sick. Indeed, I tell you now that I am feeling better than I ever hoped to feel again in all the days and nights of my life!"

"Truly?" pressed the girl, looking dubious and more than a little wan herself.

"Truly!" Katohya laughed with surprised delight as the black wolf-dog leaned from Ika's shoulder to give Ka-tohya's nose a slurping lick and a tickling nibble. An in-stant later the pup leaped onto her lap and made a lunge for the willow-wood hoop, only to be thwarted when Ka-tohya adroitly slipped the stretching frame behind her back. As it attempted to nose it out by burrowing behind her, the little animal's curling tail was up, and it was growling with determined ferocity when Katohya picked it up by the scruff of the neck. "There is more wolf than dog in you!" she informed the pup as she held it high while it squirmed and yapped in her grasp. "I think my Ika is right to have named you for the North Wind! What a squaller you are!"

"Xohkantakeh says that North Wind will be the biggest and strongest of our pack!" Ika said with motherly pride.

Katohya adjusted her position so that the stretching hoop and attached pelts were wedged tightly between the small of her back and the frame of her backrest before she placed the pup in her lap. A moment later its three siblings scrambled to join their brother in the hollow between Katohya's folded limbs. She smiled as she tussled them. "Long has it been since I dwelled in a camp in which there were dogs. I had forgotten the amusement to be found in raising pups. My sister, Mah-ree, had dogs, you know. A fine pack. In the last days of the great war between the tribes, when we first fled from our enemies beyond the edge of the world, there was sickness among the dogs, and our shaman, Chakwena, banished them from our band lest our people also sicken. They ran off into the forest and turned as wild as wolves. Your black wolf may have been the spawn of one of them, for there was much of dog song in her lonely cries. Perhaps she ran with one of them for many a long moon, until he met his end and she was left alone to birth these wolf-dog pups in this far land, crying to the leaders among the wolf kind in the night, hoping for eventual welcome among the pack."

"It must be so," said Quarana as she came to stand before her mother and sister with her arms laden with freshly aired bed furs. "Bear Slayer has said that there were no dogs in this land before First Man and First Woman, Mother and Father of all the generations of the People, came walking over the mountains of ice with dogs at their side."

A shadow fell upon Katohya's mood. The sun was going down, taking a small portion of her happiness with it. "I wonder where my sister and her shaman are now . . . if they are well . . . if they have children and—"

"They walk beyond the barrens with the sacred stone and the great white mammoth totem!" interrupted Ika with obvious awe. "Xohkantakeh says that Mah-ree and Cha-kwena have become like First Man and First Woman—guardians of the totem and of the sacred stone of the ancestors. They have to be well, my mother, because all the power of the Ancient Ones walks with them, and as long as they live, the People will live forever!"

Katohya hugged the girl. "I wish you could have known them, dear one. In many ways my sister, Mah-ree, looked like our new woman, but she was much like you. Not so tall, but strong as you are strong, and willful, too."

Ika lowered her eyes and said contritely, "I will be will-ful no more, my mother."

"We will see how long *that* lasts!" slurred Quarana, dropping the bulk of the bed furs at her sister's feet. "Help me with these, Ika. The day is done. The air grows cold. It is time for this new woman to rest."

"As though you were the only one deserving of it!" snapped Ika.

"I am the one who will bear sons to Xohkantakeh!" The young woman's declaration reeked of the smug, overstated authority she now habitually displayed toward her sister as part of her newly assumed rank. "What have you ever given to Bear Slayer except unnecessary argument, worry, and . . . and puppies!"

Ika's face paled at the insult. She seemed on the brink of a hot retort until distracted by the pups. The little wolf-dogs had vaulted from Katohya's lap. Pouncing on the fallen furs, they began a simultaneous attack. Ika's eyes widened. There, lying amidst the other furs, was the wonderful robe of twisted rabbit skins she had once yearned to possess. She reached out and gathered the little wolf-dogs into her arms. "No," she scolded gently. "You will not make war on the sleeping robe of New Woman. It was a gift to her from our mother!"

Katohya saw Ika's expression tighten as the girl fixed her sister with reproving eyes.

"These pups were a gift to Xohkantakeh from the forces of Creation!" Ika reminded Quarana. "These pups will someday pull the sledges and carry the loads of this band, including your burdens, New Woman, and those of the sons and daughters you will bear to Xohkantakeh! You have no cause to mock them . . . or me!"

Quarana's nose tilted upward. "In the Land of Grass the woman of Bear Slayer will have *real* dogs to pull her sledge and female slaves to carry her loads and answer her commands. Be careful of what you say to me, Ika, or maybe you will be one of them!"

Katohya was suddenly furious. "There will be no slaves at the hearth fire of Xohkantakeh in any camp in which *this* woman of Bear Slayer dwells!" She was aware of the giant pausing in his work to look askance toward his bickering females, but she was certain that he would stand with her in this, and so she brazened on. "As First Woman of our man, it is Katohya who warns Quarana that it is New Woman who must be careful of what she says to her sister! Through Ika's encounter with the black wolf, the forces of Creation have given a gift of great value to this band. What have you given, daughter? Yah! You have yet to prove your worth as a child bearer! So do not boast of that which has not yet come to be, New Woman, for it has been said by the Ancient Ones that the forces of Creation find their greatest amusement in teaching humility to the arrogant and boastful among the tribes of Man. Beware, Quarana—even now they may be listening! And even now they may well be preparing to make sport of you!"

That night the wind blew steadily from the northwest. It was a steady, bitter wind, and for the first time in many a long moon, there was a dampness to the air that somehow made the darkness colder. Huge, wet flakes of snow slapped across the world, as though in retribution for some wrongdoing that only the spirits of the wind might know of.

They reset the support posts of the lean-to twice that night to keep the shelter from collapsing beneath the weight of rapidly accumulating snow. And still the wind blew, and the wet snow fell, and within the lean-to, the moisture raised by their warm breaths and bodies condensed on the underside of the roof and began to drip upon the occupants and their belongings. The women and daughter of Xohkantakeh took from their pack rolls rain cloaks, made from the oiled intestines of large grazing animals, and fastened them to the undersides of the support posts to create a waterproof liner. The giant slung on his own rain cape and went into the storm to cut branches from nearby evergreens. When he had set these as additional insulation and baffling around and over the little shelter, Xohkantakeh shook off his cape and reentered the lean-to.

With undisguised disgust he told his family, "Keep the pups close. Snow slops upon the land and adheres to the trees like so much mucus blown from the nose of the White Giant Winter. Already it is above my knees, and the trees are bending so low they are ready to snap. The air grows colder. And snow is still falling fast. Before dawn ice will come. There will be no traveling tomorrow."

"But we *must* travel, Bear Slayer!" protested Quarana. "The hunting grounds of the Ancient Ones are far away, and if we are to reach the land of many helping hands before ice melts upon—"

"Perhaps the White Giant Winter will never go away," surmised Ika.

"He will go when he is ready," Xohkantakeh assured them. He drew both his women, his daughter, and the wolf-dog pups close beside him beneath the great bearskin. "It must have been like this in the time beyond beginning . . . a world of ice and snow and constant wind and cold . . . a world in which White Giant Winter was chieftain over all . . . a world in which the mountains walked and ice flowed upon the land like rivers."

"And First Man and First Woman must have sheltered together with their children and dogs within a lean-to not unlike this one," added Katohya.

Quarana shivered. "It must have been a hard cold life for First Woman, with no one to help her with her work."

"First Woman had First Man," Ika reminded her. "Why would she need anyone else? We need no one as long as our own First Man is here to keep us warm and safe in his power!"

The lean-to shivered as a gust of wind struck it.

Again Quarana shivered; in the darkness no one could see her scowl as she closed her eyes and asked sulkily, "Tell a time-beyond-beginning tale, Katohya. In the cold dark while the White Giant Winter is being sick all over us, let your words take us into dreams."

"And what tale shall I tell you, New Woman?"

"The tale of the coming of First Man and First Woman from the world beyond this world, following Life Giver, the great white mammoth totem, over mountains of ice, through corridors of storm, across forbidden lands into the land of—"

"No!" Ika interrupted again. "Tell us the story of how Wolf and Man were born of the same clan, and of how Dog was born of an ember and chose to walk with Man."

"That is your father's tale," demurred Katohya. "Among my Red World People there were no dogs, until men of the northern tribes brought them to us. Would you also hear this tale, Quarana?"

New Woman yawned. "If my Bear Slayer would tell it."

"Hmm." Xohkantakeh thought a moment, then conceded: "It is a night for tale-telling, and so, yes, let me begin:

"In time beyond beginning, in the days when the Animals and People were of one tribe, Wolf and Man were of the same clan. Together they hunted. Together they fed. Together they made young. Together they sang praise songs to Moon and Sun and to the Four Winds and forces of Creation. In peace did they dwell within the great Circle of Life, sharing meat and women and telling tales of time beyond beginning to their children even as I tell such a tale to you

now. Then came a day—and no man or wolf knows why—
two among the clan stood tall and faced each other within
the great Circle of Life and challenged each other over who
should be chief over the hunting grounds. The two fought.
The sons of one joined the father. The sons of the other
joined their father. Soon the women took sides, and even the
children joined in the battle until nearly all were dead. Yet
the two fought on, finding joy and challenge in outwitting
each other, until the great Circle of Life was awash in the
blood of the clan and the forces of Creation looked down
from the black robe of Father Above and cried:

"'You will stop this fighting among yourselves! There is
no need for one among you to be chief over the hunting
grounds! Within the great Circle of Life there is game
enough for all!'

"But the two would not listen. The fighting went on until
at last the forces of Creation called forth Lightning to strike
the two. In that moment a great chasm opened in the earth
between them, and both were transformed forever.

"'If you cannot look at one another and know that you
are of one clan, then see only what you will of one another
and be enemies forever . . . two tribes separated by a
chasm that will condemn you to walk two paths upon the
same earth, fighting for the same game, and never knowing peace until the ending of all days!' said the forces of
Creation.

"And that is how the Man Tribe came to have two legs
and hairless bodies, like ours, while the Wolf Tribe came to
have four legs and fur, like these pups. And so it is that
when Man and Wolf look at one another, each sees
Stranger, as it was on that first day when they stared across
the chasm that their fighting had set between them.

"'Who is this beast with naked flesh, flat face, and only
two limbs to walk on?' asked Wolf of Man.

"'Who is this beast with hairy skin, long snout, and too
many legs to walk on?' asked Man of Wolf.

"'Ha!' said Wolf, and spoke his name. 'This hair will
keep me warm in the cold wind and keep biting flies from
my flesh when the wind is down and warm. My long snout

will scent prey when it is yet too far away for my eyes to see, and my four limbs will be as fleet as the limbs of the grazing animals whose flesh is meat for me!'

"'Ha!' said Man, and spoke his name. 'The skins of the beasts I kill will keep me warm in the cold wind and keep biting flies from my flesh when the wind is down and warm. My flat face hides a mind as sharp as your teeth. And my two limbs are stronger than your four and hold me upright so that I will see my prey before your long snout has smelled it!'

"'And what will you hunt, Man, running upright within the great Circle of Life with no pads to cushion your steps and neither fangs nor claws to tear your meat?'

"'I will hunt Mammoth and Long-Horned Bison and Musk Ox and Great Hook-Nosed Deer! I will hunt Elk. I will hunt Caribou. Within the great Circle of Life, all of these prey animals will consent to send their old and weak and unfit young to be meat for Man!'

"'Ha! This is Wolf's meat also, and so, too, is it the meat of Fox and Raven who walk and fly in Wolf's shadow to partake of the leavings of my feasts.'

"'Ha!' said Man. 'Only if I, Man, wish to share the leavings of my feasts with Wolf!'

"'Ha!' said Wolf to Man, lifting his lips to show his teeth. 'Naked Beast with little fangs and no claws is an arrogant, half-formed thing unfit to dwell within the great Circle of Life, much less to say who among the Animals will share his meat!'

"Now these words of Wolf enflamed the anger of Man. He looked down upon his naked skin and exposed belly and genitals, and he ground his little teeth and flexed his claws that are to this day as thin and fragile as the first ice of autumn upon a summer pond. And it was in this moment that Man knew that the words of Wolf were true words, for even in his arrogance Man could see with his own eyes that within the great Circle of Life he among all the Animals had not been favored by the forces of Creation.

"And so Man said to Wolf, 'Beware, Wolf who was

once my brother, for I will hunt *you* within the great Circle of Life! I will take your hair and strong teeth and claws and use them for my good and the good of my children!'

"And Wolf said back to Man, 'Beware, Man who was once my brother, for in the winter dark when the world grows cold and there is little meat, I will hunt you within the great Circle of Life and take the soft flesh that lies beneath your naked skin to be meat for my good and the good of my children!'

"In that moment the forces of Creation were so wearied of the combative two that they sent the Four Winds to take away their bickering words. When the hateful words of Man and Wolf were scattered beyond the great Circle of Life, Man and Wolf stared at each other across the chasm their hatred had made.

"Man shouted. Wolf growled. Each spoke his hatred of the other, but their talk was no longer the same talk, and Wolf could not understand the words of Man, nor could Man understand the words of Wolf. Yet each knew that the other had taken a new name, and that name was Enemy.

"And so it is between Man and Wolf to this very day. Although we dwell together within the great Circle of Life and our hearts and spirits respond to the same clan rhythms, Wolf howls to Moon in the language of his kind while Man sings to Sun in the language of his. It is the same song; only the way of singing it is different. And now, as in time beyond beginning, Man and Wolf remain separated forever by the chasm that our warrior spirits have set between us."

"And the hunting grounds of Dog," Ika said, breathless with anticipation of her favorite part of the tale. "Tell us of how the Dog kind came to walk with the People instead of with the Wolf kind, my father!"

"Ah, the coming of Dog into the Circle of Life . . . Yes, it is a portion of the birth tale of Wolf and Man. And it begins like this . . ." Xohkantakeh allowed the words to drift and settle before continuing slowly, smoothly, in the way he had learned long ago from the tale-tellers of his youth. "In time beyond beginning, in the days when the Animals and People were of one tribe, Dog was born as an ember cast off from both Wolf and Man when Lightning struck and transformed the two forever. While Wolf and Man argued across the chasm, there was Dog, floating in the chasm . . . a glowing, red-hot, four-legged, long-snouted, hairy thing that howled like Wolf but screamed in the tongue of Man.

"'Put out the fire that burns me!' cried Dog.

"And Wind rose. North Wind! South Wind! East Wind! West Wind! All the Four Winds came together to lift Dog out of the chasm and into the sky, where they turned him around and around until the fire that burned him was put out.

"'I thank you,' said Dog, for his way from time beyond beginning has been one of agreeability and politeness.

"And seeing that Dog looked more like Wolf than Man, the Four Winds began to lower Dog into the great Circle of Life on the side of the chasm close to where Wolf was standing. But when Wolf saw that Dog's burned tail curled up like a singed sapling over his flank, and that Dog's hair had been changed by fire to the color of ashes in a fire pit that has been long used by different bands carrying different kinds of wood and fire stones, Wolf growled and said, 'The mark of Man is on that Wolf! No brother of mine will ever walk beside me with a curling tail!' And in disgust of Dog, Wolf turned and loped away.

"'Wait!' cried Dog as he landed on all fours in the footprints that Wolf had left in the ashes of Dog's creation.

"But Wolf did not wait, because Dog had spoken in the voice of Man.

"And Dog, his feelings hurt and his fur still smoking and his tail still curled up like a singed sapling over his flank, stood looking after Wolf until he heard the turn of Man's heel and called out, 'Wait, Naked Beast with little fangs and no claws! Would you also leave me alone in the great Circle of Life?'

"Man stopped. He turned and looked long and hard at Dog, then said, 'Your hair is the color of an old fire pit, and your tail curls like a singed sapling over your flank, but the look of Wolf is on you, Four-Legged Beast! The forces of Creation have placed you on the far side of the chasm. It is clear that you will be no brother of Man!'

"'But what will you hunt, Naked Beast, running upright and alone within the great Circle of Life with no pads to cushion your steps and neither fangs nor claws to tear your meat? Better for you if Dog runs at your side, to scent and flush the game and to stand with you against Wolf when he comes for your children in the winter dark.'

"And Man thought about this and said, 'If Dog would do this for Man, he must leap the chasm to show the straight way of his heart. Do this and Man will name you Brother, and we will walk and hunt together in the great Circle of Life.'

"And without another thought or a moment of hesitation, Dog leaped. High and wide Dog leaped. In a great reaching arc such as a spear takes when hurled by the strongest of men from the most perfectly balanced spear hurler, Dog hurled himself forward . . . and *almost* made the other side."

"Almost?" exclaimed Ika.

"It is so," Xohkantakeh affirmed, clucking his tongue. "The chasm between Man and Animal was wide. Too wide! Dog's front paws touched the far edge of the chasm, but the rest of him landed short." Again he paused, allowed the words to steep and settle before continuing.

"Now, we know that Dog is as strong as Wolf and as brave of heart. And so it was that Dog gripped the edge of the chasm with his forepaws and dug in with his claws and clung with his hind parts dangling. From out of the black bottomless belly of Mother Below, a voice as deep and dark as the chasm spoke his name. 'Dog! Come to me, Dog, born of an accidental spark struck by Lightning when it sundered Man and Wolf. Come, I say! You were not meant to run within the great Circle of Life! There is no place for you with either Wolf or Man!'

"Poor dog!" sighed Katohya.

"And so," agreed Xohkantakeh. "For the voice that called to Dog was the voice of Mother Below. To deny her command was to defy one of the forces of Creation, but Dog

was newly born and did not know this, nor could he understand why he should be called to end his life before he had
so much as a chance to begin it! So Dog clung to the edge of
the chasm and tried to pull himself up even as Mother Below began to shake and try to force him down. Brave was
Dog! But strong was the shaking of Mother Below—so
strong that Man's two legs went out from under him and he
fell upon the earth. Soon Dog felt himself slipping, and with
a terrible yowling yip that only the dog kind can make, Dog
lost his hold!"

"Aiee!" exclaimed Ika and Katohya as one, and even
Quarana caught her breath and levered up in the darkness.

"What happened next, my fa . . . Bear Slayer?" she
implored.

"Ah . . ." Again Xohkantakeh allowed the tension of his
tale to steep in silence until it was stretched so taut he dared
not hold back his words an instant longer. "Dog fell, but
Man reached!"

Katohya sighed with relief.

"Yes!" declared Xohkantakeh. "Man leaned over the
edge of the chasm, took Dog by the curl of his tail, and held
him fast even as Wolf heard the cries of Man and Dog and
found himself concerned for their safety.

"'How can this be?' Wolf wondered as he ran on.
'Within the great Circle of Life, I have turned my back on
Man and Dog, and yet are we not made from one flesh and
one bone? And if Man and Dog fall from the Circle of Life,
will a portion of Wolf not fall with them? Yah! I must see! I
must know!'

"And so Wolf turned and raced to the chasm that separated him from Man and Dog and arrived just in time to hear
Mother Below command Naked Beast, 'Release the tail of
that which is only an ember sundered from Wolf and Man!
Obey me, Naked Beast, and I will forget that you are also
but a half-formed thing unfit to dwell within the great Circle
of Life!'

"But as Wolf watched from the far side of the chasm,
Man held on to the tail of Dog and would not let go, for although he had no claws or fangs or pads to cushion his bare
feet upon the hunt, behind his flat face Man's mind was as

sharp as the teeth of Wolf. And so Man dared ask of Mother Below—and in the asking echo the question of Wolf—"If Dog is but an ember sundered from the flesh of both Wolf and Man, which part of him shall I allow to fall? For I would not allow that portion of Dog that is of the flesh and bone of Man to perish, lest a portion of this Naked Beast also die forever!'

"Now, the words of Man were clever words, and Mother Below, recognizing the trick in them, roared in anger until Wolf crouched low and Dog, still dangling by his tail, looked up at Man and said sadly, 'I thank you, Naked Beast, but you must release my tail or you will die with Dog on this first day of both our lives!'

"But without another thought or a moment of hesitation, Man said to Dog, 'Dog has risked his life to leap the chasm that separates him from Man, and all so that this Naked Beast would not go lonely or hungry in the winter dark! Dog has shown the straight way of his heart. Man will not do less for one who has shown himself to be a brother!'

"'So be it, then!' said Dog.

"'Yah!' declared Mother Below, moved by the selfless loyalty of Man to Dog and of Dog to Man—for, to her nurturing heart, this was proof of their worthiness to run within the Circle of Life. 'You will live!' she decreed. 'Each at the side of the other, you will run forever. Together Man and Dog will be the equal of Wolf!' And with a mighty shrug Mother Below tossed Dog and Man out of the chasm and onto the surface of her skin.

"And Wolf looked at them across the chasm.

"'Come!' invited Man.

"'Join us, my brother!' invited Dog.

"But Wolf, standing in the ashes of Dog's creation, said, 'Yes, you are the brothers of my blood and bone, but if I leap the chasm and run with you within the great Circle of Life, where will I find worthier enemies to challenge me on the hunting grounds that I have claimed as my own?'

"'You will find none,' said Man. 'Nor will there be joy for Naked Beast in the great Circle of Life if there is no Wolf to challenge me as I run within it.'

"'Let it be so, then.' And Wolf stepped from the edge of

the chasm and turned away, consenting Brother and Enemy from that day to this.

"But Dog put up his long-snouted head and, with his tail curled like a singed sapling over his ash-and-fire-colored flank, called Wolf back with the loudest, saddest howling that has ever been uttered by a dog from that day to this. 'Would you leave your four-legged brother alone with Naked Beast forever?'

"'Dog has chosen with whom he will run!' said Wolf, looking back. 'But Dog will remember me when the blood of Wolf rises in him! And on that day, leap the chasm again if you can and if you dare. Your brother and Enemy will be waiting to welcome you!'

"Now, these were strong words, and in that moment Dog looked at himself and saw more Wolf than Man. 'Wait!' Dog cried and would have leaped the chasm then and there to run with Wolf within the Circle of Life forever.

But Man held Dog fast by his tail and said, 'Dog must stay at the side of Man. Together we will be the equal of Wolf as we run forever as brothers within the Circle of Life. The forces of Creation have decreed it so! And Naked Beast will not let you go!'

"And so it is that from that long-gone time to this, Dog and Man have walked together, brothers and enemies of Wolf. But Dog has never again uttered a word to Man in the language of Naked Beast, and at night Dog will answer the call of Wolf when he hears it . . . and run to him if he can and if he dares."

"As the black wolf who carried the blood of Dog in her veins called to the wolf pack and asked it to allow her and her wolf-dog pups to run with the wolf kind," said Katohya.

"Even so," Xohkantakeh agreed with a yawn, for the tale was over now, and sleep was heavy on his lids. "Such is the way of dogs and of wolves . . . since time beyond beginning."

"It will not be the way of these pups," said Ika, lying on her side, curled protectively around the sleeping animals as she herself began to drift into dreams. "Let Wolf howl! The children of the black wolf will not know his song. They are of Xohkantakeh's band now. They will not run away."

Lying close to Xohkantakeh, Quarana closed her eyes and sent her small hand seeking beneath his shirt, across his bare belly and into the warm, furred flesh above his man bone. "Sometimes I dream of wolves . . . of a black wolf. Hmm . . . Be a wolf with me now . . ."

But the giant, wearied from the long day's trek and the exertions of maintaining a storm camp, turned away from her hand and, with a sigh, gave himself to sleep.

"He is Bear . . . not Wolf," Katohya reminded her gently. "Let him sleep, New Woman. Even a man with the spirit of the great bear living in his body needs his rest. As do you, daughter. Rest. Sleep. If the forces of Creation are willing, there will be new life in this camp sooner than any of us dare dream of."

4

Warakan had come far.

Sister Wolf was tired. The young man worried about her. Her appetite was poor, she suffered from a hacking cough, and she had lost the desire to flush game. All too often she lay down in the sledge traces, put her head on her forepaws, and stared after Warakan until he became aware of her absence, turned, and looked back along the way he had come.

"All right, old friend. We will rest again."

And so they sat together in the snow, young man and old wolf, and Warakan rubbed her skin and spoke words of encouragement until she rose of her own accord and the trek toward the high gorge and the land of the ancestors began again.

Days were as often clear as cloudy. When fog closed in, it no longer iced the trees; instead it sighed a thin, dewlike drizzle that bordered on snow but never quite froze, and bore the scent of rain. When the sun shone it was a warmer sun than Warakan had seen in many a long moon, and although there were now few hardwoods to be found amidst the evergreens, he could not help but notice that buds were swelling on every bare branch. The sound of meltwater running deep beneath the snowpack was as pervasive as the sound of a rising river.

"The White Giant Winter is leaving this land," Warakan observed, unsure if he should rejoice or lament, for although he longed for warmth and dreamed of the sun-struck grasslands of home, travel across the disintegrating snowpack was becoming even more difficult than he had feared. His snow walkers served him only in the frigid hours of evening and early morning; once the sun was high they clumped with snow and grew so heavy that he had to stop again and again to kick the webbing clean. He soon despaired of this, slung the snow walkers over his back, and went on. All too often his moccasined feet broke through the surface crust, and he found himself wallowing through knee-deep drifts that seemed intent on holding him captive. But Warakan would not be held.

He rested when the sun was high and traveled in the cold, thin light of dusk and deep into the blue shadows of morning. When darkness came down upon the world, Moon and her star children lit his way. When clouds obscured the sky, he wished upon the sacred stone for the spirits of the Ancient Ones to light his way, and, as often as not, his wish was granted.

"I *am* Shaman!" Warakan told Sister Wolf. He thought of Jhadel, feeling the old man's disapproving presence, and wondered if the spirit of the ancient Peacedreamer was not somehow conspiring with the forces of Creation to slow his progress across the land.

"No matter!" he growled to the wolf and to whatever spirits of the air might be listening. "The White Giant will leave this land when he sees fit. The Warm Moon will rise when it will. And Warakan will *not* be turned from his intent!"

The days and nights wore on.

"Soon the sledge will be useless," he conceded. He picked up the faltering old wolf and placed her on it. "My stride will be longer without you walking at my side, and you might as well ride while you can."

Shouldering the traces, he dragged the sled on. There was ample room for the wolf now, for they had long since consumed the largest portion of the moose meat, and Sister Wolf took pleasure in being carried, sitting up in a way that made Warakan think of an old grandmother of the

People taking her leisure while the man of her band dragged her along and, by so doing, displayed the respect and veneration that was her due after a long and productive life.

The comparison amused him. He did not mind carrying the old animal; indeed, in his yearning for human companionship he talked to her and engaged in daydreams that transported his mind to another plane of existence as he trudged doggedly onward across the rapidly deteriorating surface of the snowpack. He imagined that Sister Wolf was not a wolf at all—and most assuredly not an old grandmother of the People—but his young, dimpled, and most beloved Mah-ree of the Red World.

"Rest now upon the sledge, and I will bear you back into the land of the Three Tribes, woman of Warakan!" he assured the figment of his longings with a magnanimity that made his heart swell with pride, as though all that he was destined to accomplish had already come to pass.

"You must be weary after your long ordeal upon the barrens, Mah-ree, but fear not, this son of Two Tribes has rescued you from the shaman who dared steal you from me! With magic spears tipped with stone heads of white chalcedony Warakan has slain the great white mammoth totem. And now, invincible in the power of the meat and blood of Life Giver, and strong in the power of the sacred stone of the ancestors, I have made an end of the shaman Cha-kwena!"

He smiled. His words were heady, as intoxicating as the fermented drink of blood, berries, and fungi that poured from the bladder skins of his people on feast days at the end of autumn hunts. Warakan let his mind steep in the conjured liquor of his imagination as he slogged on across the snow, his body strengthened by resolve and longing.

"Yes! Jhadel swore that all this was not to be, but I have proved old Peacedreamer wrong. Cha-kwena has had my Mah-ree long enough. He should not have stood against me to keep you or to protect the totem. How we fought! How poorly he died! But, of course, how else could it have been for him when I—Warakan, son of

Masau, Mystic Warrior and high priest of the People of the Watching Star, and grandson of Shateh, shaman and high chief of the People of the Land of Grass—used the power of the sacred stone to track and slay the mammoth in the mountains of ice that rise out of the lake that is the Mother of All Rivers? Warakan is no longer the young boy Jhadel took into his care, whom Cha-kwena once dismissed as a child of no value.

"No! Warakan is now a man! And Cha-kwena was old when I killed him! Ah, yes, so very old, needing perhaps as many as three times a double hand-count of fingers to count his years, when I laughed in his dying face and ate his flesh and danced in his skin, in the way my people have danced in the skins of their enemies since our tribe was born out of the Watching Star in the time beyond beginning!"

He stopped. The fervor of his imagining cooled. Still leaning into the traces of the sledge, he shivered in revulsion. He could not recall a time when boasting in the face of loneliness or fear had not brought surcease to his all-too-often troubled spirit, but now—remembering how, as a mere stick of a boy, he had fled to his grandfather's People of the Land of Grass to escape the ruthless cruelty and cannibalistic rituals of his father's People of the Watching Star—he could almost smell the high, rank stink of human meat and was taken up short by his own misstated bravado.

"No. I will *not* eat of the flesh or dance in the skin of the shaman Cha-kwena, but I *will* kill him if he tries to stop me from slaying the totem and taking Mah-ree, the woman of my heart, to be my own!"

"Kya!" The screech of an eagle came from thin air.

Startled, Warakan looked up; there was nothing there.

"You have eaten the eyes of Eagle, and yet you will not see!"

He caught his breath as he waved a hand before his face to defend against a plummeting raptor that was not there. Yet somehow he felt the rush of its wings and the hard, sharp strike of its talons. And suddenly, as happened more and more during these long days and nights of solitude, Warakan was shaken by a rush of memory that momentarily seemed to transport him to another place and time.

He was a boy again, brash and brazen, sitting before Mah-ree and Jhadel in the musty little lodge the lost and wounded young woman had briefly shared with them until the shaman Cha-kwena had come to reclaim her as his own.

"Your man is a yellow wolf!"

Warakan winced. The words of his own boyhood anger had flown at him out of time. One gloved hand rose to the bearskin robe that covered his chest. Deep beneath the press of his mittened palm, his heart hurt, as it had then, at the thought of Mah-ree leaving him, perhaps forever, to walk with a man who was little more than a stranger.

"Warakan will be your man!" The cry tore from his throat.

"This woman already has a man . . . an always-and-forever man," the long-lost woman of his daydream told him.

"No! Your man is Trickster, brother of Coyote! How can you want to go with him? I tell you, strong in the power of the sacred stone, I will hunt the totem! I will take the magic of its blood and flesh into myself. Then *I* will be totem! And before I return to the land of my ancestors to make war upon all those who killed my father and grandfather and sister, I will take the skin of Yellow Wolf and dance in it, and you *will* be my woman!"

"Ah!" Warakan exhaled, shaken not only by the sharpness of the remembered boasts but by the sudden awareness of the vast distances of time that separated the boy who had shouted them and the man who had voiced an echo of their intent only moments ago.

"Beware of what you say, Twig of a Boy!" cautioned the long-lost woman of his daydream. "The spirits of the wind hear all things, and the forces of Creation can turn words back onto the tongue of a careless speaker like the teeth of a dog biting its own tail!"

Mah-ree's warning came back to him in all its fervor

as the wind made him straighten and turn. Was that the stench of flayed corpses entering his nostrils? Impossible! But surely nothing else could be so foul. He wondered if the phantoms he had conjured on the high plateau had returned as punishment for his outspoken boastfulness, clad in the skins of his loved ones with full intent to add his skin to theirs. But the sun was high, the day was warm, and the wind, although mild, was bringing him the stench not of flayed human corpses but of rotting moose meat.

He looked at the sledge. The aroma of putrefying meat was rising through the moose-hide tarpaulin that covered it. The scent had stirred Sister Wolf from her lethargy, and she was now groaning with delight as she rubbed herself against the hide as though its essence were as lovely as sweet grass in the spring.

"Ah! The cold has masked the worst of the smell until now!" Warakan declared. Along with other unpleasant memories of his boyhood tribe, he recalled with no small measure of disgust his people's predilection for the rank scent and soft texture of meat that had been set aside to "sweeten" with age, a preference he had never shared.

"Perhaps I am less of a wolf than they, and surely less of a wolf than you, my sister." Warakan watched the animal rub her snout back and forth on the reeking hide, then roll onto her back, twist to and fro, and, with paws flopping skyward, bathe herself in the rising essence of foul meat. At last, with a shiver of ecstasy, she vaulted from the sledge and came to his side, lifting her long dark lips in a toothy smile as she nudged his hand.

"How can you smile at me when you smell like that?" he asked. "And how can the stink of that meat be more nourishing to you than the meat itself?"

They went on.

The land was changing, rising in high-breasted, stone-nippled hills and falling into deep-bellied, boulder-filled hollows. The snowpack was broken now; it sprawled in irregular patches over broad stretches of barren scree upon which the forest stood in oddly configured islands. In some places it was composed entirely of saplings, while in others it was a confusing jumble of grotesquely shaped and stunted evergreens rising amidst broken and fallen ancients that appeared mangled as though by the press of monstrous jaws.

Warakan was disconcerted by the land and sky. He knew he had reached the edge of the barrens. Where earth and stone lay free of snow, a raw, bitterly astringent smell hung in the air, as though the skin of Mother Below had been scraped to the bone and, only beginning to heal and scab over with lichen and tender moss, was exuding the scent of her mysterious wounding. On clear days, as Warakan and Sister Wolf trudged on, the young man found the smell of the land nearly as oppressive as the stink of ripening moose meat, and there seemed to be too much sky above his head—a heavy, humid, coldly brooding and somnolent sky that seemed to press him down and make him feel small, vulnerable, and more alone than ever before, especially when, every now and then, he came across a familiar assembly of boulders, or an old fire circle he and Jhadel had made on their journey southward in search of the sun and warmer climes.

"Ah, Sister Wolf, do you remember this place?"

The wolf cocked her head, whining softly, in the way of making agreeable conversation.

"Here old Peacedreamer and I stoned the fat ground-dwelling birds whose feathers turn white with the approach of the White Giant Winter. Ah! They waddled right up to us, as though they had never seen men with lances before. And then they saw you, my sister . . . too late! What a feast that was!"

They settled in to pass a night at the old campsite. Nibbling on putrid moose meat and bundling close together against the natural windbreak of a single mammoth-sized boulder, Warakan eyed the many young trees that had sprouted from the stony earth since he had last encamped here. After a moment he found himself musing aloud, "So many young trees . . . but no new boulders. Hmm. Among the People of the Land of Grass, the old storytellers used to say that stones and boulders grew from the earth in the same way as trees and green growing things, sprouting from seeds of grit blown by the Four Winds, then maturing so slowly that the eyes of a man can never live long enough to see their growth. This boulder against which we sit must be very old. Hmm. It must have set seed in the time beyond beginning to have grown so huge! First Man and First Woman may well have sat in this very place, and have looked upon it as a stoneling. I wonder. Then again, Jhadel once told me that the wise men among the shamans of the People of the Watching Star said that the great stones and boulders walked here by themselves in the company of mountains of living ice. It was in the time of the grandfathers' grandfathers. Hmm. Jhadel himself said that he knew a man who had seen the mountains of ice slipping over the land . . . I wonder. What do you think, old friend?"

The wolf was snoring.

Warakan sighed. He was growing sleepy. The stars, gleaming through a thin haze, told him that he was viewing a springtime sky and that he was, indeed, on the pathway home. It was a comforting assurance. He dozed until the moon rose, bright and nearly full. Its light, lancet sharp, penetrated his lids and woke him. The old wolf slept on, undisturbed, but Warakan stared across moonlit distances and, with a start, saw a monstrous white mass of cloud looming along the entire northern horizon. He caught his breath, realized in an instant that what he saw was no cloud; it was ice, a towering mountain range of ice, and there, standing in the moonlight between him and the edge of that far northern world of frozen peaks, pale shapes were shifting and taking form, staring at him with the eyes of men fixed in the faces of gaunt and hungry lions.

He grabbed a moose-bone lance and leaped to his feet.

The lions turned tail and disappeared into rising mists that had already obliterated the mountains of ice. Suddenly sagging with relief, Warakan realized he had been dreaming.

The mists rose, congealed into a creeping fog that lay

writhing upon the land until well past dawn. The young
man cursed the damp and went his way until the noon sun
burned the mists away and the old wolf's step slowed and
whatever energy she drew from the stink of spoiling meat
was spent. Much as he yearned to hurry on, Warakan felt
weariness growing in his own bones. He knew he needed to
hunt again, not only to obtain fresh meat but to consume
blood and marrow and guts—for without these portions of
a kill neither man nor wolf could long hope to maintain
strength, much less survive. Besides, now that the moose
meat had gone past the point of ripening, he was not sure
how much longer he was going to be able to bring himself
to eat it.

"Ah, but I must eat of the meat of that kill until there is
no more it!" he lamented with a despairing shrug. "If I do
not, I will offend the spirit of Great Hook-Nosed Grandfather of All Deer, for he has yielded his life to me so that
Sister Wolf and I may live on in his place within the great
Circle of Life. But perhaps the spirit of Moose will not be
insulted if I take a little fresh meat to supplement the food
he has so generously given."

And so, although the day was young, Warakan prepared to make a hunting camp on high, open ground close
to a natural windbreak of good-sized conifers. He upended
the sledge, laid the moose hide upside down over a sapling
to air, then—after feeding the wolf and deciding to fast until he took fresh game—respectfully hung the remaining
slabs of reeking moose meat from the branches of a nearby
spruce to keep them safe from predators. Briefly it occurred to him that he would not be sorry if some small
nocturnal predator came creeping through the trees to
make an end of that which so revolted him, but he quickly
put the thought from his mind, for he knew it to be a griev-
ous insult to the spirit of Great Hook-Nosed Grandfather
of All Deer.

With the wolf at his side, he waded into the woods, set a
few snares in promising places, and looked about, without
success, for signs of large game. Long before dusk, a cold,
wet fog drove him back to camp. Gathering his few belongings close, he draped the moose hide over the sledge and, in

the hollow space between the bone backboard and the heavy hide, the young man and the old wolf took shelter from the damp.

The fog thickened.

A low, distant rumbling came through the gathering mists. Both Warakan and Sister Wolf tensed as, far beneath the snowpack, the permafrost trembled. Instinctively the young man knew that the rumbling had not been born in the throat of a mammoth or mastodon, or of any other animal that walked within the Circle of Life. Nor had it been the voice of Thunder.

"Mother Below is restless. It is often so with her in the spring," Warakan explained to the wolf. Remembering the violence of past earthquakes, he curled his hand around the sacred stone. "Be with us, First Man and First Woman. Keep us safe. And bring meat to our snares this night, for the land of the ancestors is yet far from this place, and we need strength if we are to reach it!"

Long did they lie together in gathering gloom, waiting for the voice of Mother Below to rumble again, anticipating the slightest shiver of her skin, but the mists were silent and the earth was still, and soon they were both asleep.

Night came down upon the world.

A pair of owls *ooh-ooh*ed to one another in the gray darkness. Neither Warakan nor Sister Wolf heard their cries. The old wolf lay close in the embrace of the young man, twitching now and then and flopping her paws as dreams took her chasing rabbits and happily digging for deer mice. Outside the warm caul of their lean-to, moisture licked at the moose hide and condensed upon the trees, dripping and pooling like rain upon the uneven surface of the snowpack and eventually bringing the stink of rotting meat to ground.

Sister Wolf smiled in her sleep.

Warakan pulled the bearskin over his head and pressed his face into its warm, tawny fur to keep the stench of putrid meat from his nostrils. In his dreams he saw himself burying the meat in a pit in the snow, piling rocks over it, and going on his way until Great Hook-Nosed Grandfather of All Deer blocked his forward passage across the land and spoke with the voice of Jhadel.

"I have given up my life so that you would be nourished. You must honor my meat. In the way of the Ancient Ones since time beyond beginning, Son of Two Tribes and Sister Wolf must eat all the flesh they have cut from my bones! If they hunt for fresh meat and leave the last of my flesh for the lowliest carrion eaters of the earth, the spirit of Great Hook-Nosed Grandfather of All Deer will walk not with Man and Wolf but with worms and larvae. Aiee! I have yielded my life to Man and Wolf so that my spirit would be honored in death. Is this how my sacrifice is to be rewarded?"

Warakan pressed a mittened hand against his nostrils and, in his dream, sat down to finger up soft green meat until, feeling sick, he called upon the spirits of the sacred stone to make the revolting obligation go away.

It was then that a loud cracking and feline screech woke the dreamers.

The wolf's head went up, a low growl resonating at the back of her throat.

Warakan held his breath as he slung an arm around her to keep her from vaulting forward.

Something was moving outside. *Something.* Warakan could feel his heart pounding as his left hand fumbled for the lance he had laid by his side before sheltering under the hide. The screech he had heard belonged to a big cat, of this much he was sure, but the sound had come and gone before he had a chance to identify the animal: lynx, or fang-toothed leaping cat, or lion. The latter he did not wish to even consider as he listened intently, heard branches settling and something being pulled across the snow. He allowed himself a breath but was quickly struck breathless again by the unmistakable sounds of chewing, gnawing, an occasional snarl, and a purring so deep and resonant that he knew it could come from only one animal.

"*Big* cat," he whispered nervously. Suddenly remembering a dream that he knew now might not have been a dream after all, he sat upright and reached for his spear, unable to bring himself to name aloud the object of his dread even though his thoughts screamed the word inside his head: *lion!*

Sister Wolf shivered; her lips were up, not in a smile, but in a quivering presage to attack.

"Hold," cautioned Warakan as he felt her muscles bunching beneath his hand. "You are no match for a lion, old friend."

But Sister Wolf was not listening. As the scent of lion permeated her nostrils, it overrode all other scents to communicate a message that aroused rage within the old animal. Although the encampment was merely one of many temporary places of rest and refuge from the weather, in the way of her kind, Sister Wolf had marked it well before retiring. Now, impelled by a deep, instinctive, territorial sense of outrage, she would tolerate no intruders. With a sudden surge of strength that took Warakan off guard, she hurled herself from the lean-to, dragging the startled young man with her.

Spear in hand, still on his buttocks, his legs stretched before him, Warakan sat stunned. To his surprise, the fog was down and much thinner than before. A full moon was standing high in the night sky; its light was so intense that it penetrated with hurtful brilliance all breaks in the mist. Warakan's right hand rose to shield his eyes. Squinting through the silvery glare, he saw that Sister Wolf had stopped in her tracks only a few paces ahead of him.

A pride of five emaciated, long-haired tundra lions was greedily feeding amidst the ruin of a large fallen tree limb at the base of the spruce on which he had hung the last of the moose meat. In an instant Warakan realized that one of the lions must have ascended the tree, crawled onto the branch from which the moose meat was strung, and ridden the branch to the ground when the wood had snapped beneath the great cat's weight. Now, after dragging its prize a short distance from the tangled debris of the broken limb, the lion was sharing the meat with others of its band.

Warakan swallowed hard. Not even in his nightmare vision upon the high plateau had he felt so alone and vulnerable to an imminent and unquestionably horrible death. But this was no vision; this was real. His gut spasmed. His entire body felt hollow, as though his spirit had confronted the specter of Spirit Sucker and chosen to abandon him to the predators that outnumbered him and had him at a complete disadvantage. He positioned the lance and prepared to use it, but it gave him no comfort. He was well within charge range of the lions, the puniest of which possessed claws and stabbing teeth that put his spear to shame, and easily outweighed him by at least three times his own body weight.

Again he swallowed. This time there was no saliva in his mouth, and his throat felt paralyzed as his thoughts ran wild in his head.

Five lions to one man! And one foolish wolf standing between us! A single swipe from any of them and Sister Wolf will never again roll in rotting moose meat, and I will be disemboweled or left without arms or legs, helpless as they eat me alive and then cache whatever is left of me in a tree for later . . . even as I cached the flesh of Great Hook-Nosed Grandfather of All Deer.

"Retreat, Sister Wolf. Be wise and wary, old friend, or your bold heart will not live to beat under another moon." His whispered plea barely scraped past his vocal chords, but he made it with his right hand pressed to the sacred stone.

The wolf stood her ground.

His words had no effect on her; they had, however, won the attention of the lions. Having already appraised and dismissed as ineffectual the threat of the blustering wolf, they were looking past her and taking measure of the bearskin-clad man out of mildly curious, contemptuous eyes. They did not rise. They did not menace. They simply stared at him as they gnawed upon the moose meat, and he knew by their reaction that—as so often happened in this far land beyond the edge of the world—they saw neither threat nor potential meal in him because they had never seen a human being before. Then, slowly, the largest among them rose, stretched languorously, and raised its massive, darkly maned head to scent him.

Sister Wolf began to growl. The lion ignored her.

Warakan met the gaze of the big male cat and knew that the animal's innate feline curiosity had won the moment. He could almost feel the lion's thoughts as it appraised him:

Smelly little beast . . . looks like a bear . . . but has a different scent, a warm, soft scent. Hmm . . . there is meat under its tawny fur. . . . Since it is stupid enough to sit there staring at me, perhaps I will take it.

"No," said Warakan. "You will not!"

The lions all flinched at his bold proclamation. Sister Wolf quivered. Her head dropped low between her hunching shoulder blades, and her growl intensified.

Slowly, so slowly that it seemed to Warakan he was not moving at all, he stood to his full height. There was only one course of action left for him to take now if he wished to live to see another dawn. He threw out his chest, brandished his spear above his head, and forced himself to speak with all the arrogance of a lion as he blustered, "I am not so small or soft as you think, Lion! Behold Warakan, Son of the Two Tribes of the Man Pride. There *is* meat under the bearskin I wear, but I warn you now that I have slain and consumed the bear whose skin now warms me in the winter wind and fog! If you would come to slay and consume me, you will taste the bite of my spear before I am meat in your belly!"

The lions were impressed—all but the big male. He was annoyed. Rolling up his lips and displaying his teeth, he snarled and roared in a way that made it clear to his females as well as to his human and canine adversaries that he was also capable of bluster and of epithets of contempt and threat in the language of his kind.

Warakan's heart sank.

The lion's insult was too much for Sister Wolf. The fog was thickening again, but Warakan could see his old companion in the congealing mist and knew by her stance that her blood was up and her sense of reason gone. The lion had come with his pride to steal and eat the meat of her "pack," and now he dared challenge her right to drive him from hunting grounds she had marked as her own. And so, without a moment's hesitation, the old wolf set herself to bluster, as both lion and man had done, but she took her threat several steps further by making a brash, slavering forward feint that brought her close to the big cat. A huge paw came swiping out with claws extended. Sister Wolf yelped once as she was batted sideways across the snow.

In that moment Warakan hurled his spear and made the best imitation of a leonine roar that any human male was likely to ever make again. He astounded himself, and he astounded the lions. The females scattered into the spruce grove, leaving the big male confounded by the spear that had snagged in its mane. Snarling, slapping at it, and thoroughly distracted by that which it perceived as Enemy, the lion was unaware of Sister Wolf getting to her feet and pounding toward Warakan as fast as her limbs could carry her. Even before she faltered and began to fall, the young man caught her in his arms, turned on his moccasined heels, and ran for their lives.

The fog embraced them.

And for the first time Warakan did not curse the mists that now concealed him from lions. He did not know how long he ran, or how far he came, before at last he went to his knees to the lee of yet another massive boulder and listened for following beasts.

There was no sound save the pained rasp of his own breathing, the shallow panting of the wolf at his side, and the occasional drip of moisture falling from the trees. Sister Wolf licked his face. He drew her close and, pulling off a mitten, checked her for wounds; finding none, he sighed with relief, then shook his head.

"Your disobedience nearly cost us both our lives," he told her. Exhausted, he sagged back under the overhanging lip of the great stone. "When the sun rises to grant light to us tomorrow, we will have to retrieve my spears and fire carrier and whatever else the lions have left us."

Warakan shivered at the thought. Tenting the old bearskin robe over himself and the wolf, he sent his bare hand questing within the furs for the sacred stone and curled his fingers tightly around it. "At least I still possess this much!" Consoled, albeit only a little, he closed his eyes and fervently wished upon the talisman. "May the lions have taken the moose meat and gone back to whatever part of the forest they came from! May we not see them again! And may . . ."

Warakan opened his eyes. A smile bent his mouth, and a low chuckle at his own expense escaped his lips as he spoke softly and certainly to the old wolf. "The spirits of the Ancient Ones are with us, my sister! We asked them to keep us safe . . . and here we are, you and I together, safe and well away from the lions that might now be gnawing our bones! But I think, too, that I may have called the lions, for although I did not speak my wish aloud, I dishonored the spirit of Great Hook-Nosed Grandfather of All Deer by wishing that predators would come in the night to rid me of the obligation of eating the last of his meat. He came to me later in my dreams. He was not pleased with me. But the spirits of the Ancient Ones within the sacred stone heard and answered the needs of both Man and Moose. In consideration of Warakan, they sent predators to consume the last of the moose meat. Not Weasel or Fisher or Lynx or Leaping Cat. No! The spirits sent a great and fearsome eater of meat to consume the last of the flesh of Great Hook-Nosed Grandfather of All Deer. And I tell you, my sister, that he cannot be less than honored to know that the portion of his spirit that does not walk with Man and Wolf will, from this night, walk with Lion in the great Circle of Life!"

The sound of migrating cranes drew his eyes skyward. For days he had been hearing and seeing wedges of waterfowl flying high overhead, but now the unmistakable *kroo-karoo* of cranes held Warakan spellbound as he watched them wing northward across the face of the moon.

"There is open water somewhere ahead. The Warm Moon *has* risen. The birds know; they speak to us in the way of their kind. Listen . . ."

"Kroo . . . karoo . . ." called the cranes.

And somewhere, not to the north but in southern skies, another bird called.

"Ika . . . Ikaree . . . Ikareeee!"

Warakan paid no heed to the cry. He was rubbing the

wolf's shoulders and looking northward as he vowed, "To-morrow, old friend, we will retrieve whatever the lions have left us and then go on our way. The lake that is the Mother of All Rivers cannot be far ahead. From its shore we will turn west, where the great river lies. In the pathway made by the light of the setting sun, we will find it . . . and the great river will lead us home."

5

Somewhere along the way they followed the wrong fork in the river.

Xohkantakeh was sure of it. Scowling, he shook back his hood, squinted into the afternoon wind, and surveyed a land that was totally foreign to his eyes. Grumbling to himself, he tried to understand how and where he had lost his way.

The land had seemed familiar, even benevolent to his eyes, as they journeyed upriver to the place where three great rivers met. Although past floods had greatly altered the run of the rivers as well as the contours of the land, he had come across familiar landmarks and soon had the band safely on the far shore of the west-flowing river. Traveling ever north, Katohya rejoiced when they reached an old campsite at the base of high red bluffs. It was good country that evoked happy memories, and their first night there was filled with storytelling and laughter. Later, while Katohya and Ika slept together under fair skies and starlight, Xohkantakeh drew Quarana to him. As she closed her eyes and yielded to his need, he savored long, slow, infinitely pleasurable hours of life making. The next morning, he lounged in his sleeping furs until the sun was midway toward noon. Ika found fresh sign, and soon he and the girl were running a herd of small, long-haired, fat-bellied brown horses toward a remembered ravine. They worked together to panic one of the yearlings into an ill-timed leap, and the animal ended its life in a broken heap at the bottom of the snow-blasted gulley. Later, prayers of thanksgiving were offered to the spirit of the horse and to the forces of Creation as the band eagerly cracked bones, sucked marrow, and supplemented the last of their supply of bear meat with fresh innards, tongue, liver, and dark, high-flavored horseflesh.

In the days that followed, the remaining meat, hide, and other usable portions of the horse were prepared for traveling. When this was done, Xohkantakeh scanned the well-remembered hills. He had known exactly where he was and, without hesitation, led his little family on.

When dusk shadowed the world, they made small, often fireless camps and, after sharing the meat of bear and horse, sheltered together until dawn. Daybreak saw them following the river across enormous gravel bars that spanned an increasingly unfamiliar floodplain. Nevertheless, using the stars and the positions of the morning and evening sun as guides, Xohkantakeh had done his best to reverse the way in which his band had journeyed downriver many a long moon before.

He kept his tracks set to the north, following unfamiliar and often confusing turns and twists in the arm of the great river, confident of the way only because the river invariably turned northward again. On and on, across a land pocked and channeled with frozen lakes and rivers, Xohkantakeh led his family along the path of Quarana's new-woman dream until now, at last, there was no denying that the great river—if it was the great river—was narrowing and veering consistently to the east.

Still scowling, the giant continued to squint into the afternoon wind. The air was cold, but the sun felt warm on his face. He was breathing hard. Little puffs of cloud were condensing and disappearing before his face as he paused above a great frozen waterfall cascading over a steep escarpment of jumbled stones and boulders that afforded a broad overview of the valley into which he had led his band. There they had encamped for the past three days while Quarana passed moon blood in the little hut they had made for her. At his back, thick spruce forest rose to high, ice-mantled mountains that cupped a frozen lake veined with long, irregular ribbons of open water that sparkled blue and silver in the sunlight. Xohkantakeh's gaze, however, was fixed on the deep river valley with its many still-frozen tributary streams, ponds, and islands of evergreens standing amidst broad open spaces of snow-covered land. He nodded to himself. The view assured him of a truth he should have confronted long before now: He had never been in this part of the world before.

And yet, what a fine valley it was. Although the nights remained bitterly cold, late each day the falls were sheened with lacings of running water, there was open water at the river's edge, and streams of blue were showing in the solid ice midriver. Each morning Ika rose early and, with a tine cut from the cast antler of a forest caribou, cracked through the thin ice along the shore so that she could bring a bladder skin of cold, sweet water to share with all.

Xohkantakeh nodded, pleased not so much by the girl's consideration as by the certainty that the White Giant Winter was in retreat. Although it did not appear as though the unusually thick winter ice would fully loosen its grip on the sleeping river for at least another moon, waterfowl were winging into the valley in greater and greater numbers, splashing down onto every opening in the ice they could find, and finding sustenance in the late-afternoon shallows at the river's edge and wherever the snowpack had melted to lay bare last autumn's grasses.

Delighting at the sight of so many birds, Katohya—whose appetite was greatly improved and who no longer turned green at the mention of meat—had taken her trithonged birding sling and armed it with carefully chosen, perfectly matched and weighted stones. With Ika at her side, she had brought down several fat geese while the girl—even more skilled with the sling than her mother—had stoned several more, and added a small heron to their take. The giant did not relish the thin, pink meat of birds, but it was a favored food of his beloved's Red World People, and it pleased him to share it with her. Coupled with the meat of the young horse, the flesh of these kills seemed to have rejuvenated her. Her color was good. She still tired easily, but she sang at every task and showed a renewed energy and enthusiasm for everything concerning the welfare of the band. Even at this very moment he could see her sitting in the sun close to the temporary lodge they had raised, busily occupied in weaving duck-shaped decoys from the dried reeds she and Ika had cut and gathered at the edge of a backwash pond that, in summer, would no doubt be a marsh.

"Many fine birds we will lure with these!" Katohya had declared. "You will see! Much fine down and tender feathers we will take for our . . . for our new woman . . . so that when she bears her first child that baby will have the softest and lightest of feathers within the liners of the winter garments we will make for it!"

Xohkantakeh's smile disappeared. He did not like Katohya's endless talk of babies. The Warm Moon was rising, and although the spirit of Great Paws lived within Bear Slayer, he had yet to set life into his new woman. This troubled him. Sometimes, when savoring penetration of Quarana, he would find himself wondering if time had sapped him of the ability to give the gift of life to a female; then the nagging spirits of doubt would move from his mind to his loins, and his man bone would go limp and refuse to sustain his pleasure, or hers. Indeed, this happened so often of late that he only rarely called her to pleasure him by day and turned his back to her in the night, preferring sleep to sexual dissatisfaction. But perhaps this would now be different.

From his vantage point atop the escarpment, the giant could see extensive bare patches in the snow where last summer's grasses were showing through, tawny and bent but nourishing enough for birds and rodents and even bison from the surrounding woodlands. His scowl disappeared as he eyed the herd. A small number of bulls grazed at one end of the valley. He knew they would keep to themselves until the rising of the Moon of Bulls Coming Back impelled them to midsummer rut. Then they would join the main body of the herd, in which calves born of their last ruttings could be seen grazing among the dark brown, shaggy, high-shouldered cows. The little ones were easily differentiated from last year's young not only because of their wobbly legs and much smaller size but by the yellowish color of their hides.

Xohkantakeh nodded, gratified by the sight of so many calves. Looking at them and then at their sires, it was easy to understand why it was said by the elders of his tribe that if a man wanted to make life on his women his efforts would be best rewarded after eating the hump meat and male parts of a bison bull, for then the spirit of the bison would cause the man sacks between his thighs to hang as low as those of the best bulls, and the life force of the slain animal would stiffen his man bone and send it seeking deep and hotly spurting the milk of life into his females.

Xohkantakeh smiled at the prospect. Only yesterday he and Ika had stalked the bulls in the way of the bison hunters of the Land of Grass. Slowly, patiently, wearing cloaks of spruce boughs to mask their scent, he and the girl had taken their strongest spears and best spear hurlers and crawled into the wind on their bellies across the broken snowpack, gradually insinuating themselves toward the edge of the herd. Then, selecting their prey, he had gestured to Ika to prepare to hurl her weapon at his command. She understood and obeyed. As leader of the band, first strike was his prerogative. He took it, and there had been no need of another. Because of his skill, last night there had been hump steaks on the skewers along with the male parts of the young bull he had slain with a single lance.

Xohkantakeh nodded again, this time with even deeper gratification. He could still taste the richness of the animal's meat. The good scent of spattering fat lingered in his nostrils, and the winter-chafed skin of his hands and face had been soothed by a liberal oiling of bison grease. When Quarana emerged from the hut of blood for her first taste of the fresh kill—denied to a menstruating woman lest the spirit of the slain male animal be profaned—he intended to feed her with one hand and with the other oil her loins and his with bison fat. He knew she would welcome his renewed sexual appetite as she had welcomed news of his kill, declaring it to be the best of omens because her Bear Slayer had accomplished it when the last of the flesh of the great slain bear had been consumed and the best portions of horse meat had been eaten.

What would Quarana say when he told her that, if the river continued on its present course, it would not lead them back to the Land of Grass at all? He would not tell her—until he was ready. In the meantime he wanted to linger a while longer in this valley. Katohya needed to rest and renew her strength before he subjected her to the rigors of continued travel. And he was not averse to a few days' rest himself. Besides, the meat of the bison would have to be smoked and preserved for the journey ahead, and he wanted to eat as much of it as he could while it was yet raw and fresh so that he would not suffer again from limpness and lack of feeling in his man bone.

His brow came down.

Katohya was singing as she wove the reeds. The wind brought the sound to him, barely audible but there, like the high hum of insect wings droning over summer grasses. His heart warmed as he watched her sitting in the sun, leaning against her backrest and happily raising praise songs to the forces of Creation while Ika, kneeling well away from the lodge and bending over the staked skin of the bison bull as she worked to flesh it, shouted what seemed to be resounding affirmations of her mother's songs.

With some surprise, Xohkantakeh noted that Ika looked like a woman kneeling over the hide, her long arms bared to the sun as she worked, her hair plaited in a single braid that fell forward over her shoulders, her long back curving gracefully to the sleek, taut roundness of her . . .

What kinds of thoughts are these! He was startled by the way his observations had led him and, squinting into the wind, took comfort in the realization that, since both his woman and daughter were fully clothed, he must have fallen victim to a trick of distance conspiring with sunlight and shadow. *Someday my Ika* will *be a woman. Someday. But may it not be until we reach the land of the ancestors, for, by the Four Winds, she is like a son to me on the hunt and*

*when it comes to carrying the burdens of the band! And if
she has not bled by now, tall and strong and plain as she is,
perhaps the forces of Creation have passed her by.*

Katohya's song continued. Xohkantakeh was grateful
for the distraction. The cadence of the song was light and
lovely, but although he strained to hear, he could not make
out the words. Feeling suddenly isolated on the escarpment,
he descended and strode back into the camp. It was not until
he walked past Ika and approached Katohya that he was
able to understand the words of his woman's song with any
clarity—words of love and life-making and of the Warm
Moon rising to enrich the spirits of the earth.

"Your song of life is a good song," he said as the welcoming smile of his Sweet-Scented Woman touched his
heart and enriched his own spirit.

"Life is good!" she said, then rose and went to the stone
fire circle. A moment later she returned with an offering
of meat.

He took it and ate slowly, watching her move to her
backrest, seat herself, and take up her weaving of decoys
once again.

She is still good to look upon, he thought and, appraising
the gentle loveliness of her features, remembered that New
Woman was not the only woman in his band and that upon
this woman he could savor a man's release free of the un-
manning pressures of a life maker's obligation.

"Come," he invited quietly, holding out his hand to her.
"The look of you awakens the power of the bear and of the
bison in me. We have not joined as man and woman since
the night before the new-woman ceremony. Let us now lie
down together. Open yourself to me, Sweet-Scented
Woman. I have need to come between your thighs."

She looked up from her work. Their eyes met, held.

"Your need is to make life," she said after a moment,
then added softly, "Tomorrow the new woman will be
cleansed of blood and ready to receive you."

"Until tomorrow I have but one woman."

Katohya smiled.

Xohkantakeh frowned. There were secrets in her smile
and in her eyes; he did not like secrets. "Come," he com-

manded, impatient now. "Great Paws and Bison Bull will not be denied!"

"They must," she told him. "Since the night you came into me before the new-woman ceremony, you have also been Life Maker."

"It cannot be," he growled. "New Woman has twice shed moon blood."

"New Woman is *not* the only woman of Xohkantakeh!" This said, she set aside her weaving and rose to her feet in one fluid sweep. Opening her robe, she bared the elk-skin dress beneath and proudly displayed the small roundness of her pregnancy. "Behold the power of Bear Slayer!"

He stared.

"It is true," she assured him, reaching for his hand and drawing him to his feet as she stepped close and pressed his palm hard against her belly. "Feel the power of Bear Slayer!"

He gaped, incredulous, until a shiver of wonder and delight went through him as the movement of his unborn child rippled beneath his hand.

Katohya laughed, a bright, loving exclamation of pure joy that held all the radiance of the sun within it. "Yes! It *is* so! Xohkantakeh is Life Maker! And although he has New Woman to pleasure him, he has put his life in me!"

Ika was stunned.

"For how long have you known?" Xohkantakeh was asking Katohya.

"Well over two moons now," replied the smiling woman. "I wanted to be sure before I spoke of it. And I thought that surely you would recognize the signs before now!"

The girl stared as Katohya and Xohkantakeh embraced and laughed together like children.

"Come, daughter. You, too, must lay your hand upon the new life that I carry for this band!" Katohya invited. "Perhaps it will inspire the forces of Creation to awaken within you. Ah, dear one, may it be soon that you know the joy that I feel now!"

Ika's eyes went wide. Her mother was not the only one who had been keeping a secret. The girl's face flushed. To know Katohya's joy she would first have to know the coming of a man between her thighs. And if they knew her secret . . .

"Come closer, Ika!" insisted Xohkantakeh. "Come and share this joy!"

Ika blanched and, with a frightened gasp, turned on her heels and made the first excuse that came into her head—that she must be quickly away to relieve herself.

Xohkantakeh laughed. "I think your announcement has shocked the child, woman!"

Katohya echoed his merriment.

Ika kept walking, her face burning. The pups had risen from their midafternoon nap and were following close at her heels. Although they were gamboling around her feet, nipping at the lacings of her moccasins, she barely noticed. What would Katohya and Xohkantakeh say if they knew her secret?

"Aiee!" she exclaimed as memories of the violence of the new-woman ceremony flared in her mind. Making a pretense of the act of which she had claimed to be in need, Ika squatted close to a stand of willows. Swatting the curious pups away, she shivered with dread and guilt. She had been a woman for three days! Early each morning she crept to the river, not out of any kindhearted desire to fetch water for the others of the band, but to cleanse herself and gather fresh mosses to replace those that had absorbed her scant show of blood, which she gave to the river to be washed away before anyone discovered them. Already her minimal flow had stopped. By all the traditions of the Ancient Ones of the Three Tribes, she was a new woman whose body should—and must—be opened to life lest the forces of Creation be offended.

Again she shivered. Her woman place tightened defensively. She did not want to be mated, to be pierced as Quarana had been pierced, to be drawn aside at any time of the day or night and opened to the insertion of that long, huge, thrusting portion of Xohkantakeh that she could find no affection for.

For days now she had lived in dread of it. On the same
morning that Quarana announced her need of a hut of blood,
cramps were gripping Ika's belly. She had said nothing.
Seeing fatigue on her father's face, she had worked with
him to raise the little lodge within which her sister must be
confined. Later, still feeling unwell, she had gone with Katohya to hunt waterbirds, but after taking a few, her
forehead had begun to ache, and she had rested her head on
her knees.

Katohya, noticing her uncharacteristic lethargy, had observed, "Perhaps your time of blood is coming. It often happens that band women will bleed together under the same
moon. And I have noticed, dear one, that your chest is no
longer as flat as it once was beneath the fall of your hunting
shirt."

Ika had not replied. For the past two moons she had
been binding her tender, rapidly budding breasts. In winter
traveling camps it was easy to hide such things, and hide
them she must or she would be mated as Quarana had
been mated, joined to Xohkantakeh in violence and
blood, and never again would she be allowed to hunt at her
father's side.

It was the latter thought that gave her the most concern. She got to her feet, picked up the closest pup, and
confided, "On the long journey northward, Xohkantakeh
has found Ika useful in ways that he will never know, for I
have carried more than my share lest his back and shoulders be overburdened, and I have been his eyes and ears
and made him think that those things he sometimes fails to
see or hear have first been discovered by him and not by
me. As it was with Great Paws, so it was with Bull Bison.
As I had distracted the great bear, so did I make a low
click with my tongue so that the bull looked up and was
tricked into baring its throat to Xohkantakeh's lance. My
father should have remembered to do this, for it is a hunting trick he taught me long ago, but he is old, my little
wolf-dog sister, and that is why Ika must always be at his
side on the hunt or on the trail, to help him to see and hear
and remember . . . and perhaps to find a way to tell him
without bruising his pride that he has been following the

wrong river since we left the floodplain north of the great
water that flows to the west!"

The pup, a brindled gray female, squirmed in her grasp
and managed to place a well-aimed slurp across her nose.
Ika returned the kiss. "Katohya has said that life is like the
great river. It must flow as it will. No one, not you or I or
even Great Father Bear in the Sky, can say where any of our
lives will pour forth in the end. Besides, Katohya and I have
no wish to return to the land of warring tribes. Xohkantakeh
has brought us to a good and meat-rich camp! And since I
have brought the children of the black wolf into our band,
my father is not so angry at this daughter. He knows that
you will soon be carrying our burdens in your side packs
and on the dragging poles. He is glad of this."

The pup licked her nose again. Ika cuddled the animal as
she confided, "Ah, South Wind, you are now a child of Ika
as well as of the black wolf. I will be a good mother to you,
I promise, for you and the children of the black wolf are the
only little ones who will ever look to me as Mother. Although I am a woman, I do not want to be mated . . . not by
Xohkantakeh, or by any man."

Xohkantakeh danced.

In the hide of Great Paws he danced. Before a fire fed
with deadwood, bison fat, and small sacrifices known
only to the dancer, he danced. As Quarana peered from the
lodge of blood, she knew that never before in all the many
seasons of life she had shared with him had she seen him
dance like this.

Xohkantakeh was old, but the vigor of his newfound
pride and hope in the future gave power to his steps as, circling with his arms raised to the sky, he lifted his voice in
thanksgiving to the forces of Creation. Then he went to his
knees before Katohya, took her hands, and kissed them.

Quarana turned away.

His song had explained his behavior. She was shaking
as she knelt in the unlighted gloom of the hastily assembled
hut of boughs. Hissing frustration between her small, ser-

rate-edged teeth, she was in no mood to greet Ika when her older sister peered inside.

"Is there anything New Woman needs before I go to my day-end rest? There is still plenty of roasted waterbird."

"While you eat bison? Yah! I have all the bird meat I can stomach here at my fire. And reed shoots to chew on! Why do you come to trouble me, Ika? Seeing to the moon blood needs of New Woman is for Katohya to do!"

"Have you not heard our father's song? Our mother carries his life inside her. He has taken me aside and told me that she cannot tend you now lest your moon blood spirits speak to the baby inside her belly and trick it into coming out before it is ready."

Quarana's face convulsed with jealousy. "She is old! How is it that life has taken hold inside of her and not inside of me?"

Ika's brow furrowed as she spoke thoughtfully, with no hint of meanness. "Perhaps because that which is tender and in need of nourishment and protection seeks a consistently warm and loving place in which to grow."

"I am warm! I am loving! Ask our father how nourishing I am when he puts his man bone inside me so that my warmth will make it grow!"

Ika's face tightened. "I do not want to know."

Quarana noticed her sister's pained expression and shook her head. Since the new-woman ceremony, Ika was beyond understanding. "It is good to feel a man inside me . . . to close my eyes and imagine that he is the Other, the one of whom I dream . . . the one to whom I—"

"Enough talk! You have the best man. It is wrong of you to imagine another in his place! If you need nothing from me, I will go to my rest. Tomorrow there is still much meat to be made. The hide needs more fleshing before it is ready to be cured, and Xohkantakeh has said that we must gather birch bark for roofing and siding the big rainproof lodge he will make for our stay in this encampment."

"What need have we of a bark lodge when we must move on again as soon as my moon blood has been shed?"

"We will not move on. Xohkantakeh has said that he has

decided to stay in this camp for a while. The forces of Creation have shown favor to him and his woman in this place."

"I am also his woman! And I say there is nothing here to stay for!"

"There is meat. The forest is rich in game. The trees are swelling with buds even as our mother is swelling with new life and joy."

"But Xohkantakeh is *old!* What if he dies before he can lead us back into the land of many people?"

Ika's eyes narrowed. "How can you speak so? He is the best of all men!"

"Yah! In this land of no people beyond the edge of the world, he is the *only* man! Do you remember nothing of the land of the ancestors, sister? Do you not remember the many young men and warriors?"

"I remember a land that burned with the fires of war."

"And I remember a land that burned with the colors of autumn! I remember painted young warriors dancing with feathers in their hair! I remember hunting grounds in which the women and girls gathered in great numbers to sing and laugh together as they worked to make the skins and dry the meat and—"

"I remember women wailing and children all dirty-faced and crying because their villages had been burned and their people slain by painted warriors with feathers in their hair."

"Yah! You choose to remember only bad things! I remember only good."

"Be it so, but even when we put our memories together, my sister, you cannot tell me that you do not remember Katohya holding us close while Xohkantakeh stood against a warrior who came in silence to fire our lodges and kill us all!"

Quarana pouted. The memory was vague, of less substance than the mists of morning. "You are Eldest Sister. You were a big girl even then. I was little, maybe not even four summers old. I do not know. You remember more than I."

Ika's features contorted. "Have you forgotten Zakeh, the bold hunter who walked with Xohkantakeh in the hunting grounds of our ancestors, a funny little man who made us all laugh, who killed wolves for meat and brought us wolf pups to make us smile in the first days that we walked with Xohkantakeh's band after we had been abandoned by our own? Ah! I had forgotten until now. Yes! Two wolf pups had we, gifts from Zakeh. Then the warrior came. He fired our lodges and crushed one of the pups beneath his heel. He killed Zakeh and all the women of our band save Katohya. And he would have killed us, too, had our father's spear not struck him down."

Quarana chewed her lower lip as an obscure recollection came through the mists. "I was on my knees, crawling from the lodge. . . . There was so much smoke. . . . I could not see."

"I saw! I saw it all! Many warriors following the first . . . the fired lodges sending sparks to fire the grass . . . flames leaping high . . . my wolf pup running away . . . and Xohkantakeh carrying us in his arms to safety and a new life beyond the hunting grounds of warring tribes! And because I remember this, I am not anxious to follow your new-woman dream back into the land of the ancestors, my sister. I am content to live at Xohkantakeh's side in this camp or any camp he chooses, especially now that Katohya carries new life."

Quarana was annoyed. "Katohya is old, too! What if she dies? Who will talk woman talk with us and—" Her words were cut short as a suddenly furious Ika leaned in and pushed her as hard as she could.

"Never speak so!" cried Ika. "Never! Would you have the spirits overhear your words and cause your fears to come to be? Aiee! What is the matter with you, Quarana? Life has been good for us since Xohkantakeh named us as his daughters. And no matter what the future brings, we have each other! We have—"

"An old man who will make babies on both of us if he can! When you come to your time to be mated, you will see how it is with him. Then, when we are both swollen and heavy with life, who will hunt with Xohkantakeh? Who will care for us if he is injured, or when he—" Again her words were cut short, this time by the fury in Ika's eyes and by the unexpected sight of the girl's upraised hand.

"*I* will hunt at his side until the sons that you and my mother may bear him are strong enough to," Ika declared. "Until then, if you do not watch the way of your tongue, I will be the 'spirit' who overhears and punishes you for your carelessness with words!"

"Yah!" Quarana dismissed her sister's threat, but not before scooting back on her heels, out of Ika's striking range. Only then did she say, "You will be old when my sons are grown. And long before then, my sister, you will be a woman with children of your own."

"No. It cannot be for me."

Quarana was puzzled by the expressions that moved on her sister's face: resolve and a shadowing of such ineffable sadness that she was touched despite her foul mood. "Ah, Ika, just because you are big and strong does not mean that you cannot be a woman! Our mother has told us how it is for women in the hunting grounds of the ancestors. There will be many young men who will smile upon such a sturdy and useful girl as you! And there will be the hands of many women to help you with your work. Ah, Ika, think of how it will be for us! If we come to them as proven life bearers—and son makers—the young men will smile at us. They will put feathers in their hair and paint their bodies and bring gifts as they dance before us so that we may choose the best among them! Surely even such a stubborn girl as you must see how good life will be?"

"Life is good now," replied Ika quietly, and turned away.

And it was so.

The day ended as it had begun, with all save Quarana dutifully consuming the last of the bear meat so that Great Paws would not be offended while they gorged on bison flesh. Xohkantakeh—who in the prime of his manhood in the Land of Grass had boasted that he could consume all but the bones, hooves, and tail of a yearling bison calf at one sitting—fell back in a blissful stupor of sated gluttony to dream of past hunts and feasts and long-gone youth.

The dreams were good, full of fire and song, of power and endless possibilities. He was Bear Slayer. He was Horse

Killer. He was Bull Bison. He was a maned thundercloud. He was a storm roaring across the earth. All things female cowered beneath his shadow and opened themselves to receive the gift of his maleness. He was Life Maker! His man bone was a lightning bolt encased in the whirling wind of a tornado. Thundering, he sent it seeking pleasure, struck the earth, penetrated deep, ejaculated rain until the grasslands turned green and the herds of game animals were as the stars in the sky, without end . . . and countless numbers of his own strong sons pursued foals and fawns and little yellow bison calves across the endless sprawl of Creation.

Early the next morning, Xohkantakeh awoke refreshed and inspired, for although he was vaguely piqued to realize that he had spent man milk in his sleep, his dreams had nevertheless proved as nourishing to his spirit as the meat of the bull bison had been. With Quarana still pouting inside the hut of blood, he worked with Ika to cut and debranch several new lodgepoles for the capacious shelter he planned to raise for his family. When the stone axes became dull and sappy, he set them aside and, after telling the girl to stay with the pups and guard the encampment, prepared to hunt again.

A perplexed Katohya asked him why. "We have meat enough to last us many a long day and night. Why not rest a while?"

"Bull Bison has spoken through the feast dreams of this hunter," he told her. "Bull Bison has reminded Xohkantakeh that he must now remember the ways of his ancestors by honoring his life-carrying woman with a traditional Land of Grass gift."

"To be a woman of Xohkantakeh is honor enough for this Red World woman," she told him. "And now that you have given me the gift of life, so also have you given to me the greatest happiness that I will ever know! I need no other gifts from you."

He embraced her, held her tight, willed his love to flow through his body into hers. "Bull Bison has shown me that there is another gift that must be yours." Intoxicated on pride and hope and the promise of dreams, he turned and went his way.

It took him most of the day to stalk and finally make his kill. He raised a praise song to the bison cow that had allowed him to take the life of her calf so that Katohya would be strengthened by its tender meat and know joy in transforming the animal's soft, pale skin into the choicest clothes for their coming baby. When the prayer was finished, he skinned and butchered the calf, deftly wrapped its meat and bones within its hide, and hurried back toward the encampment with his spirit singing.

It was very cold and nearly dark when he saw the hide-covered cone of the main lodge glowing softly against the evergreens. His brows expanded across his forehead. With not so much as a glimmer coming from the little hut of blood, he assumed that Quarana had ended her confinement and joined the others. Feeling the stirrings of man need, he laughed aloud in delight at his own renewed virility.

Soon I will make cause to hunt and bring such a gift as this to her! he vowed, knowing in his heart that the next time he penetrated his new woman his man bone would not shrivel and grow soft before he had a chance to satisfy himself; it would remain bison big and hard until he was sated, for he had proved beyond doubt his ability to set the fire of life into Katohya. Now—despite the rigors of the day and the many seasons of his life—his loins warmed and swelled as he anticipated the pleasure of taking his new woman down and coming between her thighs again.

As he came closer to the encampment, however, he was disappointed to see that it was Ika and not Quarana crouching outside with her spears across her knees. The wolf-dog pups were at her side and, an instant later, were snarling ferociously as they charged him.

"Ho! What noise and threat you make!" he declared as the animals recognized and surrounded the returning hunter with happy yipping and friendly nips. He gave each a friendly tousle as he continued into camp, smiling now, for it did his heart good to know there was not a predator, large or small, that could venture anywhere within hearing or scenting range of the wolf-dogs without arousing them into protective fury.

Ika was on her feet.

"Where is your sister?" he demanded before she had a chance to offer welcome.

"Inside with Katohya, where it is warm," she replied, shivering a little.

"Hmm. And what keeps you out in the cold?"

"My father has commanded me to guard the encampment until his return."

The girl's statement pleased him. "It seems, then, that you *have* learned to obey at last." He gestured her aside so that he could enter the lodge.

Again his spirit sang.

They were seated around a stone-banked fire—Quarana on her haunches with her face greedily pressed into a meaty bison bone, Katohya leaning worriedly against her backrest with a bone platter of uneaten meat at her side.

"Ika assured us you would be back before dark," sighed the older woman, nearly swooning with relief. "But it has been so long since you left us!"

"For good cause," he told her.

Quarana looked at him over the bone; she did not stop chewing long enough to speak a welcome to her man.

Xohkantakeh took no note; his eyes were all for the woman who carried the seed of his life, the hope of a son in whom his spirit could live on after the death of his body, the first of *many* sons who would one day hunt the great herds at his side and eventually carry on his name and memory forever. It was a hope that had too long lain dead in him, and now that it lived once more—not in his new woman but in his older and, he realized now, infinitely more cherished mate and companion—he knew he had somehow already been reborn. Shaking back his hood, he felt like a young man again as he knelt and placed his gift before Katohya.

"My Sweet-Scented Woman, I bring to you the traditional Land of Grass offering of a man to his woman when she has taken his life into her body and will carry it within herself until it comes forth as new life. I bring to you a gift! I bring to you an honoring! May the carrying and birthing of my child be as smooth and tender to your flesh and spirit as the meat and skin of the bison calf I now lay at your feet! And may the life you bear be as strong as the bison kind that

has given sustenance and hope to my people since time beyond beginning!"

Ika, entering the lodge, caught her breath as she paused
to one side of Xohkantakeh and looked down at his offering.

Quarana stopped chewing the bone. "Have you brought
no gift for me?" she said, pouting.

Again the giant took no note of her. His eyes were shining with pride as he watched Katohya look at his gift. She
did not speak; she did not even seem to breathe. A smile of
infinite satisfaction cleft his face. Vaguely aware of the
crackling of the fire and the pups happily nipping at his leggings and moccasins, he was certain that his beloved was
overcome with pleasure.

Her eyes downcast, Katohya said quietly, "I cannot accept this gift. My man must offer the meat and hide of this
calf to Fire so that they may be transformed into smoke that
will rise into the Blue Land of Sky, where the spirit of the
calf may run with the bison ancestors in hope of being reborn into this world."

The request made no sense to him. "The meat and hide
are for you, Sweet-Scented Woman, to make you strong as a
bison mother when your time comes to give birth! How can
you ask me to burn them?"

She did not move, nor did she look up at him as she
replied, "Because in the eyes of my tribe, what you
have done is an offense to the forces of Creation! I cannot
eat this meat. I cannot sew this skin into garments.
The killing of calves is as forbidden to the hunters of
my Red World people as is the taking of fetus meat or
the killing of mammoths. How can Xohkantakeh have
forgotten this?"

He was stunned. Her question was fair enough. How
had he forgotten the old proscription? It was one of
the basic tenets of Katohya's ancient tribal beliefs, and
she had never made a secret of it. Indeed, over the past
years he had gone out of his way to respect her feelings
on the subject, taking calves and consuming fetus meat
only when he was away from camp, and even going so far
as to make a covenant with Ika that they were never to
discuss these "Land of Grass kills" in Katohya's pres-

ence. The woman's gentle Red World ways would simply not allow her to understand that what they did was good and right in the sight of the Four Winds and the forces of Creation.

A tremor of impatience went through him. The child she carried was of his making. He had put the spark of its life into her belly. When that life came forth from between her thighs, it would be as a son or daughter of Xohkantakeh, and once the band reached the hunting grounds of his ancestors, it would live out its days and nights according to the time-honored traditions of the warrior People of the Land of Grass.

His head went high. Later he would wonder if it was fatigue that had roused such implacable anger in him. He was tired. He was cold. He was hungry. He had spent the better part of the day stalking his prey, and although the kill itself had not been particularly difficult for a man of his skill and experience, he had spent the rest of the day preparing it for presentation. Not once in all those hours had he—Bear Slayer, Killer of Horse and Bull Bison— doubted that what he was doing was less than right and good. He was Life Maker again at last! What he had done had been joyously and proudly performed by the men of his tribe for their life-bearing women since time beyond beginning. To be rebuffed for it now was beyond all understanding.

There was no room for contrition in his heart when he responded to Katohya's query with questions of his own. "How many moons have passed since you last saw the land of your lizard-eating ancestors, daughter of Red World chiefs and captive of the warriors of both the People of the Watching Star and People of the Land of Grass? How many camps have you shared with this man who has risked his life and chosen to live apart from his tribe in order to rescue you from slavery and keep you safe from a life of war? How can it be that you—who freely answer to the love name I have given you as you mothered my foundlings and named my band your own—still dwell within my lodge and consider yourself bound to the ways and traditions of any people other than mine?"

Her eyes sought his face. "Because we have become a band unto ourselves. Red World woman, Land of Grass man. We have made new ways, new traditions that—"

"No more!" he interrupted. "The dreams of my new woman lead us back into the hunting grounds of my ancestors, not yours! Under all the many moons we have wandered alone and away from the country of my grandfathers, I came between your thighs many times, but no life took root in your belly until this new journey was begun. The forces of Creation smile upon my intent to return to the old land and old ways. I will not anger them now! Katohya will eat the meat of this calf that has been placed before her, and she will make garments of its hide, for if she refuses, the forces of Creation will know that a woman of Xohkantakeh has thrown away the meat and hide of a bison child and is therefore unworthy to be the mother of any child of a warrior of the People of the Land of Grass!"

Quarana put down the bone.

Ika exhaled as though in pain. "My father—"

"Be still!" he roared and reached back to swat the pups away.

Katohya's eyes were enormous. Even in the warmth of the firelight, her face appeared gray as she pleaded, "Ah, man of my heart, how many moons have passed since you last saw the Land of Grass? And how many camps have you shared with this woman who has mothered your foundlings and named your band her own? Surely you must know and understand the way of my heart in this?"

His head went higher. "The way of your heart is woman weak, a Red World way, not a fitting way for a woman of a man of the Land of Grass." He paused. He knew his words were hard. Tears were welling in her eyes, and the sight of them caused a hollow to open in his heart. His love for her allowed space for contrition now, but it was a small space easily closed to pity for one whose refusal to honor the ways of his ancestors might put her at risk even as it threatened his hope of a son in whom his spirit could live forever. "Katohya *will* eat the meat of this calf! Katohya *will* accept its hide! In keeping with the ways of the People of the Land of Grass since time beyond beginning, she will do this for her man or risk losing his child and winning his disfavor forever!"

She hung her head.

He opened the hide and held a piece of meat to her mouth.

A moment passed.

And then, slowly, Katohya ate of the tender flesh, then trembled violently as she spat it out, shook her head, and cried, "May the spirits of my Red World ancestors forgive me! And may the spirit of this calf that my man has so wrongly slain somehow find a way to be reborn into the world again."

He struck her. Hard. It was a purely reflexive reaction, a single backhanded blow that sent her slumping sideways as he bellowed, "If the spirit of the calf is reborn into the world again, how will it live on in my woman to grant strength and endurance to her and to the life I have put in her belly? Yah! I will stay to hear no more of this ingratitude and this . . . this sacrilege!"

He walked alone into the darkness.

The night was not as cold as before, or perhaps the warmth of the lodge had coupled with his temper to heat his blood so that he did not feel the bite of the subfreezing air until now. Having stalked a great and furious circle, Xohkantakeh paused under the stars. He regretted striking Katohya, and yet he knew without doubt that she had deserved the blow. Glaring toward the now-darkened lodge, he wondered how much time had elapsed since he had burst from it in a fury. His brow came down. Someone was coming toward him.

"Bear Slayer!" Quarana called as she hurried to his side and flung herself against him. "You left without your spears! Ah! I feared you might not return! It was wrong of Katohya to provoke you! How ungrateful she is! Kill a calf for me and I will work the hide and eat the flesh with gladness!"

"Hmm." He looked down and saw that she had come so quickly from the lodge that she had not bothered to put on her winter cloak. "You are cold," he said, instinctively enfolding her within the fall of his heavy bearskin robe.

"Not now," she told him, pressing close and sending a small, bare hand questing under his garments, then back and forth against his belly. "I am never cold in your arms."

He caught his breath as her fingers strayed downward to curl and flex provocatively in the fur above his man bone.

"When will you kill a calf for me, Life Maker?" she sighed longingly, snuggling close, handling him in invitation.

"When you take the fire of my need and nurture it into new life within your belly, as Katohya has done."

Quarana looked up and frowned prettily. "Your need is my need. My mother is old and weak. I am young and strong. How much more like bears and bulls will be the sons you put into me! And how the warriors of the Land of Grass will envy you for possessing such a man-pleasing, baby-bearing new woman as Quarana when you return to walk like a great warrior bear among them!"

He met her gaze. She was smiling at him now, and in the starlight her face shone with the residual fat of her last meal. Her eyes were bright. Intent. Avaricious. Even without her fine black and white cloak of ermine, she reminded him of a hungry little animal, so sleek and soft and lovely to behold, and yet so sharp of eye and tooth he knew he would be bitten if he failed to control her. The observation displeased him. And he was certain that she was aware of his reaction, for she quickly lowered her eyes, raised his hunt shirt with one hand, and pressed her face to his bare torso.

"Let me give you cause to kill a calf for me," she implored as she bent to trace a wet line of fire downward with the tip of her tongue. "You have put new life in the belly of Katohya. Do not withhold it from me. I would not shame Life Giver when we come into the country of the warriors of the Land of Grass."

He was tired and irritable and knew where she was leading him. The path was familiar enough, and the sensations aroused by the moist warmth of her mouth were exquisite, but a strange and perverse mood was on him. Having just argued violently with one woman over her refusal to obey his will and having no desire to yield more of his will to another, he took hold of Quarana's hair and jerked back her head.

"It is not Xohkantakeh who will be shamed if you come flat-bellied into the Land of Grass. This man has made and outlived many sons! Now your mother carries the child of this Life Giver. Perhaps the forces of Creation have not found such a boastful female as Quarana worthy to do the same? Hmm. We will see."

She cried out, surprised by his unexpected roughness as he dropped to his knees and, after impatiently turning her, held her fast while he penetrated her from behind. It was the way in which he knew she would take the least pleasure but the way in which he now took the most—and did so with a man bone that might well have made a bull bison proud.

Katohya came from the lodge. "I am the one who deserves punishment, not Quarana," she called out to him as Ika emerged from the shelter to stand at her side.

He turned his head in amazement at the audacity of a female who would dare interrupt a male in the act of mating. She stood motionless with Ika, both of them staring, repudiating with their eyes and silence. The distraction ruined the moment for him. His release had only just begun, and now he felt sensation ebbing and his woman pleaser shrinking fast. Later he would find cause to curse the sudden, unthinking mix of anger, pride, recalcitrance, and frustration that made him roar at Katohya, "May the forces of Creation hear your words and see to it that punishment *is* yours!"

The woman went rigid, then turned and, without another word, returned with Ika into the lodge.

Xohkantakeh was glad to see them go. He continued to work his new woman, but it was no use; the milk of his passion was spent. He had gone soft and limp, and there was no pleasure left for him in the coupling. Besides, Quarana was enjoying it now. He growled, convinced he would never understand her gender.

"Too long has this man lived among women only," he snarled. Overcome by an overpowering need to know once more the company and conciliation of his own sex, he got to his feet, pulling Quarana up with him. "The forces of Creation have spoken through your dreams to call us back to the hunting grounds of the ancestors. Be it so! We will not linger in this valley. We will not make the big lodge. We will return to the Land of Grass. I, Xohkantakeh, Bear Slayer and Killer of Horse and Bull Bison, will stay in this far land beyond the edge of the world no more!"

6

Warakan greeted yet another dawn under warming skies.

He had come far since the incident with the lions. For days now he had seen no sign of the old camps he had made years before while traveling with Jhadel. He and Sister Wolf had found and were following other sign, amazing and infinitely more welcome: a series of abandoned fire circles in which ashes and the debris of past meals had long since been rendered into the earth by wind and weather; a woman's perforated bone sewing needle lying broken amidst small, telltale splinters of stone cast by a knapper's hand as he—or she—sat by the hearth stones fashioning or mending spearheads or tools; an alignment of circular depressions in the gravelly surface that looked like post holes dug to support the bone or wooden bracings of a small lean-to; and occasional stands of black spruce, alder, and willow that were scarred and broken by what appeared to be the chewing or tusking of some large, elephantine beast.

"Mammoth!" he exclaimed. "No other animal tusks up its 'meat' in such a way, unless it is Mastodon, but those tuskers do not feed in the barrens. And perhaps the scars on the trees are not all so old as they seem. The great white mammoth totem has walked in this land before us. Cha-kwena was here! And Mah-ree, the woman of my dreams, was with him!"

Warakan hurried on, carrying on his back what little the lions had left him, for they had demolished his snow walkers and bone sledge, then carried off the hide and meat of Great Hook-Nosed Grandfather of All Deer. Only his fire-hardened lances, a few lengths of thong, and his birch-burl fire carrier remained. But the heart ember of Jhadel's death fire had been lost, and he had yet to kindle flame anew in a land of endless damp and cold where there was no dry grass or standing deadwood to be found. "I am brother to a wolf, so I might as well eat like one," he said. With the White Giant Winter in retreat, he survived on the uncooked flesh, blood, innards, and marrowbones of whatever small furred and feathered creatures fell afoul of his snares and well-aimed stones.

Several times along the way, he could have sworn he smelled the smoke of a distant cooking fire and now and then heard the sound of singing, but always the source of the sound and the scent eluded him. Often he thought that if he had indeed set himself to hunt the great white mammoth and the shaman who had stolen the totem and his woman, he should think seriously about exactly how he was going to accomplish that without first retrieving the magic spearheads from the gorge where he had interred them. But the gorge was still far away, and although the mammoth and man sign that he followed was meager and old, it sometimes seemed more real to Warakan than the wolf that plodded and panted at his side. When darkness fell and he curled up with the old animal beneath the warmth of his tawny bearskin cloak, his mood was as bleak and bitter as the land. Beneath his hand, the beat of Sister Wolf's heart was often so slow he could barely feel it, and sometimes so arrhythmic that she woke, panting, and he feared she would die. His loneliness was almost beyond endurance. He would close his eyes and will himself to think of his Mah-ree—small and dimpled, antelope-eyed, beautiful Mah-ree.

"She is waiting for us to come to her," he whispered to Sister Wolf. "And when we meet again, you will love my Mah-ree as I do, for she was one who walked with the mammoth kind without fear, and knew the trust and affection of my Bear Brother, who yielded up to her a wounded paw when he was as tall as a mountain and she was as small as a little spring mushroom. But her healing powers are great, my sister. She will know all the words and ways and green growing things necessary to make you strong . . . and perhaps even young again!"

Warakan's words took him into sleep. Sometimes he dreamed; sometimes he did not. But when he did, it was always the same dream he had experienced on the promontory. He was Eagle. On broad wings he flew into the face of the rising sun, looking down on the earth: mountains, valleys, mighty rivers, a land of ice and frozen lakes and endless forests stretching away and away to a body of water so vast not even an eagle could fly over it. The Four Winds took him, turned him, and onward he flew until he saw the flickering of a single campfire glowing in distant hills, then set his own shadow across the land and upon the great white mammoth that walked below.

"Life Giver!" he cried out of his dream.

"Follow the sun into the place where the dawn is born and it shall be so!" thundered the totem.

With his left hand rising from the sacred stone to touch the time-battered golden-eagle feather he wore in his hair, Warakan sighed his grandfather's name. His dreams bore him ever eastward, but when he awoke, he spoke his heart to the Four Winds and the rising sun:

"Speak to me as you will in my dreams, but in the light of day I will turn my back to the dawn and walk into the West Wind until I do what I have sworn to do. In the name of my grandfather, Shateh, I have vowed to take vengeance upon those who betrayed him to his enemies and caused him to be slain. Strong in the power of the sacred stone and invincible in the blood and flesh of the great white mammoth, this I will do!"

Curling his fingers around the talisman, he watched the old wolf stretch and yawn and prepare to meet the challenges of the day. Her loyalty touched him. Together they had come far across the land, hunting and surviving storms and the onslaught of a pride of lions. Now they walked in the footsteps of the totem. Everything was bound to be better soon! Feeling strong in the power of the sacred stone, Warakan went his way, trusting to the forces of Creation and the Four Winds that had placed it in his care.

It was the sight and sound of reeling birds that piqued

his appetite as well as his curiosity, enticing him toward the summit of an endlessly long, high hill of bare gray stone by way of a steep, narrow, boulder-littered ravine. The day was clear, and the sun was high. Less than halfway to the top, Warakan took off his mittens, hung them around his neck, then hefted the wolf and carried her slung across his shoulders until, perspiring in his furs and heavy robe, he paused and put the animal on her feet so they might both rest, basking in the sun a while.

Shielding his eyes with the back of his hand, he watched the birds wheeling overhead . . . so many birds, of all sizes, some of kinds he did not recognize at all.

"Eee eeeka . . . eekaareee . . . eekaareee . . ."

He frowned. The call was familiar. Something born of vision, or daydreams? He was not sure exactly when he first caught sight of the small, predominantly white bird swooping low overhead, nor would he ever be able to explain what motivated him to sit upright in that moment and reach to snatch the creature from the sky. He saw the flash of startled eyes, the extraordinary grace of the deeply forked tail, and the long, mist-pale, pointed wings as the tern swept through his grasp, marking its passage to freedom as a caress against his bare palm.

"Would you drive me from this place, as in my dreams? No. Warakan walks with the sacred stone and in the footsteps of the great white mammoth. You will not turn me from my chosen path."

He went on again, climbing over the skeletal "bones" of long-dead downed spruce and ancient tamarack. The wolf clambered after him until, seeing her distress, he slung her across his shoulders again and carried her. She gave him a grateful lick. He was unaware of it as, cresting the hill, he paused and stood stunned.

The mountains of his nightmares loomed on the horizon: mountains not of stone and earth but of solid ice, rising out of a lake of such monstrous proportions that Warakan knew he had reached the Mother of All Rivers.

He gaped like an awestruck child.

The lake—enormous in his memory—loomed even larger now. He could not grasp the enormity of it. In a vain attempt to do so, he walked along the rim of the high hill until he realized that from wherever he stood, the lake looked the same. It spanned the horizon as far as his eyes could see to the east and west; only to the north was its partially thawed immensity confined by mountains of ice from which towering columns had broken away to island the gray deeps. Over these floating monoliths, uncountable numbers of birds flew and cried and settled.

Staggered by the enormity of the scene before him, Warakan dropped to one knee and placed the wolf on her feet. "The Mother of All Rivers has grown so huge that the eyes of one man and one wolf cannot see it all! And the mountains of ice—surely, my sister, they were not so close nor half so tall when last we looked upon this shore with Jhadel?"

The wolf whined. Her ears had gone flat, and her head had dropped below her shoulders as she stared fixedly ahead, neck slightly upturned, as though in obeisance to a more powerful aggressor.

Warakan was disconcerted. He could neither see nor scent the presence of any predator anywhere other than himself and the wolf. But the animal was smiling. Her nose had gone up, and her snout was quivering. This was not the relaxed grin he saw when she dreamed of chasing hares and digging deer mice; this was the grimace of a beast cowed and cornered and terrified to the point of attack, as she had been when she had faced the lions.

"Hold! What troubles you? What do you see or scent or hear that I cannot?" He followed her gaze back to the lake and the massifs of ice and caught his breath.

Now, for the first time, through the cacophony of the birds, he heard and saw distant rivers of meltwater cascading downward over the range of ice. He squinted, observing what seemed from this great distance to be small wedges of the frontal flank of the mountain dropping away into the lake, which accepted the ice with a roiling of its waters. The sound came to him after the event—through the air and moving in a wave through the lakebed and the ancient morraine beneath his feet—the same deep rumbling he had heard and felt in the forest before the lions had come.

"Ah, I see . . . I hear . . . I understand," he told the wolf, feeling better for the knowledge he had just gained. "Be at ease, my sister. Ice falls into water. It makes a sound and raises ripples in the lake and in the land. There is nothing to fear!"

But Sister Wolf turned and, with a yip, broke for the ravine.

"Come back!" commanded Warakan.

She paused for a moment and raised her head to offer a howl that was her own version of a command, then turned and ran once more, heading straight down the ravine through which they had come.

"Come back, I say! If you think I am going to climb all that long way down just to carry you up again, you . . ."

It was in that moment that the mountains moved.

Warakan would never be sure if he had sensed it happening, as the wolf had sensed deep perturbations stirring in the earth and air, or if he merely happened to look toward the massifs of ice at the instant that a vast protruding lobe surged forward, pushed the forward flank of the glacier into the lake, and sent the waters rising and surging toward him. A heartbeat later he heard the sound of the horror that was about to engulf him—a sound born in the throat of a living beast the dimensions of which not even a man born to mammoth hunters could conceive, much less comprehend. It was the voice of a dying age, only one of the uncountable, incomprehensible death screams uttered by the White Giant Winter as yet another segment of frozen muscle and flesh and blood and bone that had lain thick and heavy upon the skin of Mother Below for untold millennia slipped and yielded at last to the subtle but infinitely more powerful force of the sun.

In that moment Warakan knew that all the tales told by Jhadel and the grandfathers among the People since the time beyond beginning were true.

"The mountains *do* walk! The lakes *are* alive! They come to eat us!" he cried. He would have raced after Sister Wolf, but the tumultuous movement of ice and water sent shock waves through the earth that threw him off his feet. He saw the rocks of the morraine come up to meet him— then knew no more as the mountainous wave of water rushed toward him.

PART IV

FROM
THE DROWNED
LAND

1

The sun was high.

Xohkantakeh lay on his back beneath the open sky with his forearms crossed over his closed eyes. He called for sleep; it would not come. The feel of the sun upon his weary body was exquisite. He was aware of his females stretched out nearby, dozing as he wished he could doze. Even the wolf-dog pups were asleep after the morning's long, arduous walk up out of the valley.

The giant's mouth flexed over his teeth. It was no use; he could not sleep. A strange mood had been on him for days. The all-transcendent joy that had filled his heart when he had felt his unborn child move within Katohya's belly had turned into a brooding resentment and nagging worry. Although she had recanted her refusal to eat the meat and work the hide of the bison calf, he could not forget that she had repudiated the traditional honoring gift of his people. It was the last thing he had expected from her, and no matter how hard he tried, he could not shake the fear that the spirits of his ancestors and of the slain animal were offended.

He exhaled restlessly, pressed his closed eyes with the backs of his fingers. Light patterns swarmed beneath his lids, bright, golden, like countless little suns sparking light, beauty, and warmth. Yet Xohkantakeh was not warmed. The dark and disconcerting knowledge of his woman's sacrilege shadowed his every waking hour. Days of warmth and wind had quickly cured the flesh and hides of the bison bull and calf. Although Quarana had compressed her lips when she saw the amount of meat the band would again be carrying, she nevertheless remained anxious to move on toward the land of her dreams and had taken up her share of the load without complaint. Ika, however, had appraised him out of guarded eyes, while Katohya stood looking back at the river valley with such longing that he had almost given in and told her they would stay.

But Xohkantakeh had not given in. The incident with the bison calf had unsettled him in ways that would be long in healing. Every now and then on the way up from the valley, he had turned to observe Katohya trudging dutifully along beside Ika, and he would find himself thinking, as he thought now, *She is not young! She is not strong! The meat of the calf may have strengthened her a little, but it has also taken the happiness from her eyes and the song from her lips. Ah! We have been together so long I had almost forgotten that we are of two different tribes and two different worlds. May it be that, through her ignorance, she has not turned the forces of Creation against herself and my unborn child!*

He grimaced, remembering that midway up from the valley, he had seen fern shoots uncurling from the rock on either side of a spring and had known at once that Katohya would want to stop and gather them. He had not allowed her this pleasure but had kept on his way. He was still angry with her, and frightened for her and the baby. Tender new fern shoots would have been a welcome addition to the band's food supply; indeed, of all green growing things, they were among his favorite foods. They were a traditional delicacy enjoyed by both the People of the Red World and the People of the Land of Grass, and now he regretted denying her the few moments it would have taken to gather them. After all, he could not display animosity toward her indefinitely; he loved her too much for that. Besides, since she had made her apologies to him for refusing his gift and had partaken of the meat of the calf, the sun had been shining and the earth was definitely growing warmer. Surely, he thought, this was a sign that the forces of Creation had forgiven her.

He sighed and pressed his lids with his fingers again. He found himself remembering long-gone days when he and other young warriors of his tribe would pause on long overland hunts to rest together upon the sunstruck plains. Then, as now, he would lie on his back, crossing his arms over his face as the Four Winds swept the land and his nostrils drew in the scent of warmth and light and he knew without doubt that life was good and promised a future that seemed every bit as golden as the grasses upon which he lay.

A smile moved upon Xohkantakeh's mouth as he willed himself to succumb to the languorous warmth of the moment. When Katohya awoke he would embrace her and tell her that all was forgiven. Then, with Quarana and Ika, they would gather fern shoots together. Yes, he conceded, life *was* good! The journey to which he had set himself, his females, and the wolf-dogs was only barely begun, but there would be safety for his women and daughters when it was ended, and as Bear Slayer and Life Maker and Slayer of Horse and Bull Bison he would revel once more in the easy camaraderie of men. As for now, the valley lay far below, but the great river that would lead his band back to the hunting grounds of the ancestors still lay ahead, somewhere beyond the western hills. He needed rest if he was to reach it. Needed sleep. Needed to be free of worry for a while. And so, slowly, he drifted into dreams in which he saw himself young again, strong and confident as he reveled in the company of other hunters while they hunted big game upon the golden grasslands of home.

The baby moved.

Katohya sat up with a start, raised her face to the sun, and smiled. How good its warmth felt after what had begun to seem like endless winter. And how she looked forward to summer now, knowing that when the green growing things of the earth swelled with life and fruit, so, too, would her body swell and ripen with undeniable promise and the hope of joyous harvest! Although she was still weary from the long trek up from the valley, the few moments of sleep the active little one had allowed had left her refreshed and feeling stronger than she had felt in many a long moon. Xohkantakeh had been right about the meat of the bison; the flesh of both bull and calf had indeed restored her strength. *Perhaps he is also right about leaving the valley and returning to the hunting grounds of the People of the Land of Grass. Our new woman's dream vision calls us there. And it is wrong of me to expect Xohkantakeh to do other than follow in the way he believes the spirits are leading him.*

Katohya sighed. She deeply regretted refusing his honor gift and causing him pain. Her reaction to his offering had been instinctive, a response to a deep-seated revulsion instilled in her by the grandmothers who had taught her the traditions of her Red World ancestors. It had not been her intent to repudiate the customs of Xohkantakeh's people. As to the spirits whose anger he now feared, she had come to believe long ago that nothing men said or did affected the outcome of their illusory whims and judgments. In this world within which the Four Winds and the forces of Creation moved upon the lives of Man and beast alike—ever generating, ever destroying as they wove and rewove the terrible and glorious web of Creation—life was, indeed, like the great river, and the People like the bold, many-legged water striders she remembered from the mountain streams of her homeland in the distant Red World. How daringly those spiderlike creatures lived their lives, spreading out their filament limbs, darting here and there upon the surface of the water, courting, mating, warring, birthing, and dying in their time. But always the water bore them on, and never did any among them know where they would be carried by the river of life in the end.

Now, looking at her sleeping band, Katohya marveled at the way each individual member of her family had been snared in the great and wondrous web of Creation and brought together in this place to be nurtured by the strength and courage of Xohkantakeh. Father. Mother. Daughters. Her hand strayed to her belly.

"And son?" She whispered her longing to the sun and

sky. When the child within her moved against the press of her hand, she shivered with delight, then looked down as one of the pups came ambling from amidst its sleeping siblings to root beneath her palm. She smiled, knowing with absolute certainty that she would never be happier than she was in this moment. The child that was to be born of her body would not be dearer to her heart than the two foundling girls Xohkantakeh had brought into her life to be raised as her own, and although she had given her heart to two men before the river of life had brought her into the care of her giant, no man would ever be more loved than he.

I must show him the way of my heart!

Slowly, not wanting to disturb the others, she rose with the young wolf-dog looped in the bend of her arm. "Come," she whispered, tiptoeing around her sleeping man and daughters before she set the pup down. "We will walk back along the way we have come, you and I. Hush. Let the others sleep. We will have a surprise for them when they awake. There were new ferns uncurling among the mosses of a spring we passed midway up from the valley. Xohkantakeh passed them by, and I am not sure if he saw them. Ah, pup! Of all green growing things, new fern shoots are among the tenderest and sweetest! They will be a gift from us, eh? And my way of offering apology to my man for failing to respect his will and the ways of his people."

The way was steep but downhill, and since the hillside faced the sun, most of winter's snow and ice had melted from the stone. Katohya walked with ease and, without the burden of a heavy pack frame, with pleasure. To her right the hill slanted away, and she could see the long, narrow valley and the river sparking sunlight far below. The pup trotted boldly ahead, paws lifting and falling with a wolflike authority that belied its age. Its tail curled high over its flank in a way that amused Katohya as she remembered Xohkantakeh's story of how Dog was born of an ember and chose to walk with Man.

"Far enough, West Wind!" she called happily when she reached her destination. She paused before a span of hillside from which groundwater seeped to the surface and ran over thick green moss in glistening rivulets. The new fern shoots she sought were unfurling everywhere along the moist wall of the hill. She leaned into the earth and pressed her mouth to the moss, sucking cool spring water. It was sweet, cold, sparkling. The pup came prancing up the trail, noticed a small pool at her feet, and began to lap it up. Katohya turned her attention to the ferns.

Soon, before she had a chance to pick more than a few and eat them for her own pleasure, she was distracted by a cooling of the air and intermittent shadows falling across the earth. She looked up. Vast numbers of high flying birds were wheeling in from the north to circle in mad configurations before a suddenly misted sun.

Katohya frowned. The mist was brown. She realized that it must be dust blown high by a great wind; she had seen such dust storms when traveling as a captive in the badlands to the northwest many moons before. But today there was no wind, and in this forested land, sodden with moisture left from the rapidly melting snowpack, there was no dust. And never had she seen so many birds.

"In all this world I never thought there were so many," she said in amazement, hearing them now for the first time and sensing fright and confusion in their myriad calls. "What brings you here, winged ones, in such numbers and distress?"

She raised her hand to shield her eyes from the sun, staring across broad vistas of valley and sky. The birds were flying on now, vanishing over distant hills, while the pup began to jump up and down on its hind limbs, pawing at her leggings and yapping imperatively. Still staring after the birds, Katohya picked up the wolf-dog and spoke to it as though the little creature might answer. "Do you not wonder to what far-off land they fly? Perhaps we will see them again in some distant valley as sweet as the one we have left behind."

And then Katohya heard the strangest sound, born of both air and earth. As she felt a trembling in the ground beneath her feet, instinct warned of imminent danger. Earthquake? Her heart went cold. Holding the pup close to her breast, she listened to what at first seemed to be the low rumbling of distant thunder, but the rumbling was constant and intensifying, and it was coming closer. Huge clouds of dust billowed out of the northern sky. And then, suddenly, the ice on the river broke wide.

Katohya gasped. It was as though an invisible force had pushed the river forward, then straight up and out of its banks. Ice shattered and exploded into the air. Water boiled, embraced mammoth chunks of ice, took them down, chewed on them, then spat them out again and hurled them high as the river threw off its winter caul and began to race free and wild across the land. The sound was deafening, but it was nowhere nearly as violent or appalling as the sound and sight that followed.

Katohya was shaking as she pressed against the hill, only to find that it was shaking, too. In the rapidly flooding valley, she could see animals breaking from the cover of the trees and racing for safety that was not there.

And in that moment she saw the monstrous wave Warakan had seen, born of a glacier sliding into the lake Jhadel believed to be the Mother of All Rivers. Over uncountable hills and into uncountable valleys and streams the waters of the great lake surged across the land with a speed and force that overcame uncountable herds of terrified bison, elk, caribou, horse, and any other hapless creature that ran before it. Beneath the onslaught of its swelling power, mountains were humbled, valleys drowned, and hillsides sheared.

Somewhere high above, Ika screamed.

"Mother!"

Katohya never heard.

The land was dead.

Ika was sure of it.

She stood with the surviving pups in her arms, staring down into the darkening valley with nothing left in her heart of that blind, bright, unreasoning hope that had briefly filled her when she returned to the rim of the hill after the great wave had passed.

"Ika!"

The girl cocked her head at the sound of her sister's

summons. She made no reply; the sound and the very moment itself seemed unreal, as though time had somehow ended with the roaring of the waters and now she stood alone, one with the world and yet, strangely, forever parted from it.

The sun had long since slipped below the western horizon. It had been high when the terrible waters had come and gone, reshaping the land below and sweeping Katohya, the pup, and a major portion of the hillside with it.

Ika shivered; she did not want to think of it. Night was fast approaching. Darkness was pooling in the valley, shadowing the drowned land, but she could still see enough of it to know that the deer trail they had followed up the side of the hill was gone. The force of the flood had gouged into the land and eaten it away as though the earth's hard, stony flesh had been of no more substance than cloud. And now it seemed as though Xohkantakeh had been gone forever.

Ika dropped to her knees and allowed the pups to scatter. *He will come back,* she told herself. *He* must *come back.*

"We should raise a fire," said Quarana, coming close and hugging herself to keep warm. "He may not be able to find his way back to us in the dark unless we make light to guide him."

Ika trembled. "He will find his way," she said, and yet she thought: *He did not hear the birds! He did not hear the roaring of the water or the screaming of the frightened herds! He slept on undisturbed by the trembling of the earth! Aiee!* She closed her eyes, remembered pounding at his chest with her fists to awaken him as Quarana had run screaming for her life. And then, seeing no sign of their mother, Ika had followed her tracks and understood at once that she must have gone back down the hill to gather ferns. Racing to the edge of the hill, she had screamed her name until . . .

"He will not find her," said Quarana.

"He must find her!" cried Ika with a defensiveness so sharp it cut her heart and made her spirit bleed. She opened her eyes and looked around. The moment was real. Too real. She hung her head and closed her eyes again.

"Nothing lives in that valley now," said Quarana.

"Xohkantakeh lives. If our mother is there, he will find her and bring her back to us."

"Think what you will if it soothes your heart." Quarana's voice was as bleak as the gathering night. "The angry waters have come and gone. We, at least, are safe for now. We have the makings for a camp. We have meat. I am hungry, and I am cold. I will make fire to cook my meat and warm my bones, and to guide my man back to my side."

He did not come at dark.

He did not come at dawn.

Quarana sat glowering at the charred ring of stones she and Ika had arranged around their fire. The coals were settling. All but the heart ember of the flames had gone out, but the last of the wood was long gone, and Quarana was not about to venture alone into the forest to gather more. Carefully banking the coals, she shivered against the dank chill of morning. Ika, sitting upright in her furs with the pups in her lap, had dozed off. Quarana, on the other hand, had not slept at all. How could she rest when Xohkantakeh had left her alone with Ika? How could she allow herself to sleep when she knew that her dreams would be of devouring waters and of her childhood terror of drowning and abandonment?

Beneath the coals a small stone cracked and slumped. The coals, sagging a little, vented a wisp of smoke and a few sparks.

Quarana sent her hope rising with them.

Let Xohkantakeh come back to me! Let him not leave me alone in this land forever with only my sister to protect me!

The sparks faded.

Quarana's hope faded with them. Hunkering by the stones, she blinked back tears until her belly flexed with hunger. Reaching for the leather bag that held her traveling rations, she opened it and took out a slice of bison meat. As she greedily consumed it, she moved to nudge Ika. "Wake up. A new day begins. I will not be alone in it!"

Ika stiffened, and her eyes batted open. "Xohkantakeh has not yet returned with our mother?"

"He will come soon now, I think. He must come! In the meantime, here, take a piece of meat. Eat. You must be hungry."

The girl's face collapsed into an expression of profound disappointment. "I will not eat until our father returns with word of the life . . . or death of our mother."

"You will grow weak without food."

"Be it so," replied Ika.

With her belly full and her lips greased, Quarana felt guilty, but only for a moment. Distracted by the cries of a raven winging in from the north, she looked up, certain that the bird must be summoning others of its kind to feast upon the bodies of the many drowned animals that now lay exposed in the devastated valley. Again she shivered, this time not because of the chill air of morning but in sudden dread as she imagined bears, lions, wolves, and great, fang-toothed leaping cats, drawn by the scent of decaying meat, advancing through the forest toward the rim of the hill . . . and to this very place.

"Ah!" she gasped as she looked imploringly at Ika. "You must eat! You must remain strong! Without Xohkantakeh to protect me, who else will guard this new woman's camp?"

Ika's face was gray in the light of dawn, her wide features ravaged by sorrow. "Are you so useless, then, New Woman, that you can see no way to defend yourself without me?"

Quarana was too upset to rise to her sister's insult. Her eyes were taking in her surroundings. Her senses felt the press of the open sky, the deep, threatening darkness of the surrounding forest. Shivering and hugging herself again, she blurted tearfully, "What if he does not come back? What if—"

"Be silent!" interrupted Ika. "He will search for our mother until he finds her, or until—" She cut off the words and shook her head in the way of one who seeks to banish bad dreams. "We will wait for him. If he does not come by tomorrow's dawn we will cache what we can of our meat and . . ." She paused and eyed her sister with open disapproval that bordered on contempt. "Unless, of course, in your 'grief' over the loss of our mother you have worked up an appetite and eaten it all!"

Quarana's face flushed with shame, but she did not care. "I will not grieve for my mother until I know she is dead!"

Ika said nothing for a long while. Then, as she shook back her furs and allowed the pups to stand and stretch, she rose with a ragged exhalation and pointed. "The morning is warmer than any I have felt in many a moon. Look into the valley. The great floodwaters have run their course, but the river is rising again. As the snowpack melts, it will swell with the life of newborn water from untold streams and rivulets. Perhaps we should not wait another day. Perhaps we should seek our father now."

Quarana was aghast. "But what will happen to us if the earth-eating waters come back?"

"We will drown."

"I do not want to drown!"

"Then stay here. Guard the meat. I am not afraid to go alone in search of our father and your man."

"But who will guard me if you go?"

"Xohkantakeh should have returned to us by now, Quarana. My heart tells me that he may need help. With or without you, I will go into the drowned valley to walk at his side."

"But what will happen to me if you do not return?"

Ika's long, dark eyebrows curved downward as she took slow, disparaging measure of her sister. "You will be alone with the one you love most—yourself! So stay here or come into the drowned valley with me. I, for one, no longer care what you do!"

They worked together to dig a pit, then buried their food and belongings and piled stones and deadwood over them. The sun was well up when the cache was completed. Carrying a small supply of meat, sleeping furs, a well-stocked fire carrier, and lances, Ika and Quarana carefully picked their way down the scoured hills into the ravaged valley with the wolf-dogs following close behind.

Xohkantakeh was not difficult to track. The valley was a

silted, boulder-strewn morass of mud, uprooted trees, drowned animals, great shattered wedges of melting ice, and sinkholes filled with water. The giant's footprints were plain to see and kept his daughter and woman slogging close to the river on a circuitous path that looped around and through the debris. By midafternoon the river was running high, wild, and well over its embankments. More often than not they found themselves calf-deep in water.

"I fear it will fill the valley again before the thaw is done!" observed Ika, raising her voice to be heard above the rush of the brown, fouled river.

"We must return to the hilltop!" cried Quarana.

"Go back if you will, sister! I will continue on in search of our father lest one who survived the first flood perish in the second!"

"But . . ."

Ika would hear no more. She pushed on without looking back.

Quarana stared after her, hating her. Fear and indecision twisted her pretty face into a knot of frustration. "Ika! Please! We will both be drowned!"

If Ika heard her sister's plea, she gave no indication as she brazened on.

Quarana burst into tears. She knew all too well that the hilltop camp was now far away and that, with the river rising, the way back would be as perilous as the way ahead. She followed her sister, cursing Ika's name with every step.

Flies and birds of prey were beginning to gather on the corpses of drowned beasts when the daughter and new woman of Xohkantakeh found him, perched in his bearskin robe high on the broken, skeletal ruin of an ancient tamarack. They hurried toward him.

Xohkantakeh did not look at them, nor did he speak.

They stood stunned before him. Never had they seen him as he looked now. His face was expressionless, his eyes fixed and staring in the dark hollows of his eye sockets, his great hands hanging limply over his bent knees. Had it not been for the slow rise and fall of the bearskin that covered his chest, they would have thought him dead.

"My father?" Ika said softly.

He did not respond.

"Bear Slayer?" she pressed again.

Silence.

"Killer of Bull Bison, are you still alive, sitting in that tree?" whispered Quarana, barely able to keep down the dread that had almost choked her. "Does Life Maker not hear his new woman speak his name?"

Xohkantakeh's mouth tightened. "Life Maker?" He released the words slowly, so acidic with bitterness that both his daughter and new woman stepped back as though his very breath might burn them.

He did not move, or speak again. He continued to stare until Ika came forward and laid her hands upon his wrists.

"We have cached our belongings and meat on the high hill, my father. We must go back," she told him. "The river is rising fast. If we do not return to the heights now, we will not be able to cross the valley floor, for it will be under water again."

At last he eyed the girl and, after a moment, said calmly, "Go, then. I must wait for my Sweet-Scented Woman. Soon now, Katohya *will* come."

The sisters exchanged troubled glances. Then Ika said gently, "My father, I saw the great wave break against the side of the hills. Katohya was broken with it. Nothing save a spirit could have survived the race of such waters! The river of life has taken your woman and our mother. None of us will ever see her again except in dreams. Please, Bear Slayer, we must go. The river *is* rising again. We will drown if we stay here!"

"Be it so. I will wait for my woman."

"I am your woman!" screamed Quarana. "Your new and now your only woman! Would you let the river drown me, too?"

"I do not need either of you to keep this watch with me. Go, Ika. Take your sister and seek safety." Xohkantakeh turned his gaze to his new woman, then to his daughter. He appraised them both thoughtfully before saying quietly to Quarana, "Ika is strong. She has stood to Great Paws and not run away. She is Little Bear in my eyes. You will not be alone with Ika at your side. Little Bear will take you to the hunting grounds of the ancestors."

"But I do not know the way!" protested Ika. "Nor will I leave you alone, my father!"

Quarana felt sick. Later she would remember this moment, for it was now—in a half-swoon of fear-induced desperation—that she first spoke the lie that would give back to the man his will to live even as it would so thoroughly confound the yearnings of her heart in the days and nights to come. She did not mean to speak it; the words simply burst from her lips. "Life Maker has lost an old woman and an unborn son to this river! Would he lose this new woman, too? And would he throw away the life he has surely put into Quarana's belly?"

Xohkantakeh flinched.

So did Ika.

"You cannot know this!" Xohkantakeh's accusation was as cold as the river. "Not so much as a single moon has turned its full face to the earth and then looked away again since last you came from the hut of blood!"

"Nor will I enter such a shelter again until the life that you put into me on that very night comes from between my thighs!"

He snarled and waved a hand, disbelieving. "It cannot be!"

"It is!" Quarana insisted. "Even as a man knows when his flint has struck fire from stone, so does a woman know when a man has struck the fire of his life into her belly through the tip of his man bone. Katohya told me this. She spoke of all the signs. Would you name her Liar?"

Xohkantakeh returned to the heights in silence. For four days and nights thereafter, he kept a watch fire burning on the hill. He would not eat. He would not drink. And he would not speak, save to call the name of his lost beloved.

Only the river answered his anguished cries. Day and night it rose and raced in the valley below until, fed by the rapidly melting snowpack, it filled the bottomland and all the world below the hills lay drowned.

Ika shivered to see it so.

Quarana wrapped herself in the fine fur cloak Katohya had made for her and, seated cross-legged at the rim of the hill, scowled as she stared below. Her self-serving ambition to return to the land of the ancestors had cost the life of her mother, but that same ambition had also kept the band moving on and out of the valley in which they would all have surely drowned. Shrugging off her guilt, she justified herself to the wind. "Katohya should not have gone back down the deer trail. She would be alive now, and her unborn baby, too, if she had not gone off alone."

Ika, standing close, looked at her sister thoughtfully. "And well might they be alive had we never left the winter camp that she loved so much."

"There is no way to be sure of that!"

"No. And yet I know in my heart that our mother went to gather fern shoots for us. Xohkantakeh allowed us so little time to rest on our way up onto the hills, but I saw Katohya smile when she glimpsed the newly uncurling ferns by the mossy spring. It was always her way to think of others. And what of you, my sister? Was it out of kindness that you sought to gentle the ache in our father's heart by telling him that you carry his life in your belly? Or is it truly so?"

Quarana did not look at Ika as she replied obliquely, "It *will* be so."

"It had better be so," said the older girl. "For it is that hope alone that has given our father the will to go on living, and surely you must know that by the laws of the Ancient Ones he cannot come between your thighs again until you bring forth the life you claim to carry."

Quarana's eyes widened with surprise, then narrowed. "He will come between my thighs. When he lies down with me, he cannot help himself!"

At dawn of the fifth day, Xohkantakeh rose before the sun. Tenting the great bearskin around himself, he went alone to the rim of the hill and stared through thinning darkness into the drowned valley below. There was no wind. He listened to the race of the river, to the crashing and grinding of shattered ice floes and trees being borne downstream to only the Four Winds knew where.

His brow furrowed. Through the blue-gray haze of dawn he could see that the river was down—only a little, but enough to have left the scars of its passage in long dark bands along the sides of the hills and in new, debris-littered beaches that were emerging along the shoreline.

The soft glow of sunrise was showing in the sky above the eastern horizon. He closed his eyes.

"It is done," he said of his time of mourning. Conceding at last that his Sweet-Scented Woman would not come to him again, he turned in silence to gather what little standing deadwood was still to be found.

Slowly, with grim purpose, he called his daughter and new woman to assist him as, with the wolf-dogs watching, he raised Fire and fed the flames with the belongings of his beloved.

Smoke rose, dark and heavy and rank with the scent of burning hides and feathers, but it was not smoke that seared his eyes and made them overflow with tears; it was anguish over the loss of the unborn child he had felt moving beneath his palm when Katohya had pressed his hand to her belly and proclaimed, *"Behold the power of Bear Slayer. Feel the power of Bear Slayer. Xohkantakeh is Life Maker . . . and he has put his life in me!"*

He moaned.

Yes, he thought. *Xohkantakeh has slain a great and powerful bear! And he has put the force of his life into his new woman, but the life he made on his beloved will never know joy in the light of dawn or be sheltered in this man's arms, for that life perished before it could be born, and the one who carried it—and my heart—now walks the spirit world forever!*

Again he moaned. In sympathy, one of the wolf-dogs nuzzled his hand. A moment later Ika cried out in shock and dismay when Xohkantakeh took the female animal by the scruff of the neck, snapped its spinal column, then added its limp and lifeless body to the pyre, proclaiming, "May the female spirit of this wolf-dog find its drowned brother in the world beyond this world! May they make many more strong wolf-dogs to carry my Sweet-Scented Woman's burdens as they walk together forever upon the winds until I join them."

"Aiee!" cried Ika, and yet, with a grace that seemed bestowed upon her by the spirit of her lost mother, she spoke the required response. "May it be so!"

Xohkantakeh nodded. Then, noticing Quarana standing sullenly before the pyre, he commanded her to bring him the wreath Katohya had made for her on the eve of her new-woman ceremony.

"It was your mother's wish that on the day of her death her children would stand proud in her memory. Come, Ika. You will join your sister in this. Neither of you was born of Katohya's body, yet she nurtured you as though you were of her flesh, blood, and bone. So it is right that you burn the sacred sage in memory of her name so that, upon its fragrant smoke, her spirit will rise into the Blue Land of Sky, where she will live forever among the stars and the encampments of the ancestors—"

"Until we join her there," Ika finished as she took hold of one side of the wreath.

Quarana's mouth compressed over her teeth.

Xohkantakeh waited for her to give the expected response and frowned, disapproving, when she said instead, "May there be days and nights beyond counting until that day!"

A moment later the wreath was in the fire.

He watched as the dried sage was consumed and transformed into smoke and, with no visible show of emotion, raised his stone dagger and slowly incised a deep wound across his brow. Blood welled and ran, mixing with the tears that sheened his cheeks.

Once again, with his head thrown back, Xohkantakeh stood beneath the open sky in the furs and skins of beasts, a giant of a man on the far side of youth, telling himself that he was young again, strong again, unafraid again. But this time his assurances curdled in bitterness and defeat. He knew he was old. His beloved was dead, and her unborn child with her, not because a river had risen to proportions that would forever exceed his understanding, but because he had failed to hear the warning of the birds and the low roar of distant "thunder" that had alerted his new woman and daughter to imminent danger and should have sent him racing to Katohya's side in time to at least try to save her.

Now the dawn wind was rising. West Wind. It blew the smoke of Katohya's funeral fire to the east while Xohkantakeh stood at the edge of a world he no longer recognized or wished to be a part of. Turning his back to the rising sun, he knew he had begun to die this day. He also knew that, while he still possessed the strength, he must follow his new woman's dream; he must take her, their unborn child, and his daughter back to the land of the ancestors before the inadequacies of a failing old man cost them their lives in this lonely and savage land to which he had so foolishly led them.

"Look, my father! *Look!*"

At Ika's imperative cry he turned and sought the girl with his eyes. She had moved from the fire and was standing a little way from him, excitedly pointing down toward the drowned valley.

"Something moves!" she cried. "Something lives! Look there, upon that little spit of shore, amidst the slain trees. Something stands upright and staggers on two legs!"

His heart lurched as hope was so suddenly and intensely rekindled that he could barely breathe.

"Aiee!" Ika exclaimed with a high, wild sob of joy. "It is not something . . . it is some*one*!"

"Katohya!" roared the giant. With his beloved woman's name on his lips, he raced for the river without looking back or pausing to rest until, stumbling and gasping on a newly formed beach, he felt the last vestiges of hope die within him.

There, collapsed and tangled amidst the broken branches of an enormous, water-engorged spruce half buried in the muck of the denuded shore, lay the body not of his beloved but of a beast.

"Bear." He spoke the name in grim acknowledgment of a truth that nearly struck him down. The life of the animal must just have left it, for surely from the heights he had seen it moving, but flies were already gathering on the limp, twisted carcass. He stood staring down, motionless, accepting, only barely conscious of the moment when his daughter and new woman paused beside him. The two surviving wolf-dogs, East and South Wind, clambered onto the tree trunk and sniffed excitedly at the dead animal, growling and nipping at the sodden, mud-caked hide to get at the meat beneath.

Ika's face convulsed with sorrow. "Forgive me, my father. From the hill I saw this bear stand upright on its hind legs, and before it fell, I could have sworn it—"

"You saw only what you wanted to see," accused a scowling Quarana as she rubbed her knee, for she had twice slipped and scraped it on the way down to the river. "We have come to this place for no good purpose! There is nothing left alive here. And now we must go all the way back to the top of the hill again!"

Xohkantakeh heard petulance and impatience in his new woman's tone; both annoyed him. "Your sister is not the first—nor will she be the last—to mistake a standing bear for a member of the Man tribe. I, too, saw only what I wanted to see. But no more. Your mother is lost to us forever. Come. We must leave this place. There is nothing here for us now." This said, he would have turned and gone his way, but it occurred to him that it would be foolish to leave the two wolf-dogs to their feast; with so much carrion lying around they might soon be tempted to go their own way and never return to the band. His brow furrowed. Their value as pack animals could not be overestimated, and as male and female they would soon produce more of their own kind. "Call the pups," he commanded Ika.

She obeyed.

The wolf-dogs did not.

Xohkantakeh shook his head and, with the girl eager to assist him, moved to take the pups in hand. It was no easy task, nor was it without risk. The wolf-dogs had been wary and recalcitrant toward him since they had seen him kill their sister, and they were in no mood to be denied the meal to which they had just set themselves. The blood of their forebears was running hot in their veins. They snarled and snapped and took no heed of the commands of either man or girl until the giant grasped first one and then the other by the scruff of the neck. But as he dragged them from the bear, so did the wolf-dogs drag the hide of the bear with them.

"Aiee!" cried Ika.

"Yah!" exclaimed Quarana.

Xohkantakeh was too stunned to speak. The bear hide had come cleanly away from its body and now lay in a sodden heap at his feet. As he stood staring down, a wolf-dog dangling from each hand, he saw that the body was not the corpse of a skinned animal. Indeed, as it rolled free of the ruined hide and settled once more amidst the tangled branches, Xohkantakeh saw that it was not the body of a bear at all. It was the bloodied and broken body of a young man.

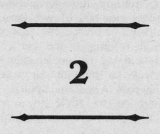

2

He was dead.

The river raced on. Ravens circled overhead. The ghosts of the Ancient Ones murmured around him. Warakan was vaguely aware of these things as he lay pinioned amidst the shattered branches of the great tree that had snared and held him fast when the flood swept them both away. Now the broken arms of the ancient spruce continued to hold him captive, refusing to release his corpse to the river or to allow his spirit to rise and flee from his drowned body even when wolves swarmed over him and stripped him of the skin of the old she-bear.

And now the ghosts of the Ancient Ones were closing around him, and he was being forcibly turned out of the warm, encapsulating hide. Pain flared—bright, excruciating pain made all the more unbearable by the shock of cold air against his exposed skin.

Did he scream as his body settled once more into the hard, unyielding embrace of the great tree? Impossible. Dead men could not scream. Nor should they be able to feel pain. Yet never, not even in the nightmare vision he had experienced after being struck by lightning and speared by phantoms on the high plateau, had Warakan felt greater agony, nor imagined that it was possible for a corpse to suffer such an appalling intensity of sensation. Perhaps he was alive after all?

No. Logic told him that neither man nor beast nor bird nor six- nor eight-legged crawling thing could have survived the raging, roaring, tumultuous cataclysm that had brought him to this moment. He *was* dead. He *had* to be dead. How else could he be hanging, immobile, suspended in the tree like an offering to the spirits? Gradually, although he faced the rising sun, an expanding inner darkness was easing his way into oblivion. He welcomed the dark path; there was no pain to be found upon it.

Ravens continued to circle overhead, summoning crows, hawks, and other carrion-eating birds to feast upon the dead.

Somewhere far away an eagle called.

Then, nearby, a bird—or was it a man?—shouted, "Eeka!"

It was the latter sound that penetrated the darkness in which Warakan's spirit drifted, diminished, all but obliterated. Slowly, surely, he became aware again of the rush of the river, of the shrieking of ravens, of other words . . .

"Can he be alive?"

"Hmm. The dead do not scream. Stand aside. Help your sister hold back the pups while I see just what the river has brought us."

Warakan's eyelids quivered against the invasiveness of sound and sunlight. The words had come blurred to his brain through the swollen, debris-clogged canals of his ears, yet he knew that the query had been spoken by a female voice, a stranger's voice, young and softly tremulous; the reply had come from the throat of a male, surly, impatient, vaguely familiar, and growling low in the way of thunder rumbling over distant mountains.

His lids batted open. The brightness of morning seared his silt-abraded eyes. Through the muddied netting of his own tangled hair and a haze induced by a rising mist, Warakan saw the ghosts of the Ancient Ones coming toward him once more.

As animals they came.

As Bear and Ermine and Fox and Dog they came. All save the latter walked upright, in the way of people, not of animals. He remembered that in the time beyond beginning the People and Animals were of one tribe; both walked upright under the all-seeing yellow eye of Father Above and the cool, serene face of Moon, Mother of Stars. So it must be with the Ancient Ones, he thought as he watched the ermine spirit fall back to stand with the fox spirit and two canine spirits that appeared to be both wolf and dog. Then he found himself in shadow. The bear spirit had put itself between him and the light of the morning sun.

A coldness touched Warakan that had nothing to do with the chill air of morning and everything to do with the certainty that he was about to be escorted from this world into the world beyond. And there, surely, the spirits of his father and grandfather awaited the coming of one who had failed to avenge them.

A tremor of remorse shook him. Shateh had not come for him, nor had Masau, or Jhadel. And where was the spirit of Sister Wolf? Surely his old friend and hunting partner had perished in the flood, so why did her spirit not come to him now? Remorse congealed into shame. Why should Sister Wolf wish to walk with Warakan in the world beyond this world when he had failed to keep her safe—much less alive—in this one? Indeed, in one way or another, he had failed all those who had ever loved or trusted him.

And now the bear spirit was hulking over him, growling to itself as it impatiently felt his bones and fingered his skin. "Hmm. No real damage here. Only bruises. Many and deep. But he has been long in the water, too long perhaps; his blood runs slow and his heart is unsteady, and, ah, here's a cracked rib or two . . ."

Warakan cried out and strained against the prodding fingers, but his protests were useless. The power of the bear spirit was overwhelming. He was helpless in the grip of a tawny phantom as huge and broad-shouldered and thickly furred as the high, rolling grasslands of his ancestral homeland. The comparison jolted him. Memories flared—and recognition.

"Bear Brother?" The question was a raw wheeze scraping over Warakan's bruised vocal chords, but he spoke on in a rush nonetheless. "Is that you, old friend, cub of the shebear whose skin has been taken from me by wolves? Ah! Did I not warn you that you must surely die if you chose to

walk alone across the country of our enemies without
Warakan to protect you? But it is good to see a friend and to
know that you have come to guide me from this world to the
world of spirits, where we will walk the wind as brothers
forever!"

"What kind of talk is this!" snarled the bear spirit as it
roughly lifted the tangled hair from Warakan's face, then
drew back with a startled cry. "Shateh!"

"Where?" Warakan wondered who was more startled,
he or the animal spirit.

The phantom was leaning close again, its eyes fixed and
hollow in a face that remained grotesquely immobile. "How
can this be? When last I looked upon your face, you were a
dead man, with your head and skin impaled on a mammoth-
bone stake in the Valley of the Dead outside the stronghold
of the People of the Watching Star. Yet now your face is the
same as when we were youths together. No . . . not the
same. You had a few hunt scars to boast of, but none at your
mouth, and your nose was high and unmarred and . . . Ah, of
course! The spirits have twisted my thoughts." The great
head moved in slow consideration. "I am no friend or
brother of yours, Warakan, grandson of Shateh, for surely
there can be no other! Look. Yes. Stare. As well you
should."

Warakan's eyes went wide when he saw the bear spirit
shake back its head and he saw—not an animal's face—
but the long graying hair and ravaged features of a man.
"Xohkantakeh! Enemy of my father! Betrayer of my
grandfather!"

The man in the bearskin snarled again, and this time
the virulence of pure hatred twisted his face and words.
"What obscene mockery on the part of the Four Winds and
the forces of Creation allows the river to puke up this
mindless spawn of the Two Tribes and present him to me
alive, when my own beloved woman and unborn child remain lost to me?"

"He must be a gift . . . a gift from the river," sighed the
ermine spirit, peeking around the side of the man and shaking back her hood to reveal the face of a woman . . . a small,
dimpled, antelope-eyed woman.

"Mah-ree!" exclaimed Warakan, incredulous.

"Quarana," she corrected. Smiling, she said to the warrior, "He *is* alive! And he is young and—"

"He is not the gift I seek," Xohkantakeh growled. "He is Trouble. In this land or any other, Warakan is Enemy to all who have ever trusted or cared for him. I want no part of him. Come away. We will leave him to the river that has left him too weak and battered to fight off the ravens and other carrion eaters of the land and sky."

"But, Life Giver, Bear Slayer, Killer of Horse and Bull Bison . . . if you know this man, you cannot just walk off and leave him alone . . . as you left Xree alone in the dark water of the marsh, alone with frogs . . . alone forever."

"What say you? There are no frogs in this place! And your little sister was surely dead! Again and again I dived into the marsh for her! Of what do you accuse me?"

"I—"

"No! I will hear no more. I tell you, this man is Trouble. He carries no blood of mine. I owe him nothing. The forces of Creation have seen fit to injure him. Now let them finish him. He is of no use to me!"

"But, my father, if we care for him, in time will he not be well and strong again?"

Warakan heard a new voice and saw the fox spirit come to stand at the side of the man. The strange-looking wolf spirits were slavering at her side; he saw now that they were half grown, but he also saw their teeth and hungry eyes and shivered with dread.

"Time?" Xohkantakeh rumbled. "Now, there is an enemy worthy of the best of us! Come. Enough talk. We will return to the hill."

"But, my father, New Woman is right! The Four Winds and the forces of Creation have brought this man to us. If he *is* a gift from the river, how can we turn our backs to him and walk away?"

"As easily as this!" Without another word Xohkantakeh rose to his feet and would have turned and walked away had the sunlight not at that moment sparked brightly on something at Warakan's throat.

Warakan saw the giant stiffen, stare, then drop to his

knees as though struck from behind by some mighty and invisible force.

"What is this?" The words went out of Xohkantakeh like blood seeping from a mortal wound. There was a fixed and feral wildness in his eyes that bordered on madness as he fumbled impatiently at Warakan's throat. "It cannot be!" he cried. "Not now! Not when I have lost the woman of my heart and all that I have ever longed for!"

Warakan gasped, strangling and hurt by the press of the man's probing fingers and then by a sharp burning at the back of his neck as he found himself jerked from the tree, then allowed to fall back hard into the branches. Pain ravaged him, left him sick and half blinded until, slowly, his vision cleared and he looked up to see Xohkantakeh raising a torn thong and a pale talisman to the light of the sun.

"What is it, Life Giver? A neck adornment of some kind?"

Warakan was soothed by the soft, tremulous voice of the one who called herself Quarana, until he heard the growl of the old warrior.

"Some would say it is more than that . . . much more," Xohkantakeh answered obliquely. "To control the power that is said to live within this stone, great chiefs and shamans have led the warriors of the Three Tribes to war against one another until the People have been broken and scattered like leaves before the winds that presage the coming of the White Giant Winter." His face tightened as his hand fisted around the talisman. "It is said that the spirits of First Man and First Woman reside within this stone. It is said that all good things come to those men and women who walk strong in its power and keep to the ways of the Ancient Ones. Perhaps, had this most sacred of all stones come to this man and his band before the flood and not after . . ." His voice broke. He looked down at Warakan and snarled again. "When last I saw this talisman it was around the neck of a Red World shaman who swore loyalty to Shateh, chieftain of my people in the Land of Grass. On that night the shaman betrayed Shateh, stole the sacred stone, and turned the spirits of the Ancient Ones against my people when he and his woman abandoned my tribe to follow the great white mammoth totem over the edge of the world. How comes this talisman into my hand now, and from around the neck of one not fit to wear it?"

From somewhere deep within the core of Warakan's being, indignation exploded into a white-hot rage that sent his consciousness hurtling dangerously close to the abyss of delirium as he shrieked, "I am Warakan! I am grandson of Shateh and son of Masau! The sacred stone of the Ancient Ones is for the one who will be shaman above all shamans, guardian of the spirit of the People. It is mine! The Four Winds and the forces of Creation have placed it in my care! It is not for such old men as you! Give it back!"

His voice seemed to slice the air. To Warakan it seemed less the voice of a man than of an animal, a high, thin, wheezing shriek, the last frenzied exclamation of a dying beast that pretends to boldness and threat. The sound faded. He felt himself fading with it, slipping once more toward oblivion even though now, for the first time, he understood that he *was* alive and had indeed survived the cataclysm that should, by all rights, have drowned him.

The magic power of the sacred stone had saved him.

But for what purpose, when the talisman—and his life— were now in the hands of his enemies?

And now, once more, Xohkantakeh was standing over him, and even as his mind slipped over the abyss into the darkness of delirium Warakan heard the giant say:

"Old man, am I? Yes. I *am* old. And you are young. But the sacred stone of the ancestors is in *my* hand now. I will not give back what the forces of Creation and the Four Winds have placed into my care. Nor, I think, will I abandon you. My daughter is right. You *are* a gift from the river. Soon, with care, you will be well and strong. Then you will be of use to me, as the wolf-dogs are of use—as a pack animal and slave to carry the burdens of my band and quicken our journey back into the hunting grounds of our ancestors."

3

The hills rose as living islands above the drowned land.

Under the glaring eye of noon, Xohkantakeh stared across a sea of devastation and fixed his eyes on the forested heights of distant ranges as he recalled the admonition of the Ancient Ones against remaining in a place where the dead had been mourned and a spirit fire raised.

"We must go on," he said. After binding the half-drowned man's battered rib cage and devising a litter for him, he prepared to set off with his females and dogs under the shadowing wings of ravens.

"Wait," the half-drowned man murmured, weakly reaching up to grip the lower edge of Xohkantakeh's bearskin. "This robe . . . it is a fine robe, made from the skin of a fine bear . . . but the skin of the head and flank are scarred by burns. How . . . how has this happened?"

"The animal was burn-scarred when I killed it. Grass fires are common enough in the land out of which it came."

The young man's hand tightened on the hide; his fever-dulled eyes widened as he stared at it. "This pelt . . . is as yellow as the hide of the she-bear that bore my brother long ago in the hunting grounds of—"

"She-bear do not birth the brothers of men! And yellow bears are as common as grass fires in the hunting grounds of the ancestors. The pelt of the animal that clothed you was also yellow. What matter?" The question suddenly resolved itself in Xohkantakeh's mind, and he pried the young man's hand free of his robe. "You will not have the hide of Great Paws in exchange for the ruined rag my woman and daughter gave to the waters when they found it beyond repair!"

"You have thrown into the river the skin of the great she-bear? Since I was a boy she has clothed me! Since the day I slew her she has shared her warmth and the gift of her life with me!"

"You are no longer a boy. It is time you learned to do without her." Xohkantakeh turned, only to be arrested in midstep when the young man again grasped the bearskin.

"Is this the skin of the she-bear's child—of my Bear Brother—upon your back?" demanded Warakan, his face and lips strained to colorlessness by the effort.

"Has the river so muddied your senses and fever so dulled your eyes that you actually imagine that the skin of a bear cub could cloak me?" Xohkantakeh demanded in turn.

"Big as a mountain was my brother when last I saw him. Shaggy as an autumn prairie, and as yellow. And his forepaw was scarred across the pad."

Again Xohkantakeh snatched the hide out of the young man's grasp. "It is the way of the bear kind to be scarred by life and battle, just as it is with men. The journey that lies ahead is long. I have no time for your senseless babblings!" This said, he took up the drag poles of the litter and led the others on.

They carried what they could of the meat of the bison and horse, leaving behind only those portions that were too burdensome, piling them high and welcoming the winged foragers of the sky to feast upon them lest the flesh of the slain animals be wasted.

"From this day we will do nothing to provoke the forces of Creation," he told his daughter and woman emphatically. "From this day we will keep to the ways of the Ancient Ones in all ways. Let no law be spurned. Let no offense be given. Let no word be spoken to invoke the spirits, unless that word be used to assure our well-being and safe arrival in the hunting grounds of our ancestors. The sacred stone has come into my care. I am no shaman, but in the encampments of my people I was keeper and guardian of sacred

Fire. Fire was kept. The sacred heart ember was not extinguished. It is said that the man who keeps the sacred talisman of the Ancient Ones is also guardian of the spirit of the People. When we return at last to the hunting grounds of the ancestors, may it be said that Xohkantakeh has kept and guarded that spirit well."

And so they went on, sobered by his words, weighted by a new sense of responsibility, and buoyed by the new sense of hope that possession of the sacred stone had given them. Dusk saw them weary, footsore, and resting amidst a rank fog. They made a lean-to on the highest, driest ground they could find, wrung out their sodden moccasins, then shared a bladder skin of oily marrow broth with their new companion, who drank greedily and vomited only half of his portion. Afterward they stripped him of his crude soiled garments. Quarana stared unabashedly, while Ika's face went red at the sight of his bared maleness as Xohkantakeh laid him on a clean fur, then rolled him tightly in it.

"If strength returns to him while we sleep, he will not be able to rise and sneak away without waking us, or try to take the sacred stone," he said. After commanding his females to bundle in their own sleeping furs, he told Ika to lie down on one side of the man while he and Quarana lay down on the other.

Quarana nestled close against the giant, sighing and languorously rubbing fatigue from his body, encouraging him to drift into sleep until she slowly slipped back the furs that separated their bare bodies and sent warm, questing hands and whispers to arouse him to wakefulness, and more.

"Life Maker, ease my need . . . and yours," she invited. "Place your woman pleaser between my thighs. Send it seeking deep . . . mmm . . . fill me . . . now . . . yes."

"No!" Xohkantakeh tensed, slapped her hands away, and, after quickly readjusting the bed furs so that a heavy layer of hide lay between them, turned from her, growling in barely suppressed fury, "Have you heard nothing of what your man has said this day? The laws of the Ancient Ones will *not* be broken! The spirit of the People and the power of the sacred stone will not be profaned. I will not come between the thighs of a woman who carries life in her belly. It is forbidden! Do not lead me in such a way again, Quarana. Never again will I allow a woman of mine to risk bringing the wrath of the forces of Creation upon herself or her band! Go to sleep, and leave this man to much-needed rest!"

She made no reply as she settled back in her furs, but if it was possible for a pout to be audible, Xohkantakeh heard it.

Ika exhaled a troubled sigh.

"Sleep!" he commanded the girl, annoyed.

"I will try," she whispered and, sighing again, snuggled closer to the wolf-dogs.

Xohkantakeh lay awake, willing his man bone back to sleep. It was no easy task, but fatigue proved a dulling agent, and soon he was relaxed and drowsy, listening to the even breathing of his daughter and woman and wolf-dogs and to the shallow rasps of the fevered, half-drowned man. Xohkantakeh scowled; by rights Warakan should not be sharing his family's shelter. Slaves belonged in separate lean-tos or outside in the weather with the dogs, but in such a dank, wet fog, even the wolf-dogs sheltered with the band, and an injured man left exposed to the elements would surely sicken and die.

In the drowned valley, the racing river set up a constant *shhh*ing that soon lulled the giant to sleep. He smiled and gave himself to dreams of distant sunstruck hills and ridges, of dry camps in which the smell of sage and sweet grass kindling rose from the fire pits. The spirits of the ancestors sang songs of praise to the tall old warrior who walked boldly along bare, stony heights with his back to the east and his females and wolf-dogs at his side, while the sun gleamed on distant icefields and he called upon the powers of the sacred stone to ease his journey and keep his females safe.

An owl called.

Another answered.

Xohkantakeh's eyes batted open. His smile vanished as he listened, remembered the night when he had set himself to hunt Great Paws under a burning sky while dire wolves howled and owls spoke of Death beyond the palisade. He closed his eyes. The owls had portended the death of Great

Paws; perhaps, he realized now, they had also foretold the death of Katohya. Now his beloved was dead, and owls were calling again. But for whom?

Whooo . . . whooo . . . whoom . . . whom?

Xohkantakeh shivered.

The human gift of the river was murmuring incoherently and thrashing in his dreams. Rambling on about mammoths and mastodons and vengeance and totems, he begged some-one named Peacedreamer to forgive him, then called for his sister. After a few moments he settled into deep sleep and lay still.

Ika whispered, "The fever spirits feed upon his body and send his thoughts upon strange and broken trails. Do you think he will die, my father?"

"Someday, surely so, but only the Four Winds and the forces of Creation can say when, daughter . . . unless I were to kill him now and make an end of his misery . . . and my own."

"But he has said that he is a grandson of Shateh, chieftain of your tribe, my father, a man whose name I have heard you honor many times. If these are true words, why do you hate him so?"

"Because they cannot be true words! Because many a long winter ago Warakan came to my tribe as a runaway . . . as a child of the cannibal People of the Watching Star . . . as a boy willing to betray his people to mine. Some said it was a good thing to be shown the weakness of ene-mies who had been usurping our hunting grounds, steal-ing our women, and slaughtering our people for endless moons, but I could not trust the loyalty of the one who had come to us at the expense of his own tribe. But Shateh trusted him as he trusted the Red World shaman, Cha-kwena, who had come to us not long before promising that all the powers of his talisman—the sacred stone of the ancestors—would be ours if we allowed him to walk as a wise man among us. Soon after, we were victorious against our enemies. Shateh celebrated the powers of the shaman and embraced Warakan as though the boy were of his own flesh. Yet the elders warned against the foreign shaman, and I knew in my heart that no child of our ene-

mies could be anything less than trouble to us. It was said
in council that no good could come of trusting those not
born to the tribe. Shateh would not listen. He named the
shaman Friend, and because he had outlived all his male
children, he called Warakan Son. Then bad times came.
Hungry times. The shaman disappeared with the sacred
stone. And a day came when Warakan went off on his
own, breaking clan law as it suited him, to take his first
bear. An elder and a youth of the tribe died as a result of
this hunt, and while Warakan was killing his bear, one of
the chieftain's women expelled a male baby from her
womb stillborn. All knew then that it was Warakan who
had wished death to Shateh's true son and brought bad
luck to the chieftain and to the tribe. War came to us again
soon after that. Many battles were lost. Shateh was betrayed and slain by one who sought to be chieftain in his
place. The friends of my youth, the last of my children,
and nearly all who ever touched my heart were killed. But
not before Warakan was cast out of the tribe and driven
into a great mad river to drown."

He paused. Memories roiled in his mind, as dark and violent as the rivers of past and present. The river into which the
boy had been driven lay far to the north and west, but it
seemed to him now that it had flowed southeast, swollen
nearly to the dimensions of the one that raced southward
now in the drowned valley. Disturbed by his thoughts,
Xohkantakeh shifted, propped himself onto a folded arm,
and glowered through the darkness at the unconscious man
who lay between him and the girl. "Is it possible that we follow the same river? Is it possible that he has been adrift in
the waters all this time, a captive of the forces of Creation, a
spirit imprisoned in this world until he could be made to
atone for all he brought upon those who should never have
trusted him?"

"He does not look like a spirit, my father."

"No. And yet if he is right about Great Paws being the
same animal as the beast he calls Bear Brother, then by the
sheer power of his will he may have sent that bear south
along the river to seek out and harass those whom he imagined to be his enemies. The sacred stone of the ancestors

was around his neck when we found him. How did such as he come to possess it unless by spirit magic?"

"If he lives, he will surely tell you, my father."

A growl rose in his throat. "Yes. And I will tell you this, daughter: If all that I suspect of him is true, then Xree is dead because of him, and for all we know, it was his dark magic that sent the waters pouring forth to devour Katohya. I will do what I can to keep him alive as a slave to serve my needs only until it pleases me to see him dead by my own hand."

A shallow sigh escaped the girl's lips. "He must have been a very small boy indeed when he caused so much sadness to your chieftain and tribe, my father. Perhaps he did not mean for the bad things to happen. After all, he *has* brought the sacred stone of the ancestors to you!"

"Too late to save Xree or my beloved!"

"Yes, but not too late to help us with our burdens when he is well and strong. Perhaps, if we treat him kindly, you need not make a slave of him, for he will prove to be a friend and—"

"Yah!" Quarana interrupted in a quarrelsome tone that made it clear she did not appreciate being roused from sleep. "What a selfish girl you are, Ika! Would you allow this gift from the river his freedom so that he can run away? Xohkantakeh is right. We must make a slave of him. Think of what the warriors of the Land of Grass will say when Bear Slayer and Killer of Horse and Bull Bison returns with the sacred stone, a baby-bearing woman, two wolf-dogs, and a strong young slave to carry the burdens of his band! Truly they will see that Life Maker is a great chief and will surely welcome him and us among them."

"But our mother was always saddened by the thought of slaves," said Ika.

"Our mother is no longer with us," Quarana reminded her.

Somewhere in the drowned valley, a lion raked the night with its roar.

Xohkantakeh imagined nocturnal predators feeding upon the dead. Cringing at the thought of his woman's body being savaged by carnivores, he lay back, saying, "It is I who called Death upon my beloved when I asked the forces of Creation to punish her for her disobedience and disrespect. My request was spoken in anger. I did not wish it to be fulfilled. But once spoken, who can say how the winds will take a man's words? And so now the punishment I willed upon my beloved is upon my head as well as hers. The 'gift from the river' has spoken truly. I *am* an old man. My one remaining wish is to survive long enough to see you—Ika and Quarana and the child my new woman carries—safe within a band large enough to protect you from the consequences of rash judgments made by old men. May the sacred stone of the Ancient Ones grant me the power to do this."

"Surely it will be so," Quarana assured him. "For when the one you call Warakan has regained his strength, our burdens will be lightened and the journey will go much more quickly! Ah, soon Xohkantakeh will be great in the eyes of men. He will be envied by warriors and women. He will be—"

"Enough," he interrupted. "I set my tracks toward the land of the ancestors for your sake, woman, and in consideration of your sister and the new life that grows in your belly. As for myself, I regret the day I left the winter camp your mother loved so much, and I have no wish to be envied or seen as great in the eyes of men. My spirit flows south with the great river that has taken my Sweet-Scented Woman and my heart. Without Katohya, my life is over."

Ika gasped in dismay. "You must not speak so! You are *my* life! Xohkantakeh is the only tribe I have ever known or wanted."

"And you are an immature girl who has lived so long beyond the edge of the world that you remember nothing of life in the camps of men," he told her.

"I remember," she disagreed. "I am your Little Bear! I have stood to Great Paws and not run away! I do not need to live among many when Xohkantakeh leads my band!"

Fatigue was suddenly heavy in him. "Go back to sleep,

Ika. We need rest to give us strength. The Land of Grass is still far away, and it will be many days before this living gift from the river is anything to us but Trouble."

They went on in the first light of dawn, with the half-drowned man still semiconscious and muttering incoherently. Xohkantakeh bound him as tightly to the litter as he had bound his ribs and, ignoring his rantings, hefted the drag poles and led his females and tethered wolf-dogs on.

The air was warmer now, but with the warmth came biting flies and evaporative mists that rose and congealed to hang blue and noxious in the morning air, ripe with the sweet stench of decomposing flesh and rotting vegetation. Beneath the travelers' feet the earth was a morass of mud, broken trees and foliage, and long, twisting dunes of debris-littered silt. The bodies of drowned animals were everywhere, and here and there carnivores drawn into the valley by the stink of death and the promise of meat could be seen feeding. Xohkantakeh did not have to tell his females that it was not safe to stop to rest.

By midday they were well onto the flanks of the first range of hills, wending their way slowly upward out of the drowned land with their backs to the sun and to the river that had so devastated the earth, and their lives.

Ika's body was aching with fatigue when Xohkantakeh at last allowed them to stop and catch their breaths. Quarana sighed in relief, sat down on a lichen-scabbed boulder, and began to rub her feet. Ika stood looking back in sorrow. The mists that had risen with the sun had thickened into a pervasive fog that now lay across the drowned land like a vast white blanket. She could not see the river or the valley, but here and there a hilltop pierced the undulating clouds. She recognized the forested ridge upon which the band had paused to rest after first ascending from the valley before the flood, and upon which they later awaited in vain the return of Katohya and then raised spirit smoke to honor her life and assure her passage into the world beyond this world.

Ika's sadness intensified. She knew Xohkantakeh blamed himself and Katohya's inadvertent offense to the forces of

Creation for the tragedy that had befallen them. But as she watched birds rising now and then through the fog—a pair of hawks, a dark eagle whose neck feathers shone gold in the light of the sun, and ravens stroking upward on long sharp wings only to bank sharply downward again, disappearing into the fog, no doubt returning to their grisly feast—she knew in her heart she was also to blame. Surely the forces of Creation knew her secret; she was a woman who had shed first blood, and still she carried a spear and hunted alongside her father even though she knew it was forbidden to do so. But what could she do? With Xohkantakeh unfit to keep them safe and Quarana now with child, she dared not reveal her secret. But what would happen to them all if she did not? Perhaps the half-drowned man would grow strong again and could be made to hunt at Xohkantakeh's side. But could he be trusted to protect the band if need arose, as she would do?

"Look there. Ah . . . do you see it?" Xohkantakeh's voice was a strained exhalation of awe as he pointed.

Glad to be distracted from her troublesome thoughts, Ika gazed out over the fog at the familiar peaks of the high, ice-mantled mountains that rose in jagged splendor above the cloud cover at the far end of the valley. In the stark sunlight, the broad, gleaming snowfields shone with hurtful brilliance. Ika squinted against the intensity of their radiance, and yet, even as she did so, her heart went cold. Something was different about the mountains.

Something was missing.

Ika was stunned, unable to comprehend what had happened to the massive blue lake the band had skirted when Xohkantakeh had first followed the river down into the narrow valley below the falls. It took her several heartbeats to grasp the realization that the lake was no longer there. In its place was a stark defile, a raw and terrible wound in the earth at the bottom of which she could see the river running in a wide, flat, shining ribbon of light that poured over a vastly widened and diminished waterfall. She stood motionless, watching the water disappear into the fog and valley below, then looked to Xohkantakeh for understanding.

"What would cause a lake to rise from its bed and disappear, my father?" she asked.

But it was not Xohkantakeh who answered.

"Mountains that walk," replied the half-drowned man from his litter. "Mountains of solid ice . . . mountains stepping forward into the lake that is the Mother of All Rivers . . . mountains calving like mammoth . . . mountains birthing smaller mountains until the great lake cannot hold them all and surges forward to push all other lakes and rivers before her as she rises to drown the world!"

Ika's heart leaped. The sound as much as the content of the stranger's words startled her and set her blood strangely racing. She turned. Quarana was on her feet, and the wolf-dogs, tethered to the drag poles of the litter, were tangling themselves in their leashes as they tumbled over the half-drowned man, so aggressive in their curiosity that he cried out for his sister while weakly attempting to push them away.

Xohkantakeh shook his head disparagingly as he moved to stand over the man, doing nothing to intervene while the pups kept at their explorations. "Are you still so feeble that you must call upon a woman to keep you from the nosings of my wolf-dogs?"

"My sister *is* a wolf!" snapped the man, gritting his teeth in a vain effort to keep from groaning as the animals stressed his injuries.

"As you are a wolf under your skin," replied the giant tersely, bending to pull off the pups. "As such you are worth keeping for a while. Soon you will walk in the traces beside my wolf-dogs and ease the burden of my band as you carry and pull your own weight and more. Now you will eat and drink. Now you will grow strong. Quarana, bring meat. Ika, bring the bladder skin. This gift of the river and spawn of our enemies must get back his strength. I will not carry a slave forever."

Ika obeyed without hesitation.

The marrow broth in the bladder skin was of her making; there was not much of it left, but it was strong and oily and more nourishing than blood or meat. She carried the container on her back in a tightly stitched packet of greased gut, with the bone spout looped by a sturdy thong over a tine of her antler-frame carrying pack. She shrugged off the frame, set her belongings on the stony ground, slipped the thong from the tine, and hurried to kneel before the half-drowned man.

He lay still, his eyes closed, his face pale and taut with pain. A bent, twisted eagle feather protruded from the tangles of his mud-encrusted hair like a tiny broken wing.

Ika could see his pulse beating at his temples, throat, and tightly clenched jaw. Inexplicably, her own pulse quickened in response, so much so that she could barely breathe as her eyes took in the tense angularity of his features: the high, wide, unlined brow; the smooth curve of his cheeks; the small white scars at the corners of his long, expressive mouth; the welting of an old break across the bridge of his nose. Everything about his face compelled empathy . . . compassion . . . and deeper, stronger, disturbingly alien emotions that fired her senses and brought her to know that no sunset or sunrise she had ever seen was more beautiful or wondrous to behold than the young man who lay before her now.

His eyes opened.

Long, lanceolate, questing eyes, heavily lashed, as black as polished obsidian hunting daggers, and as sharp.

Ika caught her breath. As she met his gaze, she felt her spirit snared in the darkness of those fevered eyes and, trembling, sighed as she yielded willingly to entrapment. *Xohkantakeh is right,* she thought. *There* is *a wolf inside your skin, a hurt and injured wolf who snaps and snarls against your captors, but soon we will make you well, and despite what my father says, he will give you your freedom, and you will be so grateful for our kindness that you will choose to walk with us, a man, no longer a wolf, and a member of our band!* A smile of happy longing curved her lips. There was something magical in the moment. She wanted it to last forever, but seconds later she flinched, disappointed, when the rasp of his voice broke the spell.

"Why do you stare? What do you want of me?"

Ika recoiled, confused by the hard, flat aggressiveness of his tone. T*ruly he* is *a wolf,* she thought, then stammered, "I . . . I b-bring marrow b-broth. Xohkantakeh says that you

. . . you must eat." She flushed, embarrassed, for her voice had come blundering from her mouth like a small, unsure little mouse that only half dared to venture from the protective confines of her throat.

"I will not eat of any food *he* would give me," replied Warakan. Closing his eyes again, he turned his face away.

Ika stared at him, her heart pounding. Pity and concern roused a deep ache in her breast. She was certain his accusations were born of fever and confused recollections of the past, but in defense of Xohkantakeh she suddenly found the strength to say, slowly and surely, "In war and battle many are slain. I know not about your grandfather, but if it *is* the skin of your brother upon my father's back, then I will tell you that if by some magic—as my father believes—you sent Great Paws here to stalk us, he succeeded only in hunting his own death. He followed this band over the edge of the world like a yellow spirit. We called him Great Paws. We wished no war with him or his kind. Always when we found his sign or glimpsed the fall of his shadow upon the earth, we broke down our lodges and moved before him. Always he followed, until one day he found the battle he was seeking. Now Bear Slayer has eaten the heart and honored the spirit of the great yellow bear, and if that bear *was* your brother, he still lives—in the body and spirit of the hunter who has slain him."

Warakan moaned. "My brother was following man scent, but he was not hunting you. He was lonely and looking for a friend he had long ago abandoned when he sought his own kind in the—"

"Sister, stand aside," said Quarana. "You will exhaust the stranger with words! Here, half-drowned man, you must eat something." Dropping to her knees on the opposite side of the litter, she held a strip of smoked meat in one hand and laid her free palm gently upon the side of Warakan's face. Lightly and tenderly her fingers stroked his hair, then moved downward across his exposed throat until a tremor went through them both and he turned his face to look at her.

Ika could not have explained the rush of emotion that went through her when she saw her sister smile and the man squint up in apparent confusion. There was no sharpness in his eyes now.

"Mah-ree?" he queried softly.

Ika's heart sank. His question was so full of hope and love that it hurt to hear it.

Quarana dimpled. "Eat of the meat I bring and I will be whoever you wish me to be."

A rumble of anger went out of Xohkantakeh. "Speak not like that to any man but me, woman!" Moving to the litter like a riled bull, he pushed Quarana away, snatched the bladder skin from Ika's hands, and took Warakan in his grip as he shoved the bone spout hard against the man's compressed lips. "You will eat! You will take the food that is offered by this band! You will do this, or by the Four Winds and the forces of Creation, I will break your neck now and leave you behind for carrion!"

The half-drowned man ate.

Quarana watched him through carefully lowered eyes as she remained on her knees to one side of the litter.

She could feel Xohkantakeh glowering at her as he held the bladder skin to the stranger's lips. He was angry with her. Very angry. Worry pricked beneath her skin. She had been foolish to speak so provocatively to the half-drowned man and knew that she would not allow herself to be so careless again, but the words had come unbidden to her tongue.

Xohkantakeh was rumbling again. He had taken the bladder skin from the stranger and was now handing him the slice of meat Quarana had dropped when he pushed her away. "Eat. Eat it all," he commanded roughly. "Or it will be the last thing you ever taste or see."

The man took the meat, closed his eyes, and, holding it in one hand, began to gnaw weakly at one end.

Quarana kept her head down. She wondered what the stranger was thinking, what it must be like to find oneself hurt, helpless, and enslaved. She felt great pity for him. And something else. Something that quickened the beat of her heart and made her tremble. The river had battered and weakened him, and fever burned in his eyes and heated his skin. But in the rank fog of yesterday's dusk, when Xohkantakeh stripped the man of the sodden pelts that covered his body, Quarana had seen the potential power of his youth laid bare: the lean, hard musculature of his shoulders and arms and limbs and chest . . . the smooth perfection of his unlined skin . . . and the cylindrical extension of his maleness lying long and limp across one thigh.

Again she trembled; her woman place tensed and moistened in readiness to receive a man—*this* man, not the old warrior, not the one who had taken and filled her again and again and had still failed to put life into her belly! Ah! What had possessed her to tell him he had? Love? Pity? Or desperation born of the fear that if he lost heart and died, she would be left alone with Ika and surely destined to die soon after?

Xohkantakeh called her name.

Quarana looked up. Her brow furrowed. The giant had just drunk deeply from the bladder skin and, after giving it to Ika, was wiping his mouth with the back of his hand as he commanded her to rise and prepare to move on. She did not move. Instead she stared at him. He looked so tired, so old. It occurred to her now, and not for the first time, that he might not live long enough to reach the hunting grounds of the ancestors. Her head went high, for it also occurred to her that, as long as the young man lived and grew strong, she did not really care.

4

They went on.

Day bled into dusk, dusk into darkness, darkness into another dawn.

And still they journeyed on.

Warakan drifted in and out of delirium. Now and then he felt himself being observed and opened his eyes to a blur of female faces. A wide face, young, full-mouthed and worry-eyed and as pensive as the full face of an autumn moon. And a narrower face, younger still, small-mouthed, hungry-eyed, as voracious as a pretty little weasel. Sometimes the faces spoke; sometimes they did not. Sometimes, it seemed, the crowns of the budding hardwoods and evergreens whispered and sighed strange utterances and mockeries. But always it was the giant, Xohkantakeh, who came to deliberately rouse him from his dreams.

"Eat! You must eat!" thundered the man as meat was shoved into Warakan's face.

He ate.

"Now drink! This broth is good. There is not much of it left, so do not waste it. It will make you strong!" The bone spout of the bladder skin was jammed into Warakan's mouth.

He sucked oily broth.

Slowly, deep within the marrow of his bones, warmth stirred and life began to rekindle, but he was not yet ready to rise to renewal. He turned his back to his tormentor and sent a hand to feebly guide his man bone as he released a stream of urine over the side of the litter, trying and failing to spatter the moccasins of the giant.

"The gift from the river is still so weak, my father. Will he never be strong again?"

"He has been many days and nights in the river, daughter. It will take as many more, I think, before the fever spirits leave his body and strength returns to his bones and blood."

And then you will die by my hand, old man, vowed Warakan. *I will take back the sacred stone of the Ancient Ones. And then, as punishment for the humiliation you heap upon me now and for your betrayal of my grandfather so long ago, I will take from you the skin of my slain Bear Brother before I piss on your body and leave you for carrion as you have threatened to leave me!*

The promise of revenge was sweet. It lulled him to sleep as the giant hefted the litter and dragged him on.

The shrieking of an eagle woke him. Did it call his name? It seemed that someone—or something—did.

"Warakan!"

He stirred on the litter, sucked air against the dull ache of his cracked ribs, and squinted as he looked up through the broken canopy of the forest. The sun was in its lodge; he saw it through a thin, opalescent haze of high cirrus cloud and observed that it was not alone. An eagle shared the lodge, hovering on broad, dark wings within the pale circle of the shimmering rainbow framework.

"Rain will come before dark, or before dawn, but it will come," observed Xohkantakeh. "Come. We must seek a place to make a dry camp before the storm comes upon us."

Warakan moaned as the litter was jostled again. He closed his eyes, curling his fingers around the battered eagle feather that had been a gift from his grandfather, and willed himself back into oblivion.

Somewhere thunder rumbled—or was it the low grumbling of the giant?

And from within the lodge of the sun, the eagle called, "Follow, Warakan, Son of Two Tribes! Kya! If you dare!"

He shivered under the furs that the giant and his two females had heaped upon him. Opening his eyes, he looked up to see trees bending above his head and recalled the arching ceilings of the smoky sweat lodges in which he and Jhadel had sought and shared communication with the spirits from the world beyond the world.

"Jhadel . . . Peacedreamer . . . Shaman . . ."

The names of the old man sighed from Warakan's lips. As they did, a soft wind grew out of them, took substance and shape, and shivered through the branches of the trees even as Warakan shivered. He felt himself borne up and knew—as in the dream-vision he had endured upon the promontory—that he was Eagle now!

On broad wings he flew.

High, higher, into the trees and beyond. Into the sky. Into the clouds and into the lodge of the sun, within which he banked and wheeled until the Four Winds took him, turned him, bore him away on vast, whispering tides of air. Mountains. Valleys. Mighty rivers. A land of lakes and ponds and endless forests and tundral barrens stretching away and away to a body of water so vast not even an eagle could fly over it. All this Warakan saw until, with a start, he hovered on the wind.

A mammoth walked below.

A white mammoth!

Huge, massive, it moved forward like a living mountain, a creature with tusks as long and wide as great trees and a voice that echoed up to him like thunder in the sky.

"Life Giver!" Warakan cried in recognition of the totem.

"Follow the sun to the place where dawn is born, and it shall be so!" replied the great white mammoth.

Warakan's breath was coming fast and sharp. There, striding beside the mammoth, was the Red World shaman, Cha-kwena, in his sacred owl-skin headdress and rabbit-skin robe. At his side walked a woman, small, sure of step, striding out as purposefully as the shaman. Warakan's heart lurched. He had almost forgotten how deceptively fragile and lovely Mah-ree was. And how much he loved her!

"Mah-ree of the Red World People!" Warakan called. "Mah-ree, I will come for you. I will make you mine, I swear it!"

She looked up, frowned, and put a finger to her mouth. "Shhh! Do not speak! Would you have them come upon us now?"

Suddenly wolves were coming for him, loping across the sky . . . leaping at him . . . bringing him to ground and back into the body of Warakan.

"Away!" he shouted, his voice rasping ineffectually from his raw throat. Although the pack scattered and ran, two of the wolves remained to devour him. He could just see them in the gloom. The sun had gone down. He was no longer on the litter; indeed, he was longer under the open sky. He was lying on his back inside a lean-to, the wolves standing over him.

Black wolf and brindled wolf. Neither was Sister Wolf. Thick-jawed, short-snouted, tails curling high over their thickly furred flanks, they set themselves to sniffing and nipping at his hands and rooting at his throat. He felt their sharp teeth against his flesh and would have backhanded them away and bolted from the little shelter, but he was shocked to find that his ankles were bound together and his right arm was noosed by the wrist to one of the stakes that held the hide coverings fast to the frame of the lean-to. And now the wolves had him. There was no escaping them. When he raised his free arm to beat them away, the jaws of one closed on his hand while the snout of the other gouged at his neck. He felt the warm wet ooze of saliva sliming his hand and caught the hot, meaty stink of their breath as he tried desperately to turn, to roll away and bury himself beneath the heavy bison hide someone had placed over him. But it was no use. He was helpless before his fate.

Then a female voice spoke, low and sharp. "East Wind! South Wind! Out! Both of you! This shelter is for the slave, not for you! Go! Join Bear Slayer and my sister! If this is how you would protect the camp while they are off hunting, I would as soon do without you!"

Confusion swarmed in Warakan's head. In an instant the wolves had gone, and now a woman was bending over him, a small, young, antelope-eyed woman whose shadowed loveliness took his breath away. "Mah-ree . . . ?"

"She is the one you love?"

His mind cleared. The woman was not Mah-ree. She was one of the giant's females, the one who had spoken her name to him at the river's edge. He did not remember it.

"I am the one who would ease your troubled dreams . . . and my own," she said, her hands gently questing over his face, caressing his features.

"Unbind my wrist and ankles."

"I cannot. That is not of my doing. Be at ease with me now. They will return all too soon."

He was too weary to argue. He closed his eyes, imagined that she referred to his dreams or to the wolves when she said "they." He allowed her touch; the light, seeking press of her fingertips was more soothing than any healing balm could ever have been.

"I have dreamed of you," she whispered as she drew the heavy hide away and, leaning closer, continued her ministrations. "Ah, yes. I have seen your face . . . and known your body . . . and longed to touch you . . . like this."

He caught his breath and opened his eyes. Only fear of pain kept him from sitting bolt upright, for she had bent to mouth his chest and belly, and her hands were venturing where no other hands save his own—and those of his long-dead mother—had ever gone. Her touch was so exquisite, so sure and warm and capable of arousing to heat and hardness that which had never before known a woman's handling that he shivered as in his dream and wondered if she was somehow not a part of it.

"Yes . . . now . . . quickly . . . and in silence!" she whispered.

And so it was done, as though in a dream: quickly, because he was too weak and inexperienced to prolong his passion, and silently, because she pressed her mouth hungrily over his while she quivered and moved violently to fulfill her own.

Then, sated, she backed away nervously. "I must leave you now. I must cleanse myself. Xohkantakeh must not know of this! He would be angry, very angry." She pulled the hide back over his body. "What has passed between us is forbidden! If we are to come together again, he must not know!"

"Again . . . ?"

"Ah, yes! I will come to you again. I will open myself and take your woman pleaser deep between my thighs and let you fill me with the heat of your need. Ah, to look at you is to want you. As I want you again even now! It is your life I want in me, not his! If only I could be sure he would not return!"

Her words enflamed him anew, but the press of her body had roused more than passion in him; it had awakened a deep ache in his rib cage. And yet, strangely, he realized now that the pain pleased him, assured him that what had just transpired between them had been no dream. He had taken the giant's woman. Half drowned, flat on his back, unable to stand on his own two feet, with one arm bound to a stake, and deprived of the power of the sacred stone, he had taken her!

Or had she taken him?

His brow came down. Gritting his teeth against the ache in his battered ribs, Warakan propped himself on his elbows and looked at her through the gathering gloom of twilight. She was young, very young, and beautiful, perhaps even more so than his beloved Mah-ree, although there was much about their features that was similar.

She crouched before the weather flap, poised to sprint off like a frightened doe, yet bravely holding her ground as she smiled tremulously and said, "I *have* dreamed of you. I *have* known how it would be between us. You are young! I am young! With you I can yield and spread myself with my eyes wide open. It is right that we should join our bodies. I will come to you again. I am your woman now . . . but he must never know!"

Warakan gaped.

She turned, ducked through the weather baffle, and was gone, her scent lingering behind.

Warakan lay back, breathed it in, and smiled. Xohkantakeh had stolen the sacred stone, but the powers of the talisman were with him still. He had survived the flood. And now he understood why.

He closed his eyes. The woman of Xohkantakeh would come to him again. He would take her again. And in the taking he would shame the giant and be assured that—until he was well and strong again—there were subtler and infinitely more satisfying ways to inflict revenge upon an enemy than by killing him.

5

The skies opened wide that night.

Rain and sleet spit against the two lean-tos of Xohkan-takeh's encampment. Thunder cracked deafeningly over-head, and lightning stung the darkness, its light so intense that it permeated the skin coverings of the little shelters. The acrid smell of ozone soured the air. The wolf-dogs tucked their noses between their tails, burrowing beneath Ika's furs, half dislodging the girl from her bed.

"It is as though the forces of Creation are angry about something!" she exclaimed, wincing against another clap of thunder. "So much rain! So much fury falling from the sky! I do not see why the pups are welcome to shelter with us when the half-drowned man is not."

"He is no longer half drowned," replied Xohkantakeh. "And he is not a man. He is a slave. He has been given shel-ter and fresh meat. It is the way of our people with slaves. It is best to keep apart from them. I do not want you or Quarana forming an attachment to one I may not allow to live if he proves to be Trouble. Go to sleep now, Ika, and trouble me no more about this . . . this 'gift' from the river!"

"Would you truly kill him, Bear Slayer?" whispered Quarana from where she lay in the fold of the giant's arm.

"He would not be the first man or slave I have slain," he told her. With a ragged exhalation he did his best to shrug off memories of war and battle and human sacrifice as he drew her closer, slipped a hand under her buckskin tunic, and laid his palm flat against the sleek tautness of her bare belly. He was not surprised when she tensed and tried to turn away—no doubt, he thought, in respect of his pronouncement against breaking clan law, for he had made it clear to her that now that she was carrying new life it was forbidden for her to open her thighs to him.

"I would not ask that of you," he said and pressed her belly slightly with his hand. With the rainstorm raging outside and the regrets of a lifetime shadowing his spirit, Xohkantakeh wanted to feel the life in her, to make real to his mind the fact of her pregnancy by touching the first sure sign of it—the hard, slender crescent mounding at the lower edge of her abdomen that would later swell and round high as his child grew toward birth. He spread his fingers, moved his hand gently, searching in vain for that which was not there.

Lightning flashed; thunder boomed simultaneously. Quarana cried out and moved as though she would leap from his arms and flee the questings of his embrace, but he held her closer still. After the horrors of the drowned valley, he knew she had every right to fear the storm. "Be at ease with me," he said, and when she caught her breath and went rigid, he stroked and rocked her as though she were a child again. "The drowned valley is behind us, my little one. We are on high ground, far from the nearest river. It is a good dry camp that we have made. The sacred stone talisman of the ancestors is around my neck; the protective power of the Ancient Ones is with me now, and with you. Listen. The even breathing of your sister tells me that she is asleep . . . as you should be. Rest now. Do not be afraid."

Quarana shivered violently until his stroking relaxed her and she lay still. He placed his hand on her belly again, telling himself that it must be too soon for the life that he had put into her to be felt beneath his palm. Yet it soothed him to think of it, deeply planted, transforming itself within her body, growing larger and stronger with every beat of her heart, uncurling like a fragile fern beneath the first tender light of the sun until . . .

He broke off his thoughts, for they had suddenly shifted

cruelly to his lost beloved, to Katohya and their unborn child, a child conceived in the passion of absolute love, not in anger-driven lust, a child lost to him forever along with the woman without whom life had lost all its sweetness.

"What is it, Life Maker?" Quarana was tense in his arms again. "What troubles you? Surely it can be nothing I have said or . . . or done since you returned from the hunt with Ika? Were the rabbits you flushed not cooked to your liking?"

Xohkantakeh turned his back to her and deliberately ignored her questions. How could he answer without hurting her? How could he tell her that, for all that she meant to him, neither she nor the life she carried touched his heart in the way his lost beloved and her unborn child had done? "Sleep," he commanded Quarana gruffly. Closing his eyes, he castigated himself for his callousness. She was his daughter! She was his new woman! And now—although she had only recently left her own childhood behind—Quarana carried his child. Surely even an old warrior who had left the largest portion of his heart in the drowned land with his lost beloved could find some semblance of sweetness in this?

The storm was over.

The sun was rising through thin, ragged clouds as Ika crept from the family lean-to under an exhausted sky. The wolf-dogs followed her from the interior only to freeze midway through their stretching and yawning, their eyes fixed ahead. The girl paid them no heed. Her gaze was already locked on the shelter of the slave.

Warakan was no longer inside. Indeed, he was staring back at her, sitting upright in what had been the entrance to the lean-to with the sodden little tent collapsed around his shoulders. His hands worked to loosen the thongs of his hobbles.

"How . . . ?" Ika was on her feet, commanding the pups to stay their ground, but her words went unheeded, for in that moment Warakan pulled the thong binding from his ankles, planted his bare feet firmly on the sodden ground, and attempted to rise. The wolf-dogs broke forward.

"Back!" Ika cried. But she might as well have tried to command the sun to set again behind the eastern horizon.

Warakan saw the animals coming for him and, pulling the hide covering of the lean-to over himself, collapsed in a protective heap.

Ika hurried to the rescue. "Away! Away!" she shouted before realizing that the pups' tails were thumping and that their manner expressed delighted curiosity rather than threat. "Back, my children, and let this half-drowned man see the rising sun and breathe the fresh air of morning!" she demanded as she pulled the hides away and again met Warakan's gaze.

"Your children?" he sputtered, grimacing against pain and openly confounded by the endearment and by the friendly nuzzling of the wolf-dogs.

Ika knelt before him and, overwhelmed by his closeness, found herself explaining in a stammering rush that set her face aflame with embarrassment. "I . . . I took the l-life of their m-mother and so, by the laws of the Ancient Ones, have taken her place. I have hunted for them and have f-fed them from my own hand and mouth. Now they look to me as m-mother of their pack and obey my word . . . in most things."

He frowned, allowing his face to be licked and his hands mouthed by the tail-thumping animals that now seated themselves close on either side of him. "It was once so with me and the cub of the she-bear whose life I took and in whose skin you found me," he said.

"Ah!" Her imagination soared as she remembered his earlier talk of bears. So he, like Xohkantakeh, was also Bear Slayer! Perhaps even the slayer of the mother of Great Paws! Looking at him now, despite his bedraggled and haggard appearance, Ika easily visualized him stalking and hunting this greatest prey of all. He was not half so tall or so massively proportioned as Xohkantakeh, but he was young and muscular, and she was certain that, when he was well and strong, he would be among the most powerful of men.

Perhaps someday he would hunt bear again. Perhaps they would hunt bear together. "Ah!" she sighed again, but this time cut off her thoughts; they made her head swim as she watched him fondling the pups, running his hands over their necks and faces and ears.

"There is the blood of Dog in you both, I think," he told them.

"Yes," Ika affirmed, "the b-blood of the dogs that once ran with the Red World shaman, Cha-kwena, when he and his woman stole the sacred stone from the chieftain, Shateh, and followed the great white mammoth totem over the edge of the world. But the black wolf was their mother, and I . . . I think that my father is right when he says there is a wolf inside your skin, for my children seem to recognize a brother in you. And did you not say your own sister was a w-wolf?"

Again he frowned. "Sister Wolf . . . ah . . ." He closed his eyes and shook his head with infinite sadness. "If she had not disobeyed me and run in panic before the flood . . . if she had only stayed at my side, close to the power of the sacred stone, she would be with me now. Alive. My old brave friend until the ending of my days."

Ika cocked her head. "She was not then a true sister of your blood and flesh?"

Warakan opened his eyes and looked at the girl as though he found it impossible to believe that anyone could have asked so foolish or offensive a question. "Not since the time beyond beginning when the People and Animals were of one tribe have men and beasts been able to couple and make young together, although I know that it is often said that my father, Masau, was more animal than man. But, then, Mystic Warrior was abandoned as a boy by my grandfather, Shateh, during starving times, and it was not his fault that he was taken in by the cannibal People of the Watching Star, or that he mated with one of their women to make me! But, no matter what Xohkantakeh may say of Warakan, I am no wolf. The only true sister of my blood and flesh was flayed alive before my eyes by the shamans of the People of the Watching Star as a living sacrifice to the forces of Creation." He shuddered against the memory. "Before my eyes they cut up Neea's body, and after the chief and shamans shared her heart—and while the high priestess danced in her skin—they divided her flesh so that it would be meat for my people . . . and for me. It was then that I ran from them. It was then that I vowed to avenge my sister and put an end to such killings. So I betrayed my tribe to Shateh and the People of the Land of Grass, for I am Son of Two Tribes, and their blood was also mine. As for Sister Wolf, I found her as a pup wandering lost and frightened in an abandoned river camp that had been fired by raiders when I was a boy forced to flee for my life after—"

Ika was shaken by the horror of his tale, but not so much that she failed to be startled by his revelation about how he had found the wolf he named Sister. "You found that pup alive in a burning river camp?"

"And another wolf pup lying dead, its head ground into the earth close to the bodies of a slain man, a pair of women, and a dying enemy warrior from whose body I took a spear before I—"

"Under what moon?" She was scarcely able to keep ahead of the sudden racing of her thoughts and heartbeat. "And what were the colors of the warrior's body paint?"

"It was under the Dry Grass Moon," he told her. "And the warrior's battle colors were as white as the many winter snows that have come and gone since that day, and as black as his own charred bones must have been after I took fire from the ruined camp and set the grasslands ablaze in a rising wind that soon consumed the camp and turned back the raiders of the Watching Star. But why do you ask about such things?"

"Aiee!" Ika exclaimed. "Surely the wolf pup you found alive that day was *my* pup, for two wolves were given to me as gifts when I was a foundling child in the river camp of Xohkantakeh. And then the black and white warrior came, crushing one pup under his heel, frightening off the other, bringing blood and death to our band before other raiders of the Watching Star followed. And we fled before a raging grass fire that . . . *you* set?"

"Yes!"

"Then you saved our lives that day."

He scowled and lowered his head. Still fondling the pups, he said, "Perhaps I did. I remember now that I had come from hiding to seek Bear Brother on the open grassland. Then, from afar, I saw the markings of your lodges and knew to whom they must belong. I saw the raiders of the People of the Watching Star coming. There were many. I moved closer, to a place from which I could shout a warning without bringing them down upon my own head, for it was no secret to them that I had betrayed them to their enemies. But by then the black and white warrior was already upon the camp. I could do nothing to stop the killing. Then I saw the giant come racing from among the trees to drive his spear into the black and white warrior and then flee south along the river with his family. I remember, too, that I was glad to see that he had survived." His tone was hard with hate. "Later I was not."

"But why?"

"Because when I thought about all I had seen, I realized that Xohkantakeh deserved to die, for he had abandoned the People of the Land of Grass and left Shateh to be betrayed and to fight his last battle alone against the People of the Watching Star."

"Shateh chose the terms of his last battle," Xohkantakeh interrupted angrily.

Startled by his voice, Ika looked over her shoulder.

The giant was coming from the main lean-to wrapped only in his sleeping hide with Quarana, bundled in her rabbit-skin robe, following close behind. Ika frowned. New Woman appeared surprised and, for reasons that eluded her, more than a little worried to see her talking with the half-drowned man. But the strained expression on Xohkantakeh's face was sobering, for it revealed that he had heard everything, was loath to believe any of it, and was furious with her for speaking to the slave at all.

"What is this, daughter?" he demanded. "Have I not told you that slaves are to be kept apart from the band? What is this loose talk between you? And how has this 'gift' of the river come to be free of his stake and hobbles?"

Ika's mouth suddenly went dry as she realized what she

had just been accused of. "My father, surely you must know that I would never—"

"Rain loosened the stake," Warakan interrupted. With more than a little contempt and mockery in his voice he added, "It took little movement on my part to pull it free. With two hands loose it was not much of a task for even a half-drowned man to slip the thongs of a hobble."

Xohkantakeh was glowering. "Be assured it will not be so easily slipped again. Nor will you again find opportunity to speak lies to my daughter behind my back."

"I have spoken only the truth."

"Bah! When you came as a boy to my tribe, you spoke of your slain sister and boasted to everyone of your bravery, but you made no claim to Masau, Mystic Warrior of the People of the Watching Star, as your father. Nor did you suggest that you shared the blood of Shateh and the People of the Land of Grass."

"I could not speak of that which I had yet to learn. But I speak this truth to you now, Xohkantakeh: Say what you will to one you think you can enslave, but Shateh *was* my grandfather, and he is dead because you and men like you among his tribesmen betrayed him and were afraid to follow him into the stronghold of the People of the Watching Star, where he was forced to fight his enemies and die alone!"

The giant's face expanded with righteous indignation. "I stood with him to the end! I would have fought beside him had he allowed it, but he would have no man at his side except Teikan when he entered the stronghold. After they were slain, the battle that raged below the stronghold was fierce, and although it is true there were some who betrayed Shateh, many Land of Grass warriors perished before we were forced to break and run before our enemies. Later those who remained loyal to Shateh's memory joined ranks again. While the others returned to the Land of Grass, we formed raiding parties to kill and take captives and—"

Warakan was visibly shocked. "You *did?*"

"Yes, of course I did, but I am a man long past youth, and soon my heart became heavy and my spirit sick of endless battle and death and mourning. And so, although my decision made enemies for me among my own warriors, I decided to take my woman and foundlings and—"

"Abandon your people to continue Shateh's war without you, with no concern to avenge the way he died."

"How do you know of the way Shateh died? And how is it that you are still alive when, long moons before, I saw you driven into a river and drowned as penalty for your complicity in the plot of the Red World shaman to steal the sacred stone and break the luck of my people?"

Warakan looked the giant straight in the eyes and declared with a cold, forthright simplicity that cut his listeners to the bone, "I was not drowned. Twice in my life I have heard the river spirits call my name from the depths of raging waters: here, in this far land beyond the edge of the world, and long ago when I was only a small boy and my grandfather's people drove me from their tribe because they falsely believed me to be a part of the shaman Cha-kwena's plot to steal Shateh's power. Twice in my life I have felt myself close to the world beyond this world, with the ghosts of the ancestors and the river spirits whispering all around, but twice the river spirits have 'puked' me up and set me on the way of renewed life and purpose." His face tightened; his eyes narrowed and grew hard. "After I was driven from Shateh's tribe, I set myself to find Cha-kwena—not to join ranks with him against Shateh, but in hope of killing him and stealing the sacred stone so that I could return it to my grandfather and the People of the Land of Grass. But the Red World shaman used his magic against me. I was captured by warriors of the Watching Star and taken to their stronghold. They looked at me and knew me all too well. They named me Traitor. The scars you see on my face were put there by them, and they would have gutted me and staked my head and skin outside the stronghold had not an old wise man among them imagined a better future for me and helped me to escape . . . but not before I saw Shateh slain while those who called him chief turned and ran away!"

"Only after more than half of us were killed! Only because we were outnumbered! Only because we knew that dead men could not hope to return to fight and win against their enemies!" The giant was shaking his head and snorting like a riled bison. "Words . . . words . . . why do I exchange words with a slave?"

"Because you know in your heart that I speak true words, and that I *am* the grandson of Shateh."

Ika looked from one man to the other; a thrill shivered up her back. The earnestness on Warakan's face was undeniable, and Xohkantakeh was taking such troubled, thoughtful measure of his features that she knew in her heart he was doing more than considering Warakan's claim; he was recognizing it.

"Hmm," rumbled the giant. "Whatever happened to you, I was not among those of Shateh's tribe who spoke against your right to live. Although I distrusted you and disliked your brash ways, I had no part in driving you into the river!"

"No. You did not. Yet always you called me Trouble, as though it were my name."

Xohkantakeh shook himself as though to be free of the oppressive weight of the past. "It was long ago," he conceded. "But I tell you now that when this man thinks back on his life he would be the first to accuse himself of many failings, but never would he say that he was afraid to stand and fight his enemies, nor was he ever less than loyal to Shateh." His head went down, and one hand curled around the sacred stone he now wore around his neck as he asked, "But tell me, if I was wrong in my judgment of you—and if you were not part of Cha-kwena's plan to steal Shateh's power and destroy my people—how came you by this talisman?"

Once again Warakan replied with forthright simplicity. "I stole it. As you have stolen it from me."

The giant stiffened, stared, then did something that made Ika relax a little for the first time since he had come from the lean-to like a great hulking shadow of condemnation or doom. He laughed.

Warakan did not appear in the least offended. Rather, he seemed vaguely distracted and discomfitted as he shrugged and said, "It seems we have misjudged one another, Xohkantakeh, but by the ghosts of the ancestors, I *have* spoken only truth to you. After the shaman Cha-kwena betrayed Shateh and fled beyond the barrens with the woman of my heart and the great white mammoth totem, I followed and stole the sacred stone from him as surely as he stole the luck of the People when he abandoned them. The Four Winds and the forces of Creation were with me on that day and on all the days and nights thereafter. They placed the talisman in my care. Old Jhadel swore that it was so, and although he took me deep into the eastern forests and raised me alone in a land beyond the edge of the world, I never forgot that I am the grandson of Shateh, or that I have vowed to avenge him. And so, when Jhadel was taken by the mountain spirits, I began my journey to the high gorge that stands between the edge of the world and the way back into the Land of Grass. There is a spearhead buried there—a magic spearhead! When I retrieve it I will travel east again, to hunt and kill the shaman who destoyed my grandfather. I now know where he has gone. I have found his sign. I will follow it, and when he is dead, with the spearhead and the power of the sacred stone I will slay the great white mammoth totem. When I have eaten of its flesh and drunk deeply of its blood, I will be invincible when at last I return to the Land of Grass as a warrior who will take revenge upon all who betrayed and deserted Shateh."

Ika was stunned; never in all her days had she heard a declaration of such savage intent.

"And you say that you know where the Red World shaman has gone?" Xohkantakeh pressed quietly.

"Yes! Not long before the great water came to sweep me away, I came across his old camps on the barrens, and often I smelled the smoke of his fires and heard the sound of distant singing. He was there, with his woman and with the totem. There was mammoth sign. Not mastodon, but mammoth! *Big* mammoth! The totem walks with him, as does the woman of my heart, to the east—in the face of the rising sun!"

Ika was unaware of Quarana's suddenly closed and unhappy expression, for the young man's words had caused in her a rush of calm. She found herself smiling as she said, "Our mother used to say that as long as the great white mammoth totem lived in the world, so, too, would the People live and their children number as many as the stars in the great Sky River."

"A People of the Red World story," replied Warakan dismissively. "All People of the Land of Grass and People of the Watching Star know a better and truer one—that the man who kills the totem becomes totem. Immortal! Invincible against his enemies! Chieftain over all! It is his children who will number as the stars in the great Sky River!"

Ika lowered her gaze, embarrassed, demeaned.

Quarana's expression changed slightly; she was staring thoughtfully at the half-drowned man.

As for Warakan, his emotional outburst had obviously wearied him, for his color was poor and his breathing thin, but he was looking at the giant as though he were seeing him for the first time. "Ah!" he exclaimed. "The forces of Creation have brought us together for a purpose, Xohkantakeh! You are not young, but you were among the wisest, strongest, and most experienced of Shateh's warriors. There is much you could teach me. With you at my side, with both of us strong in the power of the sacred stone, we could soon be invincible and immortal *together!*"

The giant's face went blank.

"Do you not believe me, old warrior?" the young man asked soberly. "You—who have heard the promise of the Ancient Ones spoken in the lodges of our chiefs and shamans, in whom the spirit of the one you call Great Paws has chosen to live again so that he could walk once more as Brother to Warakan—surely you must see that the Four Winds have brought us to this moment? Surely you believe me when I say that the forces of Creation have united us for one purpose: to avenge Shateh and bring forever to an end the cannibal People of the Watching Star."

"I believe this much of you," replied the giant evenly. "Your mind and mouth and manner are as brash as in the days of your boyhood. It is apparent that my Ika's broth and my new woman's meat and care have helped your tongue and imagination regain their strength. Now we will see about the rest of you. Come. Rise. Today you will walk on your own feet. I will carry you no more, nor, I think, will a grandson of Shateh again wear the hobbles of a slave."

Ika's heart soared.

Warakan rose to his feet; the effort caused his face to pale and sweat to break upon his brow as he extended his left hand to Xohkantakeh, palm upturned. "The sacred stone. I will have it back now."

"The river has brought it—and you—into my care," replied the giant with cool and absolute authority. "You are not yet chief over all, Warakan. I am headman of this band. I will keep the talisman of the Ancient Ones. Strong in its power, I will bring my woman, daughter, and unborn child safely into the protection of the People of the Land of Grass and to the hunting grounds of the ancestors, where my new woman's dreams have promised peace and good things to us. In this purpose alone do I believe."

"But the stone is mine!"

"And the Land of Grass is far away. Let us not waste words over this. It may well be true when you say that the Four Winds and the forces of Creation have brought us together. But for whose purpose, Warakan? Yours or mine?"

Warakan's face congested. "I will walk with your band until we reach the great gorge. Then you will return the sacred stone to me. If you do not, I will *take* it back!"

The giant took slow and thoughtful measure of the younger man. "I would not advise you to try," he said and, without another word, turned away.

6

In ever-lengthening days of cold sunlight, Xohkantakeh, Quarana, Ika, and Warakan moved on together with the wolf-dogs at their sides.

They kept to high ground as much as they could, but often they found themselves slogging across the lowlands, their way diverted by unfamiliar streams and uncountable new lakes and ponds, all grotesquely rimmed with flood debris and the corpses of drowned animals. At last the ground began to rise beneath their feet, and they traveled upward across low, rolling hills, most often in silence, amazed and troubled by the vastness of the drowned lands that still stretched below.

"Not even when the great mad river of the north rose to drown the hunting grounds of my childhood did I see the scars of such a monstrous flood as this upon the land," revealed an awed Warakan.

Xohkantakeh eyed the young man. Warakan was fast regaining strength, and although minor fractures in two ribs prevented him from carrying a back frame, he hauled a lightly loaded travois with only an occasional grimace, and not once since he had removed his hobbles had he attempted to run away. Although he required frequent rest, rare was the moment when he did not set his hand to some small useful task so that sometimes, as now, the giant found himself wondering if Warakan was not going to prove himself a gift of the river after all.

"Hmm," he rumbled as he continued to appraise the young man. "Shateh used to say, 'As the Ancient Ones lived in the time beyond beginning, we live in the time beyond the understanding of men.' Who can say why the forces of Creation do what they do? We can only keep to the laws of the Ancient Ones and hope that as we journey homeward, the Four Winds will pass more gently over our lives now that the sacred stone of the ancestors has come into the possession of this band."

Quarana stood between the two men. Her face was wan, her brow furrowed, her mouth tightly drawn. "But no matter how far we walk, no matter how many sleeps we put between ourselves and the drowned valley, the land below the hills and ridges is always the same. Perhaps even the hunting grounds of the ancestors did not escape the wrath of the great waters. Perhaps all the people there have been drowned! Perhaps all the game has been swept away! Perhaps when we arrive there after endless moons of traveling, we will find only barren earth and dead trees and great piles of fly-blackened bones and rotting flesh. Perhaps there is no longer cause for us to return into that far country!"

Ika, standing slightly behind the threesome, gasped with dismay. "Aiee! With what carelessness you speak, sister! What if the Four Winds are listening and decide to make all that you fear come true?"

"Then all who would threaten us and all upon whom Warakan would take vengeance would be dead," Quarana replied with such intense longing that she hugged herself to keep from trembling.

"Not all," Warakan asserted, frowning with obvious unhappiness at the thought of being denied the pleasures he imagined to be found in revenge. "I would still seek the—"

"Enough!" Xohkantakeh cut in. After Quarana's carelessly articulated fears, he had no wish to hear from Warakan or to make light of Ika's question. The girl had every right to castigate her sister—indeed, he knew he should have done so himself, but his new woman's words had so taken him aback that he was still stunned. "Would you wish the wrath of the Four Winds upon all our people when only a few have wronged us?" he demanded. "The Land of Grass is vast, and our people's tribe is composed of many bands. The one I seek dwells far to the north. Enemy raids were all but unheard of there. The women and girls of that far country will be your sisters, the grandmothers will ease the burdens of child raising, and the hunters will welcome this Bear Slayer who comes to them with the sacred stone of the ancestors, for with its power in our possession we will soon see the fulfillment of New Woman's dream. The great herds of mammoth and bison and horse and elk will return in endless numbers to the plains of my youth, and my enemies will lay down their spears before Xohkantakeh!"

Warakan was staring unabashedly at Quarana. "Is this truly what you have dreamed?"

She hung her head.

Worry suffused Xohkantakeh as he looked down at her. She had been behaving strangely of late. She was unnaturally subdued and sometimes so preoccupied with her thoughts that she flinched when he spoke her name. He realized, of course, that she was still grieving over the loss of Katohya and that the child he had put into her belly must surely be making itself felt by now, but after her outburst a blind man could not have failed to see the cause underlying her moody introspection. Quarana was afraid. He shook his head. "How can you, whose dreams have set us upon the path we travel, now wish to turn back from it? That which you fear cannot be, Quarana. The vision that came to you on the night before your new-woman ceremony did not portend it."

Quarana looked up. Her eyes were wide, her mouth slightly agape. "But the night of that dream seems so long ago," she said after a moment. "And so much has happened since the telling of it. Even if the great waters did not drown the people and animals in the hunting grounds of the ancestors, perhaps it is as Warakan has said, and the warriors of the Watching Star are still making war and flaying women and eating their hearts and cutting up their bodies for meat in that far country to which we journey! Perhaps my new-woman dream was wrong, Life Maker? Perhaps I was mistaken in the—"

"It cannot be!" he interrupted sharply, scowling first at Warakan and then down at Quarana. "You will not listen to Warakan. You will listen to me when I tell you now what your mother would tell you were she here to speak words to calm your heart, Quarana: First Woman and the forces of Creation speak to a first-time woman in her dreams. The things she sees and the words she then speaks are gifts from First Woman and must be accepted and acted upon lest First Woman's spirit and the forces of Creation be offended. This is the law of the People since the time beyond beginning." He paused and shifted his gaze to Warakan. "You *are* Trouble! Your tales of the cannibal ways of the People of the Watching Star have put fear into my woman. You will speak no more of their ways. Until you came to us, she and her sister were spared the details of their abominations."

"When you take them into the country of the ancestors, they will learn of them soon enough," replied the young man coolly and, leaning into his load, walked on.

Ika was in love.

She was not sure, of course, just what the emotions were that swept her spirit and warmed her body whenever she looked at, came close to, or even thought about Warakan. She knew only that there was something rare and wonderful in his presence, and she sorely wished Katohya were still alive to offer wise and gentle counsel. Quarana had fallen into such a surly and secretive mood that, no matter how much Ika yearned to share and explore her feelings with her, instinct warned that New Woman was best left to her brooding.

Now, striding out beside Xohkantakeh with South Wind close at her heels, Ika wished with all her heart that her beloved giant would stop looking at Warakan with hostility and distrust. She barely heard her father speaking to her as, out of adoring eyes, she watched the young man move ahead with Quarana trudging morosely in his wake.

"And what about you, daughter?" asked Xohkantakeh. "Are you not frightened by the tales that our 'gift from the river' has told of the People of the Watching Star?"

"Hmm?"

He repeated his question, then asked sharply, "Have you lost your ability to hear me when I speak, daughter?"

"Ah, no," Ika replied dreamily, still staring ahead. "How can I be afraid when I walk with *him?* And with you, Bear Slayer? And with the sacred stone of the Ancient Ones? Perhaps Warakan will change his mind and journey with us beyond the gorge he speaks of. Ah! He is like the warriors in your tales of the Land of Grass, my father!"

"Is it so?" Xohkantakeh looked down at her, frowning but obviously intrigued.

"Ah, yes," she sighed. "Just look at him—half drowned only days ago, and already he is growing so strong!"

"He was not as badly injured as it first appeared. Quarana tends his wounds, such as they are. The food the two of you bring to him is good and nourishing and—"

"And he is so grateful and generous to us with his words of thanks."

"Hmm. He talks too much!"

"Ah, no, my father! Think of how it has been for him all these many, many moons, traveling alone with only a wolf to share his thoughts, traversing hills and barrens, mountains and badlands, following mysterious totems and seeking magic spearheads, and all out of love for his grandfather!"

"Hmm. Love? Is that what he seeks?"

Shadows of sudden, unbidden unhappiness darkened the girl's mood as she confided, "I have heard him speak of a beloved . . . of the Red World shaman's woman. He says that Mah-ree is beautiful as Quarana is beautiful. He says she is the daughter of chiefs, and a powerful healer and medicine maker, a woman who can call the mammoths and calm the spirits of meat-eating animals so that she can walk with them and—"

"Do you not recall your mother Katohya speaking of Mah-ree, her younger sister?"

Ika was startled by quick recollection. Katohya had, of course, spoken of her past and of younger sisters, but the

memories had often caused her pain, and she had rarely
been able to speak the names of the beloved sisters from
whom she had been cruelly separated so long ago. "Ah, yes!
Truly, then, she is *that* Mah-ree?"

"Truly. And Warakan deludes himself if he thinks that
he has cast some sort of bonding thong around the heart of
that Red World woman. They are loyal, the females of that
lizard-eating tribe. Your true womb mother was such. A
good and generous woman, strong, and clever with her
hands at sewing and cooking and lodge making. In the big
hunt camps to the north, where the many warriors from the
far-flung bands of the People of the Land of Grass came together at the river crossing to await the coming of bison and
elk and caribou, I remember how your father was envied his
possession of such a useful captive."

Ika pressed her lips together at this talk of her true
mother. Her love for Katohya had been such that even now
it was difficult for her to realize that Xohkantakeh's Sweet-
Scented Woman had not given birth to her. Yet always the
memories of her true womb mother came easily, bittersweet; memories of a wide sun-browned face; of many little
lines around long thoughtful eyes; of other, deeper lines,
etched by sun and wind and sorrow, and by laughter, too.
And always Ika recalled the warmth of the woman's smile,
and the soft words of assurance to a child who, as the offspring of a captive, had never fully been part of her paternal
tribe until her father had chosen to abandon her under the
Starving Moon and Xohkantakeh had stepped forward to
take her into his own band.

"Warakan will not succeed in taking Mah-ree from
Cha-kwena," the giant was saying as he walked on, eyes
narrowed but fixed ahead now. "I remember well the night
she chose to leave our tribe and go of her own accord with
the Red World shaman into a great storm. Driving the sacred herd of mammoth and the totem before them, they
went. With the talisman of the ancestors they went. Stealing
the luck of the People they went, and although our warriors
followed, it was as though the White Giant Winter looked
with favor upon them and conspired with Snow and Ice and
Howling Wind to conceal their tracks."

Ika cocked her head and thoughtfully reminded him, "Katohya said they ran away to save the totem and the sacred herd of mammoth from those who would hunt them for meat."

"Yes. Under a Starving Moon men must hunt whatever meat they can if their women and children are to survive. Warakan is right to hate the Red World shaman and his woman for what they did that night, and yet I tell you, daughter, that Cha-kwena and Mah-ree were as Katohya and I . . . one man and one woman together in body, heart, and spirit, always and forever. Even if Warakan succeeds in finding them, Mah-ree will never walk with him of her own free will. And besides, she would be in the late seasons of her days now, perhaps even a gray-hair . . . much too old for him."

The shadows lifted from Ika's spirit. "Truly so?" She was so delighted she nearly sang the question.

Again Xohkantakeh turned his eyes toward his daughter, looking puzzled and more than a little discomfitted. "Would you take Mah-ree's place in Warakan's eyes, Ika, you who have yet to become a woman? Who, then, would hunt at my side when he abandons us at the great gorge?"

The question cut the girl, deeply. She lowered her eyes and leaned into the browband and shoulder straps of her heavily laden back frame. What would Xohkantakeh say if he knew that she was a woman now? How she hated keeping the truth from him. *Ah! He need never know. Never!* She would stay by his side to be his eyes and ears and to hold a spear at the ready to protect his pride as long as he needed her. And yet if, by some wondrous whim of the forces of Creation, Warakan were to decide to stay with the band, Xohkantakeh would have a man to hunt at his side. Might she not then reveal her secret and dare to hope that Warakan would look upon her with favor and . . . .

Ika's face flamed as she realized where the presumptuousness of her yearnings were leading. As she walked on, she found it impossible to comprehend how she—who less than a moon ago had trembled in revulsion and fear at the thought of being mated—now thrilled in happy befuddlement when she thought of becoming the woman of Warakan. *If only there were some way of convincing him to stay with the band! If only . . .*

"Are you listening to me, daughter?" said Xohkantakeh sharply. "The Son of Two Tribes may yet prove to be Trouble to us. You should be wary of him."

"Ah, yes! Of course, my father, but have you noticed that, although his face is scarred, he is so *beautiful?*"

"Beautiful? Hmm. As Great Paws was scarred, but beautiful . . . and *dangerous.*"

"But look at him as he walks beside Quarana now, helping her with her burden even though he is not yet healed. And see how East Wind walks happily at his side, as though wishing to replace the lost sister and companion of a trusted friend?"

"But what does the animal see in him, daughter? Dog or Wolf? Hmm. He has said that he will walk with us as far as the great gorge. After that, child, he will show us what he is."

Child! Ika was stung. How long had it been since he had called her that? Since before she had stood to the black wolf? Since before she had faced a charging bear and not run away? Since she had boldly hunted bison at his side? "Will I always be that in your eyes?" she asked him sadly.

He heard the hurt in her voice and seemed surprised by it. "You will always be my Little Bear. My bold Ika. In truth, daughter, it will sadden my heart when we reach the hunting grounds of the ancestors and you are no longer able to share my lodge."

Ika stopped dead in her tracks. She was not sure which shocked her more—his unexpected declaration of affection or that which remained unspoken in his last statement. "Why will I not be able to share the lodge of Xohkantakeh when we reach the hunting grounds of the ancestors?"

He paused and looked her up and down with a droll smile. "You will not be a child forever, Ika. I have seen the woman growing in you. Perhaps, even before we reach the Land of Grass, there will be two women in this man's band. And in the hunting grounds of the ancestors, there will be at least one warrior, I think, willing to take to his lodge a strong new woman in return for the pleasure of blooding himself and being first to make life on one who will serve him well to the ending of his days."

Ika's eyes widened. Her heart gave a great leap and then seemed to break wide. *He does not want me! He has taken Quarana to be his new always-and-forever woman, but he will not take me! When we reach the hunting grounds of the ancestors, he will give me away to a stranger!* She stared at him, trying to understand the reasoning behind this revelation, but suddenly her heart constricted and her emotions ran wild.

"Aiee!" she exclaimed.

Xohkantakeh was startled by her outcry. "What is it, daughter?"

She could not speak. Her thoughts were in turmoil. Before the river spirits had brought the half-drowned man into her life, she had recoiled at the thought of first blooding as surely as she had known that, despite her fear of the new-woman ceremony, she would have yielded to Xohkantakeh. She would have! No matter how the ceremony disgusted and degraded her, she would have come consenting to it, her spirit calmed by the knowledge that he would not ask it of her if it were not a good thing for them both. He was the center of her world, the Great Father Bear in the firmament of her sky and and—as daughter or woman—in this land or any other she existed only to please him. And yet now, as she looked up at his broad, craggy features and into the long, deeply set eyes that she knew and loved with all her being, a terrible sense of betrayal seared her spirit. Tears stung beneath her lids as she thought, *In the Land of Grass Xohkantakeh will have Quarana as his woman. In the hunting grounds of the ancestors Bear Slayer will walk in the power of the sacred stone. Killer of Horse and Bull Bison will soon have sons to fire his pride. And Great Father Bear will no longer need his Little Bear to be his eyes and ears, nor will he want her to hunt at his side.*

He was aware of the change in her mood. "What is it, child?"

Child! Again the hated word. Ika fought the desire to hurl it back in his face. The Land of Grass was still far away; the powers of the sacred stone had yet to show themselves.

Until Warakan was well and strong again, her father had no idea how much he needed her, and Ika loved him too much to tell him. She would not bruise his pride. It was her own sense of self-worth that needed defending now.

In a cool, authoritative tone that proclaimed her maturity more clearly than any stain of new-woman blood on her undertunic could have, she said, "If I must take a man other than Xohkantakeh in that far country, that man will be Warakan! He has taken the heart of Ika. In this land beyond the edge of the world or in the hunting grounds of the ancestors, I will have him, or I will have no other man!"

Xohkantakeh was shocked. "He is Trouble!"

"And so will I be if you try to give me away to a stranger!"

7

Warakan was not sure of the exact moment in which he realized that a most bewildering and unexpected thing had happened to him.

He was happy.

He walked with an old enemy, but the man suffered him to live and no longer treated him as a slave. The sacred stone of the Ancient Ones was worn by another, but it was close, and he could still feel its power. His body was a mass of bruises and his ribs were cracked in two places, but he was healing and regaining his strength faster than he had dared imagine possible. Sister Wolf had lost her life to the great waters, and there would always be a small, tender hollow in his heart that only her presence could fill, but the big, gangling wolf-dog pups of Xohkantakeh's band had taken to him, and more often than not he found the larger of the two walking, sitting, or sleeping beside him.

As he walked on now with East Wind trotting at his side, he saw that South Wind had loped ahead to walk with Ika. The girl carried a fully loaded back frame, and yet she looked like a young warrior walking proud and strong with her spears and sling and stone-headed braining stick. For reasons he could not explain, it pleased him to recall that earlier she had come to stride at his side to confide with a shy smile, "I think that East Wind has begun to see you as a brother, Warakan. I also think it is a good thing that the river spirits have 'puked' you up instead of taking you to the world beyond this world. And I think, too, that it is a good thing you have come to walk with us."

"Only as far as the great gorge," he had reminded her.

Now Warakan remembered that even as he had spoken the words, he had savored the girl's company as much as the flavor of her broth. He was glad his destination lay far away, for in these lean, lengthening days of spring, under Xohkan-takeh's watchful eye he was hunting small game again and using his skill at stone and bone working to make small, useful tools for the giant's females.

When night came down he sheltered under the same lean-to as the giant's little family and was comforted by the knowledge that, for now, at least, he was one of them—so much so that on a night not long ago, when dire wolves howled close by and the familiar restlessness to be away came upon him, it was unwelcome.

But Xohkantakeh, not knowing the way of his heart, had eyed him and said, "Hmm. So it has not changed with you. Look at the wolf-dogs, Warakan. They, too, heed the call of wolves. They are like you, of two tribes, encamped in one but still heeding the call of the other. Will they leave us someday to run with wolves as you have sworn to do?"

"Who can say?" he had replied. Annoyed, he had drawn the bed furs over his head and turned away. After a while the wolves fell silent, and he had been glad. It was good to be in the company of people again.

And so it was that he slept well and seldom dreamed. Often in the dawn, while the giant slept and Ika went off to check her snares and traps, Quarana would go from the lodge and gesture for him to follow. Once outside, she would draw him away, open her robe, and invite him to for-bidden pleasure. He would take all she offered. Quickly. Impatiently. There were no words between them, only lust. It was better than Ika's broth. When, only yesterday, she had whispered that in the Land of Grass it would be better between them because she would be his woman, not Xohkantakeh's, and there would be time to teach him all the many ways to please her, he had not understood or cared.

"I please myself," he told her, and did, as days and

nights passed in a slow, sure progression that he knew must eventually bring him to the high gorge and confrontation with Xohkantakeh. But now, for the first time in longer than he could remember, Warakan did not want to think about the future. He was far too content with the present.

Quarana had come to walk at his side, head down, eyes lowered so circumspectly that no one, not even a spirit of the wind or sky, would have thought twice about her manner with him.

"Am I wrong to be afraid?" she asked, her voice low, her eyes seeking his.

"Of the warriors of the People of the Watching Star? Or of your own man if he discovers what is between us?"

"He thinks I carry his life in my belly. He will not hurt me. But the others—the cannibal People of the Watching Star, the ones who scarred your face and eat the bodies of their captives and—"

"They would not harm such as you. No. Someone as young and good to look upon and eager to spread herself might even enjoy that which would be asked of you if you were taken captive. The hunters would fight over you, and you would end as some man's favorite. But the giant would be killed. Slowly. It would be a hard death for an old man, being gutted and skinned alive as though he were an animal whose head and 'pelt' were worthy to be placed on a mammoth-bone stake outside their stronghold . . . along with Shateh's."

Quarana did not even flinch; indeed, she seemed not to have been moved at all by his description of how her man might die. "I am only anxious to spread myself for you, Warakan," she said, pouting prettily.

Warakan eyed her sideways. "I am glad of that."

"Are you sure they would not hurt me and eat me, these cannibal People of the Watching Star?"

"Only in the way you like to be eaten."

Her eyes widened with surprise, then half closed again as she suppressed a pleased and knowing smile. "Xohkantakeh would skin *you* if he heard you speak so!"

"He walks with your sister and will not hear the words we speak unless we shout them. Do you think I would have him know what passes all too quickly between us after dawn when he sleeps heavily within his bed furs while Ika goes off to check her snares? In truth, though, it is your sister who should be worried about the warriors of the People of the Watching Star."

"Why? Ika is brave as a bear. And nearly as big and strong! Many times I have looked at her and thought that she should have been born with man sacks between her thighs instead of a woman's hollow, for then Xohkantakeh would have the son he so desires. I do not see why such a girl should be afraid of the woman-hunting warriors of the People of the Watching Star. Why would they want to eat her and not me?" Her smile had disappeared; her eyes were sharp with suspicion under her lowered lids. "No man would want to come between her thighs, would they? Would you, when you know the pleasure to be had when I open myself and welcome you between mine?"

Warakan was startled by her response. There was such hostility and jealousy in it that he did not know what to say. After a moment he replied simply, in what he deemed a necessary defense of Xohkantakeh's other daughter, "Your sister is a kind and pleasant girl, Quarana."

"Yah! And that is all she is, a girl, not yet a woman, perhaps *never* a woman! She has told me that she wants no man between her thighs, *ever,* so if you have looked at her with thoughts of—"

"Concern," he interrupted, annoyed by the implications of her whispered tirade and by the fact that she was hissing like a riled goose. "Your sister should worry about being taken captive by the warriors of the People of the Watching Star because they seek as their sacrifices only immature young women who have not yet been pierced by men. Xohkantakeh should not risk her life, or his own, by returning into the land of his enemies."

A sigh of relief went out of Quarana. "Ah! I understand. Yes! But *I* will not be in danger there!"

Hearing her happy exclamation, Warakan was puzzled. "Do you care nothing for your man and sister?"

She was pouting again. "Xohkantakeh has the sacred stone of the Ancient Ones to protect him and—"

"And his new woman's dream to guide him?"

"I . . . yes! My new-woman dream."

"Of a land where there will be many women and grand-mothers to do the bulk of your work for you, and where the warriors of the Watching Star and of the Land of Grass will lay down their spears before Xohkantakeh? Why is it that I do not believe you have dreamed this dream with the inner eye of true vision, Quarana? Why is it that I think you have made it up, out of your own need and desires?"

She smiled, wanly at first, then hopefully as she turned her face up to his. "You are the man of whom I have dreamed, Warakan. You are the hunter and warrior I have seen at my side in the Land of Grass. I have made myself your woman. How can you think of leaving me alone with this band in the protection of an old man when the woman of whom you dream is far away? You could have been no more than a boy when last you saw her. Did you ever join with her? Surely, even if you did, she never spread herself and pleasured you as I do? Forget her. Forget the totem. Let the Red World shaman go his way in the world. The sacred stone is with this band. I am with this band. The Four Winds and the forces of Creation have brought you to me. Forget all but the white fire that pours from your body into mine when I spread myself and take you deep. Come with me beyond the great gorge you speak of, and you will see that my dreams are as real as—"

"The baby Xohkantakeh thinks you carry?"

Her smile vanished.

And Warakan's face split with a grin. He was young and inexperienced in the ways and wiles of women, but he was learning fast. He had sensed the guile in her words and seen the lies in her eyes. It occurred to him that, even in his weakened state and with the sacred stone of the Ancient Ones around the neck of Xohkantakeh, he must indeed be a powerful and insightful shaman. And so he said, lightly and provocatively, "Do not worry, woman of Xohkan-takeh. The gorge is far. Your man often sleeps late in the dawn. Your sister is good about going off early to check her traps and snares. And until I leave you alone with your band in the protection of your old warrior, I will keep your secrets . . . as long as you continue to open your thighs to me."

Quarana stopped and faced him. When he paused beside her, she looked him straight in the eyes and allowed him to see the flashing in her own as she told him quietly and calmly, "Question my new-woman dream if you will, Warakan, but not the baby that grows in my belly. It is real enough now. You should know, for it is you who have put it there! When we reach the great gorge, you will not leave me or the child I will bear you."

His mouth gaped wide. He was stunned. "I *will* leave you," he insisted. "I want no babies, from you or anyone else!"

"Nevertheless, you have made one on me."

"I do not believe you!"

She tilted her nose skyward and smirked. "I know. But do not worry, Warakan, the truth of my words will soon be proved under the constantly turning face of Moon. And I will keep your secret . . . as long as you keep mine and promise not to leave me."

8

On a warm, overcast, oppressively humid day, they crested a stony ridge and found themselves on a high, rolling plain that stretched westward as far as their eyes could see. The drowned land was behind them at last.

Living land lay before them: grassland islanded by dark open stands of spruce and fir and occasional tamarack; tundral moor sweeping downward across the higher, north-facing hills in broad swaths of springtime colors that reflected their glorious hues in innumerable lakes, ponds, and streams, along which the tender green of newly unfurling hardwoods shimmered in the opalescent sunlight.

The sound of birds rose as a welcoming chorus. From somewhere deep amidst the evergreens came the high, unmistakable call of an elk. Xohkantakeh stood motionless, breathing in the beauty of the land as his gaze followed the northwestward sweep of a mighty river whose width and depth and fast-running substance spoke its name to him.

"The Great River," echoed Warakan, coming to stand beside the giant and observing sourly, "Only fish and otters and birds on the wing will cross those waters now. If only the river did not flow south, perhaps we could find a 'friendly' downed tree to carry us across and upstream all the way to the Land of Grass, just as the old spruce tree brought me downstream to you!"

"We will continue north along the river," replied Xohkantakeh, unamused.

Warakan shrugged. "Do as you will, but there was a night not long ago when the skies were clear in the dark of the last new moon. I came from the lodge before dawn to relieve myself and watched the star dance of the Great Bear and Great Snake circling one another around the Watching Star. I would say now that we have no more than a double hand-count of good walking days to the north before we must set our steps west toward the great gorge. The Land of Grass and the hunting grounds of the ancestors lie there, far to the west, on the other side of the river."

"Then how will we ever reach them?" Quarana was openly distraught as she slipped her pack frame from her shoulders, set it down, and seated herself heavily upon it. "Maybe you are wrong, Warakan. You said nothing to me about the star dance of the Great Bear and Snake marking the way home when we looked at them that night."

"What were you doing out of our bed skins and observing the stars with him before dawn?" the giant growled. "Warakan is no longer a half-drowned man who needs the hands of a woman to guide his man bone from beneath his garments as she helps him to relieve himself!"

Warakan's face paled.

So did Quarana's. "I . . ."

"She often rises early to make fire, my father, and sometimes Warakan helps her while I check my snares and traps," Ika told him guilelessly, spreading wide her arms and filling her lungs with the sweet scent rising from the living land.

"Yes!" Quarana gulped, nodding with more than a little enthusiasm. "I go out to make fire! Warakan helps me! Yes! And do you not remember how often Katohya went from the lodge to ease herself from the press of the baby growing inside her? It is so with me, Bear Slayer. Sometimes the force of the new life that you have put into me is so great that I must go from the lean-to lest I be sick all over our furs. Ah! Katohya would have said that such a strong mover must be male. May the forces of Creation will it so—a son for Xohkantakeh!"

He eyed her thoughtfully. The day was only half done, but he was tired, and he realized that, given her pregnancy, Quarana's fatigue must be much greater. He regretted his sharpness toward her almost as much as he regretted her mentioning his lost woman's name. The old wise men in the Land of Grass always counseled that Time was an invisible medicine spirit that would heal all wounds, but he had come to know they were wrong; there were some wounds that could never be healed. The loss of his beloved Katohya was one of them. "I *do* remember," he conceded to Quarana. "And it *is* the way of life-bearing women. Since you are often unwell in the early morning, it is good that Warakan helps you to make fire."

A muscle throbbed high at the young man's jawline as he looked down at his feet. Quarana lowered her eyes.

Xohkantakeh stared ahead, his right hand pressing the sacred stone beneath his tunic. "It is good country to which we have come. I think that perhaps the spirits of First Man and First Woman have brought us here while the river runs high so that we must pause in our journey to regain our strength. Our life-carrying woman would feel better for the rest, and for whatever fresh meat we may win on the hunt. And then, if the Great River falls within its embankments and allows a crossing during the Dry Grass Moon, we—"

"But that is many moons from now!" exclaimed Quarana, looking up, her face flushed, her eyes wide with fright. "What if you should fall injured or—"

"Quarana!" Ika snapped. "Do not even think it! Besides, Warakan walks with us now. By his presence we are all stronger upon this journey!"

The young woman bit her lower lip.

"We can still travel northward for a few days," said Warakan. "Perhaps there are narrows up ahead that will allow a reasonably safe fording of the waters. There should be only minimal danger if we are careful."

"No. I will not risk my daughter or woman or unborn child to the unknown again." Xohkantakeh shook his head, not in disagreement but in slow assent to a truth he had not considered before. "Many moons did it take us to safely reach the good and sheltering forests that lie beyond the edge of the world in the face of the rising sun. I should not have imagined that we could return to the hunting grounds of the ancestors in less. We will raise a lodge in this land. We will hunt. We will rest and grow strong. We will wait for the Great River to grow shallow under the Dry Grass Moon. If it does not, we will winter here, wait for the time when the ice spirits freeze the river solid, then cross. But I think that the White Giant may come and go and that the Dry Grass Moon will rise twice before we at last set our feet in the 'lake' of grass New Woman has seen in her dreams."

"I will not stay with you *that* long!" declared Warakan.

Xohkantakeh took slow and speculative measure of the young man before he said, "I rescued you from the river spirits that would have sent you to the world beyond this world. When you could not walk, I dragged your weight. When your strength failed you on the trail, my band rested for your sake. Our meat has been your meat. We have shared the warmth of our furs and lean-tos with you. Now that my woman and daughter have nearly healed you, how can it be that you feel no loyalty to us, no need to help carry our burdens and hunt our meat? I am no longer a young man. Your strength would be of much use to me, and to my woman and daughter, in the many moons between now and the time I bring them safely into the hunting grounds of the ancestors. Or perhaps I should hobble you again? Make no mistake, I will do what I must to protect my band."

"Band? A woman and a girl and a pair of wolf-dogs! You are not my people! It is not my purpose in life to care about you!"

"No. Your purpose is to seek the great gorge and the magic spearhead with which you would hunt the totem in order to gain the invincibility you believe will enable you to return to the land of our ancestors to kill your enemies. Bah! It is a dark and bloody vision you follow, Warakan. I, for one, have seen enough of war and death. My new woman's vision promises peace and good hunting in the Land of Grass. It is this I seek. I will not help you in your quest. But perhaps, now that I see with my own eyes the extent of your ingratitude, it would be better if you were to go. Yes. I will not have you skulking around my encampment awaiting the first opportunity to steal the sacred stone from me."

"I cannot steal what is mine!"

"No longer. The forces of Creation and the Four Winds have placed the talisman into better hands than yours. So go! Yes! Since you are neither a bird nor a fish nor an otter, try to cross the Great River while I stand on this far shore and watch the river spirits take you once again. This time, if they puke you up alive, I will throw you back as payment for your disloyalty! Bah, I say! You vowed to stay with this band until we reached the great gorge. Does a grandson of Shateh not honor his word? Or does he feel loyalty only to the dead?"

Warakan was stunned.

Even if Quarana had not looked up at him doe-eyed and given him her prettiest and most beseeching little pout, he would have been scalded by guilt. Xohkantakeh was right. Were it not for the giant he would be dead, his flesh meat in the bellies of wolves or lions, his bones stripped and scattered across the drowned land. And how had he repaid his debt to the man who had saved him? By secretly coming between the thighs of his woman and by refusing to acknowledge that any debt was owed at all. Shame burned him. He *was* the grandson of Shateh. Honor bound him to this man and band more tightly than any hobble could have done. His mouth flexed against his teeth as memories suddenly flared and within his mind's eye he saw . . .

The cave, sunlight spreading across the floor and illuminating the vaulted interior within which a withered old man sat upright beside a dark, grizzled she-wolf like a defeathered bird ready for trussing, all beaky nose and wide seamless mouth gaping in a tattoo-blackened face.

"*Jhadel!*"

"*Ah, Warakan, we thought you had abandoned us.*"

"*When have I ever given you cause to believe that I would be less than loyal? And where would I go without telling you first?*"

"*Back into the world of warring tribes! Back into the west to retrieve the magic spearhead of white chalcedony . . .*"

*a white spearhead to kill a white mammoth! It is still there,
in the high gorge, under the Watching Star. It will be the
death of you, Warakan, yet you would seek it. You would use
it. And when the totem was slain you would return to the
camps of the mammoth hunters who bore you. To the lodges
of your father Masau, Mystic Warrior of the People of the
Watching Star, and to the hunting camps of your grandfather, Shateh, shaman and chieftain of the People of the
Land of Grass!"*

"You speak of the dead, Wise One."

*"I speak of those who were enemies in life but whose
spirits live on in you, Son of Two Tribes. And I tell you now
that someday you will look with their eyes upon the land of
the ancestors, upon the hunting grounds of the People of the
Watching Star and the People of the Land of Grass and you
will see that country not as an avenging warrior—but as a
peacemaker and bringer of unity to all!"*

"Never."

He flinched. Now, as in the past, his spirit bled with renewed need of vengeance against those who had scarred his
face and sacrificed his sister and slaughtered nearly everyone he had ever loved. "Those who slew my father and
grandfather, and those warriors of his tribe who abandoned
him to his enemies, will die at my hand. This I have sworn!"

"As you have sworn to walk with this band until we
reach the great gorge," Xohkantakeh reminded him sternly.

The statement wrenched Warakan's thoughts back into
the present. Again his mouth tightened as he weighed the
two vows he had made: one to himself, one to Xohkantakeh. And again he knew that the giant was right. He *was*
the grandson of Shateh, and honor bound him to his word.
He would and must keep these two vows. But what of the
third vow?

He looked down at Quarana, who was looking at him
through lowered lashes. Her pretty face and petulant expression annoyed him to the point of disgust; he was weak with
her and knew it. How many times had she drawn him away
and welcomed him between her thighs since she had threatened to lie about him to Xohkantakeh if he did not vow to

stay with her forever? How many times had he refused her invitation? Not once. Did she carry his life in her belly, or the giant's, or no life at all? It struck him that he did not care. His eyes narrowed. By the time they reached the great gorge the latter question, at least, would be answered. When Quarana had demanded that he promise to stay with her, he had replied obliquely; could a man be held to that to which he had only implied consent? And even if he were to speak the words she wanted to hear, would the forces of Creation consider a grandson of Shateh committed to such a dishonorable purpose?

"Well?" pressed Xohkantakeh, huffing through his nostrils like an irritated bison. "What is it to be with you? Do I watch you drown yourself? Or do I hobble a grandson of Shateh because he would profane the memory of that best of all chiefs even as he insists upon dishonoring himself? Or do you keep the vow you made to me?"

"I will walk with you until the great gorge," replied Warakan. "Be it under the Dry Grass Moon or in the blizzards that are the breath of the White Giant Winter, this grandson of Shateh will not dishonor the memory of that best of all chiefs. Warakan will not break his vow to Xohkantakeh."

Quarana's frown was barely visible, a small gathering of worry lines puckering her brow. Slowly, with her hands on her lower back, she rose and stretched and prophecied sweetly, "You will not leave us, Warakan. You will see. By the time we reach the great gorge, you will find you have all the reason in the world to stay."

"May it be so!" said Ika, smiling at Warakan as though all the loveliness and promise of the new land were reflected back to her out of his face and form.

Warakan took no note of the girl. Nor did he look at Quarana as he turned his gaze to the west and made yet another vow—a silent vow—never to come between the thighs of Xohkantakeh's woman again.

The day was ending at last.

Ika laughed. The sound broke the sullen silence of her

fellow travelers as they dropped their travois and packs on high ground and stood with a thick stand of mixed spruce, balsam fir, and hardwoods at their back and the new land stretching before and below them.

"What amuses you, daughter?" asked Xohkantakeh. "It is good to see you cheerful again, but would you mock my choice of this place as the best upon which to raise our big lodge?"

"Oh, no!" she replied with unbridled enthusiasm. "My father has made a good choice! There is a spring and a fast-flowing stream close by. The trees will provide wood and bark and poles for the new lodge and break the harsh breath of the wind and wave their branches to keep biting flies away, and perhaps it is not too late to ask the birches to share a little of their sweet sap with us. The sun will shed its light and warmth from the south and west. And we are high enough above the river so that from this place we can see across the land to mark the passage of game."

"Then why do you laugh?" asked the giant.

"Because all that fills my eyes is beautiful. Because the drowned land is behind us at last." She paused and drew in a deep breath, holding back, *Because, although I no longer shine in the eyes of my father, Warakan walks with my band, and in my heart lives the hope that I will one day be his woman!* and saying instead, "Because the smell of this new land is so good and alive and green with the promise of new life!"

"Green?" Warakan was openly puzzled.

"Ah, yes," she told him. "Close your eyes and you smell the color. New-grass green, the green of moss swelling up and growing warm and happy after a long winter, the green of new leaves unfurling beneath the lengthening rays of the sun . . ."

The young man did not close his eyes, but he smiled. "As you can smell new oaks unfurling pink, and new mushrooms pink, too, and baby mice!"

Ika's heart soared. "Yes, and so!"

"Color is a thing for the eyes, not for the nose," said Quarana disapprovingly. "I do not smell green. Or pink. But look at all the little lakes and ponds that shine in the hollows of the land. There will be bogs there."

"We are on high, dry ground, New Woman," said Xoh-kantakeh soothingly.

"And look at all the birds gathering below us in the wet-lands! Herons and cranes and geese and ducks of all kinds!" cried Ika. "And do you see? Yes! There are elk coming from the woods! And look, my father, are those not bison grazing on that stretch of prairie over there? Yes! A big herd. And not just any bison, but longhorns! Was it not only a few moons ago that we feared we had seen the last of their kind? Ah, feel the sweet warm breath of the wind as the sun be-gins to go to its rest. The land itself is sweet with life. You can feel it growing . . . swelling . . . as you must feel the new life growing and swelling inside you, my sister!"

"What would you know of that?" Quarana sneered, turn-ing away and kneeling with her back to the new land as she began impatiently to disassemble her pack frame.

Xohkantakeh moved forward; he appeared in a trance.

Ika looked up as he came to stand beside her. The jour-ney was telling on him; his features were haggard, his face leaner than she had ever seen it. Despite the hurt he had in-flicted upon her, she was grateful they had come to a place where he might rest and grow strong again with no loss to his pride.

"What is it?" Warakan asked the giant. "What do you see?"

"Bison. Cows. Young. And a single yellow calf still among the yearlings. Hmm. By sundown tomorrow, if the forces of Creation grant that it be so, the hide of that one will be a gift for my new woman."

Ika's heart skipped a beat before it raced on. "They are longhorns, my father, the biggest of all bison! Surely they are too dangerous to be hunted now. You . . . *we* . . . are not as strong or sure on our feet as they, for they have been grazing long in this good land while we have—"

"He has vowed to kill a calf for me," Quarana inter-rupted, on her feet now with the oddest expression on her face that Ika had ever seen. "Would you have him shamed before the warriors of the Land of Grass when he comes to them with this baby-bearing woman and their son is not clothed in the honoring yellow hide of a bison calf?"

Warakan was eyeing Quarana as though she had begun to exude a fragrance that offended him.

Ika did not understand the look that passed between them, but it disturbed her deeply, although not nearly as much as her fear for Xohkantakeh's safety. "The bison's hides will not be prime now, my father. And they are many. We are few. The wolf-dogs have little hunting experience. Warakan's ribs are not yet fully healed. We must wait until—"

"Enough words!" the giant snapped. "Warakan honors his vow to Xohkantakeh and longs for the day when he will fulfill his vow to avenge his grandfather. Would you have Xohkantakeh do less? I have given my word to your sister. I will keep it. Since time beyond beginning it has been the way of the men of my tribe to honor the woman who has taken the fire of man need and transformed it into new life within her belly. Many times have I come between the thighs of my new woman. She carries my life in her belly. Now the Four Winds have brought us to this place. Once again the forces of Creation have placed the bison before Xohkantakeh at a time when a woman of his band carries new life. Tomorrow I will hunt for her. Not with Warakan. Not with Ika. Tomorrow Xohkantakeh will hunt alone to honor his new woman."

"And I will eat the flesh of the calf you kill for me," declared Quarana, smiling with an eagerness that flushed her face and made her eyes shine. "I will drink its blood. I will work its skin into garments for the child of Xohkantakeh. It will not be said again that a woman of Xohkantakeh has disdained the ways of the ancestors and brought the wrath of the forces of Creation upon her band!"

Ika was nearly staggered by a tumultuous wave of frustration and anger. "Be it so," she conceded. "But why must my father hunt tomorrow? He should wait until he is rested and prepared for the hunt."

"Bah!" exclaimed the giant. "The passive heart of your true mother speaks Red World words from your mouth, Ika! The words of a lizard eater! The words of one whose 'warrior' ancestors hunted nothing more testing to the spirit than ants and antelope! Would another of Red World blood ask that I offend the Four Winds? Would one whom I have raised as though she were the offspring of my blood and bone have the forces of Creation look down upon Xohkantakeh and think that he is too old and afraid to hunt for his new woman?"

Ika was so shocked by the accusations that she could not think of how to reply to them. He had seen into her heart. But what of Quarana's heart? How could her sister stand there and goad the giant to hunt when he was not at his best? And how would Great Father Bear fare on that hunt without his Little Bear to be his eyes and ears and the steadying hand that stood ready at his side to hurl a spear if his own failed in its course?

"Come," Xohkantakeh was saying. "We will prepare the ground for the new lodge. Then we will rest and eat, and while you sleep, this man will prepare himself to honor his new woman tomorrow."

Later, after Xohkantakeh had expertly felled a few young aspen and birch with his stone-headed ax, Warakan stepped in to help him debranch the trees so that they could be used as lodgepoles. Quarana watched them thoughtfully as she lounged close to the fire circle Ika had made.

One so young, she thought, *the other so old. Will they both be here tomorrow?* The premise startled her, but she made no attempt to call back the unspoken question as it wafted out of her mind into the air, as tenuous as the smoke rising from the fresh kindling Ika had gathered.

"Sister, I must talk with you," Ika said, keeping her voice low as her eyes sought her sister's face.

"You need no permission," replied Quarana. "But do not ask me to help you to prepare the boiling bag for our day-end meal. We have come far this day, and I am tired. I carry new life. And there may be a great deal of work for me tomorrow if Xohkantakeh is lucky on the hunt."

"Quarana, please. You *must* talk to him. Look at him! He is not young. Can you not see fatigue in his face and form? Aiee, sister! You alone can make him change his mind! Pretend sickness, or tell him you have seen some sort of vision, another new-woman dream perhaps, or—"

"And what makes you think I would risk offending the forces of Creation by lying?" she demanded, feigning innocence as easily as she drew breath.

"I fear for him, sister! We must do something to stop him from hunting alone, at least until he is rested!"

Quarana leveled an accusing gaze at Ika. "Would you have me shame him before Warakan, as you have done by suggesting that Life Giver, Killer of Horse and Bull Bison, and Bear Slayer does not know when he is fit to hunt?"

"Daughter!"

At Xohkantakeh's summons Ika stiffened and looked nervously his way.

"Come!" he commanded. "New Woman can tend the fire while you help us debranch the new lodgepoles!"

Ika hesitated. "Quarana, please, try to think of something to keep him from the hunt tomorrow!" she implored, handing her sister the hollow reed with which she had been blowing life into the kindling. "Please!" she repeated, then rose and hurried off to help her father.

Quarana sat motionless, watching not her sister but the two men at work. Her heart quickened as her eyes took in the grace and youthful handsomeness of Warakan, but her brow furrowed when her gaze held on Xohkantakeh. Ika was right. He was obviously tired; the slump of his massive shoulders and the sluggishness of his movements betrayed the extent of his fatigue.

Maybe he will die tomorrow? The question thrilled her as she turned back to the fire and bent to blow into it. *If he dies, Warakan will have to take me as his woman. He would not leave me. He could not leave me! Not alone at the edge of the world with only Ika and a pair of wolf-dogs to protect the one he thinks is carrying his life. Yah! How easily men are led! I have not shed a woman's blood under the last moon, and before that there was barely enough to do more than spot the moss I secretly gathered and wore! Surely there is life in me! But whose? Yah! What does it matter? I will lead them both with my promise of it, and if Xohkan-*

takeh dies tomorrow, then the same sense of honor that holds Warakan to his vow to walk with this band as far as the great gorge will not allow him to leave me. He will take me to the Land of Grass and live with me there forever. I know he will . . . if only Xohkantakeh were dead.

9

Xohkantakeh went before dawn.

He went alone, naked save for his moccasins, loin truss, hunting bag, and the sacred stone. He went without food or drink.

The chill air raised hackles on his bare skin. He paid them no heed, nor did he lament leaving his bison and bear hides behind. Both were heavy and would have weighed him down, and any lingering scent of Bear would have been carried on the slightest wind to alert his prey to danger. Besides, with his spear hurler looped by a thong across his back and three of his best thrusting spears in hand, his sure, steady stride was already working to warm him.

By the time the sun rose, Xohkantakeh was sweating, and he cooled himself down in a shallow pond that invited him to ease his thirst in the glow of dawn. He drank deeply and splashed water over himself, then rose and went on, following fresh bison sign as he loped to the nearest wallow. Here he laid aside his spear, hurler, and hunting bag, then sprawled on his belly and palmed up feces and urine-soaked mud, slathering himself in the very essence of bison, then rolling in it until he was satisfied that every bare finger width of him that might give off man scent was thoroughly covered in a wash of brown slime.

A lone wolf howled to the east. Xohkantakeh felt the

sound almost more than he heard it, crawling up his back
and under his skin. He turned to face the rising sun, perplexed, for somehow it seemed that the song of the wolf was
coming out of the sun, calling him back over the edge of the
world to the cool, sheltering green forests where he and his
beloved had raised their foundling girls in nearly perfect
happiness . . . until Great Paws had come from the snow and
the flesh of the slain bear had given voice to New Woman's
dream and drawn them westward to a new life . . . and into
the drowned land.

"Warakan's bear . . . Warakan's 'brother'!" He sneered
as he rose and, working mud and feces through his hair and
into his scalp, realized he still suspected the young man of
using the power of the sacred stone to send the bear to destroy him. The thought only served to embolden him. "The
flesh and blood of that bear live in me. The sacred stone is
mine. And this day I will hunt for a woman who respects
and keeps to the ways of the Ancient Ones."

The wolf was silent. Xohkantakeh could see the bison
now. They were well away, a small family group, no more
than twice a double hand-count of animals, with one enormous cow grazing with the other breeders, adolescents, and
yearlings.

He scowled. Where was the yellow calf? *Ah.* He saw it
now, nursing to one side of the large cow. His scowl froze
in place. The mother animal was as big as most bulls! Given
her gender and the time of year, her hump and bulk were
considerable, and although the crooked horns marked her as
female, their seven-foot span was sobering.

His breath rasped in his throat as he eyed her flanks,
the deep chest, the high, bunching muscles of her shoulders. "You will be fast, Mother . . . but will you be wise?
Hmm. Will you yield your child to Xohkantakeh and permit the strength of your kind to live on in the life my new
woman will bear me? I will honor her this day if you will
allow it. I *must* honor her. And with your consent, Mother,
I will take your life along with that of your child so that
you will not grieve for your loss, for in so powerful a
killing I will show my new woman and the daughter who
doubts my strength and the wolf-eyed 'gift of the river'

just what this onetime warrior from the Land of Grass can still do!"

Ika was dressed for the hunt and hefting her spears.

"Where are you going?" Warakan asked her.

"Come with me," she invited soberly. "I will stay in this place no longer. I must follow my father."

"He has commanded me to stay and guard his women."

"She is no woman," Quarana muttered, gathering her furs around her shoulders and settling herself irritably in the first rays of the sun. "Do you think Xohkantakeh, who so worries about keeping the ways of the ancestors, would allow Ika to use a spear if she were more than a child?"

Ika flushed. "Have you no fear for him, sister, when he puts himself at risk for you?"

"Would you have him ignore the commands of the ancestors?"

"No! Never! But—"

"Daughter of Xohkantakeh," Warakan interrupted kindly, "the hunt to which your father has set himself is one he must attend alone. I was only a boy when I lived among the People of the Land of Grass, but this *is* their way."

Ika knew he was right, and she also knew he was wrong. But how could she shame Xohkantakeh in Warakan's eyes by telling him—and in front of Quarana— that her Great Father Bear needed the eyes and ears of his daughter when he sought his prey? "You do not understand," she said. "I *must* go."

"I cannot allow it!" Warakan was emphatic.

Ika's eyes widened. She had not thought him capable of taking such a tone with her. "You are still weak from the river. You cannot stop me!" Spears in hand, she turned to go, only to find that she was wrong.

Warakan's hand was hard around her wrist. He turned her toward him and said sharply, "To follow him is to shame him, Ika!"

"But he need not know. I would not show myself unless he needed help."

"Xohkantakeh needs no help from children on the hunt!"

Ika shrank, not only from her sister's slur but from the expression on Warakan's face when he looked back over his shoulder at Quarana. Her spirit went cold. His eyes were full of hate for her sister. Never in all her days had she seen anyone look at another being like that. The wolf-dogs were up and staring, heads down, hackles up; South Wind was growling.

Warakan ignored them both. "Come!" He was tugging Ika to the overview upon which they had stood the day before, observing the new land into which Xohkantakeh had disappeared with the dawn. "You forget, Ika, that your father now wears the sacred stone talisman of the Ancient Ones. Do you imagine that he will not return to see his woman and daughter cared for until he can bring them safely into the Land of Grass after I leave you at the high gorge? The forces of Creation sweep our lives as they will, but they would not do this to me! We will wait for him here, you and I, together!"

"Ika must make fire and food for me!" Quarana said petulantly.

"Make them yourself!" snapped Warakan.

Despite her anxiety over Xohkantakeh, Ika nearly swooned in amazement and delight when Warakan slipped an arm about her waist and drew her close.

"He *will* come back!" said the young man. "By the Four Winds and the forces of Creation and the power of the sacred stone, you and I will send our prayers to the Ancient Ones and to the spirits of the ancestors, and perhaps, together, we can convince them to make it so!"

He stayed with the girl on the overview all morning. He said a few prayers while she offered up litanies to the spirits, praising Xohkantakeh and begging for his safe return. As Warakan listened, a sense of peace and well-being came over him, until Quarana came to drop a cold haunch of smoked heron in his lap.

"You will get no more from me," she snapped. "I am tired. The baby in my belly takes all my strength. And here you sit with my lazy sister, listening to her sing in a fireless camp, with the big lodge still unfinished. If Xohkantakeh should return—"

"If!" Warakan shouted at her. "He *will* return. It takes time for a solitary man to stalk bison. He will have to work inside the wind and conspire with the grass and earth to silence his steps. He will have to wait until the perfect instant to make his strike. And if, at just the wrong moment, a bird should call or a squirrel should scamper or a biting fly should bite some nervous cow on the rump, the entire herd might be off at a run, and he will have to begin all over again somewhere else. So come, Ika. We will work together to make the lodge. And we should raise up a fire and prepare drying frames. The Four Winds will see what we do and know that we trust in them for Xohkantakeh's safe return!"

She smiled. "Do you think so?"

Warakan shrugged. He was not really sure, but his suggestion seemed reasonable. Besides, he liked her smile, so in hope of seeing it again, he said, "I do! It will surely help pass the time of waiting. In the meantime, you can sing. It is good to hear you sing."

Quarana snorted. "I can sing, too!"

"Then do so," he commanded. "Sing to the spirits for your man's safe return!"

Her mouth turned upside down. "Ika has been singing that song until the skin of the sky must be bruised! I will sing another song. I will sing for the meat he may bring to honor me, and for the fine yellow hide he may bring for my baby."

"Xohkantakeh's baby!" he corrected.

Annoyed, she harrumphed and turned away.

Warakan and Ika made fire.

They assembled a few drying frames, then worked together to raise and secure the main lodgepoles. This proved to be no easy task, for Quarana refused to help and the wolf-dogs were underfoot, pulling every tie until it was undone. Twice a newly raised pole tottered and fell. With a sigh Ika tied the canine pranksters to a ground stake and scolded them. After that the structure went up fairly easily, and soon the frame was secure. Weary, Ika and Warakan loosed the wolf-dogs, seated themselves at the crest of the overview with the pups sprawled on either side of them, and patiently awaited Xohkantakeh's return while Quarana napped in the shade of the lean-to that had served as the previous night's shelter.

The day wore on.

Ika offered up prayer songs until the sweetness of her voice was strained. Then, in accommodation of her sister's grumblings, while Warakan reknapped some of Xohkantakeh's stone tools, she put small stones in the coals of the fire pit to heat while she set up a wooden tripod to hold the boiling bag. Into this went water from a bladder flask, small bits of meat and fat, and two whole songbirds that had been hanging to cure since the previous night. Then, carefully, using a pair of bone tongs, she took the stones one by one from the fire and dropped them quickly into the bag. The stew bubbled and steamed, and the meal was soon ready.

Quarana accepted the generous portion Ika emptied into the burl bowl Katohya had made for her as a new-woman gift. She ate greedily at first, then made a face and pushed the food away.

"I know," Ika said sympathetically, assuming that worry had taken her sister's appetite as surely as it had taken her own. "It is difficult to eat when Xohkantakeh is away, but we must listen to Warakan. His faith in the spirits and in the power of the sacred stone is great. We must believe him when he says that Xohkantakeh will come back to us!"

"Yah!" exclaimed Quarana. "Are you saying I do not want to believe him? Go away! The baby in my belly is not the only one who makes me sick."

Ika left her with an understanding sigh and brought the bag to Warakan. "My sister is so worried she cannot eat. And the new life she carries is finally starting to make her a little ill, I think. It was so with my mother at first. Even the smell of food made Katohya turn green. But here, if you are hungry, Quarana has left most of the fat and both the songbirds and—"

"At *first?*"

Ika thought a moment, then shook her head, for the question puzzled her as well. "Perhaps it takes longer for some new life to make itself felt. Katohya used to talk to us about life making and baby bearing. She told us how it would be for us." Her face colored, and she lowered her eyes. "Here . . . the boiling bag is nearly full."

"I will fast until Xohkantakeh returns," he told her, rising and staring off, distracted and suddenly more solemn than he had been since dawn.

She was disturbed by the change in him, but she thought she understood it. "Yes. I will fast, too. The spirits will know by our hunger that our bodies need the nourishment of Xohkantakeh's presence if we are to go on!"

Night came, unwelcome because Xohkantakeh had not returned. Quarana tossed and turned in her sleep. Warakan and Ika did not sleep at all.

Dawn came.

Quarana bundled herself in her furs again and sat in the first rays of the morning sun; she seemed to feel better and sucked the boiling bag of its contents, unheated because Ika was too distracted by worry to make fire.

Now it was Warakan who felt sick, but he dared not voice his fears. He stood looking across the land for Xohkantakeh and found it empty. *If Xohkantakeh does not come, this girl and this woman, who has goaded a good man to his death, will be mine to care for until the gorge . . . and then what? How do I retrieve the magic spearhead and go off across the barrens with a pair of females at my heels . . . one of them carrying new life—my life! No!*

"Warakan?"

He blinked. Ika was standing before him. He stared into her wide, worried face and realized with a start that he was looking into her eyes. Girl though she was, she was nearly as tall as he, and perhaps as strong. His mood lightened. *Ika*

can take Quarana back into the Land of Grass without me!
Ika is strong and bold as a bear. Quarana herself has said
it. And I want no part of any child that the woman of
Xohkantakeh will bear me . . .

"Warakan?"

He blinked again. This time Quarana had spoken. She
nudged Ika aside, and with her head held high and her face
working to contain what he knew must be a smile of triumph, she started to speak. But her words were cut short by
Ika's startled cry.

"Warakan, look! Look there!"

Now it was Warakan who nudged Quarana out of the
way, making no attempt to mask the smile of triumph that
split his own face.

Ika was already racing forward, the wolf-dogs bounding
ahead of her. "Xohkantakeh!" she sobbed. "Xohkantakeh!"

And there he was, emerging out of the distance, a spear
held high as he waved wildly with one arm, a giant of a man
dragging a flayed bison skin heaped high with meat and
draped with the unmistakable hide of a yellow calf.

PART V

THE FOUR
WINDS

1

Nothing was the same.

Everything was changing. Xohkantakeh could feel it happening, as though the world had somehow shifted beneath his feet, and now, with the sacred stone of the Ancient Ones around his neck, he knew that from now on everything was going to be all right.

"Yah hay!" He opened his arms and took Ika into his embrace.

"It was a good hunt, my father?"

"A good hunt! Mother bison was generous." He allowed the girl to slip to her feet and appraised Warakan as the young man came to greet him. "So you did not run off and abandon my daughter and woman while I was away!"

"A grandson of Shateh does not dishonor his vows."

"It seems, then, that you are to be trusted."

"As far as the gorge."

"Hmm. Still that."

"That," affirmed Warakan, looking the giant up and down with an intrigued frown. "You seem less tired than when you left us. Look at you, awash in the blood of your kills. By the Four Winds, Xohkantakeh, I know that your females call you Bear Slayer and Killer of Horse and Bull Bison . . . but how much meat can one man drag without breaking his back?"

"The power of the sacred stone is true power! And I

have left a portion of my kill as a gift of thanksgiving to the meat eaters who would have taken it from me and with whom we share this good and generous hunting ground. Better that they gorge themselves at the kill site than follow me back to camp. But I will tell you of the hunt later. Now you and Ika have come to help me with this load. Where is my woman?"

"She must be waiting for you before the lodge, my father," explained the girl. "The life you have put into her is making itself felt at last. She is feeling sick."

Xohkantakeh was too tired to sing. Too tired to dance. But he was not too tired to stand tall and bellow when they at last dragged the meat of the cow and calf into the good camp that had been made in his absence.

"New Woman! Come forth! Your man returns. Xohkantakeh comes! Bear Slayer and Killer of Horse and Bull Bison brings a gift to the new woman who has taken his life into her body. Come forth, I say! I bring to you an honoring!" He paused, sobered by memories of the last time he had spoken these words. Sorrow welled in him. He tried to swallow it down and succeeded only in tasting the bitterness of an unhealed heartbreak. Drawing in a deep, steadying breath, he reminded himself that Katohya had of her own free will chosen to offend the spirits of the Ancient Ones when she denied his honoring gift and had thus brought down the wrath of the Four Winds upon herself and the unborn child in whom had lain all his hope for a son. Now that hope had been reborn in his new woman, and although he knew that no one would ever take the place of Katohya in his heart, he rejoiced, not only for himself but for Quarana and for the child that was at last making its presence known inside her belly.

A smile of pride and euphoric anticipation cleft his face. "Come forth, New Woman!" he called again. "Hear the honoring words that the men of our tribe have spoken to their life-bearing women since time beyond beginning! Come forth and accept the gift I bring! And may the carrying and birthing of my child be as smooth and tender to your flesh and spirit as the meat and skin of the bison calf that I bring to lay at your feet. May the meat and blood of the bison mother give you strength under the moons that will pass between now and the time my child comes to live in the world of the People. Come, I say! Accept the gift I bring! There is meat to be made and hide to be worked by the hands of Bison Slayer's life-bearing new woman!"

Quarana came forth. She was pale, her face was set, and she did not look happy. "I come forth to accept the gift you bring," she said, appraising without enthusiasm the bloodied man and then the great heap of meat, hide, and horn and the limp, eviscerated body of the calf.

"And so!" exclaimed Xohkantakeh, bellowing again as he descended upon his new woman in a swoop of affection that half smothered her as he embraced her with the heart of the calf gripped in one hand and its intestines dangling from the other. "Eat! Partake of the food I bring! Behold, the forces of Creation have smiled upon this woman! Behold as she eats of the gift that has been given to her man! And behold and heed this Life Maker when he says that on this hunt the sacred stone of the Ancient Ones has restored his strength and granted him a shaman's vision!"

"Aiee!" exclaimed Ika with surprise, her face beaming with pleasure and pride in his revelation.

Warakan scowled suspiciously.

Quarana stared at the organ her man was holding to her mouth and grew noticeably paler.

"What vision have you seen, my father?" Ika was wide-eyed with expectation.

He smiled. "Since yesterday's dawn Mother Bison has led me. She drew me through fine stands of trees whose names I do not know. She beckoned me across good grass to sweet water and plains of mixed tundra and woodland, where great herds of elk and deer and caribou and short-horned bison graze amidst the bones of mammoth and horse and camel, animals that have been food for the People since time beyond beginning. And here Mother Bison paused. Here she stood with her back to the West Wind, facing toward the place where the sun rises over the eastern hills, and browsed. Here she allowed me to come upwind of her.

Here—as I waited for her to separate herself and her calf from the rest of her long-horned kind and to present her side to my spear so that I could make a killing strike that would cause her little pain and a quick death—the spirits that dwell within the sacred stone spoke to me."

Warakan cocked his head and asked dubiously, "And what did they say?"

"Not words," responded Xohkantakeh. "From inside my heart they spoke! And as I looked upon this land to which our new woman's dream has brought this band, I understood that we have come to a place where the old ways and kinds are dying and drifting away on the wind while new ways and kinds are forming and taking root. The drowned land lies behind us. The Great River stands between us and the hunting grounds of the ancestors. West Wind blows to the east, into the face of the rising sun. There is meaning in this, much meaning, for life was good for us in the green, sheltering forests beyond the edge of the world, but in those benevolent woodlands there was a lesson we failed to learn even though my lost woman warned, 'Life is like a great river. It must flow always forward, never back!'

"And so, as I looked at the river and saw the width of its waters and the way of its flow, it struck me that the river itself was speaking, inviting me to go no farther but to stay in this good new hunting ground, for here the enemies of the past are no threat to us, and the sacred stone that so many chieftains have fought and died to possess has come to us as a gift from the river."

Warakan was shaking his head. "The stone is mine, Xohkantakeh."

The giant looked at him. "Perhaps. Yes. In time. But listen to me now, Warakan, and hear the voice not of Xohkantakeh but of the spirits of the talisman. For how long have the chieftains of the Three Tribes fought one another to the death for possession of the sacred stone so that one tribe would hold power over all? It was so with Tlanaquah of the Red World. It was so with Masau of the People of the Watching Star. And it was so with Shateh! It was this ambition that ultimately led your grandfather to his death at the hands of his enemies. But behold, Warakan, son of Two Tribes! Here . . . now . . . in this new land . . . the Three Tribes are united, not through war, but through a peaceful union made by the Four Winds and the forces of Creation themselves! Yah! Even Wolf and Dog are one, as in the old tale!"

The young man frowned. "I do not understand."

"Ika's mother was a captive in the Land of Grass, a woman born of Red World People. I am of the Land of Grass People. You are of my tribe, and also of the People of the Watching Star. So, you see, in this band, the Three Tribes are united. When children are born to you and Ika, the blood of the Three Tribes will be their blood, and it will be as it was in time beyond beginning: The People will once more be one!"

Quarana's face went gray.

Ika gasped.

Again the young man shook his head. "It is Mah-ree, woman of the Red World shaman Cha-kwena, who will be mine!"

"Bah! How many seasons would that woman own to by now? Three times a double hand-count of winters? Hmm. She may not yet have become a sag-teated gray-hair with lips flapping over teeth worn down to her gums, but when you find her—*if* you find her—do you think she will be alone with the man from whom you would reclaim her? Have you not realized that by now she must surely have birthed many a brawling boy and brave girl to call her Mother? Would you truly set yourself to slay the father of her children? And if you succeed, do you imagine that either they or she will want to walk with you?"

The words settled hard on the young man. From his expression it was obvious Xohkantakeh had spoken of things he had not considered.

Seeing this, the giant smiled, and his arms went wide, dripping blood from the heart and innards of the calf as he gestured to the surrounding land. "Behold the gift the Four Winds and the vision of my new woman have given us! Stay as the hunt brother of Xohkantakeh, Warakan! And on the day Ika expels the last of her first moon blood, become my son. Make new life on her. Her face may not be as fine as my Quarana's or Mah-ree's of the Red World, but she is strong and as brave of heart as any of the children of the black wolf she has made her own. Forget the far gorge and your 'magic' spearhead and dreams of vengeance! Let the Red World shaman and his woman walk with the totem in peace, for the sacred stone has told me that the Red World People are right when they say: 'As long as Life Giver, the great white mammoth, walks in this world, so, too, will the People live and grow strong forever!' But life is so short for each of us, Warakan, and not even the mountains live forever. This is the great Circle of Wisdom, the great Joy and the great Sadness, the great and unchangeable Teaching that all must learn and abide by lest they spend themselves chasing shadows within that circle and at the ending of their days find they have become shadows, too, incapable of leaving anything of themselves behind."

He paused, fixing his gaze on the stunned expressions of his daughter and the young man she loved so well. Far across the land dire wolves were howling, summoning one another to the feast he had made for them. He smiled as he thought of his own "pack," confident that—regardless of Warakan's decision—he had reestablished its strength, and his own. He loosed yet another bellow and again enfolded Quarana in his bloody embrace. "Do as you will, grandson of Shateh, but know that I will keep the talisman of the Ancient Ones and guard its message with my life, for the spirits of the ancestors have spoken through the stone and told my heart what I must do. Xohkantakeh will not cross the Great River! I will stay in this good hunting ground to which my new woman's dream has surely led me and in which my sons and daughters will come forth from between Quarana's thighs in a land where the shadow of my enemies does not fall!"

"And I must honor my vow to Shateh!" Warakan responded. "I *will* be a warrior. My grandfather's spirit cannot rest in the world beyond this world if he is not avenged."

Xohkantakeh growled at the stubbornness of the man. "Then go! Do what you must! I will not stop you!" Distracted by a pitiful moan from Quarana, he looked down just in time to see her eyes roll back as she clapped a hand to her mouth and went limp in his arms.

Warakan watched the giant carry Quarana into the lodge. He was aware of Ika looking at him shyly, uncertainly, from beneath lowered lashes.

"Will you truly leave us?" she asked.

He could not think to form a reply. Xohkantakeh's words were resounding in his brain, and he thought the very earth and sky must be mocking him, for it was as though Jhadel had spoken through Xohkantakeh's mouth.

Peace! Unification of the tribes! He wanted no part of the old Peacedreamer's gentle vision.

"Warakan . . ."

He turned to Ika. The wolf-dogs were beside her, and the sun was at her back. He winced. Again it was as though Jhadel were speaking to him.

"For you there is one who will come out of the sun! One who will walk with wolves! One who is in danger now and for whom you must—"

"What!" he snapped at Ika, wanting to be away from her, away from her band and all its confusing, distressing constraints.

"Will you leave us without the sacred stone to protect you when you are not yet fully healed and strong?"

"Would you steal it back for me?"

"I . . ."

"Would you?"

Her eyes were enormous. After a moment she said in a voice so soft it was barely audible, "I could not steal my father's newfound strength, but if you must go, I would give you my spears and hurler, my braining club, warm furs, food, and . . ." She paused, looked to the wolf-dogs, and reached down to lay a loving palm on East Wind's dark head. "And I would send a part of myself with you, this child of the black wolf who has already chosen to be your companion and friend and protector. And if you wish it . . . I would also walk at your side."

"You? An immature girl? Why should I want you with me?"

She hung her head. "As my father has said, my face may not be as fine as that of Quarana or this Mah-ree of the Red World of whom you dream. I cannot say. But now that he has the sacred stone of the Ancient Ones and a new baby-bearing woman to fill his heart, he does not need this girl, even though I am, as he says, strong and as brave as any of the children of the black wolf. Take me with you, Warakan, and perhaps you will find I am not as immature as you might think."

He was shaken by the offer and could not say why. "You are wrong about your father. He would miss you if you left him. Your sister is useless in most ways. Besides, I would not put you at risk."

"But you will surely put yourself at risk if you leave without the sacred stone. And will you not be lonely, Warakan?"

The question cut to his heart. Despite Quarana's self-serving manipulations, these past days and nights in the company of Xohkantakeh's little band had been more nourishing to him than meat, and the thought of going out across the land alone again exhausted his very soul. He exhaled and found the excuse he needed to delay his departure and save his pride. His ribs hurt, and he was bone tired after helping Xohkantakeh and the girl drag the meat and hide into camp. "I cannot go until I find a way across the river."

"And if you cannot?"

"Then I must stay. Until the Dry Grass Moon. Or until the ice spirits freeze the waters."

"Then may the way across the river be blocked to you for many a long moon, Warakan, for I will sorely miss you when at last you go your way!"

Something stirred deep within him—pleasure, gladness. "I will miss you, too, Ika."

She smiled, a broad, white, almost reckless smile. "I am glad! But come. If you are not leaving us, my sister is sick with baby-bearing illness, and Xohkantakeh will be busy feeding her his gift meat. Let us work together and start preparing all the fine flesh of the mother bison he has brought to us, thanks to his skill and wisdom and the renewed strength that the power of the sacred stone—which you brought to us—has given him!"

Quarana was miserable.

She knelt within the partially constructed lodge and tried not to be sick while Xohkantakeh tenderly fingered out soft curd from the intestines of the calf and put it to her lips.

"Eat. It is the gentlest of foods . . . the best of foods for my baby-bearing new woman. Smile, Quarana, River Woman. It is customary for new life to make the mother sick at first. You are fortunate the illness has not come to you sooner!"

She shuddered. How could one who was so wise on the hunt be so dull-witted when it came to his woman? "I do not like this baby bearing!"

"Hmm. Many mothers say this, but the bearing illness does not last more than a few moons. And when the new life comes forth, you will be glad and proud and, when the time of suckling is done, ready to make new life again!"

"For what purpose, in this land of no people?"

"Are we not people, your sister and Warakan and Xohkantakeh?"

"Warakan will go away."

"We were a band before he came. If he chooses to go, we will still be a band without him."

Her heart sank. "Ah, Life Giver! You cannot truly mean to stay here on the far side of the river forever! Where are the warriors who will envy Bear Slayer when he comes into their hunting grounds with his new woman? Where are the grandmothers who will help me bear my babies? And where are the women who will share my work?"

"I do not need the envy of other men to know that you are a woman to take pride in. And Katohya used to say it was a woman's joy to make meat for her band in a good and sheltering camp. She taught you and your sister all she knew of woman wisdom. Ika will help you when your time comes to bring forth new life. And I will be with you. This man has twice eased a woman in birth stress—not as often or as easily as he has made life, but enough to know more or less how to help when your time comes."

"More or less? Yah! That is not comforting, Life Giver. It is not comforting at all." She glowered into her lap and silently cursed the life in her belly, wishing it would gush forth unborn so that her sickness and fear would be at an end. "My new-woman dream was not of this place. It was of the Land of Grass. You said it was. You *knew* it was! And from all you have said of it I would not be afraid to bear babies there."

"I was mistaken in my first interpretation of your dream, Quarana. The hunting grounds of the ancestors are also the hunting grounds of warring tribes. Warakan's talk of the past brought it all back to me. Now I see that the grasslands of your dreams are here, all around us. It is a good land, a better, safer land than the one into which I would have led you."

"Is Bear Slayer and Killer of Horse and Bison afraid to fight again in the land of warring tribes when Warakan—a half-drowned man less than half your years—is not?"

"I would prefer to live out my days in peace with you and the children you will bear me, New Woman."

She was annoyed; her goad had not roused his pride. "But here in this unknown land of many lakes and ponds and marshes there will be bogs under the moons of summer. Your new woman will fear every waking hour that she or her children will wander into the dark deeps to disappear and be eaten by frogs. Ah! Let it not be that when my life is done, I will be left abandoned to the bogs like Xree . . . alone forever."

He set down the intestine and drew her close. "Frogs do not eat children. And we knew not the dangers of marshes when we first traveled through them together. I will not abandon you, New Woman, ever."

She shuddered in his arms. "But you are not young. Someday you will die. Someday you will send your spirit to walk the wind with Katohya, and you will leave me behind . . . alone with the babies you will make on me."

"No," he told her. "I wear the sacred stone of the ancestors. It will keep me well and strong until the sons I make on you have grown into bold men who will protect and care for their mother until the ending of her days in this good land to which her new-woman dream has brought her."

2

Meat.

Everywhere there was meat. The drying frames sagged under the weight of it. The scent of it filled the encampment—raw meat, roasting meat, meat curing slowly under hastily raised smoking shelters that kept the blackflies away. And where there was not meat, the bones of Mother Bison and Yellow Calf lay about, divided according to kind and placed in heaps that would later be gleaned for uncountable good purposes. Already the main joints had been cracked wide and scraped free of precious marrow, and were now host to insects and small rodents feasting on the rich, oily, vascular residue. Closer to the lodge, fat glistened on the pounding stones, and the two hides were stretched, skin side up, and secured by strong thong lines to the poles of their respective drying frames. Ika worked the larger skin, Quarana the smaller, bending and stretching over the raw hides until their backs and shoulders ached and the sharp edges of their fleshing tools were thick with tissue. This they fingered off and ate, for the pulverized residue made a sweet, nutritious treat that sat well even in Quarana's finicky belly.

Ika sang and hummed to herself as she worked, ignoring Quarana, who mumbled and complained beside her.

"If we were in the Land of Grass there would be three or four grandmothers to help you flesh such a big hide. And look at the skin of this calf!" She turned her face to the left and right, making sure Xohkantakeh was not within hearing. Seeing him hard at work with Warakan on the bark lodge cover, she hissed to her sister, "What kind of honoring gift is this? It is not as good as the skin he brought to Katohya. Her yellow calf was an early spring calf, not much more than a newborn, with thick hair tightly rooted to its skin. Mine is a late spring calf, and I can tell you now that it was born moons ago, when the White Giant Winter was still on the land, because when I tried to comb it, its yellow hairs molted out in clumps in my hands! Yah! Why bother dressing it at all!"

"To honor the man who risked himself to bring it to you."

"Yah! If he did not have the sacred stone, what could he bring me, eh?"

Ika knelt back from her work. "We are here because of your new-woman dream, my sister. Long ago I warned you that it might be best to think twice before pressing our father to follow it. So stop complaining. There will be enough yellow in the hair of the calfskin to make a fine carrying robe for the new life you carry. And think of all the fine and useful things we will soon be able to make from Mother Bison! Already I have taken much sinew. And there will be thread to be twisted from the long winter guard hairs I have plucked from Mother Bison's hump, chest, and back. And because she was in spring molt, when I card her woolly underhair, it will be better than goose down when we make padding to stuff between the layered soles of the new winter moccasins we should make when there is—"

"Yah!" Quarana interrupted in a blast of annoyance. "I say there is too much work in Xohkantakeh's band for only two women! My hands are already raw from what we have done, and I am nowhere near finished fleshing the skin of Yellow Calf. I am tired!"

"Ever since we were little you have always been tired when there is work to do, Quarana!" said Ika, inexpressibly annoyed. She had just finished removing the last traces of tissue from the big hide, so she put aside her scrapers and began to untie the thongs that secured the skin to the frame.

"If you are finished fleshing Mother Bison, help me with Yellow Calf!" commanded Quarana.

"No, Quarana, Yellow Calf is an honor gift to a life-carrying woman from the one who has made life on her. I cannot touch it. You must work it yourself." As the hide slumped and dropped to the ground, Ika set herself to haul it to the nearest water.

With South Wind trotting alongside, she was soon at the stream and kneeling in a sunny glade beside the widest of several shallow pools. Into this she unrolled the skin and, kneeling on sun-warmed new grass, willed her tired muscles to relax. She watched fingerling fish and tadpoles circle and wriggle away as the clear water floated the hide, listened to the birds singing in the trees and waterfowl honking and quacking and calling to one another from the ponds and lakes that filled every hollow of the new land. Now and then she could hear Xohkantakeh and Warakan shouting back and forth and smiled, for she knew they were not arguing but working together to tie down the last of the roofing of the lodge.

Warakan has not gone away! He will stay until the Dry Grass Moon . . . until the coming of the ice spirits . . . or maybe he will not go away at all. Ah, if he stays, I will not have to worry about him stealing the sacred stone from Xohkantakeh. My father will have a man to hunt at his side, and this girl will dare to be a woman—Warakan's woman! Ah! May it be so!

Absently Ika poked the floating hide with her fingertips, pushing gently down, patiently inviting the water to take the skin deeper. A slight wind stirred the trees and set the air a-tremble so that the biting flies that were usually the bane of every waking hour were dispersed. At her side, South Wind was nosing curiously at her fingers and lapping at the water. Suddenly a fish leaped midstream, and the wolf-dog was leaping after it, running across the hide and leaving Ika in a spray of cold water.

All but soaked through, she laughed as she watched the gangling, lop-eared pup jumping and snapping and then leaping straight into the air with a fish in its jaws.

"Well done!" She applauded as the wolf-dog trotted

proudly from the water, shook herself vigorously, and settled on the grass to devour her feast. "Ha! Maybe later you will catch a fish for me! Truly you are a child of the black wolf, a born hunter."

Shivering in her wet clothes, Ika gathered several large stones with which to weight down the hide in the pool. The water was cold; it would take a while for the raw skin to absorb it. Ika did not mind. The day was young, and the sun was warm on her back. Taking advantage of the absence of flies, she pulled off her wet garments, stretched them out on the grass to dry, and, naked save for her moccasins and the bearskin pouch she had worn around her neck since Xohkantakeh had given it to her when they had left the distant winter camp, lay down on her back beside them.

She sighed. Under most circumstances she would not have been able to relax like this, alone in a wild wood, away from an encampment, but she had often been to this place and had seen no sign of danger. Besides, the wolf-dog would alert her to the approach of any animal, large or small, dangerous or otherwise. And so she lay on the moist, sweet-smelling grass and watched the wind moving in the treetops and sunlight sparking gold on the leaves and listened to the sounds of the stream and the wind and the birds and the men at work. She smiled, closed her eyes, spread wide her arms. Her breasts were tender, the nipples swollen and sore—a sure sign that her time of blood would soon come again. She sighed, resigned, knowing that before she dressed again she must don the slender waist and loin strap she always kept carefully hidden away in the bearskin pouch along with a fistful of absorbent moss.

But now, knowing she was alone and in no danger of being seen, she welcomed the caress of the sun on her exposed skin. The warm rays bathed her body and soothed her breasts and set a thousand colors and patterns ablaze beneath her eyelids. Again she sighed, raised her arms, and folded them across her face. Slowly she was drawn into warm dreams of shallow pools in which a pair of silver fish circled languorously, one expelling the milk of life over glistening eggs laid by the other . . . while blue and red dragonflies hovered overhead, netted wings shimmering,

slender bodies joined in a dance of beauty that touched her
spirit and made her expel a quivering sigh as she imagined
herself as one of them, paired . . . joined . . . mated and flying high into the sunlit vastness of the Blue Land of Sky.
Spreading wide her limbs, she arched her body as though
she would take flight and wondered at the wondrous quivering warmth in her loins as she opened her eyes and stared up
into the eyes of . . .

"Warakan!"

He stared.

Ika made a grab for her garments and was on her feet in
an instant with her damp clothes clutched in shaking hands
against her body. The wolf-dogs were jumping up on her,
but, on the brink of tears, she pushed them away and
scolded South Wind. "Aiee! Is this how you would warn
me of approaching danger? With silence? With no warning
at all?"

Warakan wanted to tell her he was not dangerous, but
he could not speak. Save for her shoulders, arms, and
lower legs, Ika's body was hidden now. And yet the vision
he had seen when he came through the trees still burned
him: lean, lithe curves and softness laid out upon the grass
. . . the breasts, full and round . . . the dark fur below
the sleek span of belly . . . the long limbs relaxed and
parted . . . open . . . open.

His mouth went dry.

Ika was looking at him, and yet not looking at him; her
head was bowed, her mouth pale and trembling, her eyes
seeking his and then looking away beneath downturned,
quivering lids. She seemed to be trying to speak; her throat
was spasming, but no words came.

After a moment he managed, "Xohkantakeh saw you
take the big hide to the stream for soaking. I thought you
might need help bringing it back, as it will be even heavier
when wet, and . . . and . . ." He took a breath. "You are a
woman under your clothes, Ika!"

She flinched and shook her head. "No. A changing girl,
that is all, but not a woman . . . not yet!"

Having set eyes on the ripe glory of her young body, Warakan did not see how this was possible, but then, of all the things Jhadel had taught him, the mysteries of the bodies and minds of women and girls was not one of them. Although he had plunged his man bone into Quarana at every opportunity, she remained an enigma, and now, as he looked at the daughter of Xohkantakeh, he realized that Ika was even more so. And the more he looked at her, deep inside his very being he felt a stirring of awesome, incomprehensible emotions that made him realize that perhaps he understood himself even less. Of only one thing was Warakan sure in this moment. "Xohkantakeh is wrong about you," he said.

Shyly, uncertainly, Ika raised her eyes. "I do not understand."

"You are as good to look upon as your sister."

She looked at him, startled.

Something in her eyes touched him. Instinctively he knew that for all her strength and courage, Ika believed herself to be less than she was and had no desire to be only strong and brave in his eyes—she wanted to be beautiful. To his amazement, as his gaze held on her wide, sun-browned face and long dark eyes and full mouth that was so quick to smile, he saw a kindness and intelligence and capacity for love that astounded him. Indeed, in this moment he knew that even had he not beheld the wonder of her body, to his eyes Ika was the single most beautiful woman he had ever seen. In a haze of near rapture he heard himself say, "Not even Mah-ree of the Red World was as good to look upon as Ika."

"Is she not the one you love?"

"I . . . yes!" The girl's question stunned him. What had he been thinking? Had the sight of her body so astounded him that he had forgotten that Mah-ree was the woman of his heart? Mah-ree! Not Ika. Ika was nothing to him. A kind girl, a pleasant girl, a girl with an awe-inspiring body; and now that he looked closely at her face again, he saw that it was not extraordinary. She was not beautiful—pretty, yes, in her way. But not beautiful like her sister or his beloved Mah-ree. No! He shook his head. Perhaps, with the sacred stone no longer in his possession, his mind was now as weakened as his body.

Warakan cleared his throat, as though he could cleanse the passage that had allowed him to defame his affection for the true woman of his heart. "Mah-ree of the Red World *is* the one I love."

Ika lowered her glance again. Her brown face seemed paler somehow. "You have come to help me with the heavy hide of Mother Bison. This is a kind thing to do. But why do you do it? Ika is strong. Xohkantakeh knows I can do this work alone. Surely Warakan must know it, too?"

"Yes, it is so," he admitted, looking down, inexplicably flustered. Her words embarrassed and distressed him. He sensed a challenge in them that he did not wish to rise to. Of course the girl was strong and capable of hard work; she took pride in this obvious fact. Why, then, *had* he come to help her? Because he liked her company. The truth was plain enough to him. So why did he hesitate to speak it aloud? He liked the company of the wolf-dogs, too, and would have owned to this fact easily enough if she had asked him. He worked his shoulders and, knowing that she was patiently awaiting a more definitive answer, shrugged off what seemed a logical reply. "The roof lines of the lodge are now secure. Quarana is not feeling strong, and Xohkan-takeh is busy tending to her needs. There is nothing else for me to do around the camp except resharpen the scrapers or make a few new spearheads, and all the best stone blanks have been used. When East Wind grew bored and began to sniff out his sister, I thought I might as well follow. And so here I am."

"I see." She pulled in a little breath and held it. When she exhaled, she looked up, face set, eyes fully open and yet, somehow, closed to him. "Turn away, then. Let me clothe myself again. Since there is nothing better for you to do, you might as well help me with the hide of Mother Bison."

They worked together in silence, hauling the heavy hide from the pool, then dragging it onto a wide span of open grass where the earth was smooth and free of stones. Here, after commanding the meddlesome wolf-dogs away, they turned the hide skin-side down and, at Ika's instructions, removed their moccasins and began to walk lightly back and forth over it to press excess water from the saturated skin. Still they did not speak, and the girl kept her eyes downturned. Warakan sought to break the tension.

"Your name—Ika—it is an odd name. I have not heard it before. What is its Red World meaning?"

"It is not truly a Red World name, and in truth it has no meaning at all."

"A name must have meaning, and yours sounds like the call of a small white bird that I have heard now and then. 'Eeeka . . . eeka . . . eekaree!' Like that it calls!"

"Ah!" She looked at him for the first time since bringing the hide from the pool, smiling now as she walked back and forth. "It is exactly that! On the morning of my birth a small white bird flew over the encampment of my father's people. No one could remember ever seeing its kind before. Again and again it circled the camp. From the north it came, winging to the south, making its circle wider and wider until my mother heard its cries and said she was sure it was telling her the birth name of her newborn. The shaman looked and listened. He was not sure, but he said that since the white bird might indeed be a sign from the spirits, my father must agree to let his captive give the milk of life to the newborn. My father was not happy, but my mother rejoiced, for she was a Red World captive and I was the first of her babies to be allowed life and a place within the tribe."

"I do not remember Xohkantakeh ever being one to expose his children, even if they were only girls."

"Ah, you forget—Xohkantakeh is not the father of my blood and bone. All his daughters and sons are long dead, slain by enemies in the Land of Grass. And so, because he grieved for these lost children, under a Starving Moon he took into his band the abandoned daughters of two other warriors."

"And so it is that you are a Red World woman, like Mah-ree, the woman of my heart."

Her smile disappeared as she said sadly, "It is so, yes, like the woman of your heart."

He was about to tell her more about the wonders of

Mah-ree when he was distracted by a *yarf* from one of the wolf-dogs and looked up in time to see the animals—evidently no longer able to contain themselves at the side of the hide—leaping onto the skin to join what they perceived to be a new sort of game.

"Off!" Ika commanded as the wolf-dogs trotted back and forth, dodging and ducking between her limbs and Warakan's as they snapped happily at each other's tails and took an occasional nip at the wet hair of the hide.

"Off!" echoed Warakan. Suddenly taken off balance and finding himself on his buttocks with the pups all over him, he showed his teeth and snarled like a wolf-dog himself as he pushed the animals away. "Off, I say! Would you damage the hide this woman has worked so hard to flesh? Away! Or I will brain you both and set your hides to dry in the sun!"

Startled, the wolf-dogs backed away.

Ika stared down at him with her hands on her hips. "I am *not* a woman," she said sternly. "But I think that my children are now certain that you must be a wolf and not a man! Surely you do not mean what you say to them?"

"Hmmph!" Warakan lay back, carefully rolled off the hide, and got to his feet on the grass, eyeing the wolf-dogs.

They eyed him back.

He lowered and extended his head.

They lowered and extended theirs.

He raised his lips to show his teeth.

The hair on South Wind's neck bristled as she slunk back a step, but East Wind stepped forward, growling.

"Ah," said Warakan, "so you would be head wolf with me? No. I am a man who has learned the ways of a wolf from my drowned sister, and I tell you, Bold One, that I was head wolf when she and I ran together in pack. So do not show your teeth and speak defiance of my will! I am Warakan. I have walked as an equal with Wolf and Bear. What are you compared to me? Ha! The curl of your tails tells me what you are. The blood of Dog is in you both. And what is Dog, eh? Only an ember sundered from the flesh of both Wolf and Man. Do you imagine that Warakan, grandson of Shateh, would allow himself to be intimidated by an ember, a cast-off spark from the lightning bolt that created—"

"I see that you know the story of how Dog came to walk with Man instead of Wolf!" exclaimed Ika, smiling now. "It has always been my favorite of all the tales Xohkantakeh has told!"

He looked at her with a confident air. "Then you should know, daughter of Xohkantakeh, that you are too easy on these children of the black wolf. You may have become their mother, but when they refuse to obey, you must remember that the blood of Dog is in them and that they are by nature slaves to Man and need to be reminded of their place."

"Ah, no, Warakan, the children of the black wolf are not my slaves. In the tale as Xohkantakeh tells it, Man and Dog together are the equal of Wolf as they run forever as brothers within the Circle of Life!" Stepping lightly from the hide, she went to the wolf-dogs and embraced them. "I will be the voice of the children of the black wolf so that those who carry the blood of Dog may speak and remind Warakan of these words from the old tale: 'Better for you if Dog runs at your side, to scent and flush the game and to stand with you against Wolf! For what will you hunt, Naked Beast, running upright and alone within the great Circle of Life with no pads to cushion your steps and neither fangs nor claws to tear your meat?'"

Warakan frowned. He did not like where her words were leading. "I need no one to run with me within the great Circle of Life. I will hunt what I choose and make my claws and fangs from the bones of the beasts I kill and cushion my feet with the skins of any animal—or man—that stands against me!"

Ika's smile vanished. "Do you mean that, Warakan? Do you truly mean that?"

He met her gaze. There was pity in her eyes. It startled and angered him. Who was Ika to pity the grandson of Shateh? Thoroughly annoyed, he decided then and there to return to the encampment and leave her to carry the hide back alone, but when he moved to retrieve his moccasins he snatched the first one so violently from the grass that its mate flew into the air. He cursed; the thing was arcing high like a well-flung spear, but with its fringes and thong ties flapping, it looked like some sort of strange, gut-wounded, featherless bird.

The wolf-dogs, reacting to the ancient blood tide of all predators, were up and after it. Ika called them back and Warakan uttered a furious command for them to return, but the sight of a large, limp, heavily fringed moccasin flying through the air was too much for the animals to resist. They ran until, with an impressive leap, East Wind caught it in midair and—momentarily brought short by Warakan's command—took one long look over his dark shoulder, seemed to smile in yet another display of defiance, then turned and ran on with his captured "prey."

"I think he will eat your moccasin if we do not stop him," said Ika. As one, she and Warakan raced barefoot across the grass and into the trees, stopping only now and then to hop about and grab at bruised heels or insteps when they stepped on stones and fallen branches. At last, in an open glade again, they were brought to a halt by a sight that made them both burst out laughing.

East Wind was looking back at them over his shoulder again, and this time there was no smile of defiance on his face. Indeed, had he been a man, he could not have looked more shamefaced as he stood snared in the middle of a low-growing span of brambles, within which the thong ties of the moccasin appeared hopelessly entangled.

South Wind came close, wagging her tail, seeking forgiveness for her part in the chase. Ika spoke low words of chastisement and looked worriedly at Warakan.

"You will not harm my dark child and use his skin to make new cushions for your feet. I will not let you."

"Your child? I thought you gave East Wind to me as a 'companion, friend, and protector' so that I would not be lonely or at risk when I left your band."

"You have not left it yet," she reminded him and, giving South Wind a loving pat on the top of her brindled head, strode forward to help the ensnared and chastened East Wind.

Warakan followed and watched for a moment, touched

by the girl's gentleness and patience with the animal. So it was with Mah-ree, he thought.

"Be still, be still, my child," Ika said. "Here. Let me loose that thong from around your forepaw. There. Now I will take the moccasin. It is not fit food for your kind, you know, and you have been foolish to chase it! Now be still again. I must lift the brambles from around your neck and shoulders. Ah! But some of these will have to be torn, and they are green and thick with sap and new tough skin!"

There was blood on Ika's hands as she worked. She did not complain, nor did she speak when Warakan, having accepted the tattered moccasin she handed back to him, moved to help her after tucking it under his tunic. Soon his own hands were scratched and bleeding, but between them they soon ripped away the last of the confining branches and lifted the wolf-dog in their arms.

Their eyes met.

East Wind licked both their faces in a display of affection and gratitude before, with a twist of his back, he indicated his desire to be free. They put the animal on his feet. South Wind came close to nuzzle her sibling, but neither Warakan nor Ika noticed.

They stood close. So close.

He did not intend to take her face between his hands. He did not intend to look so deeply into her eyes that his spirit seemed to touch and meld with her very soul. And he did not intend to kiss her.

So light a kiss: a mere touching of lips. A slow, tenuous exchange of breath.

And in that unintended melding he was undone, shattered, for as he enfolded her in his embrace, her arms went around his neck and her body and mouth opened to him, and all of Ika's love was given. Love? *Yes!* Quarana, hungry only for coupling, had never kissed or held him like this. And Mah-ree, whose memory he so adored, had never kissed or held him at all.

Slowly, as in a dream, the embrace continued, and the kiss was held until at last he drew his mouth from hers and sought once more the spirit he had seen within her eyes. It was there, open to him, a rare and shining soul so full of love he knew that in all his life no one had ever loved—or would ever love—him so.

"Do not go from this band . . . or from this *woman*, Warakan," Ika implored. "Shateh lives in you. You are all that is left of him. If you die in your quest to avenge him, will his spirit not die with yours forever? But if you stay, will the force of his life not take root through you within the body of this woman, this Red World woman, and live again in the sons you will make on me? And then will it not be as Xohkantakeh has said: that through our children the Three Tribes will be united and the People will be one again at last? This was your grandfather's hope, Warakan, the dream that was lost to him . . . and may yet be reborn through you." Tears were shimmering in her eyes as she moved to kiss him and, trembling, whispered through the kiss, "Open me, Warakan. Now, be my first and only man. I am no longer afraid to be mated . . . not now . . . not with you."

Her kiss enflamed him as Quarana's kiss and his desire for Mah-ree had never done. And yet he put her away from him. He looked into her eyes and knew that he would not take her. Not now. Not yet. Jhadel had taught him little enough of the ways of her gender, but he had not forgotten to warn that it was sacrilege to open a girl not yet come to the shedding of moon blood, for this would be a wasting of the white fire of life making. And although that fire burned for release within him now, Ika had kindled another flame that burned more deeply than the fire of passion, for it was a fire with a gentle and all-consuming flame. It was the fire of love. In this moment, as he looked into Ika's eyes, he knew Jhadel had been right all along. This *was* the woman the old Peacedreamer had seen walking toward him out of the rising sun.

"Yes!" He drew Ika again into his embrace, closing his eyes, releasing himself from the past and into the present. The spirits of the dead would understand, and surely they would release him from a vow he had genuinely attempted to fulfill and that they had never asked him to make in the first place! Now that he thought about it from a new perspective, it occurred to Warakan that if he were to die in his quest for vengeance, the life spirits of his father and grandfather *would* die with him. Then, surely, they would all have run as shadows within the great Circle of Life, and there would be nothing left of any of them when he breathed his last—except, perhaps, the small nubbin of life that was growing in Quarana's belly. The thought disturbed him. And then, suddenly, it affirmed his purpose, for if Quarana was telling the truth when she said she carried his child, did he not owe it to his father and grandfather to take Ika as his woman and make sons on her that would be worthy of the spirits of the chieftain and shamans of his line? If the woman of Xohkantakeh grew jealous, what could she do about it? If she spoke the truth, she would succeed only in revealing the extent of her own deception, a revelation that could not possibly serve her well in the giant's eyes. As of this moment the old warrior had no reason to believe that the baby Quarana carried was not his.

May it be so forever! For from this moment I will never look at that ermine-eyed, double-tongued, perpetually hot-thighed woman! She is not fit to be the woman of Xohkan-takeh! She is not worthy to carry his life, or mine. But I will be and do all that he asks of me in the days and nights to come, and perhaps, in this small way, I may begin to make up to that good man for the disloyalty and disrespect I have shown to one who has saved my life and will now be my hunt brother and, through Ika, name me Son.

"You are trembling, Warakan."

Again he put her away from him and looked into her eyes. "From this day I will be worthy of you, Ika. Yes! I vow that it *will* be so. Let the warring tribes fight on in the Land of Grass. Let Mah-ree and her many children walk with Cha-kwena and the totem beyond the edge of the world. Let the magic spearhead remain hidden in the far gorge forever! Warakan will seek it no longer. Now may the spirit of Jhadel hear the words of Warakan! Now may his ghost smile and be at peace as he rides on the back of Golden Eagle upon the Four Winds! Come, foundling Red World daughter of Xohkantakeh who will soon be the woman of Warakan! Let us return to the pool and carry the hide of Mother Bison back to the encampment. I will tell Xohkantakeh that I will be his son and brother. I will not leave this band. And when Ika sheds her first moon blood, then, in the way of the Ancient Ones since time beyond beginning, I will lie down with her and be her man forever!"

His heart was singing, and so was he, as Warakan walked barefoot and hand in hand with Ika back to the pool. The wolf-dogs loped ahead, happily sniffing out game trails while the young man and girl lagged behind, lost in the delight of each other's company and seeing the world with new eyes.

The sun was sliding well to the west when they came through the trees laughing and hugging as they talked of all that the future held in store for them now. Xohkantakeh and Quarana were waiting for them.

The grassy glade was in shadow. And so was the mood of the giant.

Despite himself, Warakan frowned at the first sight of one to whom he had intended to extend the hand of a brother. Xohkantakeh held a lance in each hand and had evidently just come from the encampment with his woman, for he was winded and flushed as though from a forced walk, and something about the way he wore the skin of the great slain bear made him appear as though he had come to do battle. He looked huge, threatening, and the expression on his face was one of pure wrath as he pointed at Ika with one of the lances and roared, "There is blood on your dress, and it is damp with sweat!"

"Sweat?" Ika asked, clearly puzzled. Looking down at her dress, she saw the splotches of blood to which he referred and tossed her head, smiling as she said, "Ah! No, my father, East Wind stole one of Warakan's moccasins, and we gave chase! The pup ran himself into brambles and was caught. Warakan and I were both scratched trying to free him. And before that South Wind took off after a fish and splashed me so thoroughly that my dress may take another day or two of sun to fully dry!"

"Yah!" cried Quarana, her face convulsing with jealous rage. "What clever lies you tell, sister! But they will not fool my Bear Slayer! I told you, Life Giver, they had been too long away! Ika carried the hide of Mother Bison to this place, and he followed and pierced her on it! I know he has! I have seen him looking at her ever since the day the river puked him up. And I have seen the hunting shirt you gave him raised up by the shaft of his man bone growing hard whenever she comes near to offer broth. Broth! Yah! Ika has been offering *herself!* And now he has seen his opportunity and finally worked up enough courage and man milk to take her . . . against her will, if we are to judge by the way she has scratched him. He has broken the law of the Ancient Ones by piercing a child, Killer of Horse and Bison. And surely the wounds on her hands and arms were not made by thorns, but in retaliation by Warakan when he returned scratch for scratch like the wolf he is!"

Warakan laughed. It was an inane reaction and he knew it, but as he stood to the scalding venom of Quarana's lies, Reason told him she had to be making sport of him. How else could he explain why a woman who had so flagrantly seduced him again and again and claimed to be carrying his life in her belly instead of her man's would now have the audacity to accuse him of raping her sister? But what kind of joke was this . . . and why was she playing it?

"Quarana, my sister, why do you speak so?" asked a stunned and befuddled Ika.

"Yah! Make her open her thighs to your inspection, Life Giver, and I am sure you will find the blood of first piercing and the man milk that he has spilled in her still sticky on her thighs!"

"Quarana!" cried Ika. "What bad spirits have entered your head and now pour from your mouth like—"

"No! You will not speak so to my life-bearing woman. It is not Quarana who has habitually defied the laws of the Ancient Ones. It is not Quarana I find alone in this place with Warakan, barefoot and stained with blood. No. It is Ika, who has made an art of defiance since the day she was born! Come to me, daughter," Xohkantakeh commanded. "Raise your dress and open your thighs and let me see if what New Woman says is truth or not."

Ika obeyed. Walking tall and proud she came to him and hefted her dress and parted her limbs and, clenching her jaw, stood her ground as he sent his great hand questing between her thighs and then drew it back and raised it high.

"There! Blood!" Quarana was triumphant. "It is as I knew it would be!"

"Impossible!" Warakan shouted. "What kind of trick is this? I have not pierced Ika . . . would not have pierced her until—"

"You . . ." The word bled out of Xohkantakeh. It was a low, dangerous sound, like the controlled growl of a lion hunkering low, eyes fixed on its prey and every muscle in its body tense and bunching and set to spring in a death charge. "Spawn of the river . . . defiler of the laws of the Ancient Ones . . . you have been Trouble since the day you were born. But no more . . . not in this man's band! You will not put my daughter and woman and unborn child at more risk than you have already done!"

"No!" cried Ika. "Xohkantakeh! Father! Please, you do not understand! He has done nothing!"

Warakan was aware of Ika's voice, unnaturally high and strained as she begged for calm and understanding. He knew that neither were possible. He could see rage continuing to build behind the giant's eyes, rising and cresting until, like the dark waters of the Mother of All Rivers when the mountains of ice had surged forward into them, it broke wide. Xohkantakeh was running at him, lances leveled in both hands.

Ika shrieked, "No! Please! No!"

Xohkantakeh ignored her and kept on coming.

The dogs, frightened and confused by the sight and scent of the giant's anger, sensed his intent and, reacting as one, threw themselves at the charging man.

Xohkantakeh kicked them away. Warakan, hearing their yelps, was instantly transformed. Unjustly accused and threatened by attack, he felt his own blood rise as his eyes focused in the clear, sharply etched definition that came only when adrenaline was racing in his veins and every nerve in his body was screaming, *Run! Flee or fight! Or surely you will die!*

Warakan did not run. Barefoot and unarmed, he knew he was no match for the giant, but he also knew that the distance between them was now so small that flight was impossible. Unless . . .

As Xohkantakeh raised his arms and descended upon Warakan with the intent to pierce him from both sides, the young man hurled himself forward with such force that he was propelled between the pounding legs of the charging man to land on the far side of him.

"Yah!" cried Quarana.

The giant whirled. He was furious.

So was Warakan. Scrambling madly to his feet, he hunched forward and balanced himself lightly so that he would be ready for whatever came. Snarling at his adversary, he gestured him forward. It was a mistake.

Xohkantakeh did not merely come at him; he flew. With his arms again extended and the great bearskin making the already huge man appear twice his size, he leaped forward with such power that, before Warakan could move out of the way, he was overwhelmed.

The giant was on him.

The world went dark. Warakan felt the breath knocked out of him and yet, somehow, managed to knee the giant's belly and groin as he forced himself up, reaching, desperately grabbing for the man's throat, jabbing hard with his fingers. He heard the garbled sound of choking as his hands sought a wider hold on the massive neck. Then, with all his strength, he levered up with his feet, burrowed his head deep into Xohkantakeh's midsection, and pulled down on the man's neck as hard as he could. His hands slipped; his fingers strained to maintain their grip, encountered a thong neckband, and, closing on it, jerked down so hard the leather broke. But not before the giant tumbled forward, leaving Warakan on his knees with the sacred stone of the Ancient Ones in his hand.

Dizzy now, shaking his head, Warakan stared at the talisman in disbelief. At that moment Ika cried his name, and he turned toward her just as Xohkantakeh's lance sang past his face. He blinked, shocked and hurt to his very spirit, for until now, despite the giant's vicious, pummeling attack, he had somehow not fully believed that the man would take his life—not now, not when the enmity between them had been set aside, not when the man had offered to name him Son and Brother, not when, only moments ago, he had held Ika in his arms and agreed to forgo his dreams of vengeance so that he might live out his life in peace with Xohkantakeh and his Red World daughter.

Warakan's heart sank. He had been right all along; Xohkantakeh *was* his enemy. Had it not been for Ika's cry, the giant would have killed him without thinking twice, and even now he was levering back for a second strike.

But Ika threw herself against her father to stay his hand. "No! No! Warakan has done no wrong! He has not pierced me, although even if he had, the laws of the ancestors would not have been violated! My father has said to Warakan that if he stayed within this band Ika would be his woman when she became a woman. But Ika *is* and has been a woman since before the great waters came to the drowned valley! It is moon blood you have found upon my thighs, my father, not the blood of first piercing!"

Silence. Absolute.

Warakan did not understand why the giant looked at the girl the way he did, or why Ika scooted back from him on her knees and touched her head to the ground. He could not have known all that had gone before, and yet he felt the weight of it and knew it was about to crush him.

"Forgive me," Ika begged in abject misery.

Xohkantakeh stood as though one of his own spears had struck him and rent a mortal blow. "You have shed a woman's blood and kept this a secret from your band? You have continued to hunt with the weapons of a man even though you have known this was forbidden to you? You have done this in open defiance of the laws of the Ancient Ones? Why, Ika? After all the many times you have been warned about breaking the ways of the ancestors, why would you do so terrible a thing?"

"I . . . I feared for . . . I mean I feared that . . . I feared you would . . ." She cut off the words; whatever was in her heart, she would not speak it now. She remained unmoving and silent at his feet.

A tremor shook the giant. "Can it be that it is you who have brought the wrath of the forces of Creation upon this band? Can it be that my beloved woman is dead because of her own daughter's selfish pride and need to hunt as a man? Katohya carried my life in her, Ika! As Quarana now carries my life! Ah! Were it not for this man your spirit would long ago have walked the wind. And now I see that were it not for this man's weakness toward you, Katohya would not be lying dead in the drowned valley, and my hope of a long life with her at my side would still be alive in my heart. Again and again I have warned you, Ika. Your life is mine to keep or throw away. And now I say that for the good of Quarana and the baby she carries, from this day I will suffer no law-breaking woman—or trouble-bringing man—to live in the camps of Xohkantakeh!"

Warakan leaped to his feet. He could see Xohkantakeh's hand flexing on the haft of his lance; the great knuckles had gone white, and the broad mouth was strained to near transparency. Slowly, so slowly it seemed almost not to be happening at all, his arm began to rise. To his horror Warakan realized that the giant was about to put an end to Ika's life.

"No!"

Warakan winced at Quarana's unexpected outcry.

"Ika meant no harm in her deception!" she exclaimed, her face contorted with confusion and dismay. "It is Warakan whom you must send from the band. He is Trouble. You have said it from the start. We do not need him. We should never have trusted him. But Ika, she has always feared being mated! She has told me this many times. And if you take her life, who will help this woman do her work and help her to bear your babies unless we return to the Land of Grass and—"

"What is this you say?" Xohkantakeh sent his gaze to Quarana. There was no softness in it, no light, only the darkness of a fixed and terrible intent from which he would not allow himself to withdraw. "Even now, at this moment, would you try to lead me to your single-minded purpose? No. I will hear no more from you on this, Quarana. You will live out your days how and where I say. And do not defend your band sister to me! If Ika fears being mated, why would she offer herself to the spawn of the river and entice him to break the law of the ancestors with her?"

Quarana was so taken aback by the question that she did not answer.

But Warakan did. There was something black in his heart, something more bitter than bile. He spat it out. "Quarana is the one who disdains the laws of the Ancient Ones! In the soft dark of dawn she has eagerly opened herself to me many times while you slept unaware. For all I know, it is my life she carries, not yours, for surely she has tried to hold me and lead me with this claim! But I care not for what grows in her belly. Now she has seen me look with a man's eyes at her sister and knows that I have no intention of becoming her man when at last she manipulates you through false dreams into taking her to the Land of Grass— where you are likely to be slain by old enemies as surely as she yearns to find a new man, a younger man, and many grandmothers to do her share of woman's work. And she wants me gone before I tell you with my own mouth how it has been between us! But now I have spoken. Now you know. Now Warakan says to Xohkantakeh that it is Quarana, not Ika, who deserves your lance in her back."

Ika looked from Warakan to Quarana and then back again like a wounded and bewildered doe. "It cannot be!"

"It is!" he shouted, not at Ika but at himself for having been so weak and willing to be led into the snare Quarana had laid for him. Now he must pay for that weakness and willingness. Now he must turn his gaze, perhaps forever, from the one he loved, for he saw rage building again in Xohkantakeh and knew he must risk losing Ika or see her slain before his eyes by her father's hand. "As for your other foundling," he sneered to the giant, "why do you threaten her? Ika has kept the ways of the ancestors. I do not know why she lied to protect me from your wrath. Perhaps because her spirit is weak when it comes to taking pity on wounded things? Who can say what is in another's heart? But I *did* pierce her! Why not? She is not yet a woman, and surely she is not much to look at, but she *is* female, and the blood you found on her thighs is blood drawn from her by the pleasure I took when I forced her to spread herself for me. Why do you stare, Xohkantakeh? Did you not name me Trouble? I am Warakan, son of Masau, Mystic Warrior of the People of the Watching Star, and grandson of Shateh, chieftain and shaman of the People of the Land of Grass. Did you not imagine that I would please myself as I will on the woman and daughter of my enemy if he gave me the chance? Have I not sworn to take vengeance on all who betrayed my grandfather? Why should I have taken your word that you were not one of them when you stole the sacred stone of the Ancient Ones from me? And now that it is mine once more, why should I fear an aging warrior who cannot see that the cause of the weakness and vulnerability of his band lies, not in the failure of his women to abide by the laws of the ancestors, but in himself?"

The giant stiffened, and with a roar of anger he hurled his lance. But the weapon flew unsteadily from his shaking hand and had little force behind it.

Warakan caught it in midair and, barely daring to believe his luck, turned and ran for his life with the sacred stone curled tightly in one fist, the wolf-dogs at his heels, and Quarana's shrieking epithets in his ears.

"Go, Liar! Go, Wolf! You are not a man! Cross the great river, and if you do not drown in it, go to the far gorge, leap the abyss like the dog you are, and run back to your own kind. We do not want you . . . and this woman has *never* wanted you!"

3

For a long while Xohkantakeh stood unmoving in the glade.

South Wind came panting through the trees, whining and circling restlessly until, realizing that no one was going to follow her back through the woods to join her brother, she went to Ika and lay down at her side.

"The wolf-dog will lead you to him," said Quarana to the giant, her face tight, her eyes wild with fury. "Why do you stand and stare into the trees? Why do you not follow? He has only a single lance! He has no moccasins or warm clothing! And he has gone without meat or fat to give him strength. He will soon be weak and sick again. But why wait? You can easily take back the stone and the other wolf-dog, and when you have left Warakan for carrion as you so wisely wished to do when we first found him, we can go on as before and—"

"No, Quarana," he interruped, looking at her. Wondering at the absence of anger in him, he said quietly, "We cannot go on as before. Everything *has* changed. And yet I see now that *nothing* has changed. It is as it was in time beyond beginning. The People and Animals are still of one tribe. Warakan and Xohkantakeh are both men who walk in the skin of Bear. We have both walked with wolves, each in our own way. But the spirit of Bear is in me, while it is Wolf who runs in the blood of Warakan. Our bands must walk separate paths. Perhaps it is the will of the forces of Creation that we must be enemies forever. I cannot say, but I tell you now, woman, that although he has betrayed my trust, there will be no death for Warakan at Xohkantakeh's hand. I have looked into his eyes and have heard and believed his truths. From this day we will walk separate paths beneath Sun and Moon and the great Sky River. Warakan will go into the West Wind to fulfill or fail to fulfill the vow he has made to the ancestors. Xohkantakeh will stay in this good camp on the far side of the Great River. Here we will rest. Here we will grow strong. Then I will take my woman, daughter, and wolf-dog and return across the drowned land into the sheltering forests that lie beyond the edge of the world. I should have listened to Katohya. We should never have left the winter camp. Life was good for us there in the face of the rising sun. Perhaps it will be good again? Only the Four Winds can say."

"Aiee!" cried Quarana. "It cannot be! My new-woman dream has called us to the Land of Grass, where there will be many warriors to hunt at your side and many women to help me with my work! Surely you would not risk your unborn child to—"

"I do not know whose child you carry, Quarana. The moon beneath which it enters the Circle of Life will speak its father's name. I will know if it is a child of Xohkantakeh or of Warakan as surely as I now know in my heart that your new-woman dreams were lies made to serve your own laziness and selfish need to shame me with a younger warrior. So speak no more lies to me. If the life you carry was made on you by a wolf, I will smother its first cry and deny it life as surely as I will take you back to the land where there are no two-legged wolves. There, if the forces of Creation grant it so, I will put life into you again . . . *my* life . . . a son for Xohkantakeh before it is too late and my spirit dies forever. This I will do. And you will be grateful. Yes. Because by the laws of the ancestors it is my right to brain you now and throw your life away as penalty for what you have done. But I will not do this, nor will I blame you for all that has befallen us upon the journey into the West Wind, for Warakan—although he has proved himself a wolf with you—has spoken great wisdom to me this day. In the light of his words I have seen Truth reflected back to me as an image seen in water on a clear day. And so I say, before the sacred stone of the Ancient Ones came into my hand, was I not Bear Slayer and Killer of Horse and Bull Bison?"

Ika, still on her knees and staring fixedly toward the trees into which Warakan had disappeared, looked up at Xohkantakeh out of pained and guarded eyes.

"Now the stone is with Warakan," he continued. "Let him run with it before the Four Winds and chase the meaningless shadows of revenge forever across the land of our enemies. He has understood nothing of the Great Circle of Wisdom. Even if he succeeds in all he has sworn to do, he will have spent his days as a shadow pursuing shadows, and in the end he will have slain the great white mammoth totem and put an end to all the Peoples' dreams, including his own. But I, Xohkantakeh, know what he does not—that those who seek to take the life of the great white mammoth invariably discover at the end of their search that they have found their own death."

Ika shivered.

Quarana, sobered by the giant's threats, reminded him, "But he has taken the sacred stone and walks strong in the power of the—"

"I need no talisman to make me strong," Xohkantakeh interrupted. "I have seen my place in the Great Circle of Wisdom. And it was the insult of Warakan that showed it to me. I *am* an aging warrior. Until this day I have allowed my fear of this truth to determine the way in which the Four Winds would blow upon my band. No more. From this day I will look no longer to talismans for power or to dreams for direction, nor will I blame others for my own failings. I will face my weaknesses and accept them for what they are, but I will look also to the strengths that the forces of Creation have left to me. Enough to allow me to walk in the skin of Great Paws! Enough to send me forth to be Killer of Horse and Bull Bison! In this wisdom I *will* be strong. And until Ika becomes a woman, she will be warrior enough to hunt at my side in those good hunting grounds Katohya loved so well."

"But there are no people in that far land!" Quarana said

querulously. "Ika will become a woman someday! Who will hunt with you then? And what happens to me when you die and I am left alone with—"

"The great white mammoth totem walks in the face of the rising sun, Quarana. The shaman Cha-kwena and his woman walk with him. Maybe they will weary of the cold and come from the barrens someday. Maybe we will walk with them and their children. Maybe. Who can say what the Four Winds will bring or how any of us will end our days . . . or which of a man's daughters will work against his will to betray and shame him for her own purpose?"

Quarana shrank in her furs. Then, quickly, desperate to have her way despite all that had just happened, she feigned wounding by his words. Wide-eyed, she batted her lids in pretended astonishment, swung her head in slow denial, and pouted prettily until . . .

Xohkantakeh slapped her so hard across the face that she spun around and, stunned and off balance, fell to her knees. "Look not in my eyes again, Quarana, until you are sure I will see no guile there! Do you imagine that I have not seen you look at him as though the very sight of him fed your spirit? And can it be that you do not know that I have suspected what was between you from the time I heard your words to him on the first day you brought him meat? The instigation was yours, not his, Quarana, and afterward I sometimes woke after dawn and thought I caught the smell of mating on you when you crept back into the lodge after making the morning fire. I know now that I should not have slept so easily, but an old man guards his pride and does not readily suspect his woman when she is young and good to look upon and has made him dare to dream of spring again."

Quarana's hands were on her jaw, testing and rubbing it as she succumbed to tears.

Xohkantakeh took grim pleasure in her discomfort, then became aware of Ika staring off into the forest again. With a start of self-recrimination he felt his heart soften toward her. "I have accused you wrongly, daughter. Forgive an outraged father. And yet you *did* lie for him. What was I to think? Lies . . . they twist and confuse the spirit . . . set us all to purposes that cannot ever lead to a straight path. Let no lies come between us again, Ika. You have seen what they have put between this man and your sister."

Her jaw tightened. "I have seen."

He was discomfitted by her manner—so contained and detached, as though a part of her spirit had gone from her body and she was lighter somehow, not quite the same strong, bold girl she had been before. "Has Warakan hurt you badly, child?"

She did not move. "Yes," she said. "Warakan has hurt me badly."

"Your mother would have known what salves or green growing things to use to ease the pain of a forced first piercing. I am sorry. I do not know the secrets of such female things. But in the medicine bag within the lodge there must be—"

"No salves will heal the hurt that has been made on me this day."

Again that contained, detached voice, the voice of a stranger. Xohkantakeh did not like the change in her. He did not understand it. "Come, Ika," he said impatiently, for he was now feeling the onset of fatigue for the first time since his confrontation with Warakan. "You are not yet a woman. Do not grieve over this. I warned you that he was Trouble. It is good he has gone. We will go back to the winter camp now. It was your favorite of all our hunting grounds, the place where I slew Great Paws! Do you remember that day, Little Bear, when we shared the heart of that yellow thief and you said we were like Great Bear and Little Bear in the sky and wished we would always hunt together?"

She turned and looked up at him. "Yes. I remember. And you said 'May it be so . . . until Ika becomes a woman and can hunt with a spear no more.'"

"Perhaps the Four Winds heard our words that day."

"Then may they hear this woman's words now!" whimpered Quarana, on her feet now, still rubbing her jaw as she moved out of striking range of her man. "If my Bear Slayer will journey back into the forests beyond the edge of the world, then may it be that Ika never becomes a woman! For when Xohkantakeh dies, who will hunt for me and help me care for the sons I will bear him?"

It struck the giant that she was right, that what he was proposing was, in its own way, as reckless and selfish as anything she had done. It also struck him that he did not care. He was Xohkantakeh, Bear Slayer and Killer of Horse and Bison. His woman had shamed and deceived him. He was tired of being reasonable and putting the welfare of others above his own. Quarana deserved punishment; he would punish her and please himself in the punishing. As for Ika and any sons Quarana might bear him? Ika was strong; she could take care of herself. And if there *were* sons . . . he would worry about them when they came.

"Take up the hide of Bison Mother, Quarana," he commanded. "We will return to the lodge and prepare ourselves for the journey that will soon lie ahead."

"But we have just made the lodge! And the hide of Bison Mother is for Ika to work! It is far too heavy for—"

"Bison Mother gave up her life and the life of her calf to honor you, Quarana. I see no reason why your sister should continue to ease your workload when, by your behavior with Warakan behind my back, you have shown that you are stronger than you would own to. Take up the hide, I say. Until Ika becomes a woman, she will need all her strength to attend to her own responsibilities and to hunt at my side. She will not carry your loads or make your meat, New Woman, for from this day your wheedling words will no longer win pity in my eyes!"

He waited.

In the woods close by the brambles where they had savored their first kiss, Warakan held East Wind close and wished upon the sacred stone for Ika to come.

"You will see, Bold One. She has seen through my words and understood the way of my heart. She will know why I spoke of her the way I did and that I had to lie to save her. But what of her lies? Where was truth when she told me that she was no woman, and then showed her father blood upon her thighs? It was real enough, and you and I know full well that I did not put it there! I do not understand. Quarana said Ika was afraid to be mated, but she did not seem so with me, eh? Ah. She will explain. I will explain. She will come, you will see. Soon now, she will come!"

The wolf-dog, restless since South Wind had cut back through the trees to join the others, raised his head and scented the wind, then lay down, panting, wanting to be away.

"Stay with me a while, friend. Just a while. If she does not come . . . she *must* come!"

Darkness came instead, cool and damp. Warakan shivered for want of Ika, and for want of a warm robe and a complete pair of shoes. He huddled close to the wolf-dog. "Stay with me. I need your warmth. Stay."

He dozed. He dreamed of sneaking back into the encampment, tiptoeing into the lodge, and seeing Ika bound hand and foot. He saw Quarana smirking, inviting him to forbidden pleasures the thought of which set his loins to shriveling and the hackles rising on his back. *Not with her. Never again with her!* He saw Xohkantakeh sleeping and, without hesitation, drove his lance deep into his vast back, killing him as he slept. But it was not a man he killed; it was a yellow bear, Bear Brother, and Warakan was confused. Quarana cried, and this confused him more, for it did not seem possible that she could cry, for a bear *or* for the giant. He ignored her and held his hand out to Ika. "Come! We will walk together now. Ika and Warakan, always and forever!"

"And where shall we go, Father Slayer and Sister Defiler?" asked Ika in his dream. "I cannot walk with you within the Circle of Life. There is no place for me in the encampments of the enemies whom you would bathe in their own blood and yours."

"Mine? No! I have taken back the sacred stone! I will retrieve the magic spearhead and place it on the lance of Xohkantakeh. I will hunt and kill the great white mammoth totem. You will be with me. Together we will be invincible!"

"No. You will be alone. And if you keep to your ways, Trouble, you will bring death to us all!"

Warakan awoke. East Wind was gone. He could hear Xohkantakeh chanting in the encampment, the song of the Fire Keeper, a litany of hope in the continuation of life. It

unnerved him as the dream had unnerved him. Moonlight
bathed the wood. An owl called, and another answered. He
wondered when he had last felt so lonely. Shivering again,
he rose and crept back to the glade, where he found his
abandoned moccasin. But Ika was not there. Xohkantakeh
had stopped singing.

"Now she will come," he told himself, speaking low,
feeling better for the sound of his own voice. "When the
others sleep, she will be free to leave them." He laced on the
moccasin as best he could with a thong tie ripped in half by
East Wind's frolic through the brambles. But a half-tied foot
covering was better than none at all on a chill night.

"Ika will bring another pair of moccasins, and a robe,
and food, and . . . Why does she wait?"

He rubbed his arms and hunkered low, missing the
warmth of the wolf-dog. "I thought you had chosen me to be
your brother. Hmm. You are not so loyal, Bold One . . . perhaps she is not so loyal either? No! She will come."

She did not come.

The stars began to shift toward dawn. "I will go into the
camp and bring her out! If the giant stands in my way, I will
kill him!"

He advanced slowly, careful to make no sound, for he
was only vaguely confident that the wolf-dogs would not
hear and betray his presence. Moving to a place from which
he could see and yet not be seen, he waited and watched.
The lodge was dark. Quarana had not risen early to make
fire this day. His mouth tightened; he realized he hated her.
On the power of the sacred stone he wished pain and a slow
death to her and the life she carried in her belly, even if that
life was a part of him—surely he did not want it!

The sound of movement caused him to catch his breath,
to hold it, to strain his senses. The dogs were stirring before
the lodge, and someone was coming out. *Ika?*

Yes!

She was alone. Tall and erect in the starlight, she took a
few tense, cautious steps forward, turned slightly, and stared
toward the trees, looking . . . for him.

Warakan rose. His heart was pounding in his chest as,
like the girl, he took a few steps forward.

Their eyes met. Held. He could see that she had a lance in one hand. His heart leaped. The dogs were up now, aware of him. He saw her bend, place a hand on the shoulder of one, but already the other was coming forward. *East Wind! Yes! Come to your brother. And now let Ika follow!*

She did not move.

He raised an arm, waved a broad and generous greeting and kept on waving as he waited for her to rise, to wave a greeting of her own as she hurried forward with South Wind at her side and whatever else she had managed to bring from the lodge that would help them on their way.

Warakan's brow came down. Distance prevented him from seeing her clearly in the moonlight, but Ika seemed to be clothed only in her dress; no sign of a robe or pack or bag. *No matter. Come to me, daughter of the Red World, and we will make our way together with nothing but the dogs and our lances and the power of the sacred stone to guide us!*

He waved again, more broadly than before, imperatively now. *What is she waiting for? I know she sees me. I can feel her gaze upon my face! Why does she not wave back to me?* East Wind was already at his side, rooting for a pat on the head. He gave it, and then went cold. Ika was standing tall again, rigid, head held high in a stance of cold repudiation. Then she turned on her heel and disappeared into the lodge with the wolf-dog. His mouth and hands went dry, and he was suddenly cold and shivering again. *She will come out. She will come to me.*

But Ika did not reappear. Warakan's hand was curled so tightly around the sacred stone that his flesh burned and then began to go numb, but if the spirits within heard his silent invocation and felt the yearning in his heart, they did not answer.

"She has chosen with whom she will walk," he whispered to the wolf-dog. "She will not forgive me for the lies I have spoken or for what has passed between me and Quarana. She is right. I do not deserve to walk at her side. And you are her 'child,' not mine. Go. Why do you stand here? I may carry the sacred stone of the Ancient Ones, but you do not belong with me!" He paused, angry now; self-pity had turned to righteous indignation. "Go or stay, wolf-dog! I am Warakan, grandson of Shateh, and I have sworn on the Four Winds and the forces of Creation that I will take revenge on those who have slain my grandfather and dishonored his name! I have accomplished this here. Now I will go my way."

This said, he turned and walked steadfastly into the dying night. Not once did he look back.

Ika sat in darkness.

Xohkantakeh and Quarana lay asleep, their backs to each other. After his solemn chanting was done, the giant had asked Ika to keep watch in case Warakan was foolish enough to return with malice in mind. She obeyed, and deep in the recesses of her heart where secret hopes were born, a part of her had wanted him to come, had known he would come—not to burn the lodge, or to strike Xohkantakeh down while he slept, or even to take Quarana as his own. *No.* Ika had seen hate for her sister in Warakan's eyes and had known in that instant that all he had said of what had been between them was true. And she had seen something else when he had looked at Xohkantakeh—an expression of betrayal and lost trust and deep pain. But then, when he had turned away and spoken the lies that brought the full wrath and hatred of the giant upon him, she had heard only "weak" and "not much to look at" and such utter contempt for her in his tone that, shattered, she had understood nothing of what he had done, or why he had done it. Only later, when it was too late to call him back or defend him to Xohkantakeh, she had understood that he had lied to save her life at the cost of everything he had truly hoped they might share together. And so she had awaited his return. She had known he would come. And she had known what she must do when she saw him.

South Wind yawned and laid her head across the girl's folded thighs. Ika patted her and closed her tear-filled eyes as she sent her longings into the dark and hoped that the spirits of the night would take them across the miles.

East Wind, child of the black wolf, walk now with

Warakan, for he will be so lonely in the days and nights ahead. Love him as Ika loves him. Be at his side, because I cannot! Soon Xohkantakeh, my Great Father Bear, will walk into the face of the rising sun with my sister and her unborn child—Warakan's child—and I must walk with them. If I do not, who will hunt beside Xohkantakeh and be his eyes and ears and his strong right spear arm when he falters and grows too old to hunt? And who will help Quarana birth her baby and nurture it with love if Ika does not stay?

4

Now the Four Winds blew.

For Warakan they were bitter and chilling to his spirit even though he walked beneath the Warm Moon. Traveling northward under the eye of the Watching Star, he soon reached a place where he might dare to cross the Great River.

The water was wide and deep, but he could see the current cutting crosswise into a broad, debris-littered bar and then, after a series of eddies, cutting crosswise again to the far shore. If he could find a way to keep his head above water, he knew he might stand a chance. At his feet, bobbing in the wake of the current, was a piece of driftwood the size and shape of an elongated camel. Appraising it thoughtfully, he remembered the last two occasions when rivers had carried him, tangled in the branches of buoyant downed trees.

"I wonder," he mused aloud.

East Wind had fallen into the habit of whining in response to the young man's musings.

Warakan looked down at him. "The time has come to return to your band, Bold One. I do not know if I can make my way alone across these deeps, but the river spirits have been kind to me in the past and may well be so again. I have come this far. The sacred stone of the Ancient Ones is still with me, and my vow to Shateh has yet to be fulfilled. I must make a try at this, for I cannot bear the thought of waiting until the Dry Moon or until the White Giant returns to freeze the river. Go back, child of the black wolf. I have lost one wolf to the river spirits and would not lose another, even if you are half dog."

East Wind had picked up something in Warakan's tone that he did not like, for his brow furrowed in the way of his kind when understanding is elusive. He watched, whining in puzzlement as Warakan, gripping his lance, pushed the floating trunk away from shore and stretched out upon it.

"Go back, East Wind . . . into the rising sun. Tell Ika that Warakan has not forgotten her!"

The wolf-dog barked, excited now and nervous; he did not need another wolf to tell him what was happening now. He took a few steps into the river in pursuit of the man, then turned back, whining and yipping until, impelled by a need not to be left behind, he leaped and swam madly in Warakan's direction.

Warakan kicked his feet, pushed sideways with his free arm, and, looking back just in time, saw East Wind fighting for his life. Without a second thought he released his hold on his lance and managed to grab a hank of canine shoulder hair just as the wolf-dog was about to be swept past him. He pulled in hard and had the struggling animal crooked in an elbow. "Thank you," he said facetiously. "Now I am unarmed. Would that your Red World mother were as loyal to me!"

The river took them. Fast, cold, roaring, it swept them downstream, past the bar and into the eddies, whirling them around and around before shifting hard and sending them downstream again in a tumult of white water. East Wind yipped in terror and managed to find purchase with his forepaws. Warakan gripped him so hard he thought his arm must surely snap with the strain. Then, with a massive bump that tore loose their hold on the tree and sent them flying, they found themselves flailing in shallows, exhausted but safe on the far shore.

For a while man and dog sat stunned in the water, tongues lolling and heads sagging. The shadow of a circling eagle drew Warakan's eyes upward. Squinting, he watched the familiar form, half expecting it to be a spirit bird that would speak in the voice of Eagle Woman and mock him for his effort to return into the west. But the eagle was only an eagle, and it soon found an updraft and was gone. Warakan was glad; he was in no mood for omens and started to say as much, but East Wind was no longer sitting beside him.

Warakan turned and, with great relief, saw that his canine companion had sloshed to the shore and was now lifting a leg and sending an arcing yellow stream of urine to mark new territory upon an exposed tree root. Warakan raised an eyebrow, rose unsteadily to his feet, waded to his "brother," hefted his hunting shirt, and matched the wolf stream for stream. "It is fitting," he observed. "For on this side of the river we may well soon find ourselves in enemy hunting grounds, and we would both be wise to remember the wolf in us, or we will surely die."

They went on.

South now, and then west. Warakan was certain the spirits of the Ancient Ones within the talisman were guiding him as before, but for reasons he could not understand, his enthusiasm for the quest was not the same, and every time he was sure of the way it soon confounded him.

"The gorge should be close," he told East Wind. "We are approaching the hills that I remember bulking up to the high pass. Or are we?" The spirits of the stone were silent now.

Days were passing in a long, slow tedium that frayed his nerves and often made him so restless he did not sleep well at night. His dreams were always of Ika, not of revenge but of a loss so deep that he would wake to the first birdsong of dawn with a hard, hurtful ache in his chest. Sometimes he simply lay on his back and wondered if he was dying.

He lived as before, alone with an animal. Had East Wind been more wolf than dog, the animal might have gone mousing or rabbiting for his human brother, but he did not share his kills, and Warakan went hungry if he did not hunt for himself. He devised snares of strong cordage made with long fibers pulled from the inner stalks of certain plants. He armed himself with a stone dagger chipped by his own hands and made stabbers, scrapers, and perforators from flakes cast from his stoneworking and from the fire-hardened bones of small animals. With patience and difficulty he made fire and stored the sacred heart ember in a partially gnawed ram's horn that East Wind sniffed out for him one day. And when he roasted the flesh of rabbits and hares and squirrels, he passed the time by telling East Wind of Wise Father Rabbit and Hook-Nosed Grandfather of All Deer and of all the animals that had given themselves as meat for him on his long journey out of the eastern forest.

"Surely it affirms my purpose," he said to the wolf-dog. "We will find the gorge. Soon. You will see. We will unearth the magic spearhead and journey to the barrens to hunt the mammoth, and then we will come back to take vengeance on our enemies. Never again will we walk in fear of them or—"

He stopped speaking. The words suddenly sounded hollow to his ears: onward to the gorge, northward to the barrens, then back to the gorge and down across the Land of Grass into the hunting grounds of the Two Tribes. And then what? An exhalation of weariness went out of him. The journey to which he had set himself suddenly seemed longer than a man could endure in a single lifetime, and yet he had vowed to endure it. He *would* endure it. To avenge Shateh and Masau and his sister, Neea, and all those who had ever suffered or died at the hands of his enemies. For what better purpose could a man spend his life?

Warakan considered this question.

He closed his eyes. Ika's smiling face filled him with an inner warmth that made him smile in return. It was as though she was with him, reaching out to him, calling his name. He opened his eyes with a start, expecting to see her, wanting to see her, but he was alone with a wolf-dog in hills he did not know, and Ika was far away. Forever.

"Come," he said to East Wind. "We will go on our way. What else is there for us to do?"

And so the days passed in an endless search for the right rise of hill, for the downsloping curve of a valley he was sure he remembered, for a stand of trees or a circle of boulders in which he might find sign of an old camp, for anything that would point the way to the high gorge. But in the ten long years since Warakan had walked out of the sunset into the face of the rising sun, either the land had changed or the distorted memories of a nine-year-old boy led the man he had become awry. Nothing was as he remembered, as though great living phalanxes of trees and shrubs and green growing things had deliberately advanced over the earth to clothe it and hide all landmarks from him. At night he lay awake watching Moon turn her face to him and then, gradually, turn away again and again while the great Sky River flowed inexorably across the black robe of Father Above and the stars pursued one another across ever-changing and never-changing pathways. If the spirits within the sacred stone were speaking, telling him how to follow those pathways home, Warakan could not hear them.

And then, early one morning, in woods flushed with the first faint coloring of autumn, Warakan sat with East Wind and watched the sun rise over the lands out of which they had come. As on so many other mornings, he thought of the distant forest that lay beyond the edge of the world and found himself yearning to be back under the rich green canopy of the trees with the good smell of woodsmoke rising from the cook fires he and Jhadel had made each morning. "Ah, East Wind, how Ika would smile to see and smell the color of those woods. Ika!" He spoke her name and missed her so that he nearly cried. "Ika!"

The wolf-dog rose, circled, looked for the one who had raised him as her own, and, not finding her, turned to the east, ready to go back for her.

"To what would we return, Bold One? She does not want me. *They* do not want us. They do not *need* us!"

Need. It was that word that made him remember Quarana. Looking around, he was suddenly intensely aware of the yellow edging on the leaves. He gauged the position of the rising sun. *She must be great with child by now,* he thought. If it was Xohkantakeh's baby it would come with no more than the rising of two moons. Would the giant suffer her to carry it to term? Or would he be like the stallions of the grasslands of his youth and bludgeon the offending life that was not his from her belly so that, if she did not die of his cleansing, he could impregnate her with the milk of his own life?

He was troubled. He told himself he had no cause to be. *Quarana has brought this on herself. But what if she carries my life? What if it is the only life that any woman will ever bear me? Is it not a part of myself living in her, and also of Shateh and Masau and all of those brave chieftains and shamans whose spirits will die forever if Quarana is not allowed to give birth? And what will happen to my son or daughter out there beyond the edge of the world with only an old man and Ika to care whether it lives or dies? And, now that I think of it, it is not a good thing to live life alone and imagine oneself dying alone with only wolves to howl over your bones before you are eaten and your spirit is lost forever! Perhaps Quarana's need to be safe among the grandmothers when her babies come was not so terrible a thing.*

He raised his head. The smell of smoke was in the air. He had not conjured it; it was real. And it was not the smoke of his own cooking fire, for he had made no fire this day. It was the smell of burning grass, and hide, and flesh—not meat—and hair and bone. It was the stink of war.

Warakan was on his feet, reaching for the hunting bag he had made and his bone and hardwood lances. He commanded East Wind to follow, but the wolf-dog was already on the scent and disappearing uphill through the trees.

He ran.

Even before he came breathless and panting to where East Wind had paused upon the heights, he knew he was there at last.

The great gorge!

He had found it! The spirits of the stone had been leading him all along.

The undergrowth was higher and thicker than before, but he knew the ancient grove and recognized the patterns

of the lichens on the gray and red rocks. And there, among
the man-tall boulders, was the place where he and Jhadel
had last sheltered before turning their backs on the setting
sun forever.

But if there was joy in Warakan's heart—or a desire to
go to the spot where he had buried the magic spearhead
deep in a pit of duff and loam—it was gone in a breath
of time.

There, far below, the grasslands stretched away to distant, glacier-clad mountains. Beyond those lay the hunting
grounds of the ancestors and the Two Tribes. But now, below in the gorge, he saw two encampments, one far, the
other near. The closer of the two was burning. He stared, incredulous, as in his nightmare upon the promontory. In
body paint and war feathers, with their ankle-length hair
loosened for battle and streaming in a rising wind, the tall,
tattooed warriors of the People of the Watching Star waged
battle on the painted warriors of the People of the Land of
Grass, who fought to protect their burning lodges. The bodies of their dead lay strewn, mutilated, turning the grasslands black with their blood.

The sight of it turned him cold.

He had been seen. One warrior was pointing, another
turning, staring up along the flanks of the great gorge, and
now all eyes were on Warakan as a roar went up from the
throng.

"Warakan!"

He flinched. Who called his name? Was the voice real or
imagined? He could not say, but Reason counseled that his
enemies could not possibly have recognized him after so
many long winters, and from such a distance. And yet,
somehow, it was as though he stood again on the high
plateau and the nightmare phantoms of Vision were shouting up to him, "Yah hay, Warakan! Is that you? Can it be
that you still live?"

"It is I, Warakan," he shouted back. "The grandson of
Shateh still lives! And behold, the sacred stone of the ancestors is mine!"

"We will take it!"

"Come and try!" he challenged.

"And so we shall, for behold! The grandson of Shateh stands rooted and quakes like a sapling in the wind!"

"It is fear that shakes him!"

"Then let us cut him down. He has called to us upon the sacred stone! We have come at his command to answer his need for vengeance. We will come to him now! We will take the talisman of the Ancient Ones from around his neck and follow him beyond the edge of the world to hunt the great white mammoth totem and to strangle his women and children and all who have dared to walk in his shadow!"

"I have no women! I have no . . ." The protest died in Warakan's mouth as, thinking of Xohkantakeh and Ika, Quarana and her unborn child, he realized what he had just done. The enemy warriors were real enough, but their threats had been born of his own mind and fear. They would never have recognized him had he not told them his name.

East Wind was growling, the hair standing high along his back and shoulders.

From out of nowhere, it seemed, an eagle plummeted down. "Kya! Set yourself alone against the combined forces of the warriors of the Two Tribes, would you? Kya! Now Warakan will see where his self-centered need for vengeance must lead him!" The eagle banked and disappeared into the trees, but not before dipping its broad wings to slap the top of Warakan's head so hard he was nearly brought to his knees. "Follow!" the bird commanded. "Or has Jhadel wasted these past many years on one who rightly names himself Fool? Can it be that the Son of Two Tribes prefers to die rather than commit himself to the peaceful reunification of the tribes and the fulfillment of Jhadel's hope for the future of us all?"

Warakan was stunned. Peaceful reunification of the tribes in the face of advancing warriors who, now that they had seen and recognized him, seemed unified against him? Commitment to the future when, at this very moment, spears were flying from below and the war cries of enemies were thundering up the gorge to him?

His heart was pounding. His hand went to the talisman. All the visions he had sought and the portendings he had denied were alive in him now as memories of Jhadel's promise came to him.

"The spirits of those who were enemies in life live on in you, Son of Two Tribes. And I tell you now that someday you will look with their eyes upon the hunting grounds of the People of the Watching Star and the People of the Land of Grass, and you will see that country not as an avenging warrior—but as a peacemaker and bringer of unity to all!"

And Xohkantakeh's revelation: *"We have come to a place where the old ways and kinds are dying and drifting away on the wind while new ways and kinds are forming and taking root. . . . For how long have the chieftains of the Three Tribes fought one another to the death for possession of the sacred stone so that one tribe would hold power over all? It was this ambition that led your father and grandfather to their deaths at the hands of their enemies. But behold, Warakan, son of Two Tribes! Here . . . now . . . in this new land . . . the Three Tribes are united, not through war, but through a peaceful union made by the Four Winds and the forces of Creation themselves! When children are born to you and Ika, the blood of the Three Tribes will be their blood, and it will be as it was in time beyond beginning: The People will once more be one!"*

Warakan felt sick.

The warriors were coming up the gorge, waving their spears, shouting their threats. The stink of war was in his nostrils. He wanted no part of it, but not because he was afraid for himself. He had come across the Great River from Xohkantakeh's camp with no thought of concealing his trail. It was there now for all who would follow to see. And they would follow. They would come with their spears and their braining clubs and their war dogs and all the mindless hate that had moved their kind since time beyond beginning. They would find the encampment of the giant. And Xohkantakeh would stand to them like the warrior he was—Bear Slayer, Killer of Horse and Bison—until they struck him down, raped and enslaved his woman and daughter, and bashed the brains of his child—Warakan's child—into the earth.

He ran.

He whirled on his heels and broke for the cover of the trees, not stopping to retrieve the magic spearhead. It was nothing to him now. Those who followed on his trail would not seek it; they did not know it was there.

"May it lie hidden in the skin of Mother Below forever, a white spearhead that will *never* slay a white mammoth!"

Behind him voices were shouting and clamoring on the heights. A spear came hurtling along the ground; he picked it up without breaking stride.

Soon the day faded into dusk, and night followed with a brilliant full moon setting a silvery sheen across the sky, veiling into insignificance all but the brightest points of starlight: the vast, arching sweep of the Sky River; the sprawl of the Great Bear; the flexing length of the Great Snake, whose open jaws pointed to the one star around which all the others turned—the Watching Star, the North Star, the star by which a man could find his way or lose it forever.

Warakan kept on. He would not allow himself to slow his pace though his breath snagged in his throat and his muscles burned and the wolf-dog at his side looked up at him as if expecting him to fall.

"We must go on. All that is bad comes from the north . . . all that is dark and cold . . . all that has to do with death and danger. We must warn Xohkantakeh of what comes for him. We must bring the sacred stone of the Ancient Ones to him before it is too late for him or Ika or Quarana and my child! May it not be born before I return . . . for by the forces of Creation he will have every right to kill it!"

On and on he ran, loping like a wolf now, strengthened and renewed. The moon was soon so bright he could no longer see the Watcher, but he knew it was there, watching him, and he hated the star and all it represented. Although he had been born into a tribe whose chieftains and shamans had looked to it as a source of eternal power, all that had ever been hard and cruel and painful in his life had come to pass under the cold, glinting constancy of its authority: the death of loved ones, the shaming of self, the loss of everything that had once centered his life and made it worth living . . . until, standing at the crest of the great gorge, he had discovered the renewal of spirit that came to a man when he committed himself to life and hope in the future.

"I will warn them in time," he vowed to the wolf-dog. "I must. Too long have I given them cause to name me Trouble. Run on with me, Bold One. We are of one kind, you and I, meant to run in pack, not alone!"

He did not know how long it took him to reach the Great River. The Dry Grass Moon was full, and he had successfully maneuvered his pursuers onto one of several false trails that he had laid for them when at last he smelled the moisture of the river and hurried toward it. A day later, he was there. The river was down. He crossed it as he had before, floating atop a fallen tree with the wolf-dog tucked under one arm. But when he reached the place where the encampment had been, he saw at once that the big lodge had been broken down. A brief search for tracks told him what he wanted to know. Xohkantakeh had taken his woman and daughter and headed back into the face of the rising sun, back perhaps across the drowned land to the winter camp in the deep, sheltering forest of which his daughter had spoken with such love. Relief filled him. They would be safe there, for now, at least, and difficult to track for anyone who did not know the forest. He hunkered down on his heels and rubbed the wolf-dog's head. "We can relax now for a while. As we follow, we will do what we can to cover their tracks. It will be all right. We will find them in time. The White Giant Winter will come soon. Snow lies deep in the forest, and the warriors of the Two Tribes will not have snow walkers. I think perhaps they will lose heart and turn back. And perhaps they will turn on themselves and kill each other before they have a chance to return."

The thought amused him, until another turned him cold with dread. "Quarana will bear our baby when the White Giant comes. If I am not there, will Xohkantakeh allow it to live? Ah, Bold One, we must go! May the Four Winds be at our back! For if he kills my child, I swear I will strike him down, and all that I have hoped for the future will not come to pass, for Ika will surely never forgive or look at me again!"

Time.

How slowly it passed! How great were the distances the giant had put between himself and Warakan! And yet the young man blundered on. Now and then he saw an eagle circling high, but no matter how he strained his eyes, he could see no glint of gold on the broad, dark neck; instead he saw the sheen of a white head and tail and, one night in his dreams, heard the voice of Golden Eagle and the spirit of Jhadel sighing on the wind.

"We can journey with you no longer, Warakan. We must fly on the back of West Wind into the hunting grounds of the ancestors. You must follow in the shadow of our kindred, White-Headed Eagle, into the great forests and across shining waters into the face of the rising sun. Go there . . . into a new dawn . . . if you are not afraid!"

But Warakan was afraid—not only for himself but for Quarana and their baby. And increasingly—as Moon turned her face to earth and looked away again and again, until the White Giant Winter came roaring down from the north in company with the Cold Sisters, Snow, Ice, and Howling Wind—he began to fear he would never see Ika again.

It was the cry of a white bird flying low overhead that led him to her on a day when snow fell, bandaging the scars of the drowned land but failing to conceal the smoke from a cooking fire or to muffle the wail of an infant or the low sobbing of a woman.

And then he saw her.

"Ika!"

She rose, trembling, as he came to her. The wolf-dogs ran to each other not like brother and sister but like startled lovers, and East Wind stopped to sniff at the pups that came to greet their sire. Warakan took no note of them. The infant had not cried again since he first heard it. Ika's face was as

white as the snow, and her eyes were red-rimmed and
swollen from weeping.

"Where is Quarana? Where is the giant?" he demanded,
his hand tight on his spear.

She gestured off. "There . . . the baby . . . its coming has
taken so long. Quarana has been so brave and suffered so
much, and yet . . . Warakan, wait!"

He did not wait. He burst across the little compound, the
blood of rage at the back of his mouth. "You have killed my
child!" he roared, flinging back the weather flap and storm-
ing inside, only to be brought short.

The smell of blood and birth fluid overwhelmed him,
but no more so than the sight of the giant sitting amidst
soiled bed furs, holding Quarana tenderly in his arms while
she suckled a newborn child. Bloodied from the birth of the
infant, Xohkantakeh looked up. "You! Go away, Trouble! I
have no wish to look upon your face. My new woman has
had a difficult birth. With my own hands I have brought
forth a son from her body. Behold!"

Warakan stared as Quarana smiled wanly and allowed
the man to take the child from her breast. The infant
squalled and squirmed like a flesh-colored little storm cloud
when Xohkantakeh held it high. Warakan swallowed hard,
for this was undoubtedly the healthiest and surely the
biggest baby he had ever seen.

Xohkantakeh laughed. "Do you not know how many
moons it takes to make life come forth, Warakan? Hmm.
Why do you stare? Did you think it was yours? Ah. You
have cause, yes, and you thought I would kill it if it were. It
was in my heart. But as we walked into the face of the rising
sun, I thought of my Katohya and the child I had lost, and it
came to me that life itself is a precious thing. A child does
not ask to be born, but when it comes forth into the Circle of
Life, wisdom teaches a man that it must be allowed its
chance to chase a few shadows. And a baby-bearing woman
who has been made to work too hard and carry too heavy a
load by an angry man sometimes bears early, yes? Or later.
Who can say? Who can judge? Only the forces of Creation,
and they are the makers of life. I know only that this child

has come forth from this woman between moons that would surely have named his father. And so Xohkantakeh accepts this son of his band. My son or Warakan's? Not even Quarana can tell us that."

"I have dishonored you," Warakan acknowledged. "I have come back to tell you that. And to walk with you and hunt with you as a brother and as a son if you will have me. It is your right to turn me away, or to strike me down. I will not fight you. But I will tell you now that I bring the sacred stone to you, to place it in the care of a wiser and worthier man than I. It will keep you strong and safe in the days and nights that lie ahead. For the warriors of the Watching Star have followed me over the edge of the world. They hunt me. They hunt you. They hunt the great white mammoth. If they come, I will fight with you. I will—"

"Ah, Warakan, this man learned long ago that the forces of Creation shape men and the world as they will. From the time beyond beginning the People have warred and scattered like seeds before the storms that beset us all. The Four Winds blow. And life *does* flow like the great river. It has brought you to this band. Now, if it is the will of Warakan to walk with us at last, be it so. Xohkantakeh will not turn his back on a friend."

"I have been no friend to you."

"Bah!" he rumbled and, giving the baby into Quarana's loving embrace, rose and came to sling an arm around the young man's shoulder. "There would be little joy for this Man in the great Circle of Life if there were no Wolf to challenge me as I run within it. We will walk into the face of the rising sun together. We will seek the great white mammoth and the band of Cha-kwena. Mah-ree's children should be half grown by now. And she would be the next best thing to a wise and caring grandmother to look after my fearful new woman."

Warakan was overwhelmed. "I do not know what to say."

"Then say nothing."

"I have shamed you!"

"Yes, and yourself. But the circle turns, Warakan. To-morrow the sun will rise over the edge of the world, and who among us can know where the waters of life may pour forth in the end? Go. Our days are short in this world, and we have both chased too many shadows in the Circle of Life. Leave me with my woman. The white bird has been heard in this camp this day. Go to Ika, Warakan. Let the People be one through you. She has been waiting for you."

AUTHOR'S NOTE

This novel has been inspired by the ever-growing archaeological record of man in Pleistocene and Holocene North America, and by continuing research into Native American history, traditions, and mythology.

The white bird that calls to Ika is an Arctic tern, symbolic of a people born of the cold northlands of the high Arctic and yet destined to migrate and "set shadow" over all of North, Middle, and South America to the very tip of Tierra del Fuego.

I have drawn my descriptions of the Pleistocene forests, tundra, broken grasslands, and muskeg not from existing habitats but from the pollen records and from a surviving remnant of Ice Age forest found preserved in the glacial debris along the ancient shoreline of Lake Michigan. When referring to the map at the front of the novel, readers should realize that the journey lines are meant to give only an approximation of the travels of Xohkantakeh and Warakan across a land that has been scoured and reshaped by the Laurentide Ice Sheet at least four separate times during the Wisconsin glaciation. Major land features as well as many tributary streams, lesser rivers, and lakes are therefore not shown, and the boundaries of the ice sheet are also only an approximation. The Great River is, of course, the Mississippi. The disastrous ice surge and resultant flood that drowns the valley in which Xohkantakeh has raised his "good" camp is based on occurrences that were common-place during the Pleistocene.

Some readers may question the "old woven matting" upon which Jhadel lies and which is buried with him when the ceiling of the "cave beyond the edge of the world" collapses. Would a man of that ancient epoch possess knowledge of weaving? Would he not be reclining instead upon a rough assemblage of skins and furs? No, I think not. Although the storyline of *Face of the Rising Sun* unfolds approximately twelve thousand years before the present era, research continues to affirm this author's certainty that the people of that long-gone time were far more "technologically" advanced than currently believed. Indeed, the media at large may well continue to portray Ice Age man as a slouching, savage, unkempt, and ignorant brute, but the scientific record continues to prove the opposite: By the time the first bands of Paleolithic hunters set themselves to following the vast Ice Age herds of caribou, bison, and mammoth eastward out of Siberia across the Beringian Refugium, they had already domesticated the dog and advanced the skills of stoneworking to an art. Certain decorated bibeveled rods of proboscidean bones found in Washington State's Columbia River Valley hint strongly of ideographs and of the use of sleds by Clovis hunters more than eleven thousand years ago. Fragments of basketry found in Gypsum Cave, Nevada, date to the time when that desert landscape was lake country and home to mammoths as well as mammoth hunters. Paleolithic Oregonians of this period donned summer sandals of woven and pounded yucca fiber. And, if radiocarbon dating can be relied upon, a piece of plaited matting of human manufacture was charred by fire in a south-facing cavern some twenty-nine miles southwest of Pittsburgh . . . over nineteen thousand years ago.

The description of the cave in which Jhadel and Warakan take shelter has been inspired by this cavern. Meadowcroft Rockshelter in today's western Pennsylvania is one of the most fascinating and controversial prehistoric sites in North America. Here, on the north shore of Cross Creek in the upper Ohio Valley, man has indisputably been taking shelter almost continuously since "time beyond beginning" when—at the height of the Wisconsin glacial maximum—Meadowcroft lay less than forty miles south of the terminal moraines of the miles-thick ice sheet that sprawled across the entire northern half of the continent.

For all that I have managed to glean on the subject of this extraordinary site, I must extend my heartfelt thanks to Dr. J. M. Adovasio, Professor of Anthropology, Archaeology, and Geology and executive director of the Mercyhurst Archaeological Institute and Archaeology Research Program, for his generous sharing of time and data. This novel has been enriched immeasurably by his willingness to discuss at length the surroundings of Meadowcroft Rockshelter during the Pleistocene and the extraordinary finds unearthed in Middle and Lower Stratum Level IIa.

Thanks must also go again to Charles Cline for his unstinting support and assistance; to Sally Smith for her confidence; and to my editors at Book Creations, Pamela Lappies, editorial director, and Elizabeth Tinsley editor, for their all-enduring patience. My deepest appreciation to Joost Bloemsma, president of Uitgeverij Het Spectrum, publisher of the Dutch editions of FIRST AMERICANS, for his graciousness and his support for the series both here and in Europe.

Thanks once more to Dr. Richard Michael Gramly, curator of the Great Lakes Artifact Repository, Buffalo, New York, Clovis Project director at Richey Clovis Cache in Wenatchee, Washington, and organizer of the American Association for Amateur Archaeology, for his continuing enthusiasm for the FIRST AMERICANS saga, and most especially for making available to this author Eva Jane N. Fridman's "Of Domestication, Dog-Husbands and Dog-Feasts: Human-Canine Interaction in Native North America" (master's thesis, Harvard University, 1989).

WILLIAM SARABANDE
Fawnskin, California

THE SAGA OF THE FIRST AMERICANS

*The spellbinding epic of adventure
at the dawn of history*

by William Sarabande

FACE OF THE RISING SUN

___56030-1 $6.50/$9.99 Canada

___26889-9	BEYOND THE SEA OF ICE	$6.50/$8.99
___27159-8	CORRIDOR OF STORMS	$6.50/$8.99
___28206-9	FORBIDDEN LAND	$6.50/$8.99
___28579-3	WALKERS OF THE WIND	$6.50/$8.99
___29105-X	THE SACRED STONES	$6.50/$8.99
___29106-8	THUNDER IN THE SKY	$6.50/$8.99
___56028-X	THE EDGE OF THE WORLD	$6.50/$8.99
___56029-8	SHADOW OF THE WATCHING STAR	$6.99/$9.99
___57906-1	TIME BEYOND BEGINNING	$6.50/$8.99

Also by William Sarabande

___25802-8	WOLVES OF THE DAWN	$6.50/$8.99